THE RED BOOK

For a preview of upcoming books and information about the author, visit JamesPatterson.com or find him on Facebook, Twitter, or Instagram.

THE RED BOOK

JAMES PATTERSON

AND DAVID ELLIS

Little, Brown and Company

New York Boston London

The characters and events in this book are fictitious. Any similarity to real persons, living or dead, is coincidental and not intended by the author.

Little, Brown and Company
Hachette Book Group
1290 Avenue of the Americas, New York, NY 10104
littlebrown.com

First Edition: March 2021

Little, Brown and Company is a division of Hachette Book Group, Inc. The Little, Brown name and logo are trademarks of Hachette Book Group, Inc.

ISBN 978-0-316-49940-8 (hardcover) / 978-0-316-59330-4 (large print)
LCCN 2020946234

Printing 1, 2021

LSC-C

Printed in the United States of America

For Sue, Jack, and Red
–JP

For Abigail, Julia, and Jonathan Ellis
–DE

BOOK I

CHAPTER 1

LIGHTS, CAMERA, action.

This could mean everything to Latham. It could be his ticket out.

But it could ruin him, too. It could land him in prison.

Or worse. It's the "worse" that jars him awake in the middle of the night, heart pounding, bedsheets soaked in sweat.

If Shiv ever found out. Shiv wasn't the forgiving sort. Shiv didn't have a sense of humor.

Just ask Joker Jay, who one day last summer made the mistake of joking around a little too much with Shiv's woman. They found Jay in a pool of blood by the field house in Clark Park. Shiv had decided to take Jay's nickname literally and slice open both sides of his mouth.

Jay doesn't joke around much anymore.

And that's just for messing with Shiv's girl. Messing with Shiv's business?

If anyone figures out what Latham's doing, he's a dead man. Shiv will make an example of him, beat him, torture him, leave his bloody corpse for all to see. This is what happens when you mess with Shiv. This is what happens when you mess with the business of the K-Street Hustlers.

Lights: easy enough, the sunlight of late afternoon pouring

through Latham's bedroom window, up on the fourth floor of the apartment building.

Camera: a small one, hidden inside the AC unit perched halfway out his window, overlooking the street to the south.

Action: a silver BMW sedan slows at the intersection down the street, then turns left, driving north on Kilbourn toward Latham's position.

A Beemer, Latham thinks. *Promising.*

Using the toggle, Latham zooms in on the license plate, then widens the view and captures the intersection's street signs, Kilbourn and Van Buren.

Then he returns the focus to the street, where the BMW crawls along Kilbourn before pulling over to the curb on its left, exactly where Latham knew it would stop, just past the alley, by a brick two-flat, only four doors down and across the street from Latham's apartment and his hidden camera.

A young African American in an oversize Bears jersey and tattered jeans—that's Frisk—strolls by, does a once-over of the idled sedan, then looks up at some people sitting on the porch of the brick walk-up. Latham doesn't bother moving the camera. He knows what's going on. Frisk is looking for the green light from Shiv, sitting on the front porch.

Shiv must have given it, because Frisk ambles over to the sedan and leans against the driver's door. The window rolls down. Latham toggles the camera down and focuses in. The driver is a white man, probably midthirties, dressed in a suit and tie. He talks to Frisk for a minute, then hands him some cash, folded over once. Frisk palms the money like an expert, still leaning in close, then gestures down the street, to the spot where the driver will score the drugs he wants. Heroin, presumably; it's cheaper in the city than it is in the suburbs.

The car moves on. Latham stops the camera, downloads the short video onto his laptop.

Picks up his cell and calls his cousin Renfro, in his third year at the DMV since graduating from Farragut. Reads him the license plate.

"Registered to a Richard Dempsey," says Fro. "From River Forest. That's cash, my brother. And a BMW?"

Latham agrees: it could be a real payday. Guy like that, dressed like a professional, in a fancy ride from a fancy suburb, probably a doctor or lawyer or financial guy. A guy who'd have a hard time explaining that video to his bosses or his wife.

He'll check out this Richard Dempsey. Will go online, look at his house, find out his occupation, search him up on social media. You can't get too greedy. Gotta be something they can afford.

But yeah, Latham's seeing dollar signs. Ten thousand? A guy like that, to protect his dirty little secret? He might pay that.

Shit, ten thousand dollars—that's more than halfway to the tuition for film school. More than Latham could make in six months at Best Buy.

"Peace." Latham punches out the phone. Thinks about the money.

Thinks about film school.

I'd like to thank the Academy, he'll say one day, clutching his Best Director Oscar, *and I'd especially like to thank the men and women who made this all possible by traveling the Heroin Highway.*

CHAPTER 2

TODAY'S THE day. The roiling in my stomach is supposed to signal excitement, not dread.

I open my eyes to the water damage on my ceiling, the paint splintering and soggy, which should be a metaphor, though I can't make it work. I can't make much of anything work. My head is banging like a gong; my tongue feels like shag carpeting; my stomach has erupted into civil war. I warned myself when that third bourbon slid across the bar last night. By the sixth, I was pretty confident the morning would be a challenge.

You're avoiding, my shrink would say, the shrink the department made me see during my "vacation" from the force—paid administrative leave while the department shook out from the scandal, indictments, calls for reform, reassignments. I was the hero and the villain in the story, depending on your point of view, though most of my comrades on the force put me in the latter category. They couldn't fire me after my one-man wrecking ball to the police department that made Sherman's march through Atlanta look like a sightseeing tour. I'm the face of reform now!

"More like the face of death," I mumble, getting a load of myself in the bathroom mirror. Hair standing on end, dark circles, pale complexion. I have . . . what, twenty minutes to look presentable?

But how presentable do I have to be, sitting behind some desk or assigned to traffic duty? Who knows what the superintendent's going to do with me? I'll be about as welcome in his office as an IRS audit.

"You don't have to go back," I say to my reflection. "But what else are you gonna do? Work private security? Roam the earth as a shepherd?"

I'm not sure which side won that debate, but twenty minutes later, I'm driving to headquarters, at 35th and Michigan, still considering that shepherd thing. Does it have to involve sheep?

Police headquarters is a long low-rise building that looks like a high school. Not a bad analogy, because this mandatory meeting feels like being sent to the principal's office, though far less pleasant. I'd rather be visiting my proctologist, and he has a criminal record.

Most people don't notice me as I walk the halls in my sport jacket and blue jeans, shield on, just another cop, not one who opened the wrong closet door and found a bunch of department skeletons inside. Not one who got a bullet to the head and a murder indictment for his trouble. And my biggest crime? That I overcame all of it. I was supposed to go away, surrender, but instead I fought back and won—if returning to a job where you're persona non grata counts as a victory. Good thing I'm not bitter.

"Detective Billy Harney for the superintendent," I say to the receptionist when I enter the vaunted anteroom of the Chicago top cop's office. He might also be Chicago's top asswipe, though a lot of people are competing for that prize.

I glance at the clock to make sure I'm not late. I'm late by two minutes. Aces.

"You're late," says the supe before I've even entered the room. He's alone behind his desk. Makes sense. No eyewitnesses.

I think you can be a shepherd without sheep. You just wear

flowing robes and say something deep once in a while. *Fear not what you do not know but that which you do not endeavor to know.* That's not half bad, and I just pulled that out of my keister.

"Have a seat, Detective." Superintendent Tristan Driscoll, though the top cop in full dress this morning, isn't a cop in any real sense of the word. He's a politician. He somehow managed to survive the destruction I caused, which also took down the person who appointed him, the mayor of Chicago. Not to mention the top prosecutor in town, the Cook County state's attorney. It was a big wrecking ball.

But Tristan, who must have had sadistic parents for giving him that name, managed to stay in the graces of the new mayor and avoid the chopping block himself. And all while Chicago is making a name for itself as the murder capital of the free world—Beirut-by-the-Lake. His knees must be sore. The walls surrounding us are lined with framed photographs of him standing next to people whose asses he's kissed.

"We can forgo the pleasantries," he says to me.

"That's a relief," I say. "I couldn't think of any."

His mouth zips into a tight smile. "Always that mouth, Harney." He looks down at a file on his desk. "Your psych evaluation says you're ready to return to the force."

"I was always ready. I wasn't put on leave because I couldn't work. I was put on leave while you figured out if you could fire me. Then you realized you couldn't, because it would look like retaliation against the reformer. The media would have you for lunch."

Never hesitate to say that which is true over that which is comfortable but false. Shit, I'm really getting the hang of this. Where do I buy flowing robes?

Driscoll grins and leans back, rocking in his high-backed leather chair. "I own you, Harney. I can put you on traffic duty. I can make you Officer Friendly, wanding high school students and patrolling crosswalks." He shrugs. "All I have to do to make that happen is to say you've been damaged psychologically. Forget about the union filing a grievance. Nobody's taking your side. Nobody would challenge me. As long as I don't fire you—so the media doesn't 'have me for lunch.'" He uses air quotes, playing my words back to me. "I can make your life a nightmare. And I will."

My hands ball into fists, blood rushing to my head. My head was already hurting; now it feels like it's going to burst.

"So whaddya say, Harney? You retire, you get a full line-of-duty pension, and I don't have to deal with your fucking bullshit for one . . . more . . . day."

He actually maintains his smile throughout.

The part that really stings—he's not far off. Do I really want back in? With a shitty assignment and nobody wanting to work with me? The line-of-duty pension isn't half bad, and I'm still in my midthirties—I could think of something. A fresh start.

But maybe it took this moment, this opportunity to walk away with a clean bill of health and some money in my pocket, to realize it: I still want to be a cop. If I did something wrong to deserve getting the ax, I'd own up to it. But I didn't. I did my job. Why should *I* leave?

And those flowing robes? They'd be a bitch to keep clean, I bet.

"No deal," I say. "Put me where you're gonna put me."

Driscoll loses that smarmy smile. He Frisbees a file across his desk. I catch it in my lap and open it. I read it. I read it again.

Then I say, "You've gotta be freakin' kidding me."

CHAPTER 3

I STARE at my transfer papers, still unable to believe it, rechecking that it's my name and star number at the top of the page, that there hasn't been some kind of mix-up.

"Believe me, Harney," says Driscoll, "it wasn't my idea."

The Special Operations Section. I've been assigned to SOS.

"We just announced it last month," says Driscoll.

I saw the presser, Superintendent Driscoll making the announcement with the mayor by his side. The Special Operations Section is an "elite strike force" assigned to major crimes throughout the city. But its focus will be the West Side, terrorized by all the shootings that have given Chicago a nationally recognized black eye and made a lot of local politicians nervous.

Ah, the new mayor. He must be the one who made this assignment happen. Never met the guy, but he must've said, *Hey, that Harney guy, let's put him in this unit, show everyone how committed to reform I am.* Ever the suck-up, Driscoll would've heartily endorsed the idea. He probably even gave the mayor a congratulatory hand job even though he privately wanted to coerce me to retire. He took a shot at getting me to quit just now, but I didn't take the bait. So now he has to bite his tongue and promote me to one of the best assignments on the force. It must be killing him.

"You're in the spotlight, Harney, right where you like it."

I look up at him. Still in shock—this was the absolute last thing I expected—I'm unable to come up with one of my trademark one-liners. "I never wanted the spotlight. I just did my job."

"Well, you got it anyway, Media Sweetheart. But the thing about the spotlight? It can be warm and comforting when you do good. It can be harsh when you screw up."

That's one thing he didn't need to tell me.

"There's nothing the press likes more than a fall from grace," he says. "A hero cop who turns out to be a fuckup."

That's two things I already knew.

"That line-of-duty pension's still on the table," he says. "Walk away with some bucks in your pocket, move on with your life."

"And get out of your hair," I add.

"That, too."

Yeah. Driscoll's the type who throws dead weight off the boat without a moment's hesitation. He'd take the first opportunity to burn me if it suited him. And for all I know, that's what this whole thing is—I'm being set up to fail.

So I'll just have to make sure I don't fail.

I give him a wide grin. "I accept the assignment, Mr. Superintendent, sir. Your Excellency."

He gives me a sidelong glance. "Oh, you're gonna last a *real* long time with that attitude, hotshot. Your boss is going to *love* you."

I knew about the creation of SOS. But I never heard who'd be running it.

"Who's my boss?" I ask.

CHAPTER 4

MEET THE new boss. Same as the old boss.

"Don't look so happy to see me, Harney," says Lieutenant Paul Wizniewski, working the unlit cigar stub in the corner of his mouth. The Wiz has a melon face, a salt-and-pepper mustache, and one finger always testing the political winds of the department. He has a knack for predicting curves in the road and always makes sure he's in the correct lane of traffic. That was always a problem between us when I used to work under him. I tended to lead with my chin; he always wanted to know whose ox was getting gored, map out the whole thing first, before making a decision.

He also once arrested me for murder, so there's that.

"I'm speechless," I say, deadpan.

"That'd be a first. Listen," he says, leaning back in his chair, looking at me over his chaotic desk—he couldn't have been in this assignment more than a week, in this shiny new space at North and Pulaski, and already the papers are piled so high they topple over onto each other. "It sure as shit wasn't my idea to bring you here."

"I'm getting a lot of that today."

"Well, you're gonna get more. If you have the smarts I think you have, you already know that."

"I think that was a compliment."

He scratches his stomach, something I wouldn't recommend watching. "Look, the past is the past. You thought I was a lowlife. I know you did; it's okay."

"I wasn't going to deny it."

He chuckles, shakes his head. "Harney, what, you think cuz you got shot in the head and charged with murder—"

"By you," I add.

He pauses on that. "Well, I didn't shoot you in the head."

That's true. Just the murder accusation.

"Okay," I say, "well, thank you for not shooting me in the head."

"You're welcome." He comes forward, elbows on the desk, nearly knocking over a Styrofoam cup of coffee. "I know you're a good cop, Harney. I might've had my suspicions about you once upon a time, and they might've been wrong—"

"They *might've* been wrong?"

He looks up at the heavens, exasperated. "I'm trying to, you know, make peace on this."

"Turn the page?" I say.

"Yeah."

"A new chapter?"

"Right. Because here's the thing, my friend. You know what SOS stands for?"

"Yeah, Lew, I do," I say, using the nickname we all called him. "It stands for 'no fuckin' around.'"

He points at me. "That's exactly what it stands for. The supe is this close to losing his job over the shootings on the West Side. The blacks out there are howling, and our new mayor is a very sensitive-type guy. The SOS is supposed to start getting solves and getting solves quick. And I got a cop standing before me right now who, all things being equal, is the perfect guy for this assignment. One of the first people I'd choose, to give you the God's honest."

"But all things aren't equal," I say.

"Right. You're a parasite around here."

"I think the word you're looking for is *pariah*."

He glares at me, even allows a smile. "That's the one, yeah. Okay, Mr. Word of the Day, so listen up. I've got a good team here. Some of the best in the city. Every one of them's looking at you wondering if you're going to screw it up. So don't."

"I won't, Lew."

He removes the cigar from his mouth, which usually means he's about to say something serious. "The only way we're going to stop the carnage out there is to solve murders. We solve murders, then the gangbangers don't think they can do whatever they want, whenever they want. The police stop being a joke to them. Witnesses start talking to us again. All that shit on the West Side's gonna stop. Because Special Ops is gonna *make* it stop. You hearin' me?"

He's probably waiting for another wisecrack. But that corny stuff? The stuff about how we're here to protect the good people who just want safe streets? That's what gets me every time. Every day that I was on paid leave, staring at my star, wondering if it was worth coming back to the force with all the baggage I'm carrying—every single time, all I had to do was think about why I wanted to be a cop since the day I could walk.

"I hear you, Lew. I won't let you down."

He stares at me until he's sure I'm being straight with him. "Okay, Harney, good. So get to it." He looks down at his desk, miraculously locating the file that had held his attention before I walked in. "Oh, and, uh..." He waves a hand absently, not looking up. "I apologize in advance for your partner."

CHAPTER 5

THE SUV is curbed along Cicero just north of the expressway, near a long brick building with the word FURNITURE stamped across the window, the store all boarded up and caged. "Turn that shit off," says Disco, alone in the back seat, to the men in the front, playing obnoxious dance music. "Or... move it to the front of the car."

"I don't know how to move it to the front." The two men in the front seat, dressed, like Disco, in shabby clothes and baseball caps, fiddle with the dashboard, trying to figure out how to transfer the music from the rear of the vehicle.

"Then turn it off!" Disco snaps, bowing his head, tapping his finger to his earpiece.

"The last customer just drove away," says the voice in his earpiece. *"It's been a busy morning. They were lined up six cars long an hour ago."*

"And everyone's outside?"

"Yeah. Shiv's on the porch with the girl."

"And you're ready with the backup?" he asks.

"Ready."

Disco glances at the men in the front seat. *Do we look like three dopeheads?* Close enough, he figures—three white guys in casual clothes. They come in all shapes and sizes these days. Addicts wear business suits and turtleneck sweaters and trendy clothes and torn shirts and sweatpants. They are lawyers and accountants and housewives and students and homeless junkies.

Do they look too much like they're *trying* to look like dopeheads? Disco, for his part, is wearing a sweatshirt he bought in a sporting goods store yesterday that he slept in last night, so it wouldn't look too nice and fresh.

He stretches his arms, shaking out the nerves. "Okay, let's go."

The men in front straighten up, check their weapons. One of them kills the music. The SUV—an eight-year-old model with a dented fender—pulls off the curb and turns onto Van Buren by a convenience store littered with spray-painted graffiti. The signs advertise two-liter bottles of pop for ninety-nine cents and lotto cards and Marlboros and an ATM.

"They have lookouts past the alley by Kilpatrick, north side."

"Okay. Boys," Disco calls out, "say something to each other and laugh. Look like you're not worried."

Disco sits back, playing it calm, seeing three African American girls jumping rope on a sidewalk, eyeing the SUV as it passes. Otherwise, Van Buren is quiet this time of day, shiny and bright from the noon sun, almost tranquil in outward appearances despite the dilapidated homes, the vacant lots littered with garbage.

His partners in front are doing as he asked, joking around, trying to smile—pulling it off better than he would've expected—as the SUV turns north onto Kilbourn.

"Backup is ready?" Disco whispers into his earpiece.

"Ready."

Here we go.

Disco removes his earpiece, throws it to the floorboard.

The SUV rolls northbound on Kilbourn. The men in front grow quiet. Disco's pulse thumps like a bass drum inside him. They pass an alley, a row of brick flats, a Dumpster. The vehicle pulls over to the left side, near a two-story brick walk-up where Shiv sits on the porch with the girl. A man idles by on the sidewalk, or pretends to be idling by, in an untucked Chicago Bears jersey. He glances up at the porch, at Shiv, who nods back. Then the man ambles over to the SUV.

"Roll down your window," Disco tells the driver, bracing himself.

"How you fellas doin'?" says the man, standing a few feet away, bent at the waist.

Disco slowly moves his head in the direction of the porch. Shiv, wearing a tight black shirt, long basketball shorts, and high-tops, sits on a step up to the porch. The girl, wearing a T-shirt too long and drooping over her shoulders, sitting next to him, arms wrapped around her knees.

Wait till the cash changes hands.

The driver hands over the cash. The man sweeps it away, tucks it into his pocket, and turns and tells them where to go, up the street and around the corner, to pick up the heroin.

While the man gestures up the street, the cash transaction already completed, Disco's right foot lifts up, raising the AR-15 at his feet. He grabs hold of it without moving his head or shoulders, tipping off nothing. Tucks his finger under the trigger.

He rolls down the window, sticks the barrel out the window, and starts firing.

The bullets rattle the front porch, splintering the wood, ripping across the chests of Shiv and the girl before they have a chance to react, shattering the window behind them and spraying the house's interior.

"Go! Go!" he hears himself shout as the SUV peels north.

CHAPTER 6

I WORK my way through the squad room, well lit, high ceilings, shiny new laptops at each station, one for each of the detectives brought in from all our twenty-five districts over the last month. There is a little bit of a first-day-of-school feel to it, as I look around and see some familiar faces. Some of them nod to me but show no inclination to do anything more. Some of them avert their eyes. A couple of them purse their lips or raise their eyebrows.

Not the warmest of receptions, but not unexpected. I'm a cop who took down other cops and exposed a scandal. Cops are a tight-knit bunch generally, an us-against-them bond that's never been more tangible than it is now, with the press routinely questioning our practices, citizens with cell phones trying to goad us into doing something stupid for the YouTube crowd, consent decrees requiring us to fill out reams of paperwork every time we frisk someone or remove our sidearms from their holsters. It's bad enough when the shit comes from outside our band of merry brothers and sisters, but when the damage is caused by one of us—by me—the instinct is to expel the Benedict Arnold from the circle. Or at least give him the freeze-out.

Whatever. I always lived by the motto *Just do your job*. Keep it simple.

"Excuse me, sir, only cops are allowed in here."

I smile before I turn my head as Detective Lanny Soscia wraps a beefy arm around my neck and threatens to knock me over. I've known Sosh since we were cadets in the academy. We worked patrol together, got our first detective's assignment in the same branch. He stood by me when all the walls came tumbling down on me. Both times, actually. First, when my wife and daughter died, four years ago, then this last year, when I got caught up in the spiderweb—nearly killed by a gunshot to the head, then charged with murder, with high-ranking officials falling like dominoes in my wake.

"Look at this detective in this elite new unit," he says after he lets me go. "I'm referring to myself, of course. How'd *you* get in here?"

"I have to shine the supe's shoes once a week," I say.

"That all you're shining?"

Someone calls out Sosh's name. He gives me a forearm shiver to the chest, then points at me. "Drive the speed limit for a while, right?"

I nod. It's good advice. I'll watch my step around here until I get the lay of the land.

I find my desk near the back, passing other people who eyeball me before finding themselves engrossed in conversation or fascinated by their phones. The woman dropping a box on the next desk over is around my age—midthirties—with kinky dark hair stopping just short of her shoulders, dark-complected with a spray of freckles across her cheeks. Biracial, I'm thinking. Or maybe Latina? There's no way in hell I'm going to ask her.

"Detective Harney," she says, turning to me.

"Hey, that's my name, too."

She blinks, swatting away the innocuous joke. No smile. "Detective Griffin," she says, sober as an undertaker. "Carla Griffin."

I shake her hand. “I was just... kidding around. Call me Billy.”

“Fine,” she says.

And should I call you Carla? No? Nothing?

“I look forward to working with you,” she says with a level of enthusiasm that tells me she’d look forward to a root canal more. I’ve seen statues with more animation.

“You, too. So... where you come from?”

“The second,” she says. “Wentworth.”

“Nice.” When I see she’s not seeking any return information from me—probably because she already knows it—I clap my hands together. “Well, let’s make the most of this assignment. I think we can really make a difference out there.”

“That’s my plan,” she says. “I hope it’s yours, too.”

She holds her stare on me.

“It is,” I say. “I just said that.”

“But I hope you mean it.”

“You got some reason to think I don’t?”

Down, boy. You knew this might be the reaction.

She goes back to her box, pulling out framed photographs and supplies and placing them carefully on her desk. A young boy is prominent among the photos. No man, though. Maybe she isn’t into men. Something else I won’t ask her.

“Let’s just... try to get through this as best we can,” she says.

Oh-kay.

I don’t have a box of stuff. I didn’t know where I was getting assigned. I thought, by this time of day, I’d be on horseback, or with a whistle in my mouth at the corner of Clark and Huron, or inventorying evidence behind a cage door.

All I have is a bottle of ibuprofen. I still get headaches from the bullet to my brain. No seizures yet, though they’ve been promised to me—*Could be a year or so after; you never know*—but headaches on an almost daily basis, yeah.

She's putting everything just so on her desk, a little extra thud on every item she drops down, indicating her state of mind.

"Let me ask you a question," I say. "How many times you turn this down? Partnering with me?"

She shakes her head, a smirk on her face, but doesn't look at me. "Nobody asked me my opinion."

"But you gave it anyway," I say. "How many times?"

She shoves the drawer closed with a bang, turns, and faces me, her expression hotter.

"Harney! Griffin!" Lieutenant Wizniewski, standing outside his office, wiggling his fingers toward us.

I look back at my new partner. We hustle to the Wiz's office.

"Three times," she says to me before we enter.

"A shooting in K-Town," says Wizniewski. "Four victims. You two will take the lead. Harney's the senior."

"Got it, Lew," says Griffin.

"This one's bad," he says. "It's gonna be very, very bad."

CHAPTER 7

WE SPEED to the crime scene over the pockmarked streets of the West Side, its wide boulevards where commerce once boomed now lined with boarded-up buildings, payday-loan and dollar stores, fast-food joints and liquor stores and gas stations, nothing big box or upscale. The West Side was once an enclave for the wealthy—then came the immigrants, then came the black migration from the South—before it was beaten down by one economic downturn after another over the course of decades, by the flight of professionals and the highly educated, leaving behind a skeleton of poverty and desperation, crime and unemployment.

K-Town is among the most violent of West Side neighborhoods, the gangs feasting like vultures, the summer nights a shooting gallery.

Though this shooting happened in broad daylight.

We park on Van Buren, just east of Kilbourn and short of the squadrol barricades. It's already a zoo, the residents spilling out of their homes to see the spectacle, a few reporters I recognize already on the scene. *Okay,* those media types will be saying, *let's see how good this SOS unit really is.*

Not that we needed more heat; it has to be in the mideighties out here, everyone wilting under the afternoon sun. In other circumstances, I'd probably lose the sport jacket.

A supervisor with Patrol, a woman named Bryant, grabs us as we walk under the yellow tape. "Hey, Billy," she says.

"Hey, Mary. Detective Carla Griffin, Mary Bryant," I say by way of introduction.

Forensic Services is just getting here, placing down evidence markers.

"It was a drive-by," says Bryant.

Right—so there won't be much in the way of evidence at this crime scene other than bullets and casings. We walk under a tree on the east side of Kilbourn that provides some relief from the heat. When we emerge on the other side, we cross the street and reach the house where it happened, a brick two-flat. We duck under the tape and stop, get a big-picture view.

A dreadlocked African American male in a Bears jersey and long shorts is facedown on the sidewalk amid a pool of blood, his lifeless eyes oblivious to the flies buzzing around him. He's wearing number 22, the one worn by our old running back Matt Forte, but bullets have ripped six or eight holes in it. Peeking out of his shirt, on the back of his neck, is a serpent coiled around a machete.

"He was a Hustler," I say.

"This is Stanley Wilson," says Bryant. "He went by Frisk. Yeah, a Hustler, low-level. Lookout, front man, courier, a guy who took orders."

"He approached the car?" asks Carla. "This was a drug buy?"

"Probably," says Bryant. "No drugs on him, but he had some tens and twenties in his pocket. So he was the screen, the pay window."

"Where's the pickup window?" Carla asks.

Bryant allows a grim smile. "I'm fairly sure they packed up business for the day. But you know how it works. It was probably around the corner, on the way back to 290. I took the liberty of sending out officers up and down Kilbourn and Van Buren—I assume you approve."

"Yeah, sure, Mary, thanks," I say before Carla can say something about chain of command.

So that's the first victim. Three more.

We carefully step around the Bears jersey and approach. On the right side of the porch—our right, that is—the dark wood is splintered everywhere, pockmarked from bullet holes, with spatters of blood and a deep pool of it on the top step.

"The man sitting on the porch stairs was Dwayne Sears," Bryant tells us. "Goes by Shiv. He's in surgery at Loretto. Multiple GSWs to the chest. No idea what his chances are. He was a lieutenant in the Hustlers. He was the real deal."

And he was probably the reason this happened. Whoever did this wasn't here for the courier by the sidewalk. Shiv must have been the target. And yet he's the only one who survived, at least so far.

The third victim, splayed out awkwardly on the walkway to the porch, is a young white woman. Blond hair still up in some kind of fashionable messy bun, her head resting on the top stair, lifeless eyes gazing into the beyond, her mouth open in a small circle. An oversize white T-shirt that falls to her thighs.

We lean over her. She's young—late teens, early twenties—and skeletally thin, unnaturally so, suggesting malnourishment. Four bloody gashes where gunfire ripped open her chest. Track marks on her bony arms. Encircling her throat is a necklace dangling a charm that looks like some kind of shepherd dog. A gold-studded watch marked CHANEL on its face, surely a knockoff she bought on the street for a hundredth of the retail price. And above her ankle, a small tattoo of a black flower.

I stifle the urge to cover her, to shield her, to swat away the buzzing flies.

"No ID on her," says Bryant. "Someone thinks, but isn't sure, she went by Evie."

Judging by the direction of the bullet holes battering this porch, I figure the girl was sitting next to Shiv when the shooter drove by. And judging by her position, I expect she hardly had the chance to move before the bullets riddled her body. She was dead before she knew what happened.

Inside the house, wailing, a woman's anguished howl.

Carla and I look at each other. "Ready?" I ask.

She goes first as we steel ourselves before we see the fourth victim.

CHAPTER 8

WE STEP inside the house: squeaky hardwood floor; mismatched, torn furniture.

An African American woman, early twenties—the mother, Janiece Moreland—tears streaming down her face, cradling her young daughter in her arms, as if she were a newborn, not a four-year-old girl. The little girl—LaTisha, I'm told—head in her mother's lap, pigtailed and chubby-cheeked, dressed in a red T-shirt with what appears to be a large squirrel on the front. Her eyes are closed peacefully. Her lips are pursed as if she were blowing a kiss. She would look like nothing more than a cute little girl sleeping in her mother's lap if not for the dark, mushy wound above her pigtail where the bullet hit. The white wall behind them is spattered with blood and small fragments of little LaTisha's brain.

I open my mouth, but words don't come out.

"Ms. Moreland," says Carla, "I'm Detective Griffin, and this is—"

A garbled cry from the mother, fresh tears. "You're not taking my baby. Ain't nobody taking my baby!" She lowers her cheek against her dead daughter's, that cherubic face.

I feel it across my chest first, radiating heat, then a *thud thud* pounding between my ears, sweat bursting from every pore, the images everywhere—

The memories from four years ago:

The hospital smells of iodine and bleach. The gentle beeps and whooshes and gurgles from the machines keeping her alive.

Her tiny hand engulfed in mine. My mumbling whispers: *C'mon, you can do it, wake up, honey, please wake up.*

Knowing she'd never wake up.

Praying to God to bring her back. Begging and pleading and bartering with Him. *Take me instead of her.* Berating and threatening and shouting at Him. *How could you let my three-year-old daughter die?*

An elbow pokes my arm. My daughter's face dissolves into the past. I turn to Mary Bryant as if jarred awake from a dream, her eyebrows creased in concern, a curt nod of the head, as in *Get a grip* or *You okay?*

I snap out of it, nod, draw a breath. I traveled there and back, but my feet are still planted where they were, next to Carla, who is squatting down, speaking with the mother in hushed tones, the woman struggling to answer amid heaving gasps.

I wipe my arm across my greasy forehead, useless and shaky, a spectator in my own investigation. I'm joining the conversation late, but I get the gist of the mother's story, most of which we already knew—she was at work, left LaTisha here with Shiv, her boyfriend. Got the call to come home and hasn't let go of her daughter since.

I follow Carla and Mary outside, feeling better with fresh air, no matter how thick and humid. Hoping that my new partner didn't notice me getting lost in there. She has a low enough opinion of me already.

"Poor woman," says Bryant. "No one's been able to find it in their heart to make her let go of that little kid."

I see Detective Soscia and his new partner slip under the yellow tape, heading toward our scene. That's good. I could use a friendly face on this one.

"So the only eyewitness is in surgery and might not survive," I summarize.

Bryant nods. "Unless one of the neighbors saw something. Anyone taking bets?"

Her skepticism isn't far off; there will be plenty of *nope-didn't-see-nuthin'* in our canvass. But there are a lot of people out here who don't want to live among this violence and who will stick their necks out, even at risk to themselves. We just have to find them.

"Keep us posted on the canvass," I say to Mary. "We're gonna do some of our own."

"Will do." Mary walks carefully down the porch steps.

I look at Carla, blinking away tears in her eyes. At least I wasn't the only one affected. "Both girls were collateral damage," she says, clearing her throat, nodding at the young woman lying on the porch. "And the courier wasn't the target. It had to be a hit on Shiv."

"Looks that way, yeah. Why hit a lieutenant with the K-Street Hustlers?"

She shrugs, looks out over the street. "We can hope he owed someone money, or he was doinking someone else's lady."

That would make it easier, if this whole thing was personal. Maybe LaTisha's mommy inside used to go with another guy who wasn't too pleased when Shiv stole her away. That would be easy.

But Carla doesn't think that. Neither do I.

No, this doesn't seem personal. This feels like business.

I tap her on the arm. "You didn't say 'turf war.' I didn't say 'turf war.'"

Because if the gangs are fighting over territory, this would be only the first shot in a long, bloody fight.

CHAPTER 9

THIS ONE is different. We know it immediately.

There are dozens of shootings a week in the city, headlines every Monday morning—19 SHOT OVER BLOODY WEEKEND—grim faces from our mayor and superintendent. We grunt with despair and mumble that *somebody really has to do something* before pouring our second cup of coffee. Next weekend's the same thing.

No names, no faces. Just a bunch of black people dead on the West Side.

But this one's different. Within an hour the crowd has swelled, filling a city block in each direction. Megaphones and chants: *Justice for LaTisha!* News trucks by every barricade, news copters buzzing overhead.

Because this time it was a cute chubby-cheeked little girl. Perfect for television. Somebody has already obtained a photo of little LaTisha wearing a ruffled chiffon dress, pigtails, and a radiant smile, and her image is showing up on cell phones everywhere.

The murder scene is mobbed. We try to bring order, to find out if anybody saw anything, but it's like trying to find a dropped penny on a crowded, sweaty dance floor. Our officers work a door-to-door canvass, but nobody's at home. They've all joined the crowd outside, the spectacle.

Nobody saw nothing. Or everybody saw everything.

The K-Street Hustlers did it. Those boys by Clark Park. Those folks who drive in from the suburbs for their dope. Someone saw a red sports car. Someone else, a blue SUV. It was three Mexicans. They were African American. It was two white guys. It's probably the Cannibals that did it, or the Jackson Street Crew, or the Nation, or the Disciples, or some crooked cops, angry they didn't get their payoff last week.

One woman yells at me about the burglary at her house two weeks ago, took the cops over an hour to show. An old man tells me we need to put in cul-de-sacs like they do on the South Side to prevent drive-bys.

Carla is finishing up an interview. I look over just as she slips a hand into her pants pocket. It comes out as a fist that she raises to her mouth, as if she's coughing, but instead she slips something between her lips before lowering her hand back down to the pocket. She glances around and catches my eye, does a double take, like I caught her doing something. But doing what? What did she slip into her mouth?

Cough drop? Aspirin? God, don't tell me Carla's a pill popper. Is that what Wizniewski meant when he apologized "in advance" for my partner?

What do we want?

Justice for LaTisha!

When do we want it?

Now!

My head ringing, made no easier with the sun beating down and several hundred people chanting and shouting while I try to take witness statements.

Detective Soscia, red and sweaty, grabs my arm. "We got some POD footage!" he shouts into my ear. Police observation devices, he means—closed-circuit cameras, usually mounted on traffic-control devices around the city. "There's one on Kilpatrick north of here by the park. A better one's near Kolmar on Van Buren. Just around the corner."

Screw it. It could be a lead. We're not getting anything from this crowd. We'll be lucky if all their anger and frustration doesn't turn this thing into a riot.

"Let's go check it out!" I shout back.

"We got no rope on this one, Billy Boy," Sosh says. "We need this solved by yesterday."

CHAPTER 10

"YOU GOT informants, work 'em," I say to the roomful of detectives and uniforms. "You need informants, pick 'em up on whatever you can and flip 'em. Tell 'em the CPD is holding a tag sale, 99 percent off for information leading to an arrest. Route all information through Soscia or Officer Bostwick. And let 'em know about the hotline number, too.

"Gang Crimes," I say. "We have a UC in the K-Street Hustlers?"

Nobody knows. SOS is a new unit, just up and started, not local. But it's likely the cops in the Eleventh would have an undercover with the gang.

A guy shouts out, name of Jimenez. "Don't know about any UCs, but I'll find out."

"Great—do it," I say. Nobody should have a better idea of who hit the Hustlers than the Hustlers themselves.

I check my watch. It's nearly 5:00 p.m.

"Eight bells, tomorrow morning, we're back here in this room. Eight and five, every day, until we solve. But we'll have this wrapped up by tomorrow, right?"

Yeah, probably not, but it won't be for lack of trying.

Lieutenant Wizniewski takes front and center. "This is why you're here," he tells the room. "This case is the exact reason we have SOS. They already have a protest rally planned, day after tomorrow, at Daley Plaza. Father Pfleger, Jesse Jackson—even Reverend Al is flying in for it. Let's have a solve by then, ladies and gentlemen."

The crew breaks up. The Wiz levels a stare on me. "Get this solved, Detective."

"Will do, Lew."

That's what I keep telling myself. I've been gone a long time, after the shooting and recovery and then that fun little murder charge filed against me. I'm rusty. Figured I still had it in me, but you never know. Until you're back, until you're in the shit again, you don't really know.

I still don't. The docs swear to me up and down that I don't have any permanent damage from the shooting. Headaches aside, that seems right. Visibly, at least. Arms and legs work fine, reflexes seem okay. I can still hit a target with my Glock. I don't slur my words, no droop on one side of my face. But I'm a rebuilt car, and I've never seen a wrecked car come back as good as new. This is a hell of a case for my first test run.

But I won't show it. I can't. You show fear, hesitation, uncertainty, you're nothing on the street or in this house.

My phone buzzes in my pocket, a new text message:

Don't keep me in suspense!

This from my sister, Patti, also a CPD detective. I promised to let her know when I got my new assignment. I haven't had a chance to get back to her. She's been shooting me notes all day. What's your horsie's name? Just say no to illegal left turns. Crossing guards are people, too! Real supportive stuff.

You won't believe it, I write back. SOS.

No fn way, she types back.

Same reaction I had.

The lead teams—Carla and I, Soscia and his partner, Mateo

Rodriguez—head to Mat's desk, where he's got the POD footage pulled up.

"Shiv's dead," Mat says. "Didn't survive the surgery."

Great. Another casualty. Another potential lead lost.

We reach his desk, where he shows us what he found.

"That's gotta be it," Sosh says. "That's gotta be the car."

Sosh and Mat did the initial run through the POD footage. One at Cicero and Van Buren, one on Van Buren near Kilbourn. Closest thing to triangulation we can manage.

Best bet, the shooters drove east on Van Buren, probably from Cicero, and then took Kilbourn north. That's how the suburbanites buy their smack, and it wouldn't draw attention. The Heroin Highway does a brisk business.

The POD footage is black-and-white, herky-jerky—the camera rotates every three seconds—and grainy. So we can see the vehicles but not their colors. We might get partials on license plates at best. And we usually can't see the occupants inside the vehicles.

Still, we have five vehicles in our sights. Sosh thinks it's the last of the five, captured by the Van Buren POD only four minutes before we received our first 911 call about the shooting. He's probably right.

"Pretty sure that's a Toyota 4Runner," says Rodriguez. Like me, Detective Mateo Rodriguez comes from a family of cops. Until today I'd never met him or heard of him, but Sosh says the word is Mat comes from good people, and Sosh has sources everywhere. Me, I usually assume the best about people until they give me a reason not to, which usually takes around ten minutes.

"Let's run that partial against stolen vehicles and vehicle regs."

"Now, why didn't I thinka that?" Sosh smirks. "Waiting on a call."

"And we need to ID the dead girl on the porch. Mat, you got the DNA sample to Forensics?"

"Done."

Sosh answers his cell phone, gets a look on his face. “The 4Runner,” he says. “Reported stolen last night in Melrose Park.”

“Great.” That’s it. That’s the vehicle.

“My cousin’s deputy chief out there,” he says. “I’ll go now.”

Mat reaches for his phone. “Lemme text my wife.”

Sosh clasps a hand on Mat’s shoulder. “Detective Rodriguez, take it from me: it’s better to ask for forgiveness than permission.”

“Marital advice from a guy with two divorces,” I say. “You should probably carry around a recorder so you can memorialize all these pearls of wisdom.”

“I don’t need my wife’s permission,” Mat insists.

“Sure ya don’t.” Soscia winks at me and grabs his sport jacket. “C’mon, Rodriguez, we’ll get a beef sandwich at Johnnie’s on North Avenue. My treat.”

“Write that down,” I say. “When the bill comes, he’ll forget he ever said it.”

They take off, leaving me and Carla. She’s over by her desk, throwing some things together and popping another pill in her mouth, her back turned.

Jesus, that better be aspirin. Or a vitamin.

“Feeling okay?” I ask without looking at her.

“I was gonna ask you the same question,” she says. “When we were inside that house, you were looking a little wobbly.”

Nice deflection. She’s quick on her feet.

I shoot a glance her way. “That right?”

“I mean, I get it, with your past, your daughter and all. Anyone would understand.”

I throw on my sport jacket. “Detective, we’re on the clock. You got something to say, say it.”

“I just want to make sure nothing’s gonna slow us down. This is too important.”

I turn to her. She’s looking right at me.

"Am I slowing you down so far?" I ask.

"Hey." She opens her hands. "I'm just saying. This is the deep end, Harney."

"I didn't forget how to swim, but thanks for your concern." I snatch my keys off the desk. "C'mon," I say.

"Where we going?"

"You'll find out," I say. "If you can keep up."

CHAPTER 11

DISCO PULLS his convertible up to the curbside valet and throws it in Park. "Do not speak unless you are spoken to," he says to Nadia. "This is one of the finest restaurants in Chicago."

"I know." Her tight purple dress worn off the shoulder, hair slicked back into a bun.

"What do you know about fine restaurants?" Nothing, that's what she knows.

He turns the rearview mirror toward himself, his hair gelled and coiffed, two days' worth of stubble on his face, small circular eyeglasses. Nailed it.

He sucks in his stomach and walks toward the simple black door to Domaine—the name of the restaurant spelled out in fashionably minimalist small-block lettering. This place is, indeed, one of the city's finest, if you believe *Time Out Chicago,* but Disco's not much of a foodie. He just likes being seen in one of Chicago's finest restaurants.

Business always comes first, always, said the general years ago. *But you must make time to enjoy life's comforts, too.*

Besides, one day he might be running more than Chicago. He could get the entire Midwest. That would mean millions. He might as well get used to consorting with the elite.

Inside, low-hanging lanterns wash simple wood tables in dim orange light, while casual-cool patrons sitting in black chairs listen to retro music playing from the overhead sound system. Most of the men are wearing jackets over T-shirts or open-collar dress shirts, some in jeans.

Disco frowns. He overdressed. But he still looks good, and enough heads turn at Nadia and her sleek figure to make him feel better, keep his chin held high. She was the right one to bring. Nadia is probably his hottest girl, certainly one of the most popular.

And besides, fuck all these people and their stares. How many of them left their native country as he did, moved to the States, built an operation from scratch, got a law degree even though English was his second language?

None of them.

How many have killed eighteen people, including three this morning?

Zero, that's how many. He has more balls than all these trust-fund babies and tech millionaires combined.

He had preordered a 2006 Allemand Cornas, which he chose from the online menu after checking reviews in *Wine Enthusiast*, *Wine Spectator*, and some wine-tasting blogs. The sommelier pours the first taste for him and waits.

He drinks it as you're supposed to drink it. As he's seen the general drink it. Appreciate the glass. Hold it to the light. Tilt it. Sip the wine. Suck on it, swirl it.

Disco swallows the sip, looks at the sommelier. "It needs to open up," he says.

He's heard the general say that.

"Yes, sir. Shall I decant it?"

Disco trips over that. Decant? But he quickly and casually says, "Yes."

The waiter leaves with the bottle.

Nadia doesn't understand. She wouldn't. She is beautiful and sexy when she is dressed up, but she is stupid, just like the rest of them. Good for one thing and one thing only. "Read your menu," he tells her, as if she's capable of reading it. She's been here four years and has picked up English only from what she's been told and what she's seen on the television in the basement.

Disco is in the midst of checking his phone under the table, looking up the word *decant,* when it buzzes.

His other phone. His burner phone. The phone for which only three people have the number.

Probably Nicolas, still worried about today. *You fired too many shots,* he complained after they sped away. *You killed too many people.*

He had to smack Nicolas to get him back in line. *Nobody cares about a bunch of black drug dealers,* he explained to him. *They shoot each other all the time.*

But it's not Nicolas texting. It's Augustina, with a link to a news article in the online *Sun-Times*.

He stops breathing. He knows from the headline alone. He thought he killed three people today in K-Town. But he didn't. He killed four.

He opens the link: FOUR-YEAR-OLD AMONG VICTIMS IN WEST SIDE SHOOTING. The story is the headline on the page. A photo of an African American toddler, wearing pigtails, a fancy dress, and a beaming, innocent smile.

No. No. But yes. The 300 block of South Kilbourn, midday.

He clicks over to the *Tribune*'s site. The same lead headline, the same photo. Four-year-old LaTisha Moreland among the victims of a drive-by shooting, believed to be drug-related. A protest rally planned for the day after tomorrow at Daley Plaza. The mayor pleading for calm The police superintendent vowing to bring the killers to justice.

He dials Augustina on the burner phone, his hands shaking. He crouches inward, cups his free hand around his mouth. "She was not out there," he says when Augustina answers, noting the shake in his own voice. "I saw no little girl outside."

"She was inside house," says Augustina. *"You must have shot through window."*

He closes his eyes. Of all the luck. There are shootings on the West Side all the time, but when *he* does it, it's a headline story?

"I call Boho?"

"No!" he hisses, catching the harshness, the fear in his voice. "Do not call the general. I will handle this. Understand?"

He cuts out the phone, straightens up, runs a shaky hand over the stubble on his cheek. What is he going to do now?

The sommelier places down a long goosenecked glass vessel holding the red wine.

"What is this?" Disco snaps. "I do not want this. Take this away."

"I'm sorry, sir, you wanted to open it up—"

Disco lashes out, backhands the decanter off the table, wine splashing on Nadia, glass shattering on the floor. The heavy din of conversation ceases abruptly.

"There—now it is opened up." Disco gets to his feet, rocking the table. He pulls a wad of money from his pocket, counting out twelve hundred-dollar bills, throws them down on the table. He grabs Nadia by the arm.

"Hey, excuse me!" The next table over, a man standing, brushing splattered wine off his slim-fitting shirt. "You spilled wine all over us, guy."

Disco pivots, fixes a stare on the man, grips the man's flimsy bicep, squeezing, his fist like a tourniquet. The man's indignation immediately turns to alarm. "You should sit back down," Disco says, "before this becomes embarrassing for you."

He shoves the man back into his seat. Turns to the waiter, who backs away, hands up in peace.

Disco straightens his suit jacket. Turns and leaves, Nadia following.

On his way out, he dials his phone. "We have to meet," he says. "Right now."

CHAPTER 12

"YOU KNOW about the protest rally day after tomorrow," says Lieutenant Wizniewski over the speakerphone of my cell.

"Right, you mentioned."

"'Cops don't care about black victims.' 'Cops don't protect the West Side.' 'Justice for LaTisha.' Read me?"

"Read you," I say.

"The supe's putting the entire force on riot duty. They're gonna shut down the courts and the government buildings, evacuate the downtown. I don't gotta remind you what happened last time."

The last time this happened, a year and a half ago, after a cop shot an unarmed African American kid, what started as a peaceful protest turned ugly. Some blamed the police for overreacting. Others blamed the protesters. Either way, everything went to shit. The Daley Center was smashed up, there was a fire down by the Old Post Office, protesters flooded and shut down the Eisenhower Expressway. Multiple dead and dozens of casualties, damage to businesses in the millions.

"It's gonna be a fucking mess, Harney. Unless."

Unless we solve this case by tomorrow.

"We're working on the 'unless,' Lew."

"Keep me posted."

"Will do." I punch out the phone. We're speeding along the West Side, close to our destination.

"We should call ahead," Carla says from the passenger seat. "This could get us shot."

She might be right. But I don't think so. "Andre's not gonna shoot us."

She glances over at me. "What, I make a comment about your daughter, and you not being up for this assignment, and now you have to show me what a hard-ass you are?"

"Yeah, Griffin, you nailed it again. You've got me figured, all right. We got the biggest heater we've seen in years, with a dead little girl, a riot about to break out on the West Side, the mayor and the superintendent breathing down our necks, but all I'm worried about is your opinion of me."

She goes quiet, conceding the point. She's wrong about my motives, because I wouldn't give two shakes of my weenie over what she thinks of me, but she may be right that an unannounced visit to Andre Oliver isn't the best idea.

"Your daughter was three when she died?"

"Oh, good, we're gonna talk about that again."

"And you lost your wife the same day?"

"Jesus," I sigh. "Yes. Just to get this over with. Yes, my wife and daughter died on the same day."

She lets out a breath of her own. "Life can be cruel."

"Gee, yet more keen insight from you. What's next? The weather's unpredictable?"

"Doesn't give you the right to be an asshole, Harney."

I veer the car over, put it in Park at the curb. "My daughter died of a stroke, okay? A fluke. One in a million. A three-year-old had a fuckin' stroke. Nothing we coulda done. Never coulda seen it coming. That's life being cruel."

She nods.

"My wife, she had depression, and then this thing with our daughter hit, and she couldn't handle it. And I was too caught up with my daughter to realize how much it was killing my wife. So her eating a bullet? That wasn't life being cruel. That was me fucking up. That was me failing her. You got that all down on your scorecard? Is get-to-know-ya time over?"

Not sure where all that came from. Those feelings about Valerie have always lurked under the surface, but I've rarely said them out loud. I don't know why I picked now, with Carla, to unleash them. Probably the lateness of the hour, the stress, the fact that she's been busting my balls all day with this passive-aggressive bullshit.

"My father had depression," she says. "A chemical imbalance. It took him—it took us—a long time to realize it. It's not always easy to recognize."

Especially if you never see your wife because you're working the night shift while she works days, trading off responsibilities for the baby. And then your daughter has a stroke, and you turn every ounce of your attention on her, ignoring your wife at the very time when her suffering has exponentially multiplied.

"And you know how many homicides I've solved since that happened, four years ago?" I say. "I'll tell you, because yes, I keep count. Thirty-one. Thirty-fucking-one. So yeah, seeing a dead girl today, maybe it brought back some memories, and maybe my knees got shaky for three seconds. But I'm gonna put on my big-boy pants and solve this one, too."

She looks over at me but doesn't speak. A truce, détente.

"Let's go say hello to Andre," she says.

I remember Andre Oliver from when I was a high school kid. He was my age, but he went to Simeon, where he played power forward and drew the attention of virtually every Division I program in the nation. He was the next Magic, the next Jordan, graceful and powerful, a beautiful touch on the ball. He got a ride to U of

I, which back then attracted most of the Chicago talent, but got kicked off the team freshman year after a rape charge, followed by a B and E that ended with him punching out the cop who busted him. He did some time, went to Europe to play, blew out his knee, and came back home, still a hoops legend but with an asterisk.

Now he's involved in several ventures—basketball camps and a nightclub and his own rap label—but more important for our purposes, Andre Oliver is the undisputed leader of the K-Street Hustlers, who lost two of their soldiers today in a drive-by.

"So tell me why we don't call ahead," she says. "Andre's gonna have a battalion covering him tonight."

"We don't call ahead because cops don't call ahead. We show up when we want, where we want. We don't ask permission."

That's not what she meant, but she takes the point anyway. We have to show we're in charge.

I slow the car as we get close to his house, two miles away from K-Town. The streets are quiet, but they're not deserted. We catch plenty of eyes as we pass.

Sentries. Andre's gonna have 'em out in full force tonight. He's hunkering down for an assault right now while planning one of his own in response.

I drive the speed limit, use my signal when we turn. Last thing I want to do is come storming up to the house.

I curb the car in front of Andre's house, turn to my partner.

"Ready?" I say to her.

CHAPTER 13

THE BLOCK is covered on both sides with parked cars, most occupied by young men, heavily armed, who'd be letting everyone see their weapons if they hadn't just been told that a cop car was coming around the corner.

The K-Street Hustlers are circling the wagons tonight, after the drive-by, preparing for war.

Andre Oliver's house isn't much to look at from the outside, a two-story brick building with a small lawn and wraparound porch. Two men on the porch stand up as Carla and I get out of our car. Our stars hang from lanyards around our necks, as if the flashing cherry on the dash and every other single thing about us didn't already signal that we are cops.

"We need to talk to Andre," I say before these guys say a word.

"He's not available," says the guy on the left, tall and wide, probably early twenties. Dreads hang to his shoulder, gold chains from his neck. A bulge under his T-shirt for his hand cannon. Once upon a time, that was cause for arrest right there, but the Supreme Court changed everything when it said guns are a constitutional right.

"Does 'not available' mean he's here but busy?" I say. "Or he's not here?"

"He's not available, Officer."

Behind us, a couple of car doors open. I look behind me, but casually, the men watching me by their car doors, automatic weapons within arm's reach.

"Go get him," I say to the man on the porch. "Tell him Chicago police detectives want to ask him some questions. You have thirty seconds."

"You officers have a warrant?" he asks.

"Oh, good, you have an education," I say. "That means you can count. We're down to twenty seconds now. Wanna guess what happens in twenty seconds if Andre doesn't come out?"

"We'll start with the two of you," says Carla. "Then your friends over there hiding by their cars. You guys all have permits for your weapons? That'll be the first question." She shrugs. "Either way, even if you're clean, we take all of you in for questioning. Is that what Andre would want? Half his crew taken in for the night? Seems like he wants his people nice and close right about now."

The tough guy blinks. His left hand, near his sidearm, opens and closes.

"Don't even think about it," I say.

The other guy on the porch, shorter and heavier, tenses up, his legs spreading apart.

Maybe Carla had a point about calling ahead.

"Five seconds," I say, watching the first one's left hand, separated by a thin piece of shirt cloth from his handgun.

But he's saved by his right hand, where his phone bleeps once. He looks at the phone, then looks away. "Follow me," he says.

CHAPTER 14

WE INTERRUPTED a summit, a meeting of the Hustlers' top brass, a war council. A number of men emerge from the basement door, all tight shirts and biceps and gold chains and tats, each one making it clear that they aren't intimidated or even impressed by the police in their presence.

Andre's home, not surprisingly, is much nicer on the inside than it would appear from the outside. He knocked down some walls, opting for an open floor plan, a nice family room with a sectional sofa, a large TV mounted on the wall, a fancy Oriental rug. Photos of him are everywhere—framed pictures from his high school days, showing him flying through the air toward the basketball rim; headlines announcing that "Sir Andre" committed to the U of I; a gigantic "Mr. Basketball" trophy he won for being player of the year.

Our guide takes us down a flight of stairs with plush purple carpeting to a basement with the same carpet laid from wall to wall. This man cave of man caves contains a fully stocked bar, a basketball hoop, two big-screen TVs, sports memorabilia, and pornographic posters.

Andre Oliver is spread out on a purple couch—six feet and six inches of solid muscle and attitude, dressed in long basketball shorts and a T-shirt, giving Carla a good look-over before even acknowledging me.

"Ain't a great time for this," he tells us. "I got nothin' to do with what happened."

Yeah, we didn't like Andre for shooting up his own people. That's not how a leader disciplines his crew. If Shiv and Frisk needed a lesson, it would've been given behind closed doors, not in a drive-by shooting.

"Looks like you're hunkered down for a war," I say.

He allows one shoulder to lift. "Don't look for no war. One's declared, I don't back down. Can't back down, am I right?"

"Who declared the war?" I ask.

He likes that, chuckles, runs his tongue over his teeth. "Who you think?"

"The King," Carla says.

"Smart, too," he says to me, gesturing to Carla.

Jericho Hooper is the leader of the largest street gang currently operating in the city, the Imperial Gangster Nation. King Jericho, so it goes, or just the King.

"How do you know it was Jericho?" I ask.

"Oh, the brother wrote me a full confession." Andre pats the cushions around him. "Gotta be here somewhere. He told me to give it to the po-lice when they show up."

He's pretty happy with himself. But it's all a show. He's feeling serious heat. The Hustlers don't have the firepower to take on the Nation. Andre knows that better than anyone.

Problem is, it won't stop him from retaliating. He doesn't have a choice now. Jericho killed two of his men in audacious fashion. If he doesn't answer, his blood's in the water.

"Give us the shooter," says Carla, "and we tie it back to Jericho. Put your competition outta business. Without you guys shooting each other up."

Andre puts a finger to his temple. "Now, why didn't I thinka that?" He leans back against the couch, puts his feet up on an ottoman.

I kick the ottoman out from under his legs, forcing him forward.

"Andre, use your brain," I say. "You go to war with Jericho, you lose. What you're not seeing is that you have a chance to win."

"We catch the shooter," says Carla, "maybe we flip him. He gives up Jericho."

Andre's not buying it. "Ain't nobody gonna flip on Jeri-Curl."

"You sure?" I ask. "Why not give it a chance? If we can make that happen, you don't have to do anything. We do your work for you. We put Jericho behind bars. And you don't lose any more soldiers."

He takes his time. It'll be on his terms, after he runs his tongue over the inside of his cheek some more, pops in a toothpick and works it around.

"Give us forty-eight hours," I say. "Don't do anything for forty-eight hours. Give us time to catch the shooter."

He pulls out the toothpick, looks at the floor. "Twenty-four," he says. "And then there has to be an answer, know what I'm sayin'?"

I look at Carla. Twenty-four hours before both sides start shooting.

"Think we can solve this in twenty-four hours?" Carla asks me once we're back in the car.

"I can think of one way," I say. "But it's a long shot."

I look through my phone directory for a beat reporter with the *Sun-Times*. "I need a favor," I say. "I need a phone number."

CHAPTER 15

DISCO CURBS his car along Monticello in Albany Park, the city's northwest side. Gets out of the car, buttons his suit jacket, and walks down the alley. He passes four garages. The fifth one is open, a Range Rover parked inside. He stands still for a moment to make sure he isn't surprising anyone.

Then he walks into the garage and gets in the car, hit immediately with the scent of aftershave.

"You fucked up. You fucked up royally."

Disco hasn't even planted his ass in the seat before the rebuke comes. "The little girl was inside the house. I did not see her."

Dennis Porter is dressed in a cotton shirt and dark slacks, a baseball cap on his head of gray hair. He was at home having dinner with his family, apparently, when Disco called him from the restaurant. "Well, it's a fuckin' shit show now. They're running it out of SOS, the shiny new top-notch crew. You better find a way to fix this."

"*You* better find a way," says Disco. "You're the cop."

Second in command of Internal Affairs, to be precise. Captain Dennis Porter has proved himself both useful and resourceful. Disco is going to need both of those traits.

Porter wags a finger. "You don't pay me enough to work miracles.

You killed a fuckin' *toddler*. You didn't even tell me you were gonna do this."

"I need your permission now?" Disco comes back. Always the battle over who's in charge—the dirty cop or the gangster paying him.

"You got some nasty business you gotta take care of, yeah, you tell me first. Maybe I can show you a better way. And you couldn't have picked a worse way."

"It was an accident. A mistake."

"Yeah, *your* mistake, not mine. Not my problem."

Always the negotiator, Porter. He's not really saying he won't help. He's saying it won't come for free. He'll want a bonus.

Disco grabs Porter's forearm, a vise grip. Porter turns and looks at him, first with a cop's indignation, aggression, but his expression quickly softens, adjusting to the reality that the situation is a lot more complicated than that.

"My problem," says Disco, "is your problem."

"The fuck are you doing?"

"I want to hear you say it."

"Let go . . . of my *fucking* arm." Jaw clenched, lips hardly moving, watery eyes.

"Not until you say it, Denny. Say it for Amy. Say it for Jay and Laura."

"You don't want to threaten me, my friend."

Porter can play it tough, but he has to know that Disco's right. He can trust Disco for one thing and one thing only—to pay him handsomely to protect Disco's business. If he fails in that regard and Disco goes down, why wouldn't Disco make life easier on himself and cut a deal to implicate the cop who protected him?

The dirty cop's dilemma: once you're in with the bad guys, you're in all the way.

"Yeah, we gotta figure this out together, okay? Fuck." Porter yanks his arm free, Disco willingly releasing it. It was close enough to a full concession.

The stick having been shown, it's time for the carrot. Disco hands over an envelope full of cash. "This is double the usual. Because of our problem."

The money usually helps Porter's attitude. Porter takes it, counts it, confirms it. Nods his head with reluctance.

"You have someone in SOS?" asks Disco.

It takes a moment for Porter to recover his pride. "I got someone everywhere," he says. "It's the benefit of my position." As Porter always likes to say, Internal Affairs knows everything.

"Who is your source at SOS?"

"My source is my source. You don't need to know. I ever let you down before?"

No, he hasn't. If Porter's capability wasn't clear before, it certainly was after he managed to survive the fallout of the recent CPD scandal, which took down several members of the Bureau of Internal Affairs.

"I got an idea," Porter says. "I got a way to fix this. But it's gotta be quick. And it's gotta be you that does the heavy lifting."

"Me? That will not work."

"Well, it's gonna *hafta* work, pal. This thing's a fuckin' nightmare. My people can't be anywhere near it. We'll put the finishing touches on it. But the legwork? It's gotta be you."

No sense in arguing. This is where Porter excels. If Porter says it has to be Disco, it has to be Disco.

"And it's gotta be tonight," says Porter.

CHAPTER 16

THE VIBE is off tonight, she notices as soon as she walks in.

The Hole in the Wall is a copper's joint, co-owned by three guys who were on the job and put in their twenty. Half-off drinks for the men and women in blue, which is around 90 percent of the population in here, so it's not so much a discount for cops as it is a double charge on civilians for the privilege of mingling.

The mood's typically loud and merry, a place to blow off steam, to bitch about department politics or the YouTube crowd just itching to catch coppers in a bad moment, out of context, so they can post it on social media. You're among friends at the Hole.

But it's tense tonight, and Detective Patricia Harney knows why. The shooting in K-Town. It's got every politician in Chicago spooked, so it has the department spooked, too.

She's not here to drink. She had a couple with two of her friends in Lincoln Park before coming here, and that's enough for her these days, now that she's gotten serious about marathon training. She has a six-miler planned for tomorrow morning.

She's here to see her twin brother. But Billy isn't here. She half expected to see him on the makeshift stage in the corner, where anyone can grab the microphone and do a few minutes of stand-up. Billy's the best. He'll grab the mike and just start being funny, without prep; she doesn't know how he got that gene for fearlessness and quick thinking, the one that escaped her entirely.

Lanny Soscia's here, though, holding court with some young ones, drinking out of a tall glass, something that looks like cola.

"Patti-Cake!" he says, throwing an arm around her. "Haven't seen you in a dog's age."

"Got a minute?" she says.

They find their way to a booth in the corner. "Rookies, scatter," he says, and the new patrol officers clear out of the booth, just like that. It always amuses Patti how the seniority system works in here, as if they're still at the academy. "And get us a couple whiskeys."

Sosh drops into the booth like a load of bricks. "I can have one," he says.

"Just one?" That would be a first for Soscia.

"Just got here from the station," he says. "This shooting. Jesus." He runs a hand over his thinning hair.

"And Billy's lead?"

The whiskeys drop on the table, one for each of them.

"He's doing fine," says Sosh. "I admit I was worried, too. But he just hopped back on the bike and started pedaling."

"You guys partners?"

"No. I got Mat Rodriguez. Good seed. Good cop. Your brother, he, uh..." Sosh shakes out a laugh. "She's a real piece a work, that one."

"She?"

"Yeah. She's about as fun as a case of hemorrhoids. I don't know much about her, except that I didn't see her smile once today."

"Huh," says Patti. "A quadruple murder, including a dead little girl, and she didn't find a reason to smile? That's weird."

"You know what I mean."

She knows what he means, sure, but does anyone say that kind of thing about a man? A guy who keeps a stiff upper lip is stoic, maybe rough around the edges. A woman who does it is a frigid, humorless bitch.

"Okay, look," Sosh says, after he throws the whiskey back. "No, it wasn't a festive occasion today, but she hardly said two words. I mean, we're a team, right? We jaw a little. We gotta have, y'know, camaraderie. Get to know each other. She didn't say shit."

"Who is she?" Patti takes a sip of the whiskey, makes a face, slides it across the table to Sosh.

Sosh takes it and downs it. "Name's Carla Griffin," he says.

Patti does a double take, falls back in her seat. No way.

"She's from Wentworth," he continues. "She worked Narcotics—"

"I know who Carla Griffin is," she says. She puts a hand over her face.

"You know something I don't?"

This is a first. Sosh knows everybody in the department. He's privy to the gossip, the grapevine. He *is* the grapevine. This seems to be the exception. He doesn't know about Carla Griffin.

But every woman in the department does.

Billy said all along the superintendent would try to screw him. He figured he'd get some crap traffic assignment or a desk job. Instead, he got Carla Griffin.

"Shit," she mumbles to herself. "He's being set up."

CHAPTER 17

THE CHURCH looms large and silent near midnight, with its massive arches and sharp angles, looking much like a beacon on the city's South Side.

The massive parking lot is not empty. A black Cadillac is parked near the entrance. Flanking it on both sides are Chevy Blazers filled with heavily armed men.

Mike Spaulding, one of the city's top defense lawyers, who's made splashy appearances in political corruption cases, mob prosecutions, and celebrity trials, greets us on the sidewalk in front of the church, shaking hands with Carla and me. He is dressed down, having taken my phone call from his home in the Gold Coast, rushing out here on short notice.

Not that I gave him a choice. Either produce Jericho Hooper within the hour, I told him, or we come looking for him. He quickly agreed that a covert meeting was preferable for any number of reasons.

"We met in court," Spaulding says to Carla. "You worked Narcotics? The thing out of Cal City a few years back?"

"Don't remind me," she says, trying to make that sound friendly.

"He's inside." Spaulding heads up the stairs to the door.

"They open churches for him now, do they?" Carla mumbles to me.

Apparently. We follow Spaulding through massive oak doors. The interior is spacious, covered in red carpet, filled with stained-glass windows and oak pews. On the carpeted steps leading up to the altar sits King Jericho, dressed all in black silk—matching shirt and pants—and sandals.

"Pajamas?" Carla whispers out of the side of her mouth.

"Who knows? He's probably telling us how unimportant we are."

"Doesn't help that we're coming to him," she jabs.

True, but we need to handle Jericho differently from the leader of the Hustlers. We just asked Andre Oliver to give us some breathing room before he retaliates. We're going to ask Jericho for a lot more than that.

Jericho stands slowly, shorter than I expected, no more than six feet, and extends lanky fingers in my direction. He's nothing impressive to look at, but everything about him—his posture; his impassive, calculating eyes—radiates power as if it were a distinctive cologne.

"I've explained to my client that he's here to listen," says Spaulding.

Jericho nods his head, covered in gray braids, a soul patch on his chin.

Jericho Hooper committed his first murder when he was fourteen, too young to be prosecuted as an adult. He learned well in juvenile detention. He beat a second murder charge when he was twenty-two—the witnesses had sudden changes of heart—and was in and out of Stateville on convictions for residential burglary, aggravated battery, witness intimidation, and possession with intent to deliver heroin. But for the last seven years, Jericho has had no arrests. He thinks of himself as untouchable now. The feds estimate his net worth at eighteen million dollars. He launders the gang money through the typical avenues—two nightclubs, three convenience stores, and a handful of laundromats.

Forty-two years old, and this kid from Cabrini-Green is rich beyond what he ever imagined, the head of an empire.

I only have one chance to do this, so I better do it right.

CHAPTER 18

"I'M NOT here about justice," I say. "I'm here to talk about business."

Spaulding and his client Jericho remain impassive.

I pull a photo of LaTisha Moreland out of my jacket pocket and hand it to Jericho. "That photo's everywhere," I say. "The papers. The local news. The national cable networks. Everyone wants justice. The mayor, the superintendent, they aren't going to stop until they get it. It's a political thing. The superintendent, he'll lose his job if we don't get a solve and get it quickly. I will, too."

"Not to mention Andre Oliver," says Carla. "The Hustlers are gearing up for battle with you."

Spaulding nods, impatient. "There's a point to this?"

"The Nation was behind this," I say. "Jericho wants the Hustlers' turf. And if a little girl hadn't been killed, this case never would've made it to SOS. It probably never would've been solved. But you did kill a little girl. And now it *has* to be solved."

Spaulding opens his hands. "If you're suggesting that my client was responsible for this—"

"I'm not suggesting it, Counselor. I'm saying it. It's not up for debate. So the question is, what's Jericho going to do about this?"

"Sounds like you're about to tell us."

"I am. Jericho's going to give us the shooter, and we're going to arrest that individual."

A chuckle bursts from Spaulding. "That's—I mean, listen, Detective—"

"If he doesn't by tomorrow, we're holding a press conference," I say. "We will announce that we like the Nation for this shooting. The turf war, the whole thing. Easy for the public to understand. And the mayor will demand that CPD declare war on the Imperial Gangster Nation. Jericho's name will be plastered all over the papers. He'll be famous."

Jericho blinks, looks away. There is probably some appeal to Jericho's ego in that. But there's a reason why Jericho has been successful. He's flown under the radar, quietly building his empire. He doesn't want to be a household name.

"This conversation is ridiculous," says Spaulding, "and it's over."

"We're here to listen. So let's listen." Jericho finally speaks. Just a few words, but enough to sweep the legs out from under his lawyer.

Spaulding has no choice here but tries to recover some of his dignity by saying, as if it was his idea, "I guess you might as well finish your ridiculous proposal."

"I have all the resources I need," I continue. "For this case? With this kind of heat? I could post a patrol car on every corner of every block of your turf. We'll have a battalion of officers itching to knock down doors."

"Feds would want in on this, too," Carla adds. "So add the FBI, DEA, ATF. We'll come at you from every angle."

"We'll miss as often as we hit, but so what?" I say. "We don't have to bat a thousand. Christ, you hit .333 in the bigs, they give you a twenty-million-dollar contract. The point is, we'll be watching every move you make. The other street gangs will know that associating with the Nation is bad for business. Your own people will start to wonder whether it's worth it. Any new territory you've been adding to your little fiefdom, that's over. And you'll probably have a mutiny on your hands."

"Maybe so," says Jericho, still a wall of stone. "Maybe not."

"Yeah, but you're nothing if not a smart businessman," says Carla. "You're risk-averse. You have to be. Why bring all this on yourself when you can cure it by giving up a couple of your men?"

"Men who fucked up royally," I add, "by killing that innocent little girl. By bringing all this heat on you."

Jericho doesn't speak, but he inclines his head, taking our points.

What's left unsaid, and will remain that way, is that we all know which lawyer's going to show up to represent the shooters if we arrest them: Michael Spaulding, Esquire. He'll protect his meal ticket. He won't let those boys utter one word about Jericho.

I hand Spaulding my card. "The anonymous number's on there," I say. "Nobody has to know how I got my information. Nobody knows this conversation even happened. But I need it by tomorrow."

"We have video of the shooting, by the way," Carla says. "So don't try to pin this thing on Pope Francis or Bozo the Clown."

We don't have video of the vehicle occupants or the shooting itself, only the car. But it's good improv by Carla. Smart. If Jericho thinks we have faces on video, he can't just give us some patsy; we'll get the actual shooters.

If we get anything at all.

"I need it by tomorrow," I say. "Make a good business decision, Jericho."

CHAPTER 19

DISCO LIGHTS a cigarette while he sits in his car. He had vowed to quit. He hasn't lit up in three weeks. But all that changed after the call from Augustina at the restaurant, after reading about the death of the four-year-old girl with the pigtails. Now's not the time.

There's never a bad time to quit. Sure, but whoever said that didn't have the entire Chicago Police Department after him.

He rubs an eye with his knuckle. He didn't bother trying to sleep. No chance. Anyway, he needed to be up by three, pick up Nicolas and Trev by three fifteen, stop at the drop-off point, then make it to the location by four, while it's still dark.

Out of the apartment building comes Nicolas, long and rangy, a flat nose and dead eyes, his hair buzzed tight, dark circles under his eyes at this hour. Like Disco, Nicolas was recruited out of Berkut, the Ukrainian secret police, mostly covert missions to suppress political opposition, anything from surveillance and intelligence gathering to assassinations and torture. Nicolas came to the States years after Disco, each of them chosen by General Boholyubov, who ran Berkut before it disbanded. Nicolas was especially fond of the Berkut rape rooms, which is probably why Boho brought him here.

Nobody scares the girls more than Nicolas.

"How's Trev?" Disco asks in their native tongue. Disco normally has a rule that they speak English, but that's another exception he makes under the circumstances.

"Scared to death," Nicolas answers, also in Ukrainian. "He watches the news, reads the internet. He thinks we're all going to prison."

Trev could be a problem. Unlike Disco and Nicolas, he's not Berkut, not someone trained. He came fresh from the army in Ukraine. Physically capable and morally flexible. But lacking fearlessness. Or, more accurately, lacking the ability to harness fear.

Five minutes later, they pick up Trev—smaller, darker, boyish, though looking worn out, aged well beyond his twenty-six years. "It's all over TV," says Trev. "It's all over the internet."

"Then stop watching TV," Disco replies. "Stop reading the internet."

Disco drives up to the northwest side, finds the alley, pulls over to the side of the road. Neither Nicolas nor Trev has ever seen the actual meeting place. Disco likes to keep some things to himself.

Nor have they ever met Dennis Porter. Nobody will meet his contact in Internal Affairs besides Disco.

Anyway, Porter won't be there. This is only a pickup.

Or at least that's the plan. You can never be sure. The shooting in K-Town shook up everyone, Porter included. From a strategic standpoint, he can't see the logic in Porter's ambushing him here, trying to kill him. But if there's one thing Disco has learned, it's that you can never fully understand the motives of your "friends."

Disco draws his Ruger and holds it at his side as he approaches the alley. He stops, listens, hears nothing but faint sounds of trains, some birds chirping.

Disco walks the alley, heads to the same garage, fifth one down. This time, the garage door is down, but it's not locked, and the automatic opener has been disabled. He raises the door with an abrupt yank and jumps back, crouches, gun aimed inside.

The space is empty. His adrenaline decelerates.

In the middle of the garage, on the ceiling, a plastic enclosure covering the controls for the door opener. He uses a ladder, reaches up, lifts the enclosure carefully, and unhooks it from its moorings. With his other hand, he reaches in and pulls down the heavy paper bag.

He closes the enclosure back up, puts away the ladder, and looks inside the paper bag.

A SIG Sauer pistol. A suppressor. And a crushed cigarette butt in a plastic bag.

He breathes a sigh of relief. Porter came through.

CHAPTER 20

THE HOUSE is in Englewood, on Union Avenue south of Marquette, as rough a neighborhood as they come. An A-frame with aluminum siding. On one side an alley, on the other an empty lot where a house once stood. Disco scouted it earlier tonight, after meeting with Porter.

They decide on the back door. Disco is the expert on locks, having focused more on covert work with Berkut than Nicolas, whose talents for brutality made him better suited to interrogations and torture.

Behind him, Nicolas and Trev are quiet, tense. Weapons out. Like Disco, each of them wears rubber gloves.

Disco works the dead bolt open, turns the knob, opens it a crack while keeping hold of the knob, not letting the latch snap back. Listens for an alarm.

No alarm.

There's a chain on the door, though. Disco could kick in the door, as he often would in Ukraine, boldly asserting himself, but this isn't that kind of moment. You don't do that in America unless you're a cop.

He uses bolt cutters to snap the chain. Stops. Listens. Hears no sounds from the darkness inside.

Turns and nods to his men.

He pushes the door open and quickly walks through a small kitchen, the sink filled with dishes. Hears the faint sounds of canned laughter, identifies it as a television, moves toward the sound.

The bedroom. A man and woman, asleep, illuminated by the television's light.

The man is in his twenties, African American, with braids, dyed bright red, tight against his head. The woman is—well, who knows? Who cares?

The man awakens with a start just as Disco sticks the SIG Sauer, suppressor attached, into his face, grabs a braid, and holds him down.

"Hello, Junior," he says, so this man, wide-eyed and terrified, will understand that Disco knows his name, or at least his nickname.

Nicolas grabs the woman, covers her mouth with a gloved hand, holds her down, looks at Disco expectantly.

"Where are your car keys, Junior?" Disco asks.

Junior angles his head to the right, to Disco's left.

"Ah, look at this, right on the nightstand."

"Let me do it," Nicolas says in Ukrainian to Disco, holding the woman down. "A few minutes, at least."

This is no time for getting your jollies, but as Disco thinks about it, it could help paint the picture. "Go ahead," he tells Nicolas in Ukrainian. "But keep your pants on. Just use your hands. And keep the gloves on."

No DNA, in other words.

Disco turns on the man, Junior. "If you stay quiet, I will let you live," he says.

Junior, sweaty and breathless, nods once.

Disco stuffs a handkerchief in Junior's mouth. Then he shoots him in the shoulder, the sound muted by the suppressor, the man's cries by the cloth in his mouth as he bucks and squirms. Disco shoots him in the other shoulder, all but disabling his upper body.

Nicolas, with his free hand, lands a solid punch to the woman's face, the sound of bones crunching, then switches hands, holding down her head with his right hand while yanking down the bedsheet with his left. The woman thrashes about as Nicolas forces his hand between her legs.

Christmas came early for Nicolas this year. An unexpected bonus.

"My friend is going to have some fun with your girlfriend," says Disco. "What do you think about that, Junior?"

Junior is about to go into shock, his eyes turning glassy while he makes guttural sounds through the handkerchief.

Disco shoots him in the upper right thigh. Then the other. Junior's mouth opens, letting out another scream but then gagging on the handkerchief as it moves toward his throat.

Trev is standing back, keeping an eye on the scene.

Nicolas is doing a serviceable job of muting the woman's screams with his hand, but it's getting to be too much. They've made their point.

"Enough!" Disco stands up, holds the tip of the SIG's suppressor against Junior's head, and puts him out for good.

"A few more minutes," Nicolas says, enjoying himself.

"No." Disco aims the pistol at the woman. "No."

Nicolas steps off the bed, panting like an animal himself, his eyes wild. Disco puts a suppressed bullet through the woman's temple.

"Let's go," he says. "We have to hurry."

Back outside, Disco pulls the paper bag out of his pocket, which still contains the cigarette butt that was left for him. He drops the butt on the back porch. Then they find Junior's car, an old beater Ford sedan parked in the rear. Disco uses the car keys to pop the trunk. He removes the floorboard and finds the spot where the spare tire would normally be.

Nicolas, who went to their car, returns now, holding the AR-15 that Disco used in the K-Town shooting. Disco drops the assault rifle in the trunk, replaces the floorboard, closes the lid, returns the car keys to the bedroom.

Then they get the hell out of there. They drive back to the northwest side of the city in silence. Disco returns to the same alley, to the same garage, places the SIG and the suppressor back in the paper bag, and puts the bag back up in the enclosure of the garage door opener, just where he found it.

There, he thinks to himself. *Porter can take it from here.*

This better be fucking over now.

CHAPTER 21

VALERIE?

You call out her name, your voice shaky, your throat clogged with emotion. You just kissed your little angelic daughter, your beautiful Janey, for the last time, said your good-bye at the hospital.

And her mother wasn't there.

She's dealing with it, you tell yourself. Dealing with it in her own way.

But she couldn't have been there? She couldn't have answered your phone calls?

These thoughts while you climb the steps of your home, calling out her name again.

Valerie. Valerie.

Open the bedroom door. Empty. Light's on in the bathroom.

Valerie, you whisper.

You know it, somehow, before you reach the bathroom, before you see her legs. Her body turned awkwardly to the side. Blood spatter on the walls.

The gun, your service weapon, in her limp hand.

I draw a gasp of air, my eyes popping open, stinging from sweat. I push myself from the drenched pillow, shivering as I sit up, checking my phone for the time. My alarm was just about to go off anyway, so at least my nightmares have good timing these days.

I head into the bathroom and turn on the shower, my body reeking from slimy perspiration, my mouth dry as dirt. My heartbeat slowly decelerates, my breathing evens out, as I put my face under the pulsating water and let it wash everything away.

They've been dead for four years. *You've had four years to get past it.*

And so much has happened since then. I returned to the job; I even fell for another woman; I was almost killed; I stood trial for murder; I unearthed a scandal that took down all kinds of major players. Why am I back to having nightmares about Valerie? I never stopped thinking about her, of course; not one day has passed that I haven't. But it's like her death is front and center again for some reason. Why? I've got the whole freakin' city breathing down my neck to solve this murder, and I'm dreaming about Valerie again.

"Why now?" I whisper. "Why are you back?"

CHAPTER 22

TODAY'S THE day. We're already well into the twenty-four-hour cease-fire that Andre Oliver promised us. And the protest rally, for which the city is already preparing, is tomorrow.

Praying that my meeting with Jericho Hooper will bear fruit.

The sky is a brilliant orange as I drive to the station just before six in the morning, sipping a large black coffee, no more than three hours of sleep under my belt.

The front pages of the *Trib* and *Sun-Times* are all about LaTisha, all about the gang violence, all about the new Special Operations Section, all about how black people have to live in drug-infested, violent neighborhoods, with cops only paying lip service to their problems.

I don't know a single cop who doesn't care about what's happening on the West Side. We see the victims, and it hurts. We go after the perpetrators and okay, sometimes we go overboard, maybe because we can't get out of our heads the images of dead children or drugged-up addicts choking on their own vomit. Sometimes we cross lines. We pay for that. Courts throw out evidence. People hold up their smartphones and record us. Then we can't solve cases, so people stop helping us. They figure, *Why should we, if it's gonna be for nothing? Why stick our necks out, even risk our lives, to bear witness against criminals who aren't going to be caught anyway?*

The station house is all but empty. SOS isn't a typical district headquarters with a traditional overnight shift. But Carla is already at her desk. And—what the fuck?—popping something into her mouth.

I'm just walking in as this happens, as she's throwing her head back and swallowing. She spots me and clumsily screws the lid back on the bottle and throws the bottle in her work bag in a single fluid motion that is supposed to be casual, nonchalant, no big deal, nothing to see here.

I say the prayer again: *Please don't give me a pill popper for a partner. Please let that be vitamins or ibuprofen.*

She nods to me. She looks strung out—thin, too thin; dark circles under bloodshot eyes. She looks more likely to vomit than solve a case. But what the hell—she got no more sleep than I did last night, so bright-eyed and bushy-tailed was never on tap for today.

Whatever. I don't have time for that right now.

Sosh and Mat Rodriguez are in by six. We're meeting with the whole squad in two hours, but I'm reporting to the superintendent and my lieutenant in one hour, and I wanna see what we have so far.

"Tox screens came back on the victims," says Rodriguez.

The dead carrier, Stanley Wilson—Frisk—tested positive for cannabis. So did the presumptive target of the shooting, Dwayne Sears—Shiv. The unidentified dead girl on the porch had heroin in her blood.

"Stolen 4Runner in Melrose Park's a dead end so far," Sosh tells me. "Family that owns it, it's there when they go to bed, gone when they get up. Melrose Park has shit for POD cameras, at least on the residential streets. We're still reviewing the ALPRs and the PODs on the Eisenhower."

"All right, so where's Ronnie Lester?" I ask.

Lester walks in as if on cue. Ronnie's a UC in the Fifteenth—the Austin neighborhood—in the heart of Nation territory. He must be in his midtwenties at least, if not thirty, but I swear he could pass for a teenager. Short and wiry, his kinky hair sprouting like a fountain off his scalp to his shoulders, a black White Sox jersey and tattered jeans and high-tops. Without the lanyard around his neck holding his star atop a series of gold chains, you'd make him for the Imperial Gangster Nation drug dealer he's pretending to be.

"Griffin, shit, I know you." Ronnie gives Carla a fist bump. The rest of us introduce ourselves.

"I got five minutes," he says, not taking a seat. "If you're lookin' for word on the shooter, I don't got it."

"Nobody's talking?" Sosh asks.

"Shit, everyone's *talkin'*. But nobody *knows*."

"Jericho wants K-Town, though," Carla says. "Right?"

Lester makes a face, as if she just said the most obvious thing in the world. "Jeri-Curl wants the whole damn city, girl. Probably get it, sooner or later." He looks over the squad room, new and shiny, so different a workplace from the one he has on a daily basis, on the streets of Austin. "Whatever happened, man, we're gearing up now."

We. He's been undercover a long time. Hard to get out of the role. Better that he doesn't, in fact. So not *they* but *we*.

"Gearing up for the Hustlers," I clarify.

He lifts a shoulder, yes. "Everyone's puttin' it on us, so Jericho's got us preppin'. Shit's gonna get thick." He spends two syllables on that last word.

"Say we catch the shooters," I say. "What are the odds we get them to talk about Jericho? We got any chance at all?"

Ronnie smiles at me as if I'm an idiot.

"So no chance," I say.

"You remember Stevie Lewis? Stevie Woo-Woo?" He can tell we don't. "Kills a Disciple in Harvey. We pick him up, got him dead to rights on the shooting, he says he's willing to give up Jericho for ordering it. His throat accidentally runs into a knife in county lockup. But Jericho, he don't stop there. They shoot Stevie's brother coming out of a liquor store. They tag his face so many times we need DNA to ID him. They find Stevie's mama, they pull a train on her—okay, sixty-year-old woman—then strangle her and leave her naked corpse in the middle of Augusta Boulevard. And then, in case anyone didn't get the point, they burn down the motherfucker's house."

So nobody talks.

Ronnie points to us. "Only way you're getting those shooters is if Jericho gives them to you."

He doesn't know we're already working that angle, and I'm not gonna tell him. For his sake.

"Think he'll do that?" I ask.

He shrugs again. "With this heat, could be. Didn't expect to kill no cute little baby girl." He looks at his phone. "Gotta move. Don't think I'll have anything for you, but if I do, I'll get word to you."

He looks back at Griffin. "SOS, huh?" He makes a fist of congratulations.

"I'll walk him out," she says when he's halfway to the door. "Maybe he'll tell me something else."

"Why would he do that?"

"Because I was a UC, too."

Like it's a fraternity, a bond. Carla pops out of her chair. It spins when she does so. Resting on her chair is one of the pills she's been taking. Must have fallen out when she tried to hastily put them away as I walked into the station.

We break up our powwow. I walk over to her chair, scoop up the pill, and drop it in my pocket.

I have a right to know.

Just as a patrol officer, Officer Bostwick, rushes into the squad room.

"Detective Harney," he says, "I think we got something on the tip line."

CHAPTER 23

DAMIEN PEPPERS, a.k.a. Junior, stares at the ceiling with lifeless eyes, a gunshot wound to his forehead with stippling, suggesting it was close range. Of course it was close range. He was executed.

But not before he was tortured, shot once in each shoulder, once in each thigh.

"But why?" asks Carla. "For information or punishment?"

Neither of us knows yet. We don't even know yet if Junior was responsible for the K-Town shooting. We know he's Nation through and through, one of Jericho's top "troopers," or gunmen. Assassins. Jericho needed someone dead; Junior was one of his boys.

Kudos to Officer Joe Bostwick, overseeing the tip line, who listened to the woman calling in anonymously just a few minutes before six this morning. He got the name, ran his sheet, and realized it was credible. He passed it to me. Our team—Carla, Sosh, and I—headed straight over, while Mat Rodriguez rushed to the emergency judge for a search warrant just in case we needed it.

Nobody answered at the house, but Carla stood on a crate and peeked through a window and saw blood spatter and spent shell casings on the carpet. Exigent circumstances. We entered the front door at around the time the judge was signing the warrant.

They did more than shoot him. They made him hurt first. They did a number on his girlfriend, too. Evidence of sexual penetration, vaginal trauma, says the ME on the scene, before they put a bullet through her head, too. So to Carla's question: Why?

Could be this was the Hustlers' work. Andre Oliver learned that Junior was one of the shooters, or maybe just suspected it, and sent some boys over for a combination of retaliation and the extraction of information—information like who was in the car with Junior at K-Town.

Maybe. But I don't think so. That would mean that "Sir Andre" violated his promise to me of a twenty-four-hour cease-fire. Not that I'd expect him to be honest. But I would expect him to be smart. I don't see how it helps him to piss off the Special Operations Section. He could've waited twelve hours and done the same thing.

But who knows how people think? Maybe, against all reason, Andre thinks he has no choice but to retaliate, and he didn't want Junior caught—he wanted him dead.

"No, this is Jericho cleaning up his own mess," Carla says. "The extra gunshots and what they did to the girlfriend was to tell Junior that's what you get for screwing up and killing a four-year-old."

That's where my money is, too.

The techies are working the scene now, lifting prints and pulling fibers, snapping photos and examining the victims. I take another look at the back door, where the entry was forced. They picked the lock and snapped the chain clean.

We step out onto the back staircase, where someone's flagged a crushed cigarette butt by the door.

"You smell any cigarette smoke in there?"

Carla shakes her head no. "Faint smell of reefer, maybe. Didn't see any packs of cigarettes, either."

"Westbrook!" I call out.

Diane Westbrook, from Forensic Services, comes out from inside the house.

"Diane, bag this cigarette butt and run it over now. Upload a DNA sample onto the database. Maybe we get lucky with a match."

"Got it," she says.

"Diane," I say, making sure we're eye to eye. "This goes to the head of the line. Anyone has any doubts about that, you call me. I'll have the supe on the phone within minutes. Head of the line, Diane. I have these results by lunch or someone's gonna lose their job."

"Roger that," she says. "Believe it or not, I can be a bitch once in a while."

"You, Diane? No."

Soscia is standing by the sedan parked behind the house, Junior's key ring dangling from his index finger. He's already peeked in through the windows and seen nothing. He pops the trunk. Nothing of interest initially—a food wrapper, blanket, jumper cables.

But underneath the floorboard, an AR-15.

Soscia lifts it out of the car like he's holding the Holy Grail. The dozen or so cops, detectives, officers, and techies out here—everyone wants in on this—all but break out in applause.

"I'm gonna personally run this to Ballistics," he says.

Carla and I watch Sosh drive away with the prize.

"Well, gee whiz, Harney," she says, "your little stunt with Jericho may have worked."

CHAPTER 24

BACK AT SOS, the house is buzzing with the news, an extra skip in everyone's stride. We aren't saying anything officially yet. Everyone thinks there was more than one person involved in the K-Town shooting. It would be hard to pull that off solo.

Which means there's at least one other man at large.

Mat Rodriguez pulls paper from the database. The list of known associates of Junior Peppers reaches the double digits. We start cross-referencing, lining up addresses, and getting patrols ready.

And getting an affidavit ready for a warrant. We just need the name to fill in.

Superintendent Tristan Driscoll is camped in Wizniewski's office, working on an official statement he'll make, presumably taking complete credit for solving this case, if that's what we're about to do.

Reporters are camped out downstairs, having heard some murmurs about a suspect taken into custody.

Sosh calls in at ten o'clock. "Ballistics are a fuckin' match!" he shouts.

"Match," I mouth to Carla, who gives me a high five, the most animation she's shown. So the AR-15 we found in Junior's car was the one used in the K-Town shooting.

One down, at least one to go.

"Great—now get your ass back here," I tell Sosh.

Carla and I break the news to Lieutenant Wizniewski and our favorite superintendent, Tristan Driscoll.

"And you're confident there's a second offender involved," says the supe.

Carla takes that one. "Hard to imagine one person would drive up and open fire," she says. "More likely, there was a driver and a second guy in the back seat."

Driscoll nods. "And where are we on that?"

"Hopeful for a DNA match," I say. I tell him about the discarded cigarette butt. "It looked fresh, and neither Junior nor his girlfriend appeared to be smokers."

"A full DNA analysis could take a while," Carla adds. "But submitting a sample to a database for a match, at least a preliminary match—we should have that soon. Enough for a warrant, at least."

"So when am I releasing a statement?" he asks, which was clearly all he wanted to know. How quickly can he take credit for this?

"Prefer you hold it," I say. "We'd prefer that the first our guy hears about it is when we're knocking on his door."

"I can only hold it so long." He leans back in his chair. "The press is already hearing about a suspect in custody."

"Hold it as long as you can," I say. "And let me know when it's going to drop."

He raises an eyebrow. "I'm taking orders from you now, Detective?"

"Pretty please," I say. "With sugar on top."

"What Detective Harney means," says Wizniewski, dressed today in a full suit and tie, I notice, "is he'd appreciate a heads-up, sir."

I point to the Wiz. "That's what I meant."

Out of the corner of my eye, I see Diane Westbrook come bounding into the squad room.

"Excuse me," I say.

We pop out of Wizniewski's office. Diane is out of breath.

"We have a preliminary match," she says. She looks at the printout in her hand. "Prince Valentine."

"That an alias?"

"That's his given name. Prince Allan Valentine. Got a sheet a mile long, including a juvie murder, agg batt, some drugs. Reputed member of the Imperial Gangster Nation." She sings the last words, proud of herself.

"Diane, I could kiss you." I nod to Carla, catch the eye of Rodriguez. "Mat, run the affidavit over to Judge Peters. We're not screwing this up on a procedural."

Diane walks over and confers with Mat while we read his rap sheet. Diane's right. Violence and gangs all over. This is our guy.

"Gear up," I say. "Let's get a solve."

CHAPTER 25

PRINCE VALENTINE lives on the far West Side, on the third floor of a yellow-brick apartment building in the middle of the block with an alley to the north. I don't like alleys. Alleys cause problems. So we have a cruiser—driven by Officer Bostwick, who deserves to be in on this, along with three of his fellow patrolmen—blocking the alley a ways down, out of sight from Prince's alley-side window but close enough to respond within seconds if we need it.

Carla, Soscia, Rodriguez, and I sit in the Taurus, curbed down the street, waiting. Someone could've made us already. Our "unmarked" vehicles don't fool anyone who knows what they're doing, and this is a neighborhood that's seen plenty of crime. I'm pretty sure we broke up a drug deal on our drive here, four guys standing on a sidewalk, scattering as we approached.

"No roof access," Sosh says. "Fire escape's half falling off the building. The ladder to the roof is swinging on one hinge."

Mat has the warrant. I had a pretty good sense we could've gone in without one, but better to be careful, a case like this, all the attention it'll get. And the time to wait didn't cost us. We had patrols watching his house within five minutes of getting those DNA results from Forensics.

"Don't knock and announce," Sosh says.

"We're gonna knock and announce," I say.

"Better we surprise him."

"Yeah, if you're last through the door, like you'll be. How about if you're first, Captain Courage?"

"Fine," Sosh says. "You wanna use Betsy? I'll go fuckin' first."

"*Mierda,* it's like I've got two more children," Carla interrupts. "Harney's lead, so we freakin' knock and announce. Next time, we'll do what you want, Soscia. I promise."

"There," I say. "Let's go." We get out into the blazing heat of high noon and hustle up the sidewalk as a woman walks out the front door of the apartment building. "Excuse me, ma'am," I say, meeting her as she comes down the porch steps. My shield is already dangling from a lanyard, but I hold it and show it to her. "Help us get through that front door, would you?"

The woman, middle-aged and tired, dressed in a waitress outfit, looks up from her purse and sizes us up, one eyebrow lifting. "Is there gonna be trouble?" she asks.

"No, ma'am. Just a routine inspection. Not your apartment, of course."

"Mm-hmm." She eyes the battering ram Sosh is holding at his side, which he named Betsy after his first wife. She walks back up the steps, finds the right key on an impressive ring, and lets us through the outside door.

Carla radios to Bostwick to watch the alley; we're heading up. We take the stairs as gently as four people can take stairs that creak and moan with every step. No matter. As we hit the third floor—the top floor—we hear music, some poppy dance stuff.

"Prince Valentine? Chicago police detectives." I stand to the side and pound on the door.

Footfalls from within the apartment. The probation reports say Prince lives alone. No children, no spouse.

"Just wanna ask you some questions, Prince!"

My three partners have their guns drawn but down while I stand at the door.

"Hang on," he calls out from within the apartment, yelling over the music.

Then more noise: a whining noise, then a crash of wood on wood, then a body in motion, feet pounding. But not on the floor.

I draw my weapon and wave to Sosh, already hoisting Betsy.

"Fuckin' told ya," he murmurs.

CHAPTER 26

SOSH RAMS Betsy against the door. The door splinters, but the hit wasn't square, so it busted the door but not the lock. Sosh cusses and rears back, slams the ram against the door with more violence, this time hitting the target, busting through the lock, the door swinging open.

I go through first, shouting "Police!" into the empty apartment. Turn to my right, the bedroom window, closed and secure. To my left: a ladder, coming down from the ceiling. He has roof access from inside the apartment. And a head start.

Carla calling in to Bostwick, "He's on the roof!"

I bound up the ladder, pause before popping my head through the open skylight, then peek out. Yep, a big head start.

I jump onto the gravel roof.

"He's got a weapon!" Carla relays. Someone on the ground must've seen it.

Prince Valentine is in full sprint, heading south toward the other end of the building. I call out "Police!" again, as if that wasn't the whole reason he's running. "We just want to talk to you!" I yell, as I hold my weapon down, running as fast as I can, which is not as fast as Prince can.

He doesn't break stride as he runs toward the other end of the roof. What's his play here? Any second, he's going to have to stop, turn around, his brain overtaking his instinct to run, and realize he has nowhere to go. I have to be ready when he realizes that.

But he doesn't stop. He jumps off the ledge, like a long jumper, hands and legs making wide circles, and disappears from sight.

What the—

I keep running, and I see him. He jumped onto the neighbors' roof, a two-story building. He's coming out of his landing now, recovering, jumping to his feet and running again.

I don't think. I don't stop. Knowing that it might be the dumbest thing I've ever done. I holster my weapon as I speed up, moving as fast as my legs will take me, plant my foot on the ledge, sail into the air, a narrow alley beneath me—that sickening feeling of being airborne with nothing but a hard alley pavement three stories below—and land hard on the other roof, fifteen feet below, my weight pitching forward, my hands scraping against blacktop and a thin layer of pebbles. Flat on my stomach. The wind knocked out of me. I look up, see the suspect slow down, pivot, and turn to his left, past an AC condenser and toward a small roofed enclosure.

He had an escape planned out. He's going to go through a door down into the building.

I get to my feet, draw my weapon, and jog in the direction he fled. I clear a wide circle to improve my angle and keep my weapon up, just in case—

He pops out from behind the condenser, a one-handed grip on his weapon, aiming it where he expects me to be, to my left, quickly adjusting but giving me that split second of time—

A flash from his weapon as I rip off one, two, three shots, a force hitting my torso so hard that I'm thrust backward, falling to my back, a blue sky, the sun hitting my eyes.

A sound behind me, a body landing, scrambling. "Harney!

You okay?" Carla sweeps past me, her weapon trained forward. "You okay?"

I don't answer. I can't. I roll to my side, see Carla move toward the suspect, lying motionless on the ground. She approaches him with caution, kicks the weapon far from his body, reaches down, and feels for his pulse.

Another body landing on the roof behind me. "Suspect is down!" Rodriguez calls. "Officer is down!"

CHAPTER 27

BY THE time I sit up, my legs out in front of me, the roof of the building next door to Prince Valentine's apartment is littered with uniformed officers. Carla has holstered her weapon and walks over to me. "We need to get you to an emergency room," she says.

I shake my head. I'm fine. I put three bullets into Prince's chest; he put one in my ribs. I was wearing a bulletproof vest; he wasn't. I'm alive; he's dead.

"Anything hurt?" she asks.

"Only when I breathe." An old joke, but I'm not kidding. Ribs aren't broken, though, just a little sore. I also hit my head pretty hard on the fall and got a good ringer to show for it.

The aftershock is just now hitting me, the adrenaline rush, as I consider in hindsight what happened so fast at the time.

Starting with the beginning: if we'd surprised him, rammed the door without notice, Prince Valentine would probably still be alive.

Soscia appears on the roof, the last of our four-person team. He wipes his sleeve against his forehead. It's only then I become aware of the intense heat, the sun on my face.

He comes over, stops, appraises me, nods his head. "Welcome back to the force, Detective Harney."

"You took the stairs, I see."

"Don't want to overextend myself," he says. "Doctor said to cut down on roof jumping."

Sosh was the last one through Prince's door—his weapon wasn't drawn because he used the battering ram—and the last one in secures the apartment. Not that Sosh would have been able to clear that alleyway space between the two buildings anyway. If he'd tried, we'd have two officers down, one of them on the pavement of the alley.

Sosh squats down, looks me in the eyes, cups a hand around my neck. I swear I catch some mist in his eyes. The guy's a teddy bear at heart.

"You did good here, Billy. Real good."

I'm not sure that's true. "If we surprised him, like you said—"

"You don't know what woulda happened." An emphatic shake of the head. "Guy could've had the gun on him. Probably did. We surprise, he starts blasting at us inside the tiny apartment. Instead, you gave him time to run. Shit, the guy was probably hopped up anyway after the shooting drew so much attention."

"Assuming he was the shooter," I say.

Sosh winks at me. "Guess what we found in a false floor in his closet?"

"Tell me."

"Heroin," he says. "About fifty bags."

I nod. Not what I was hoping for. "That could be why he ran."

"Maybe," says Sosh, holding back a grin. "Or maybe he ran because of the SIG pistol and suppressor we found under his mattress."

CHAPTER 28

LIFE IS good again. Disco soaks up every word on his phone.

The online *Sun-Times* says, POLICE NAB SHOOTERS.

According to the *Tribune*, LATISHA MORELAND SHOOTERS CAPTURED, KILLED.

The story: Damien "Junior" Peppers and Prince Valentine, known enforcers for the Imperial Gangster Nation, performed the shooting in K-Town that claimed the life of LaTisha Moreland and three others. Prince then killed Junior, worried about the intense police manhunt, worried that Junior might implicate him. The police raided Prince's apartment, where Prince ultimately died after a shoot-out with police.

Perfect. Just as Porter called it.

Well, not the last part. It was just dumb luck that this Prince person died in the shoot-out with police. Still, Porter directed this to perfection.

Disco wasn't so bad himself, now that he thinks about it. He cuts out his phone, feeling high with relief, as he pulls his car off 122nd Street and turns into the old industrial park. It was once owned by an auto-parts company in the fifties, an entire city block of factories and buildings connected by an underground tunnel. The general, through a sham corporation, has kept the electricity on in this place for the occasions when Disco needs it.

Like tonight. With a new arrival.

Augustina, middle-aged and heavyset, with tiny eyes and cheeks like small balloons, her hair dyed fire-engine red and pulled back tight, meets him at the heavy doors, sucking on the straw of a McDonald's coffee drink and holding a thin manila folder.

He opens the folder and reads the contents. The girl is fourteen years old. From an orphanage in northeastern Moldova. A brother, still there, two years younger. The photo is promising. "When did she arrive?" he asks. Back to English only. Now that things are normal again, the old rules apply.

"Three hours ago."

"Has Nicolas seen her yet?"

"No, he wait for you."

"Good." He moves past Augustina into the back room, unbolts the door. When he opens it, a young woman seated on an overturned crate startles to attention. She is wearing a tattered coat buttoned to her neck, an equally tattered suitcase next to her.

She looks younger than fourteen. Most of them look older when they come over, scarred and weathered from a difficult life. It's nice when you can get them before life ages their faces. They're so much more valuable when they look young and pure.

She is trembling, despite the coat, despite the stuffiness of this cramped staff-only room. Her eyes, wide and piercing blue, look up at Disco with a combination of worry and hope.

He can't see much of her body yet, only that angelic face, a nice swan neck.

Men will fall in love with that face. They'll want to protect her. They'll pay handsomely. Fifteen hundred a night? Certainly possible, but he can't use the hotel, not with a girl that obviously young. It will have to be the condo building, which tends to draw the lower-paying clientele. Or the ones who like them young.

"Does she speak English?" he asks Augustina, who joins him.

"Only a little."

"Tell her to take her clothes off."

Augustina speaks to the girl in Romanian. The girl doesn't seem as surprised as Disco might have expected, but she shakes her head, not so much defiantly but as if there's been a misunderstanding. She answers in Romanian, then says one word in English: "House... keeper?"

It's all Disco can do not to laugh. "Tell her again," he says.

Augustina and the girl speak some more. The girl's eyes well up.

Disco walks over and kicks the crate on which she's sitting. The girl is forced to her feet. Disco makes a gesture. "Off," he says.

She says, "Please," in English.

He grabs her coat and works the buttons. She doesn't resist. She stares off into the distance as a single tear falls down her cheek.

He pulls the coat off her. Underneath, she's wearing a long-sleeved shirt, gray. He grabs it and raises it up. She stiffens in response but again doesn't resist, ultimately even raising her arms to allow him to take it off. This can't be her first time, not if she's been raised in that orphanage.

That leaves only her bra and jeans. Disco steps back. Her breasts are underdeveloped, but that works fine.

He was going to name her Cassandra. But seeing her in person, that doesn't work. Too voluptuous. Up close, she looks much more like the young girl she is than a slutty vamp. What would be a good name?

"Tell her... her name is Katie," he decides.

Augustina does. The girl says her real name back, only now her voice contains more than a quiver, closer to panic.

Disco reaches out and takes her face in his hand, pinching each cheek like an angry parent giving a scolding. "Katie," he says. "Katie. Yes?"

One of her tears drips onto his finger. He pushes her back and wipes his finger on his suit jacket.

"Tell her she owes us twenty-five thousand dollars for getting her out of Soroca and bringing her here, plus the lodging and other expenses. Tell her she needs to repay the debt. Tell her the housekeeping work will come later—after she pays off her debt."

Augustina translates to the girl, who has shrunk now, slightly bent at the waist, trying to cover her upper body with her hands. But she responds to Augustina. Disco doesn't speak much Romanian, but he can grab bits and pieces, mostly about her brother.

"Tell her we will send for her brother after she pays off this debt," he says.

Augustina does. The girl bursts into tears, spilling out words in a high pitch, pleading. Augustina starts to translate. "She says she had agreement—"

"Why do I care what *she* says?" He starts for the door as the girl crumbles to the floor, shoulders heaving, crying so hard she chokes up.

"Nicolas should come in now?"

When Nicolas breaks her in, she'll understand her new line of work. Her customers will seem nice by comparison. She'll be an addict within two weeks, if not sooner, and then she'll do anything they want for another score. She'll be making them good money within a month.

"Yes, send Nicolas in," he says. "But tell him not to touch that face."

CHAPTER 29

BETWEEN THE interviews that come with any officer-involved shooting and a mandatory trip to the emergency room in a hospital in Oak Park—mandatory because Wizniewski ordered Carla to drive me there—I don't return to the station until close to five in the afternoon.

When I walk in, Wizniewski is out of his office, in the squad room. He puts his unlit cigar in his mouth and starts clapping. Before I know it, the whole room erupts in applause. Wizniewski puts a hand on my shoulder, beaming. I haven't seen him this happy since he arrested me for murder once upon a time.

High fives all around, deflections by me about a team effort. It feels good. I can't deny it. A week ago, I wasn't sure I'd ever be a cop again. I wasn't sure I'd still have what it takes, even if they let me back. And I didn't know if my brothers and sisters on the force would ever welcome me back.

Fast-forward a few days, and everyone in the squad room is shaking my hand, beaming at me, applauding me. This was my case. I was the lead. They dropped the heater of all heaters in my lap. And we solved it in less than two days.

"Ballistics came back on the SIG in Prince's apartment," says the Wiz. "It was used on Junior."

Soscia throws an arm around my neck. Every part of my body hurts, but I don't feel it. There's no better painkiller than this—this adulation, this palpable sense of relief, this feeling that I am finally back, really back, really a cop again in every sense.

So right now, I don't feel the stabbing in my ribs. I don't feel the shooting pain down my back. I don't feel the bell ringing between my ears.

I don't feel that itch I can't quite scratch, that sense that something just doesn't feel right here.

CHAPTER 30

I COLLAPSE in the chair, my head swimming, everyone drunk with relief, feeling suddenly exhausted. There will be paperwork to do tonight, then festivities later, no doubt, at the Hole.

A bottle of Maker's Mark is passed around, which probably isn't the best idea. Soscia hands it to Carla, who turns away, puts up a stop signal with her hand. "I don't drink," she says.

"You don't *drink*?"

Apparently not. She looks like she's about to puke.

Which reminds me. The pill I found on Carla's chair this morning, before everything happened. Feels like a lifetime ago now.

I head over to the coffee station to give myself a little space and pull out the pill. It's an oval gelcap, the word VIT-A-GIN on it.

I stuff it back in my pocket and do a search on my phone. Vit-a-gin is a gelcap of purified ginger root extract.

I take a breath, relieved. I had it all wrong. I was afraid she was on Oxy or something. But she's no addict. She's taking ginger pills. My wife took ginger to battle nausea when—

Oh. *Oh*.

That explains the nausea, the haggard look, the no drinking, even her attitude. It's hard to be in a good mood when you have morning sickness.

My partner is pregnant.

CHAPTER 31

DRINKS AT the Hole. We probably started around seven, coming straight from the city hall press conference announcing our solve. The Hole is wall to wall with cops. Everybody wants a piece of this. Everybody deserves it, as much as we get shat on.

Even Superintendent Driscoll, at the press conference, shook my hand and told me, "Well done, Detective," before he took credit for the whole thing in front of the bank of microphones.

I've turned down more shots tonight than I've drunk, but I've drunk plenty. Why not? Last time I was here, half the coppers turned their backs on me or mumbled something under their breath. Now I'm the man of the hour. That's fine. It makes the job easier if you're on good paper with other cops. But I won't forget who my friends are, the ones who were there during the rough patches.

I spot Carla, who's basically standing alone. Not drinking (of course) and not really socializing. Looking like someone who feels like she's supposed to be there but doesn't really want to be. Valerie always retired early during her pregnancy and slept in fits.

Maybe I'll never get Carla Griffin. But at least I have some window into her life now, whether I'm supposed to or not. And thinking of her jumping down onto that roof to stay with me, to do the job, even though she's carrying a child, and feeling like crap—I've got to cut her a lot more slack.

I tap her on the shoulder. She turns and tries to smile. It just isn't really her. "Good work today," she shouts to me, the only way we could hear each other. "If I didn't say so already. Great work, actually." She doesn't look me in the eye as she speaks. It must have taken a lot for her to say that.

"Right back atcha," I say. "A good team effort."

She nods, but she's not done. She looks at her feet. "I... sometimes, y'know, take a while to—"

And then I'm mugged, lifted from my feet, carried away as a chant starts in the room, *Har-ney! Har-ney!,* and suddenly I'm back on the stage in the corner, someone shoving the mike in my hand, just like old times, Billy Harney in the house.

The crowd goes quiet. I wasn't really up for this, but what the hell.

"First of all, I'd like to thank the entire team that made this happen," I say into the mike. "Lanny Soscia—where are you, Sosh? There he is." Sosh raises a pint. "I'd like to thank Soscia for getting us through that door with a battering ram. It only took him six or seven tries."

Everyone seems to like that.

"I'm not saying we lost the element of surprise, but the offender showered, packed a suitcase, and did his taxes before we got in."

I wait for the laughter to subside. "That's not to say Sosh is out of shape, but the guy breaks out in a sweat if he jumps to a conclusion. I've seen turtles with better lateral movement.

"Rodriguez still here? Mat?" Rodriguez shouts out from the crowd, hand cupped around his mouth. "There he is. Your wife let you stay out tonight?" He waves me off with a smirk. The crowd likes it.

"I'm not saying Mat's henpecked. The other night, his wife told him to be home by eight. But she wasn't gonna tell *him* what to do. No, sir. He was home by *seven*.

"But seriously," I say after the laugh. "Mat's an assertive guy. He comes right out and says exactly what his wife tells him to think." Someone puts Mat in a headlock. I'm not the first one with this observation. "But no matter how much he argues with his wife, Mat always, *always* has the last word." I lower the mike, nod at Rodriguez, then bring it back up. "That word is, *Sorry*!

"You know why Mat goes to a female dentist? It's a nice change to have a woman tell him to open his mouth instead of shut it."

I make an attempt to bow, but it doesn't go so well. I've had better balance on a pogo stick. Someone figures out that it's time to get me off the stage. Maybe this would be a good point in the night to slow down on the booze.

At ten o'clock, everyone shushes as the local news comes on. The stunning anchor breathlessly relates the "breaking news" as a photo of little LaTisha pops up alongside her. Within seconds, the screen cuts to the press conference from earlier today—the mayor and the superintendent, several leaders of the African American community, and behind them, our team: the Wiz, Carla, Rodriguez, and the two pale white guys, Sosh and me, as the bookends.

A cheer goes up. Elbows thrown my way. Sosh hollers out about the camera adding ten pounds. Someone asks if I lost my comb. They show us a couple of clips from the presser, the mayor taking credit for starting the Special Operations Section and saying it's "time to heal," a minister telling us "there's more work to be done." Then the anchor's talking again as they run some footage without audio of Superintendent Driscoll at the mike.

Sosh doesn't miss the opportunity to mimic the supe, his best Poindexter voice: "I'd just like everyone to know that I had absolutely nothing to do with the solving of this crime, and that I'm currently wearing ladies' undergarments."

I spot Joe Bostwick among the revelers, throwing back a pint with the lads. I grab his arm. "First of all," I say, "great work today, Joe."

He shakes my hand. "Learned a lot from you today, Detective. It's been an honor."

"Bright and early tomorrow morning," I say, "we recanvass."

"For real?" Patrol officers don't usually question orders. He seems to realize he stepped over the line. "I mean, we got our—"

"Coulda been more than two people in the car," I say. "Probably was."

"But we talked to practically every person in the neighborhood."

"Is *practically* every person the same as every person?"

The next story on the news: PROTEST RALLY CANCELED, and I can't really hear what they're saying, but apparently the solve of the case has led the community to change the rally from a protest downtown to a "peace vigil" outside one of the South Side churches.

Jeez, I guess that makes all this a happy ending.

Yeah.

Yeah, maybe.

CHAPTER 32

LATHAM JACKSON'S eyes are open before his alarm goes off Friday morning. Feels like he hardly slept. His stomach is still churning, and not from hunger or from the two or three bites of his mother's hamburger pizza he forced down last night.

No, he's hardly eaten, hardly slept since he saw the shooting outside Shiv's house two days ago.

He assumed it would be another run-of-the-mill drug buy. He handled it same as always. He started the video rolling as a vehicle turned from Van Buren onto Kilbourn, used the toggle on his computer to move his video camera, hidden inside the window AC unit. Followed the car until it stopped outside Shiv's house, where Frisk casually approached the vehicle to get the customer's order.

Then zoomed in on the license plate. Then upward, into the vehicle, the front-seat occupants.

The windows were partially tinted, meaning that a lesser, grainier camera wouldn't capture them. But Latham has the best equipment, one of the perks of working at Best Buy. He could see them well enough.

The guys in the front seat were white. They wore baseball caps and kept their chins down, but they were white.

He remembers the small adrenaline burst when he zeroed in on them. White people, so there was a better chance they had money, and tinted windows, meaning they were particularly careful about being seen. Latham was seeing dollar signs. These people, he was sure, would pay good money to keep this video a secret.

And then everything went wrong. With the camera toggled in nice and close on the occupants, Latham couldn't see anything at first, but he could hear it out his window, the unmistakable *rat-a-tat-tat* of automatic gunfire.

Without thinking, he pressed down on the toggle, widened the frame, to see a flame shooting out from the car's back-seat window. The occupants on the porch—Shiv and some white girl—rattled with bullets, the surrounding wood splintering from gunshots. Frisk, the courier in his Bears jersey, momentarily stunned, then turning to run. Gunfire hitting him, his back arching from the bullets as he fell face-first to the sidewalk.

It all happened so fast. Before Latham could process what he'd seen, the car was gone. And he'd captured a thirty-second horror movie on his laptop.

He was an eyewitness to the crime. He had proof, video. Now what?

His first instinct, of course—hand it over to the police. But they'd be wondering what he was doing, videotaping drug buys. What would he say? He was making a documentary? Nobody would believe that. It would take the cops two seconds to realize that Latham was blackmailing suburban drug addicts. He could go to prison.

And say the cops didn't figure out his scheme or didn't care. Latham would still be a witness. He'd have to testify in court. He wouldn't be safe. His mother wouldn't be safe. *Snitches get stitches,* sure, but these guys with their automatic weapons weren't messing around. Forget stitches. They'd put a bullet through his brain.

He could send the video anonymously to the police, but with

the camera angle, any halfway decent cop would figure it came from his building.

The good news—the only thing that has sustained him the last two days—is that he could always do it later. He could wait. Maybe the cops would solve it without him. This case was a big deal, right? They'd put a lot of resources into it. Yeah, he told himself, this video might not be necessary.

And there you go: within twenty-four hours, the Chicago PD identified the vehicle used in the shooting. It was in the newspaper reports, which Latham was following closely. So if they knew the car, most of what he could show them was stuff they already knew, right?

Right. He pinballed back and forth like that. They'll figure it out; they don't need the video. Still, the video would help—maybe they could use facial recognition on it. But it's not Latham's problem. He's no cop, no avenging superhero.

And then, last night, finally—the word came that they caught the shooter.

Latham gets out of his bed, puts on a T-shirt and jeans, and wakes up his laptop. He has the photo from the newspapers, the mug shots of two young men, Prince Valentine and Damien "Junior" Peppers, enlarged before him. Two young *black* men.

It's possible, he told himself. Just because the two guys in the front were white doesn't mean the guys obscured in the back couldn't have been Nation gangbangers. Who says black and white people can't ride in a car together?

And what if it's otherwise? What if the cops really *did* get this wrong? It's not like Latham can bring Peppers and Valentine back to life. What good will an exoneration do them now?

The Chicago PD thinks they solved the case. Why should he tell them otherwise?

Yeah, keep telling yourself that, he thinks as he heads down the hall into the kitchen. All the rationalizing can't remove the uneasiness in his stomach, constant since that day. And he knows why. It has nothing to do with Prince Valentine or Junior Peppers.

It has everything to do with that innocent little girl. Doesn't she deserve justice?

He pours cereal into a bowl, stares at it. He knows he has to eat. But he can't imagine doing so.

He hears a knock on a door. Not his door; another apartment down the hall. You can hear just about anything in this building, with its paper-thin walls. Sit in the living room after ten o'clock and you can hear the next-door neighbors going at it in their bedroom, the grunts and moans, the bedpost banging against the wall.

He hears a word that sends a shiver down his spine. "Police."

The cops have been all over this neighborhood since the shooting. Latham's managed to avoid them. His mother was at work when the shooting happened and has since told the officers that. Latham has never been home when they've stopped by. The day of the shooting, he ditched out through the alley, driving to work, even though he wasn't scheduled to be there for several hours. He told his mother that he'd already left by the time the shooting happened. She doesn't keep tabs on his ever-changing work schedule.

His heart begins to pound. He thinks of that little girl. Thinks of that pain in his stomach that just won't go away.

He opens the door, peeks into the hallway. A patrol officer, a white guy, big and wide, standing by a door, making a note on a clipboard.

"Excuse me, Officer," he calls out, realizing he's just passed the point of no return.

CHAPTER 33

"HOLY SHIT," the officer mumbles, sitting at the kitchen table, having watched the video twice on Latham's laptop.

"You can't see the shooter in the back seat." Latham states the obvious. "And I'm not sure the guys in the front seat—I'm not sure you could identify them."

"Maybe..." The officer, squinting at the laptop screen, shakes his head. "And how'd you say you got this?"

"I—like I said, I got this camcorder." He holds up a camcorder—not his new one, in fact, but his old one. "I was trying it out."

It's a lie, of course, but the cop—young-looking, especially now, seemingly overwhelmed by the video he's just watched—isn't paying attention to the niceties of Latham's story. "I... have to call the lead detective," he says.

The cop sounds nervous, too. He must be new. Living where he does, Latham is no stranger to the police. He's never gotten into any real trouble—props to his mother, whom he fears more than any cop—but he's been questioned by cops and received plenty of cool stares from them over the years. The young ones make him more nervous than the old ones. More intense, less sure of themselves.

The cop walks down the hall and into Latham's bedroom,

pulls a cell out of his pocket, talks quietly, nothing Latham can make out.

Latham takes a breath. He's scared, no doubt, but more than anything relieved. And convinced he did the right thing.

Still, he lied about why he shot that video. He considered going with his original lie, that he was making a documentary. But he didn't want the Chicago PD getting its hands on his new camcorder or his laptop. They'd confiscate them as evidence. And who's to say they wouldn't figure out his blackmail scheme, landing *him* in trouble, too?

So he made a spur-of-the-moment adjustment and said he was trying out his "new" camcorder when he just happened upon a shoot-out. He realizes, in hindsight, how convenient—how ridiculous—it sounds.

A few minutes later, the officer returns, looking at a clipboard flipped over a few pages, holding the cell phone against his chest. "Your mother told us you were at work when it happened."

A slight edge to his voice, more suspicion. The initial shock has worn off. Maybe something the detective said to him on the phone.

"That's what I told my mom," Latham rushes to say. "She didn't know about this video. I didn't want to get her involved. I was, y'know, scared—"

"Can we talk to your mom?"

"I mean, you can call her at work if you want. She doesn't get back till six, six thirty tonight."

The officer returns the phone to his ear and retreats into Latham's bedroom.

Latham drums his fingers on the kitchen table. Did he just get his *mother* in trouble? "My mom didn't lie or anything," he says to the cop when he returns to the kitchen.

"No, I got that, I got that." The cop, the name BOSTWICK

tagged to his shirt, pulls out a notepad. "Okay, so who else has this video?"

"Nobody," he says.

"Who else knows about it? Anybody else we can talk to?"

"Nobody else knows about it," he says.

Bostwick gives him a stare, cocks his head.

"Nobody," Latham insists.

The cop nods. "Okay. You have it on your camcorder and that disk drive stuck into your laptop."

"Yeah."

"Nowhere else? You sure?"

"I'm totally sure." One lie on top of another on top of another.

"All right. I'm gonna need to take those with me."

It's what Latham figured. It was the whole reason he told the cop he used the old camcorder, not his new, hidden one. He figured he might never see it again, at least not for a long time.

"Can you... can my name be kept out of this?" he asks.

The officer sighs. "We're gonna try. The detective, he told me, those videos speak for themselves. It doesn't really matter who took them. But really, it's up to you, Latham. You sure you haven't told anybody about this?"

"I'm sure, yeah," he says.

"Okay. So I'm gonna need you to come downtown with me." Bostwick raises his hand. "Don't worry, they just want to interview you. You can drive your own car if you don't want to be seen in the patrol car. So go ahead and clean up, get your things together. I can wait."

Latham sighs. He picks up his bowl of cereal and takes it to the sink. So far, so good, he supposes. What the cop said makes sense. The video shows what it shows. It doesn't matter who took it. He grabs a plastic bag from under the sink and drops in the camcorder and the mini disk.

He looks around. Where's the officer?

"Latham!" Bostwick calls out. *Shit.* He's in Latham's bedroom. "You got a lot of cameras and equipment in here."

Shit!

"Yeah, it's mostly old stuff," he says quickly, scurrying toward the bedroom. He's ready with a whole explanation when he walks into the bedroom.

He's not ready for Officer Bostwick, holding a handgun, extended by a suppressor.

"Sorry," says Bostwick, his hand shaking as he pulls the trigger.

CHAPTER 34

THE FIRST time I ever met her was in court.

I had to testify in a drug case. I was a second-year, still green enough to find the whole thing exciting. Especially when the prosecutor prepping me told me that the public defender on the case was one of the best in the building.

I took my seat, got sworn in. When the lawyer at the defense table stood up, I forgot everything about the case. I could barely speak. I felt like someone had turned on a heat lamp inside my chest cavity. I suddenly wished I'd checked myself in the mirror before I came in, finger-combed my hair or something.

Her navy-blue suit, athletic figure, dishwater-blond hair pulled back with a few strands refusing to comply, falling to her cheeks. Normally, a woman who looked like that, my first instinct would be picturing her naked, writhing in bed under me. But this wasn't carnal lust. The warmth in her eyes, her easy smile, a confidence that was quiet and nonthreatening. I knew it instantly. She was kind. She cared. And if I fought her, she'd fillet me like a fish on the witness stand.

Didn't catch her last name, but her first name was Valerie.

* * *

"Hey, sunshine." Sosh snaps his fingers at me. "You drifting off on us?"

"Paperwork may not be fun," Rodriguez joins in, "but it's an important part of what we do here, Detective Harney."

I snap out of my trance. It's probably just sleep deprivation. Or too greasy of a lunch, to help with the hangover. Or meeting with my union rep over the officer-involved shooting.

"No word back on the recanvass?" I ask.

"Haven't heard," Carla says.

"Still don't get why we're recanvassing," Sosh contributes. "You need to look up the word *solved* in the dictionary."

"They're called unanswered questions," I tell him.

He makes a face. "I got unanswered questions about my second marriage," he says. "You don't see me calling up my ex to chat."

"I know. It's a real mystery why she wouldn't have stuck with a prize like you."

"Detective Harney?"

I turn at the sound of the woman's voice. This must be the FBI agent who called an hour ago, Special Agent Clara Foster. I force my bag of bones out of my chair and shake her hand.

"Good to meet you," she says. She has a low voice and a no-nonsense approach. Some of these FBI agents are okay, but most of them take themselves way too seriously and look down on us Chicago cops. Agent Foster doesn't give off an impression either way, which probably means she's good at her job.

I introduce her to the other detectives. I offer her a chair, but she prefers to stand.

"We got the DNA sample and prints of your Jane Doe," she says. "Along with the photos. No hits on the prints or the DNA. Best we got from DNA is that she's from eastern Europe."

From a visual standpoint, it's surprisingly hard to determine things like nationality with dead people, even if they're recently dead. It's like the things that made them human drain away almost instantly upon death. The young white woman dead on the porch was from eastern Europe? That could work, yeah.

"What's it to the Bureau?" asks Sosh. Lanny Soscia views FBI agents much as my father used to view the boys my sister, Patti, brought home—he doesn't like them and trusts them even less.

"I'm on a joint task force with the county," says Foster. "Human trafficking."

"Human trafficking," I say. "You think that's what we have here?"

"Good chance," she says. "Nobody's claimed her?"

"Nope. She could be a runaway. She's probably old enough to be emancipated."

"Could be," but her tone tells me she likes her idea better. "Pretty girl. Agreed?"

"Yeah, I'd say so."

"Undernourished? Drugs in her system? Track marks on her arms?"

"All of the above," I say.

Agent Foster smirks, not in a good way. "Sounds like a 'lost girl.'"

"A lost girl."

"Someone smuggled over here. No record of her. Forced into prostitution. Hooked on drugs."

"Then what was she doing with the K-Street Hustlers? They're into that?"

She takes that question almost as a joke, though none of us is laughing. "Human trafficking is everywhere. A neighborhood street gang wouldn't be smuggling girls into the country, if that's what you mean. But they could be protecting the trade. Maybe even getting a little taste of the action. Some of these traffickers bring the girls in and run them, pimp them out. But others sell them as soon as they arrive."

Agent Foster slides a glossy photograph out of a manila folder. It's a close-up of the dead girl's leg, her ankle. A tattoo of a black flower just above her anklebone. I remember seeing it the day of the shooting.

"She was branded," says Foster.

"Do you recognize the brand?" asks Carla.

Foster shakes her head. "Never seen it before."

"It looks like a lily," says Rodriguez. "A black lily."

"Martha Stewart over here," Sosh mumbles. He throws Mat an elbow. "I gotta toughen you up. Take you to a Hawks game."

"All we know about our Jane Doe," I say to Foster, "is that she went by the name Evie. Honestly, we haven't focused on her. We figured this was a gang shooting. She was collateral damage."

Foster puts the photo back in the envelope. "You're probably right. But we try to learn their identities. Then we can work backward, figure out where they came from, try to put together how they got smuggled here. Try to locate the source."

"We'll try to get her identity," I say. "And let you know."

"Thanks." Foster nods. Her eyes are heavy. I have the sense she isn't expecting much from us, that a lot of the lost girls stay lost.

CHAPTER 35

FRIDAY NIGHT, we put the band back together. My brothers, Brendan and Aiden, come into town. Patti and I meet them at home. By "home," I mean the house on the South Side where we grew up, a house that is now empty in light of our mother's death years ago and the recent incarceration of the patriarch of our family, dear old Pop.

The thing about my wrecking ball to the department—the scandal I unearthed a little over a year ago: one of the casualties was my father, the chief of detectives. He was ultimately convicted on around two dozen federal corruption charges and sentenced to life in prison. It ripped our family apart and almost destroyed Patti.

After Pop's arrest, we didn't know what to do with the house. Luckily, the mortgage was paid off, so we just paid the real estate taxes and hired somebody to mow the lawn. Patti dropped by in the winter to run the faucets so they wouldn't explode.

None of us talked to Pop. We went through his lawyer. Pop agreed to sell the house and use the proceeds to pay off his lawyers. Patti found a real estate agent. We're going to get our personal stuff out this weekend so we can put the house on the market.

We hired packers to throw everything into boxes. The price was exorbitant, but we split it four ways, so it was manageable. And well worth it. None of us wants to admit it, but it's painful being here. The less time here, the better.

We're grilling brats, about the only thing we're good for, on the Weber in the backyard. The heat, the buzz of mosquitoes, the smell of charcoal and grilled meat—it's like I'm sixteen again.

Aiden, the second oldest, a workout freak who coaches high school wrestling and runs a gym in St. Louis, nearly decapitates me with a football I didn't see coming. That'd be something. I've survived a gunshot wound to the brain and took a bullet to the vest-protected ribs yesterday, and I die from a pigskin chucked at my noggin.

Brendan, the oldest, already having crossed the Rubicon of forty, presides over the grill. He got Pop's looks more than anyone. The licks of gray at the temples and a midsection that seems to expand every time I see him only enhance that effect. He has a wife and two kids outside Dallas, where he works as a financial planner. He's the grown-up among us, but he seems to like being here, where he can just be the brother again, drinking and belching and cussing like the rest of the Harney clan.

"So you're, like, the hero," says Aiden, dressed, as always, as if he's about to pump iron, wearing a shirt two sizes too small. He gets into a crouch and wiggles his fingers at me. "C'mere. Let's see how tough you are."

"I would if I wasn't wounded in the line of duty," I say, raising up my shirt to show the bandages on my ribs. "I'd drop you like third-period French."

"But I'm only going to use my thumb." Aiden, doing his best Sean Connery in that movie with Meg Ryan.

"I got another idea what you can do with that thumb."

"All right, you savages, let's eat," says Brendan.

"No bun for me," Patti, the low-carb girl, announces, conveniently ignoring the fact that she's drinking beer.

"How do you train for a marathon and not eat carbs?" Aiden asks her.

"I carbo-load for long runs."

"I've got some powder you'd like." Power lifter and bodybuilder that he is, Aiden has all kinds of supplements and enhancements, most of which smell like shit and taste even worse.

Brendan makes a face and nods at me. "Am I the only one who's getting fat gracefully?"

"Give me time," I say, recognizing the obvious, how much weight I've lost, but not for good reasons. "I'm not old as dirt like you."

"When's the last time you worked out, B?" Aiden asks Brendan.

"When your girlfriend came to visit last week." Brendan dishes up the brats and buns, puts them next to the huge bowl of chips, which only he and I will touch. "She's a wildcat, that one."

"Our Aiden has a girlfriend?" Patti didn't know that. Neither did I. The night just improved significantly. If Aiden has any brains, I mean any cerebral activity whatsoever, he will take the Fifth immediately, keep his lips shut so tight that the Jaws of Life couldn't pry them apart. But he won't, cuz he's our Aiden.

"I'm seeing someone, yeah," he says.

"Does she see you?" I ask. "Or do you just peep through her window and jerk off?"

"Hey, go easy on the lad." Brendan to the rescue. "The windows at the psych ward are tough to see through."

"Just kidding, A," I say, sitting down. "Seriously, what's the lucky fella's name?"

Aiden spears a brat and drops it on his plate. "She's a teacher at the high school."

"What's she teach?" Patti asks. Aiden's gonna tell us now. He shouldn't. He really, really shouldn't.

"Special ed," he says.

"Oh, you're one of her students," I say, low-hanging fruit. Patti likes that one, spills some beer down her chin.

Aiden raises his beer. "To Pop," he says. "For not being exposed for the corrupt motherfucker that he was until we were grown up and out of the house."

We clink bottles on that one, all of us except Patti, who shakes her head and frowns. It's never going to be that simple for Patti.

"That's fine," says Brendan to Aiden, "but you ain't changin' the subject, meatball."

It goes on like that for an hour. We slowly extract every detail of Aiden's girlfriend's life, devouring each nugget with any number of helpful comments. By the time we're done, this woman has a harelip, male genitalia, a criminal record, Alzheimer's, and a scorching case of herpes.

Good to be back with this crew. If nothing else, it takes my mind off Prince Valentine and Junior Peppers. It takes my mind off my Jane Doe on the porch, probably a victim of human trafficking, says the FBI.

Wherever she came from, however she got here, she deserves to have a proper burial, with her name on a tombstone, not a pauper's grave.

So I decide, as I sit at the old table on our old back porch, drunk and sentimental, that I will give her that much.

I'm going to give Jane Doe a name.

CHAPTER 36

WALKING DOWN into the basement brings back everything from childhood, even though after we kids moved out, my parents replaced the wrestling mat with an area rug, the dartboard with artwork, the foosball table and weight bench with a love seat and couch.

We're quiet at first down here, drunk and more emotional than any of us wants to admit, Brendan trying to break the ice with an occasional wisecrack, one or another of us turning away at times to hide the mist in our eyes. We brought a bottle of Jameson down here, and everyone's partaking.

Patti will take this the hardest. She and I were tight, as twins usually are, but for her Pop was on a pedestal. And she was on his pedestal, his only girl. The boys got an occasional smack when we stepped out of line, even the belt once in a blue moon, but Patti always got delicate strokes of the hair and gentle admonishments.

But Patti's also had the longest time to adjust. She worked with the movers more than I did. She's been checking on the house since Pop went away. Brendan and Aiden, on the other hand, they don't even live in Chicago anymore, so being here is a big deal for them.

We don't spend too much time looking through the boxes.

Thanks to Patti, they're well organized. Aiden, the biggest puppy dog of all, just peeks into the boxes to make sure they contain his stuff. He'll "go through it later," he tells us, which probably means the boxes will sit in some closet in his house, untouched, for the next decade.

"Look at fuckin' this." Out of a tall moving box, Brendan pulls a Santa Claus suit—the red velvet, the black-and-white trim, the long cotton beard.

"God, was I pissed at Pop," I say. There's a story there: Santa Claus always used to come visit on Christmas Eve, bearing a present for each of us kids, while we sat, mute and awed. It was a big deal every Christmas at our place, with the rest of the crew there, too—Uncle Mikey and his family from Bridgeport, Aunt Marcy and her brood from the North Side, Cubs fans but otherwise good eggs.

Anyway, I'm six, and we're done with dinner, same as always when Mom did Christmas—roast goose with boiled potatoes, cabbage, and brussels sprouts—and we're all talking about Santa coming. Four of us little kids mean it, we still believe, and the older ones just go along with it.

For some reason, I head into the garage, probably for a Pepsi, but I don't really remember why. And there, standing next to the Chrysler, is Pop, one foot already in the Santa suit, an *oh-shit* expression on his face as we locked eyes.

Needless to say, I'm beside myself, running through the house, calling everyone liars, letting the few of us who didn't already know (including Patti) in on the big secret.

"You didn't talk to Uncle Mikey for, like, a year," Aiden says.

That part I don't remember. "Why Mikey in particular?" I ask.

"For wearing the Santa costume," he says.

"God, he felt so bad," says Brendan, chuckling, shaking his head. "Remember? Mikey tried to tell you that night that Santa asked him to fill in because of the snowstorm."

I look around the room. Everyone's enjoying the memory, but… "Pop was wearing the costume," I say. "Not Mikey."

"No, it was Mikey, dumbass," says Brendan. "He had the better stomach for it. At least back then."

I look at Patti. "It was Mikey," she agrees.

I put my hands on my hips. "The fuck you guys talking about? I was the one who saw him. I was the trauma victim. I looked Pop straight in the eyes. I can picture him, totally, halfway into that Santa costume."

"Yeah, okay," says Brendan out of the side of his mouth. "Or maybe it was Angelina Jolie in that costume, and you banged her. I mean, as long as you're making shit up, it might as well be worth it."

"You guys are fucked in the head." I head into the back room of the basement, the storage area.

"Yeah, all of us are wrong," Aiden calls out, "and you're right."

It was Pop. I distinctly remember it. I mean, I can picture it like it was yesterday.

The back room—the storage area and utility room. The boiler, which must be fifty years old. Pop was so proud of that thing. He said that boiler would outlive us all.

Next to it, the hot-water heater, nearly as prehistoric, a big beige contraption with a little slot in the back that opens, the place where they put the thick set of instructions, out of sight but there if you need them. I know this detail only because I needed a place to hide my *Playboy* magazine when I was a teenager, and my bedroom held no secrets from Mom.

What are the odds that it's still there? I have no idea if I ever removed it. The feds, with their search warrant, went through the house with a fine-tooth comb after Pop's arrest, tore the place apart. Maybe, in addition to finding troves of incriminating evidence against my father, one of the agents came away with a centerfold of Lexie Karlsen.

What the hell. I step around some boxes and reach around the water heater. Using muscle memory, I push up on the latch. The door falls open, and I reach in.

No magazine. Some other kind of printed material. A hard cover. A book.

I move closer, so my hand can grip it better, and slide it up and out.

Yeah, a book. A small inch-thick book with a red cover. A ledger of some kind.

A flutter passes through my chest.

I leaf through it quickly, confirm it's what I think it is—some kind of record Pop was keeping of payoffs. It's his handwriting. Not prose but words, numbers, codes, written in pencil. I stop on one page, glance at the initial entries.

- S3925P—Rio Fly—250
- S2607R—V Disc—300
- W3827K—Bobby Jay—250

I close it up. I don't want to read it. That chapter, if you'll pardon the pun, is closed. The feds missed this ledger, this little red book of secrets, but then again, they had enough to put him away for a life sentence anyway.

So what's the difference? I consider putting it right back where I found it.

Instead I head back into the main part of the basement, where the siblings aren't done with me, still throwing out guesses about who donned that Santa costume in the garage thirty years ago. Wilford Brimley? Caitlyn Jenner? Pee-wee Herman?

Nobody notices as I slip the small red book into one of my boxes.

CHAPTER 37

PAVLO DEMCHUK was a thug, but he was a thug with a sense of honor and dignity. When I put the cuffs on him almost eight years ago, he wasn't exactly giddy with joy, but he didn't complain, didn't whimper, didn't beg or plead. There was a sense of resignation about him, as if he knew this day would come but hoped it wouldn't come so soon.

After he pleaded guilty to one count of running an illegal gambling establishment over in Portage Park—but before he was sentenced—I went to visit him in the lockup. I had a real hard-on back then, hoping to make detective, and I wanted the mobsters above him on the food chain. I thought Pavlo could give me that, because Pavlo knew everybody; his uncle had been one of the top Russian mobsters in Chicago, and though Pavlo never reached those heights or even tried to, he had his finger in plenty of things, and I suspected that very little happened that he didn't know about.

Pavlo was a perfect gentleman, complimenting me on my police work, readily admitting to his own involvement, but he smiled politely when I asked him about anyone else. "I understand your curiosity, but I will not speak of others," he kept saying in that thick Russian accent. I went through my routine: I could talk to the prosecutors; we could reduce the hell out of your sentence; why would you protect people who didn't even bond you out when you were arrested—the full charm offensive.

Over the three trips I made to the lockup, always with some version of that same pitch, Pavlo's expression never changed. He just nodded, let me say my piece, and politely declined to say anything further. I came to respect the guy, even admire him—at least how he handled adversity.

He got five years with his priors. He's out now, but still on MSR, so I knew the address on his sheet must be current. I called ahead to make sure he was home.

Pavlo lives in a bungalow in Norridge, a decidedly middle-class neighborhood full of A-frames and Georgians on small plots, not far from Harlem Irving Plaza. Pavlo is standing at the door when I pull up. It's been years, and I don't know what I expected, but he's aged more than I would've thought. I remember the bald top, but the sides were bushy and dark; now they're snow-white and cut tight. His stomach used to hang over his belt; now he's svelte, unnaturally so, which makes me think of illness.

"Mr. Harney," he says, still with the heavy accent. *Mee-ster*.

"Pavlo, thanks for seeing me," I say.

His eyes glance at the bag hanging from my shoulder. He couldn't have thought this was a social call.

We shake hands. "This isn't about you," I say. "I just wanted your help on something."

"How could it be about me?" His eyes widen, his hands spread. "I am committing no crimes."

I wonder if that's true. Finding work, straight work, after a felony conviction is ridiculously hard. The probation officer thinks he's a cook at a Polish restaurant in Broadview. I'm sure he is. I just doubt that's his only source of income.

He shows me into the first room, painted a bright yellow, family photos decorating the walls, many of them black-and-white, most from his homeland. If memory serves, Pavlo came to America in his teens, in the midseventies.

We take two chairs by the window, separated by a small pedestal table that looks like a relic from his childhood. He's made coffee. Feels like it would be impolite to decline, so I accept a cup, even though I'm sweating from being outside for only two minutes.

"I'm trying to get an identity on a young woman," I say. "Late teens, possibly early twenties. They have her from eastern Europe by way of her DNA. The FBI thinks she was a victim of human trafficking."

Pavlo nods, his brow furrowed, but I don't know how to read him. I doubt he was ever into that kind of activity, but I suspect he knew people who were, once upon a time. He probably still does. But that doesn't mean he's going to tell me.

"This is all off the record, Pavlo," I say to put him at ease, if he's worried about blowback for cooperating. I slide half a dozen glossies out of an envelope and hand them to him, hoping to give him an attack of conscience.

I nod toward the photos. "That woman didn't do anything wrong. She's an innocent victim. She deserves a proper burial, Pavlo."

His expression eases. "And this is not all," he says.

"Come again?"

"You wish to identify this girl, yes, but you wish for more than this. You wish to find out who used her."

"Busting up a human-trafficking ring isn't my assignment," I say, but he's not convinced. Say what you want about the guy, Pavlo's no dummy.

He looks down at the top photo, a gruesome close-up of Jane Doe's face. "Ah, how young she is," he mumbles. He flips to the next one, panned back farther, a waist-up shot, part of the battered porch. "This I never did. Girls, never."

"I believe you," I say. "But you have good ears, my friend. If girls from eastern Europe were coming over here, it would be the Russian mob, right?"

"The Russian mob." He says it like it's a joke. "There is *some*... organization, yes. But you must know this, Mr. Harney. There are... freelancers?" He flips to the next photo and grimaces.

He's right. There isn't much organized crime anymore, only small pockets of Italians and Russians trying to score in their tiny fiefdoms. But girls and drugs never go out of business. Someone's doing it.

"If you are looking for names, Mr. Harney, I cannot give them to you." He flips to the next photo. "Not because I won't." He flips to the next one. "But because I—"

He stops midsentence, his eyes glued to the photo. It's the close-up of the woman's leg, the tattoo of the black flower above her ankle.

"I... cannot help you," he says.

"You recognize that tattoo," I say.

"I do not." He hands me the photos. I don't take them at first, but he shakes them. "I cannot help you."

"Pavlo, it's off the record."

The color has drained from his face. His eyes have an intensity I've never seen. This guy took five years with a polite smile. The look on his face now, you'd think he was staring at the Angel of Death. "No, I—I do not know anything to tell you. Please. You must leave," he says. "Please go now."

CHAPTER 38

"YOU CAN see yourself out," says Pavlo. He heads out of the room. I follow him through the kitchen and out his back door, the sweltering heat again.

"Nobody will know it came from you," I say, stepping onto his back porch, passing a dingy gas grill, a hot tub covered with a tarp. "Just give me a lead."

"I have no lead to give you." He stops walking, standing in his lawn, his back to me. "This is the truth. I do not know the names of these people."

"But you know about them," I say. "The black flower. The lily," I say, thinking of what Rodriguez called it.

The answer is yes, but he hasn't said it yet.

"They brand their girls," I say. "Why do they do that?"

I have a feeling I know the answer to that, too, but he's giving me nothing so far.

"Pavlo, please."

His shoulders rise and fall, his back still to me. His head turns to the side, so I have his profile. "I say the truth when I tell you I do not know who they are. I only know that they are organized, and they are protected."

Protected. That can only mean one thing. And it explains why they brand their girls.

"People have died," he goes on, "trying to investigate them. They will kill. Just for asking questions, they will kill."

"I'll take my chances," I say.

He turns to me. "But *I* will not."

"Who died?" I ask. "Give me the names of the people who asked questions and got killed. There must be an investigation opened. Your fingerprints won't be on it. I'll just be a cop opening a cold case."

He considers that. Shakes his head, just his general anxiety, I think, because his eyes have drifted off. He's thinking.

"There was a lawyer," he says.

"A prosecutor?" I say. "An assistant state's attorney? A federal prosecutor?"

He shrugs. "Lawyer is all I know."

"And that lawyer was murdered," I say. "In Chicago?"

Pavlo closes his eyes and nods.

Okay, so that would be a big deal, if a prosecutor in Chicago were murdered. There would be a file opened, no question.

"Can you give me any specifics?" I ask. "His name? Any dates?"

He shakes his head again. "No, I do not believe there would be any specifics. There was no . . . investigation."

"Why not?"

Pavlo runs his hand over his bald head. "I tell you that these people are organized. They are very smart. I . . ." He puts up his hands. "I have said too much."

"Why wasn't there a murder investigation, Pavlo?"

"Please, I must go. I have work." He walks back up on the porch, tries to pass me. "If I do not go to work, they revoke my probation."

I put my hand on his chest. "Why didn't the police open a mur—"

"Because they did not think it was a murder," he spits out. "Now, please."

He tries to pass. I push him back.

"What did they think happened?" I ask.

He sighs, looks away. "Suicide," he says.

It was staged as a—

Seeing colors before my eyes. My hands shaking, my throat closing up, dry as sand. "Was the lawyer a... man or woman?"

Pavlo Demchuk looks at me like he's seeing a ghost. I know how he feels. "I know nothing else. I do not know her name."

Her name. *Her* name. My heart pounding so hard I can't breathe.

"This was several years ago. I was still in Stateville. I only *hear* things, Mr. Harney. Please. Please, Mr. Harney—"

I grab Pavlo by the ear. With my free hand, I draw my weapon, place the barrel against his forehead. "What was her name?" I shout. "Tell me her fucking name!"

He cowers, his knees buckling. "Linder... I do not know this. Linder-something. Linderman? I do not *know*, Mr. Harney! Please, I swear to you I do not know..."

I release my grip, pushing him back. He collapses to the porch.

I reholster my gun.

"Blinderman," I whisper.

She wasn't an assistant state's attorney. She wasn't a federal prosecutor. She was an assistant public defender who kept her maiden name professionally.

Valerie Blinderman was my wife.

BOOK II

CHAPTER 39

FOUR YEARS ago.

Billy, seated next to her in the office of the Cook County medical examiner, catatonic, expressionless, immobile, as the office door opened and clanged shut.

Dr. Fernando Cruz—Doc Fern, the cops called him—the county's chief medical examiner, a long, tired face, gray hair combed back, reaching the back collar of his lab coat. "Billy," he said. "This is my final report. Again, I'm so sorry for your loss."

"What's the verdict?" Patti asked, taking Billy's hand in hers.

"Suicide," said Doc Fern. "No question about it."

Patti pushes away that memory, breaks ten different traffic laws on the way over. Her SUV flies into Billy's driveway, bouncing harshly over the curb, screeching to a halt only inches from the garage door and its peeling beige paint.

She has a key to his town house. She always has.

She pushes open the front door and starts to call out his name, but she hears her brother in the family room. She walks in and finds Billy sitting on the floor amid a mess of papers strewn over the hardwood, in piles on the area rug, stacked on chairs.

Going through Val's old files, her legal work. Looking for clues.

"Oh, kiddo," she whispers.

He looks up at her, his hair, short as it is, standing on end as if deliberately mussed. His eyes shadowed, his expression...

She's seen that look on his face before. She saw it when she came to this very town house some four years ago, as Billy sat in the master bathroom, his dead wife's head cradled in his lap, rocking her as if she were a child. He never looked younger, she remembers thinking back then, never more vulnerable.

Billy blinks. "You think it's—"

"No."

"—true?"

"No," she repeats. "I do not. Of *course* not. Val took her own life. She had depression. She'd just lost Janey, for God's sake. She... did this to herself, Billy. You know that. Deep down, you know that."

His eyes drift. He shakes his head absently. "Do I? What do I remember? I don't... I don't even remember it. Not really. The details, I mean. It's... like a fog."

That must have been exactly how it felt after watching Janey die and coming home to his wife. He wasn't in investigation mode. He wasn't in cop mode.

She reaches into her purse, unfolds the final autopsy report, stares at the first page.

Office of the Medical Examiner

County of Cook, Illinois

Report of Postmortem Examination

<u>Name:</u> Harney, Valerie Blinderman

She flips to the back page, folds it over.

<u>Cause of death:</u> Self-inflicted gunshot wound
<u>Manner of death:</u> Suicide

She drops it down next to him. "Doc Fern was the best ME we ever had in Cook County," she says. "He called it a suicide."

Billy picks up the report and flings it at Patti. "Don't show me that."

"What do you mean—"

Billy leaps to his feet, lunges toward Patti, fire in his eyes, his contorted expression. She startles and draws back. It's the first time in her life that she fears her own twin brother.

He stops just short of her. "Don't fucking show me that report! How do you explain what he told me?"

"What, that guy Pavlov? Some ex-con who—"

"Pavlo," he spits. "Pavlo Demchuk."

"Okay, whatever, Pavlo. This guy tells you a tattoo of a black flower is the symbol for some Russian sex-trafficking gang, and so now you think Val was murdered? And maybe your K-Town shooting wasn't just some street-gang turf fight? Your whole life has to turn upside down now, just because some thug you put away—"

"How could he have known what he knew? He knew her name, for chrissake. A female lawyer named Blinderman, killed four years ago, made to look like a suicide. You're gonna tell me that's a coincidence? Huh?"

He stares at her, chest heaving, sweat on his face, eyes glistening. It's more than rage. He's pleading with her, she realizes. He *wants* to be wrong. He wants her to make this right, to make this all go away.

She's not cut out for that role. It's always been the other way around. Billy was always making it right for *her*. "Billy," she whispers.

"No, don't *Billy* me." He jabs a finger at her. "Tell me one possible reason why I shouldn't listen to what he told me. *One!*"

His breath hot on her face. She opens her hand and smacks him across the cheek.

"Hey, brother, you wanna take it down a notch or two? You want a reason? You wanna stop yelling at me and listen?"

She shoves him backward. Billy stumbles a bit but keeps his feet.

"Listen to what I have to say," she says.

CHAPTER 40

"WELL GO ahead," says Billy. "I'm listening."

Patti puts out her hands, stalling while she puts it together. "Okay, maybe this *super reliable* ex-con buddy of yours is right, and Val was looking into some Russian traffickers," she says. "So they were nervous. And then Val committed suicide, just like Doc Fern said, just exactly like it looked, for the obvious reason that she was grieving and depressed over the death of your daughter. The two things happened together, yes. But they were totally unrelated."

Billy flaps his arm. "And then—"

"Shut up and let me finish," she says. "So these Russian traffickers, these guys have reputations to keep up, right? They want to be feared, right? They want to be tough guys, right? So they spin the story like they killed her. Not only killed her—but killed her and made it look like a suicide. So they look ruthless *and* brilliant."

Billy shakes his head. "You don't believe that."

"Right, because it would be the first time in the history of organized crime that some mobster told a fib. That's what these guys do. They lie and bullshit and con their way through life. They took credit for her death, Billy. It doesn't mean they actually killed her."

"Bullshit." His hands on his hips, his head shaking furiously, the reservoir of rage quickly refilling. He walks in a circle, then lashes out, knocking a mess of papers off the coffee table. "That's bullshit, and you know it!"

He gets his hands under the coffee table, a wide circular walnut job, and turns it over, a plate and glass of water shattering on the hardwood floor, papers flying everywhere. He kicks one of the upturned legs of the table, nearly knocking it from its hinge.

Jesus, she's never seen him like this.

He drops into a crouch, taking gasping breaths, a deep moan.

"And if I heard you right over the phone," she says with trepidation, afraid that if she says it, it will be true, "you think these same Russian traffickers were behind the K-Town shooting? That it wasn't the Imperial Gangster Nation? It wasn't a turf war?"

Billy doesn't answer, buries his head in his hands.

"So..." She shakes her head. "So in addition to reopening four-year-old wounds, probably for nothing," she says, "you're *also* going to take a wrecking ball to a solve that just made you cop of the year and basically guaranteed you a career on the force."

Billy gets out of his crouch, turns his back to Patti. "When I make their acquaintance, I'll be sure to ask them if they shot up that house in K-Town."

"You're not going to *ask* them anything," she says, walking toward him. She can't believe she's about to say these words, but she's never believed anything more.

"You're going to kill them," she says.

Billy remains still, quiet. When he finally responds, his voice is robbed of all inflection, all emotion. "You should leave now, Patti."

"Billy." She walks to him, puts a hand on his shoulder. "You could lose everything. You've worked so hard to get back on your feet, and you could lose it all."

He nods his head but says nothing.

"Billy—"

"Then I lose everything." He jerks his shoulder, moving her hand off, then turns to her. "I'm going to find out what happened to Valerie. I don't care what it costs me." He grabs her by the arms. "Now go home, Patti. And forget this conversation ever happened. You don't want to be involved in what happens next."

CHAPTER 41

SEVEN YEARS ago.

The gambling problem started after the divorce, or at least that's what he claimed. He was fifty-four, their only son out of the house, and he felt incredibly alone when his wife left.

Jesus, Patti remembers thinking back then. *Why not just surf porn on your computer or get into some online chat room for losers?* Never really made sense why that led him to fall in with the high-end poker rooms, throwing away his money. But there it was. He was a good man, a longtime public servant, who'd made a mistake. But a mistake, nonetheless, that threatened everything.

"Twenty-seven thousand dollars and change," he said, his face falling into his hands, the words coming out through sobs. "I have nowhere else to turn. I don't have the money. They're going to kill me."

"I'll help you," Patti told him. She didn't tell him the next part, the part that he didn't need to be told: he would owe her.

A shiver runs through Patti as she starts up her car, reverses out of Billy's driveway, and drives. The streets in Lincoln Park are filled with people with so much less on their minds, people younger and happier, unburdened by the things she sees every day on the job—the burned babies and the bloodied, bruised spouses; the desperate, angry juveniles; the gangbangers who spit at her. People who don't have to wonder what's behind every door they enter, inside every vehicle they approach.

She reaches her apartment and parks in her designated space in the back lot. An apartment she wouldn't be able to afford were it not for the fact that the landlord likes having a cop in the building.

The engine still running, she turns on the dome light and pulls out the autopsy report filed by the ME's office, reads its conclusion one more time.

> Cause of death: Self-inflicted gunshot wound
> Manner of death: Suicide

"Fuck you, Val," she whispers. Billy might have made excuses for her, but Patti wouldn't have any of it. How could Val spend one minute away from that hospital room while her daughter was lying in a coma? While Billy was suffering, too?

Sure, okay, maybe Val had some depression issues. They'd all seen it. But what more could Billy have done? He took the night shift so Val could work days as a public defender while he took care of their little girl. Billy and Val hardly saw each other. He was holding down a brutal overnight shift and caring for Janey during the day. He was sleeping two, three hours out of every twenty-four. And when Janey had the stroke, he got family leave, walked away entirely from his job—more than Val could say. What, her job was more important than his?

No, Billy had done more than enough. None of this was his fault.

And now this? Now he has to relive this whole thing? Because of some stupid fantasy about a Russian human-trafficking ring? Where the hell did *that* come from?

She gets out of the car, uses the key to enter the back entrance to the four-story condo building. Ignores the smell of cannabis coming from the first-floor unit, her stoner neighbor Jamie and his buddies. Heads up to the second floor, walks into her lonely condo, and enters the bedroom.

Four years ago.

"The scene was pristine," Patti told Dr. Fernando Cruz. Only the chief medical examiner in Cook County would be assigned the case of a cop's dead wife.

"You've seen the photos," she told him. "No gunfight. No forced entry. No evidence of struggle."

Doc Fern removed his glasses, pinched the bridge of his nose. "The angle," he started to say.

But she interrupted him. "Angle shmangle. There's no manual for how you shoot yourself."

"And the GSR," said Doc Fern.

"Bullshit and you know it," said Patti. "Billy wrapped her up in his arms when he found her. He gripped her, hugged her, held her. That could've easily removed any residue.

"And don't forget Val's depression, Fern. That's documented. And for God's sake, she'd just lost her daughter. Of *course* it's suicide."

Inside her bedroom, Patti opens the closet, turns on the light. Reaches up to the top shelf and pulls down a long plastic box. She opens the box. Lifts the other documents—her birth certificate, a savings bond from Aunt Marcy, a thin family album—and pulls out a file from the bottom.

She removes the document from the file folder, the same fourteen pages, the same heading (OFFICE OF THE MEDICAL EXAMINER), the same title (REPORT OF POSTMORTEM EXAMINATION), the same subject (HARNEY, VALERIE BLINDERMAN). But it's not the same document.

No, this version bears a red stamp in the corner spelling out one word: **PRELIMINARY**.

And that's not the only difference. The last page, too, the conclusion.

> Cause of death: Gunshot wound
> Manner of death: Indeterminate

Indeterminate. That cruel, ugly word, meaning we can't be sure, Billy; she might have been murdered, Billy; more investigation is needed, Billy.

Imagine, she thinks, if Billy had ever seen this preliminary version of the ME's report.

Imagine, she thinks, if Doc Fern hadn't had that gambling debt a few years earlier, which Patti used her badge to help work down from twenty-seven thousand dollars to six thousand dollars, stripped of all the vig and placed on a reasonable repayment schedule.

Imagine if Patti hadn't called in that favor with Doc Fern.

Patti takes the preliminary report and walks into her bathroom, the report still flipped over to the final page. She picks up the Bic lighter resting behind a scented candle on the counter. She flips on the lighter and raises it to the report, the flame illuminating the words:

> The angle of the gunshot wound and the sporadic presence of gunshot residue on the decedent's hand and forearm are not necessarily suggestive of suicide and could lead to a reasonable conclusion of homicide.

The paper curls as the flame spreads, turning those words to ash. She holds the document as long as she can, until the flame almost licks her fingers pinched at the edge of the document, before she drops it into her metal garbage can and watches it curl and flicker into indecipherable black ash.

The last remaining copy of that "preliminary" report, never made public.

If Billy will no longer believe the suicide conclusion, maybe she'll help him pin it on these Russian traffickers, whoever they are. At least that would give Billy closure.

But he can't ever know what really happened.

CHAPTER 42

"YOU'RE LEAVING," I said to Valerie as she removed her hand from Janey's.

Valerie, eyes heavy, neck aching after spending the night by her bedside in the ICU. "I'm going to work," she said.

I didn't want to argue in the hospital room. I followed Valerie out into the hallway. "You're going to start back to work?" I asked. "Your office said take all the time you need."

"These kids need me," she said.

"Janey needs you," I said.

One in the morning. Heading west in my car. Blasting the radio to drown out the echoes.

I drive over the North Branch of the Chicago River and head a few more blocks west before pulling over. It won't take long. This is a decent neighborhood by day, industrial, working-class. By night, it's one of the places you go if you're looking for white girls.

The first girl who passes looks Asian. Maybe my information is outdated, my short stint on Vice ending years ago. The woman stops, bends over, peers into the car. I shake my head no.

* * *

"What if she wakes up today?" I said. "And you're not here?"

Valerie's head dropped. "You and I both know that's not going to happen."

Anger, bitterness, always brimming near the surface during this whole ordeal, took over. "Then go," I said. "Because those kids need you. The rapists and murderers and drug dealers—they need you."

"It's not that simple," she said. "I'm on to something, Billy. There are girls, girls I might be able to help—"

"What about that girl?" I hissed, pointing toward the hospital room. "The one who happens to be your daughter? What about helping her?"

Her eyes brimmed with tears, her face hardening. "We can't save her, Billy. Don't you dare pretend we can. Don't you dare be that cruel—"

"Fine—then go. Go save those other girls. If it's okay with you, I'm going to worry about one beautiful little girl who needs her parents right now."

I turned my back on Valerie and returned to the room.

The third girl who passes looks the part. Blond hair teased up, slinky outfit showing off her legs, sidling awkwardly up to my car on her high, chunky heels after we make eye contact.

I buzz down the passenger-side window.

"Hi, handsome," she says. If the nose and cheekbones didn't do it, the accent does. Eastern European. "Want some company?"

I nod. She opens the door and gets in.

She doesn't tell me her name. I don't tell her mine. No point in either of us lying.

She runs her hand high up my thigh, long purple nails scraping denim. "What would you like to do, handsome?" Her voice sultry, comforting, like I'm the man she's always fantasized about, like she can't believe her luck, meeting me.

"I have fifty dollars," I say.

She tells me what that will get me. She tells me to drive, turn at the next right. After three blocks, we're in a vacant lot by an abandoned manufacturing plant.

I put the car in Park and turn on the dome light, surprising her. "Lemme see your feet," I say.

A quick arching of her eyebrows, but no more than that. This poor kid probably sees everything, fetishes of every kind. "You want to see my feet."

"I like feet," I say. "And heels."

So she leans back against the passenger door and turns those spindly legs toward me, putting her feet and heels in my lap next to the steering wheel. I pretend to admire them, caress them, turning them from side to side as if appreciating fine art.

Nope. No black flower tattoo above her ankle. No black lily.

"Okay," I say.

"You are funny," she says.

I show her my shield. She doesn't think that's as funny.

The whole enamored-with-me facade immediately leaves her face, replaced with defiance, an eye roll. "Oh, c'mon, cop," she says. "I give to you for free."

I shake my head. "What's your name?"

"My name is . . . Cherie."

Yeah, and mine's Leopold. "Cherie, I have you on solicitation. But you answer a couple questions and you walk away. Or I take you in, find out what your real name is, and you get a free night in the clink, maybe more depending on your record. What's it gonna be?"

She doesn't answer. But that's an answer. I reach down to my feet, grab the file folder, remove the photograph of my Jane Doe's ankle. "You see this tat?"

She takes the photo and looks at it.

"That mean anything to you?"

"No." She shakes her head, shrugs. She's being straight. No fear in her eyes, not the kind of fear she'd register if she recognized this.

"You ever see a girl with this ink on her?"

"No."

"Ever heard any talk about 'black lily girls' or anything like that?"

She shakes her head again, hands me back the photo, concern on her face. Pretty obvious that it's a crime scene photo, a victim photo. Prostitutes see a lot of kinky and dirty stuff, and they are no strangers to violence, but murder isn't an everyday occurrence.

"I have one more question," I say.

I ask her. She doesn't want to tell me. Tears well up in her eyes. But eventually she tells me, with my promise that it won't come back to her.

I drive her back to her spot on West Armitage and hand her a hundred dollars, all I have on me. She takes three of the twenty-dollar bills and stuffs them into her skirt. She takes the other two and slips them into her shoe, tucked under her foot, money her pimp will never see. She better hope he doesn't.

Then she looks up at me, appearing several years younger than she did when she sauntered up to my car door twenty minutes ago. Looking like a young girl, a scared young girl.

"You have something else you could do?" I ask. "Somewhere else you could go? A family or friends or something?"

That seems almost amusing to her. "You are going to save me, Mr. Police Officer?"

"I'm just saying— "

"There is nowhere else to go." She opens the door and gets out before I can say another word.

I watch her disappear into the shadows. Then I put the car in gear and start driving.

CHAPTER 43

JOSEF DROPS his cigarette to the sidewalk and stubs it out, counting the bills as he blows out smoke through pursed lips. "Forty? Only forty?" He shakes the bills in his hand. "For an hour?"

"That's all he gave me, Yo."

The woman, who uses the name Martina on the street, red-and-blue dyed hair in a bun, shifts her weight from one side to the other, knowing Josef is angry, knowing she screwed up.

"You get the money up front," he says, gesturing with his hands. "I always tell you to get the money up front." He shoves Martina backward. She nearly falls, balanced precariously enough already on her high heels.

"I did," she says. "I told him he had half an hour. But he made me stay longer."

"He made you stay. He made you..." Josef points to the car. "Get in. Now."

"Yo, I told him—"

"Get in the car *now*."

She walks past him, giving him a wide berth, wincing, but he doesn't touch her. Not yet.

"The back seat," he tells her when she tries for the front-seat passenger door.

"Yo, please—"

"Get in the back seat now." He lunges for her, making a fist, feigning a strike. She rushes into the back seat, closes the door.

God, these girls. He walks around to the other side of the car, removes the leather strap tucked into the back of his pants, and gets in.

"Yo, please," she says before he grabs her bun and shoves her face against the front passenger seat. Holding her in that position with his left hand, he gathers up the leather strap in his right, gripping each end in his fist, a makeshift whip.

Always the back, which the men don't notice. Always through her shirt, the less likely to break skin. She takes the first strike between her shoulder blades with a whoosh of air, the second with a loud whimper, the third—

The illumination coming from the streetlight disappears, the interior of the car suddenly dark.

A shadow by the car, blocking the light. A man standing at the window.

CHAPTER 44

I SMACK my Maglite against the rear window, the glass shattering on impact. I drop the flashlight and reach through the window into the car, the man with the belt in his hand turning in my direction.

I grip his slimy hair in one hand and cup my other hand under his chin, yanking him backward, toward me, away from the girl he was whipping. I step back, using my body weight, pulling with every bit of force I can muster, a tug-of-war, yanking his head toward the shattered window. I keep pulling, leaving the scumbag with the choice of a broken neck or reluctant compliance.

His hands claw desperately at mine, but I have the leverage. His mouth forced shut, he is reduced to loud grunts of pain and surprise. My forearm cuts on the jagged shards of glass in the window's frame as I yank his head through the window and keep pulling with everything I have, leaving him no options.

He tries to raise an arm free, but I yank his shoulders through the frame of the window, barely fitting, pinning his arms at his side. The upper third of his body hanging out the window, facing upward into the dark sky, pure shock on his face.

He tries to adjust, to look at me upside down. I slam my fist down on his mouth, a pronounced crack, busting teeth, popping his jaw out of place. He takes the blow badly, having no cushion to receive it, his eyes rolling back, his head lolled backward, dangling.

I pull him the rest of the way out of the car, his body limp, his feet smacking the ground, and throw him to the street, face forward. He lands like a lump of cement, not breaking his fall, a loud puff of air escaping him. Stuffed in the back of his pants, a Glock. I remove it and stuff it in mine. I take out his wallet, too, and check his ID.

Josef Alexander Sablotny.

I flip him over, a garbled cry escaping from him, the stench of body odor and tobacco and fresh blood. Facing up now, his head lolling from side to side, eyes shut in pain, his jaw off its hinges like a broken puppet. His mouth bloody red, like a wolf after devouring prey. Not as fun when you're the hunted, not the hunter.

I drop down on top of Josef. He issues another pained grunt, which causes him to open his eyes, trying to focus on me, dumped on his torso, pinning his arms down with my knees.

"I have questions, Josef. If you answer them, you live."

Josef's head rolls to the side. He tries to spit out blood, but with his jaw malfunctioning, most of it dribbles onto his chin.

"Fuck...yourself," he hisses, not moving that jaw, spraying more blood.

"You're a tough guy, no doubt about it. Especially when you're beating up defenseless girls." I find the Maglite on the ground, raise it, and strike him in the chin, right where it would hurt the most. The wounded-animal cry he releases would make *National Geographic* proud.

I stand up, grab his arms, and pull him to a sitting position. He probably lacks the ability to fight back now. But I hope he tries.

Instead, he rocks, swoons, then vomits into his lap. That's hard to do with a busted jaw.

I reach into my bag and pull out the photo of my Jane Doe's

ankle, the same one I showed one of his prostitutes, Cherie, an hour ago. "Tell me what you see," I say, holding it near his face.

It takes him a while. He catches his breath, wipes his mouth tentatively, and finally focuses. I watch his face. He reacts to the photo, a change in his expression.

"You recognize it," I say.

He closes his eyes, nods his head.

"Who runs these girls?"

"Don't...know. I don't, I don't." Raising a hand. "I...swear." Speaking without jaw movement.

"Of course you do, Josef. They're your competition."

"No." The way he says it, not a desperate denial but an assured statement of fact. "Not my comp—competition. They do not...walk streets."

"What, they're higher-end? Call girls? Escorts?"

He nods, still taking wet, heavy breaths.

"Where do they work? Where do they live? *Who runs them?*"

"I..." He shakes his head. "I don't—please..."

There are girls, girls I might be able to help.

These kids need me.

"Please?" I repeat. "*Please?* You want mercy from *me*?"

I reel back and kick him in the ribs, audible cracks, as Josef doubles over in pain, grimacing and broken, curled into the fetal position.

"You think I won't kill you?" I shout down at him. "You think I won't?"

"Nobody...knows," says Josef, wincing, gritting through the pain. "Is not...my business."

"Bullshit. Bullshit!" I remove Josef's Glock from my waistband, crouch down over him, pressing the barrel of the gun against his left eye. "You know a name. Or a club. Or a hotel. Something. You have till the count of three, or I put a bullet through your brain."

A moan of protest or pain or both.

"One," I say.

Behind me, the roar of a vehicle, a flashing red light. Josef, with his free right eye, sees the lights behind us.

"That's not gonna save you," I say. "Two."

Tires screeching to a halt, the flashing light now bathing us, coloring Josef's face.

A door opening. "Police! Police officer!"

Footsteps approaching, shuffling. "Drop that weapon! Drop it!"

"No! This isn't your business!" I shout back. I press the gun harder against his left eye. "You little fuck! Tell me! *Tell me!*"

"Drop that weapon now! *Now!*"

My body trembling, I hiss through my teeth. *"Tell... me."*

Josef cries out, spitting more blood, coughing.

I Frisbee the gun to the street and take Josef's jaw in my hands, like I'm going to rip it off his face. "Tell me what you know!" I shout over his high-pitched squeal of pain. "Tell me what—"

One arm wraps around my neck in a choke hold, the other under my armpit.

"No!" I shout, but I have no leverage, being pulled backward out of my crouch, wrestled backward, unable to get my feet under me. "No! Let go!"

I end up thrown against the bumper of the vehicle with the flashing light.

"What the fuck are you doing?" I spit.

Patti bends down and looks me in the eyes. "Are you out of your *mind*?"

CHAPTER 45

PATTI DISABLES the cherry on her dashboard and tosses it in the back seat. We peel away in her car.

"You have got to get it together, little brother," she says. "You have any idea how many ways that could've gone wrong? You know how lucky you are?"

"The only one who's lucky is Josef."

"Yeah? So what's the plan here, Wyatt Earp? Kill every pimp in Chicago?"

My body shaking with post-event adrenaline. Still wishing I had my hands on that guy. "I didn't kill Josef."

"Would you have, if I hadn't shown up?" She turns to me, concern more than anger on her face, her eyes brimming with tears.

If I had an answer to that question, I'd give it. "I told you not to get involved," I say.

"Well, I shared a womb with you," she says, "so I guess that makes me involved."

I punch the side door of the car. Punch it again.

I rub my hand. My forearm, I notice for the first time, is bleeding from Josef's busted glass window. My hands are bloody, though it's not my blood.

"Would Val—" Patti's throat closes. Muffled sobs. "Would Val want this?" she manages. "Throwing your life away over this?"

There are girls, girls I might be able to help.

These kids need me.

"She'd want me to find these scumbags and stop them."

Patti swerves the car over to the side of the road and brakes hard, the seat belt locking me in place.

She puts the car in Park and turns to me, tears on her cheeks, but no grief in her expression. Determined, resolute.

"Then let's find them and stop them," she says. "But do it smart. Keep your eye on the prize. No bull. No china shop. No Charlie Bronson. Let's make a plan."

CHAPTER 46

"ONE THING you need to be clear on," Patti says after we've adiosed the scene, doubling back now to drive me to my car. "The force isn't going to back you up on this. They get one hint that you're shitting all over the K-Town solve, they'll put you down."

The adrenaline slowly drains away. Patti's right. I can't shoot or fight my way through this. I need to be smart. Still, I'd be ready, willing, and able to go back for round 2 with Josef the pimp right now.

"Got that covered," I say. "The story is that I'm trying to ID the Jane Doe. It gives me an excuse to go looking for these guys. The whole black-lily tattoo thing."

"That won't hold for long."

"Maybe I won't need very long. Or maybe my partner buys into my plan."

"Your partner," says Patti. "Carla Griffin?"

"Right. We didn't hit it off so well at first, but I think she's okay."

Patti steals a glance in my direction. "Carla Griffin is *not* okay. She's bad news."

"Says who?"

"Says a lot of people."

I look over at her. "Don't tell me she's IAB."

"No, nothing like that."

Thank God. That's all I need right now. I'm not sure how I'm going to figure out who killed Valerie, but I do know it's gonna involve fracturing some laws and bending a few rules into pretzels. I don't need Internal Affairs sticking its long, hairy snout over my shoulder.

"She burned a lieutenant in Wentworth," she says. "Guy named Franco. You hear about that?"

I didn't. I've been out of the gossip circle for a long time. Hell, I was never in it. But Patti, she's a different story. The women on the force tend to stick together, having to deal with so much bullshit, the double standards and everything else.

"Lieutenant Ron Franco," says Patti. "Married, buncha kids. Anyway, Carla was sleeping with him. He ended it; she didn't like it. So she accuses him of sexual harassment. He denied it, said everything was consensual, but the department, well, they didn't want the publicity. Neither did Franco, because he didn't want this getting back to wifey. So he took an early retirement. And Carla, voilà, gets promoted up to SOS."

"Sounds like a he said, she said."

"That's the thing," Patti says, stopping at a light. "It was a *they* said, she said. Half the coppers in the Second knew about the affair. A detective I used to partner with—remember Gunner?—he said it was common knowledge. And they all went to bat for Franco. But it didn't matter. She screams 'sexual harassment,' everyone runs for cover. She had him by the short hairs, and she pulled hard."

"So now we're feeling sorry for a guy who stepped out on his wife?"

She makes a face. "Screw Franco. I don't give a rat's ass about that scumbag."

"And the Me Too movement?" I ask. "Where's that feminist who shared that womb with me?"

"See, that's the thing," says Patti. "Sexual harassment? That shit happens all the time on the force. Blatant stuff, subtle stuff, all shapes and sizes."

"To you, too?" I ask. "You don't tell me that." She's mentioned a few things here and there, but not like it's a constant thing.

She rolls her eyes. "Billy Boy, if I told you every time I get a comment on my ass or an 'accidental' brush-up or a captain staring at my tits or rubbing my shoulders or asking me if I've ever been with another woman, it would be all we talk about."

"Fine. Then why you have a problem with Carla?"

She sees my car by the curb, pulls her car over. "Because," she says, a new edge to her voice, "when someone like Carla comes along and makes an obviously false accusation, it hurts the rest of us. It makes it harder to complain about something real."

"Okay, well—I don't know what I'm supposed to do with that. Sounds like none of my business."

"It *is* your business," she says, "and I'll *tell* you what you're supposed to do. Watch out for yourself, that's what you're supposed to do. Look, Billy, I don't think it's an accident you got assigned Carla Griffin for a partner."

I apologize in advance for your partner, Wizniewski had said to me.

"Our good ol' Superintendent Driscoll was looking to burn you. And she'll do it, brother. Don't give her a reason."

"Maybe." Not hiding the doubt in my voice.

She slams the gear into Park and turns to face me. "The point being, this plan of yours to find these Russian traffickers?" she says. "You can't tell anybody. You can't trust your partner. You can't trust anybody on the force. Not a single person."

I nod and reach for the door handle.

"Except me, of course," she adds.

CHAPTER 47

ANTOINE STONEWALD.

It takes me the rest of the night, a pot of coffee, hours of going through Valerie's old work files, dawn shooting beams of sunlight through the window of my family room, but eventually I fix on it.

Antoine Stonewald.

Charged with felony murder, an armed robbery that went bad. He killed Nathan Stofer, age forty-five, some real estate developer, inside a parking garage in downtown Chicago as Stofer was walking to his car near ten o'clock at night. The case was three weeks out from trial, which is when Valerie would have dived into it full throttle.

An accordion file's worth of documents, more than Valerie would normally have kept at home, but back then, life wasn't normal—she was spending half her time at the hospital with Janey and me, trying to keep up with work at home as much as at the office.

A rough draft of a motion for continuance, half completed. Valerie was going to ask the judge to push the trial back, give her more time. A mention of "undersigned counsel's young daughter" being treated in "intensive care," which I gloss over because I can't think about that right now—I just can't.

A folder entitled "Att'y Notes." Random notes. Valerie's handwriting. Valerie's smell on the paper. I close my eyes, breathe it in, think of the small of her neck, those eyelashes, the soft moan when I touched her—

No, can't do that. Not right now.

Her notes. Focus on the words, her thoughts, things nobody would ever see, confidential work product.

AS denies involvement. Must mean Antoine Stonewald, her client. Not exactly a shock; he denied the crime. But Valerie was a pro.

Left job at 9:30 and went to parking garage. Heard gunshot on floor below him. Went down and found victim dead. Ran. He was scared, a black man standing over a white professional guy.

Cassietta says AS called and was going to pick up food on way home. Didn't sound nervous or excited. No motive, she says. Didn't own a gun, she says.

Cassietta must be the girlfriend or wife.

Motive motive motive ???

Words below it:

Stratton?

Boho?

Several pages of trial prep, the beginning of a written examination of Antoine Stonewald, some points about cross-examination of the responding police officer, part of a closing argument (a good trial lawyer writes the closing first, she always told me, then works backward to make sure she can support that argument through the evidence).

The next page, a full page with a color photograph, probably printed off her camera phone. A view into an alley. A Lincoln Town Car. A man dressed in black, wearing shades and a chauffeur's hat. The back door opened. A woman, dressed in a slinky gown, hair in a fancy updo, stepping out a door and into the town car. Valerie's handwriting, noting the date and time: ***5/5 7:00 p.m.***

The next page, same thing, but different woman, again a Lincoln Town Car, maybe the same one—too grainy to read the license plate, and the whole picture darker, later in the night. The woman's dress is off the shoulders, her hair pulled back. A different woman, but coming out the same alley door into a black town car. Valerie notes the date and time, again, with a Sharpie: ***5/5 8:30 p.m.***

Twelve more pages like that, several photos each for May 5, 6, and 7. Same setup—various women dressed to the nines stepping into a black town car.

Valerie must have been using her phone. The photo quality is poor. I can't make out license plates or faces. Can't make out an address or any detail in the foreground or background that would indicate a location. Just an alley, like thousands in Chicago. Nothing whatsoever of note. Can't even make out the ages of the women.

There are girls, girls I might be able to help.

I close the folder. This is it. She was preparing Antoine Stonewald's defense, and she stumbled onto a human-trafficking ring. Something in these pages will tease out the answer.

Inside, I'm boiling, my hands balling into fists, my pulse thumping so loudly that it drowns out all other sound. But it has to be a controlled boil. Patti's right. Keep your eye on the prize. Be smart. Don't show your hand. Keep a low profile and snoop around. Do it off the books. Act like everything's normal. You can do that. You've done it before. Be the wisecracking comedian. Be everyone's buddy. All good. No problem here. Be the guy who just solved the big case, the aw-shucks routine, the team player.

But find these people. Billy the funny guy will find these people.

And then we'll all find out together how funny I am.

CHAPTER 48

MONDAY MORNING, the sky like orange sherbet, the air mild.

Before work, I go to the crime scene, looking for things I didn't look for the first time around, when by all appearances, the K-Town shooting was nothing more than a turf battle between street gangs.

That still may be the case. The shooting might have had nothing to do with my Jane Doe and her black-lily tattoo. If I find out different, so be it, but all I want right now is to learn more about Jane Doe.

The house is still roped off, surrounded by police crime-scene tape, but I stopped at the station and checked out the key to the house before coming here. I walk under the tape and slide the key into the door.

Inside, it smells like blood, like body odor, like death. I ignore the blood spatters on the wall and head back to the bedrooms. From what we know, this house wasn't really a place where Shiv lived so much as the place where he ran his drug operation. But it was enough of a home for his girlfriend to sometimes leave their daughter, LaTisha, with Shiv while she went to work, a decision that will haunt her the rest of her days.

The bedrooms generally look like actual bedrooms—twin-size

beds, simple nightstands, closets with some clothes hanging in them, and dressers. We cleared out all the drugs from the place, but the other stuff is untouched.

I snap on gloves and start with the bathroom. It doesn't take me long to find what I'm looking for. Tampons, a purple box. So some female was living here, at least part-time.

Lip gloss, too, resting inside a medicine cabinet—also says female. I drop that into an evidence bag, in case I need DNA testing. We already have Jane Doe's DNA, but I might be needing some evidence off the official record.

I hear the creak of the door from the front of the house. Footsteps entering.

I draw my piece but keep it low at my side. "Police officer!" I shout. "Who's there?" I move slowly down the hallway, peek around the corner.

A young African American woman, twenties, braided hair—takes me a second, but it's LaTisha's mother, Janiece Moreland, staring at the bloodstain on the wall. She doesn't even acknowledge me as I turn the corner, holstering my weapon.

The last week has not been kind to her. She buried her daughter and got to spend a whole lot of time thinking about her decision to use her drug-dealing boyfriend for day care.

"Ms. Moreland," I say.

She nods absently, still looking at that stained wall. "Saw you come in."

"You were parked outside? Any particular reason why?"

She takes a long breath. "I come here every day. First time it's been open." Her head slowly turns in my direction. Her eyes are heavy, purple bags that could almost pass for bruises. "You're the one that caught the shooter. You're the one that shot him."

"I am, yes. I was hoping to take him in, question him, find out—"

"I'm glad you killed him." She considers what she said, lets out a bitter chuckle. "Not s'posed to say that, am I? Not s'posed to *answer violence with violence,*" she says, as if it's something people have been telling her. "Try losing your baby daughter first."

"I understand. Would it be okay if I asked you a couple questions?"

She doesn't say anything. Her body in a slight tremble, a tear falling down her cheek. She's in a blue uniform, on her way to work, less than a week after her daughter was killed. She has three other children, older than LaTisha, and she has to provide.

"The woman that was shot on the porch," I say. "Anything you can tell me about her?"

For a time, I think she won't answer, as she stares off. It must be agonizing to be back here, to see the blood and brain matter of your daughter splattered against a wall and onto a couch. But there's no manual for suffering. We torture ourselves.

"Evie," she says, a short *e,* rhyming with "Chevy."

"You have a name besides Evie?"

She shakes her head. "Evie," she repeats.

"Was Evie staying here?"

"'Bout a week or so, yeah." Still with that far-off expression, her eyebrows up.

"Who was she? What'd she do? Where did she come from?"

"Fuck if I know. Dwayne said he wanted to help her, give her a place to stay for a few days. Said she ran from something ugly." She turns to me again. "Take one look at her, you know what she was."

"A prostitute," I say.

"And a junkie."

"Right, but—anything else you know? We're trying to identify her. We don't know anything about her."

"Neither do I, mister. Neither did Dwayne. I figured he took her in so she'd pay the rent, know what I mean?" She shakes her head.

"But Dwayne said it wasn't like that. He said he didn't touch her. Said he felt bad for her."

"So she was running from something. Something ugly."

"What she said, mister. Don't make it true." She wipes at her face. "I gotta go to work."

"Sure, Ms. Moreland." I slip her one of my cards. "If you can think of anything else, please let me know."

She nods and leaves, a lifeless stoop to her posture, carrying a burden that will probably never lift.

I close the door behind her and begin a search of the first bedroom. I'm getting short on time before work begins.

Ten minutes in, my phone buzzes. Caller ID says it's Carla.

"Hey," I say when I answer, the content, easygoing, wisecracking partner, nothing amiss here, no, sir.

"Lew says he has something for us," she says. *"You close?"*

"Maybe half an hour," I say. "Sorry; I overslept. You wanna take the assignment, and I'll meet you?"

"No. I'll wait. You're on your way or still at home?"

I close the dresser drawer I was searching and head for the door. To be continued.

"Just leaving now," I say. "Walking out the door."

Which is technically true. I pull open the front door, step onto the porch.

And there on the sidewalk is Carla, phone against her ear.

CHAPTER 49

WHAT NOW, smart guy?

"Hey." I nod to her, nonchalant, as if she didn't just bust me in a lie. "What are you doing here?"

"Me? I'm just looking for my partner. What are *you* doing here?"

I walk down the stairs. "Trying to ID the Jane Doe," I say. "We never really checked out the interior of the house. Thought I'd get a head start on it."

She stares at me, wanting more, expecting more.

"Figured I'd do it off time," I add. "Save regular time for the new stuff. The Wiz gave us a new assignment?"

She smirks. *Nice try,* she's saying without saying it. *But I'm not chasing that shiny object.* "What's in the evidence bag?" she asks, nodding at my hand.

She's batting me around like a kitten bats a ball of yarn. I got nothing here. But I take a swing anyway.

"Lip gloss," I say. "Figure it must be hers. It wouldn't be Shiv's."

"We already have her DNA," Carla observes. "You need a second sample?"

"Yeah, good point."

Fuck. This is getting ridiculous.

"So you're checking up on me," I say.

"So you're *lying* to *me*." The smirk gone now. "Why didn't you want me to know you were here?"

I shrug. "What's the big deal? I was doing a little extra work to identify this girl. I feel sorry for her. Is that a crime?"

"No crime," she agrees. "No big deal. I feel bad for her, too. So why lie about it?"

"Shit, Carla—lay off, okay?" I walk past her, head to the car.

"You're keeping something from me, Harney. I don't like it."

"Yeah, it really sucks when a cop hides something from her partner. But you wouldn't know anything about that, would you?"

"What the hell is *that* supposed to mean?"

I spin on her, raise a finger, but think better of it. "Nothing," I say. "It doesn't mean anything."

She steps toward me. "I want to know what you meant."

"No, you don't. Y'know something?" I pat my chest, filling with rage, the easygoing, good-natured partner receding far into the shadows. "Say what you want about me, but I'm an open book. My history with the department? Everyone knows it. My corrupt bastard of a father, my former partner, everything was well covered in the press. And you made it *more* than clear that I was on thin ice with you from the start, that you'd rather be tarred and feathered than partner up with me. Like your record is spotless."

"My record? What *about* my record?"

"Just get off your high fucking horse, Carla, okay? Don't act like your shit don't stink, too."

I leave her again, heading for my car, hearing her rush up behind me. "Harney, I swear to God, you walk away from me, I'm drawing my weapon."

"As long as you don't accuse me of sexual harassment."

The footsteps behind me halt abruptly. I can't believe I just said that, but I'm too amped up right now on adrenaline and anger and frustration, and my brain is telling me to stop, to turn around and apologize, to let her know that rumors are rumors, I don't believe everything I hear, but all I want to do right now is take her down a notch, which it seems I have done in spades.

I get in my car and drive to the station, feeling like an asshole.

CHAPTER 50

THE NEIGHBORHOOD is about as south and east as Chicago gets, near the Skyway, mostly industrial—most of it *formerly* industrial, slowly abandoned during the various economic downturns over the last century. The small pocket that's residential runs about two-thirds black, one-third Latino. The white population is almost entirely gone these days.

I turn off 95th and drive south a couple of blocks. The street is lined with trees and filled with single-story homes on small lots. I squint through the oppressive afternoon sunlight to find the right house. It's a mix of yellow brick and aluminum siding, a tiny front lawn divided by a walkway up to a porch.

"You Mr. Harney?"

A boy in the front yard, skinny, maybe ten or eleven, dark-complected, wearing a purple T-shirt that hangs on him and shorts that pass his knees, a baseball in his right hand and a mitt on his left. The same purple color on a baseball cap that is too big for his head.

"That's me," I say. "What's your name?"

"Samuel," he says, throwing the baseball up in the air and catching it. "Wanna play catch?"

"Why not?" I put out my hands and keep my distance. His arm reels back, and he tosses it, hitting pretty close to the target I put out for him, stinging my hands. "Nice arm," I say. "The Sox are looking for middle-relief help." I flip it back to him.

"I'm in the minors," he says.

"What position?"

"We play all the positions." He throws it to me again.

"You wanna keep that elbow up," I say.

He raises his elbow up high, a one-arm chicken dance. "Like this?"

"You want the ball up about ear level," I say, showing him. "Then you bring it over and down, snapping your wrist." I do it, making sure not to throw it too hard. "The power of your throw's mostly in the wrist action."

He catches the ball. His tongue peeking out of his mouth, he holds the ball up high, elbow up, and flings it overhand, snapping his wrist. He doubles the velocity on this throw, though it flies far past my reach.

"I'll get it," he says, racing off.

"No, I can—"

"It's okay. I know to look both ways." He scoots past me, chasing the ball into the street. "Mom, can we go to the park and play catch?"

Mom? I turn and see Carla, standing on the front porch. I didn't even hear the door open. She changed out of her work clothes, going with a tank top and shorts, after deciding to miss work today—a sick day, she called it.

"Hey," I say, ever the brilliant conversationalist.

She nods back. I took a personal half day and called ahead, told her I was coming. She didn't say yes. She didn't say anything at all. I half expected her not to be here.

"I had no right to say what I said. I'm sorry." I want to get that in before Samuel returns with the ball.

"Can we, Mom? Can we go to the park?"

"You go. Mr. Harney and I will catch up." She looks at me. "Let's take a walk," she says.

CHAPTER 51

CARLA'S BOY, Samuel, starts jogging down the street. There's a square block of a park just ahead, complete with a baseball diamond where kids are playing. Carla and I walk in lockstep down the sidewalk.

"I should've fronted it," Carla says, her arms crossed in front of her. "You should've heard it from me. I should've figured it would get to you. It probably got to everyone. So much for confidentiality."

"Welcome to the CPD," I say.

She grunts a laugh. "So what did you hear? His side, probably."

"Probably."

"Let me take a guess," she says. "Ron and I were doing the nasty for a long time, just having a grand old time, his place, my place, hotels, the back seat of a squad car, wherever we could. Couldn't keep our hands off each other. Then he breaks it off. I'm crushed, just absolutely *crushed* not to have the honor and privilege of screwing that lumpy piece of shit. But he won't take me back. So I'm hurt, and I retaliate. I'm a 'woman scorned.' I make up some BS story about him sexually harassing me. And the department? Well, these days, they can't have that kind of pub. Doesn't matter if it's true. Doesn't matter if I'm some 'irrational woman.' So they give me whatever I want, as long as I'll keep quiet. They early-retire Franco, and I get a big promotion." She looks at me. "How'm I doing so far?"

"That's more or less it," I say. "How much of that is true?"

"The part about me keeping quiet."

Samuel, up ahead, joins a pickup game of baseball. Couldn't be a better day for it. We stand to the side, watching like parents at a Little League game.

"I never touched Ron," she says to me. "Except when I was pushing him off me. He came at me ten different ways. Always trying to get me to work late or take some special assignment involving only him. Always brushing up against me and making comments. Calling me at home. All that I could handle. You just have to take some of that or you'll spend all your time complaining."

Sounds like something my sister would say.

"Anyway, he started getting more forceful. Started talking about lieutenant exams coming up, he could help, but he needed to know I was a 'team player.' You get the idea. What am I supposed to do, spit in his face? Knee him in the balls? He's my boss. I just tried to discourage him without telling him to go jump in a lake."

"Understood."

"So one time, we're in his office late—he kept me late. He calls me in, and I can tell right away he's been hitting the sauce. I can smell it all over him. He tells me it's time to stop being such a tease, that kind of thing. He's all over me, more aggressive than he's ever been before. First time I've actually been, like, scared."

She sounds scared now, her voice trembling, reliving it.

"You've told me more than enough, Carla. I don't need—"

"So suddenly he's got his hands halfway up my shirt, he's pressed up against me, and I'm thinking he's going to do this, right here in his office—he's going to rape me. So I fought back. I just—I just went crazy."

"You kick him in the balls?"

"No, but he walked with a limp for a week. And he had a pretty good shiner." She glances at me and actually chuckles. "I should've kicked him in the nuts."

"I'm sorry. Sorry about all that. And what I said before—"

"So then I knew that it was every man for himself," she goes on. "I had to beef him, because he was going to beef me. So yeah, I filed a sex harassment, and that's when I come to find out how devious he was. He'd been telling people for months that we were sleeping together." She shakes her head. "So when I beefed him, all his buddies figured they already knew the truth. I was a liar; he was righteous. Nobody believed me. Nobody. I'd lost the game before it even started."

On the diamond, Samuel fields a ground ball and throws it to first, throwing it like I told him to. He looks over and chicken-arms his elbow at me. I give him the thumbs-up.

"Least you got out of there," I say. "And you got into SOS." I turn to her. "Only to get partnered with a burnout like me."

She laughs, elbows me. "You're not so bad, Harney. I admit I was worried. I thought they were promoting me and punishing me at the same time. But you seem like a guy that calls it straight. That's all I care about."

We watch the game for a bit, some clouds moving in, providing a brief respite from the sun. Samuel can hit better than he fields, driving a ball between the shortstop and third baseman.

"As long as we're all kumbaya here," I say, "can I ask you another question?"

She makes a noise like yes.

"Are you pregnant?"

"Pregnant?" She draws back, looks at me like I grew a second head. "Why would you think that?" Unconsciously, she looks down at her stomach, as if I was suggesting she had a belly. She doesn't. She's thin as a rail. Hard, too, like she trains.

"I couldn't help—one day, you spilled . . . a . . ."

She rolls her hand over, like get on with it.

I blow out air. "You left a pill on your chair. You take a lot of pills. So yeah, I looked at it, and it was a ginger pill. My wife, when she was pregnant, she took ginger for morning sickness, first trimester. I wasn't snooping," I insist, seeing the look of horror on her face. "It just fell out. I just looked at it."

She puts a hand to her mouth.

"Okay, maybe I was snooping," I admit.

Ashen, looking violated. I wish I hadn't said anything. But . . . she's not pregnant?

Finally, she shakes her head. "Well, I guess there aren't going to be any secrets between us, Harney," she says. "Yes, they're ginger pills for nausea. But I'm not pregnant, thank you very much."

I put up my hands. "Okay, sorry I—sorry I asked. Really."

She pinches the bridge of her nose. "The nausea pills are for chemotherapy," she says. "I have cancer."

CHAPTER 52

DENNIS PORTER drives on North Broadway, half past six, having called Amy an hour ago to tell her he'd miss dinner again tonight. Used his standard line for why an IAB captain has odd hours: *Crooked cops don't take evenings off*. He tries not to think about the irony in that statement.

Besides, it's not like the cops who *don't* work IAB are on the straight and narrow. If they were, he'd be out of a job. If they can get their taste of the action, why can't he get his? He's no more a hypocrite than the rest of 'em.

He likes this gig, being on top of the perch, where he can see everything, control everything. Especially after last year's scandal cleared out most of the other brass. Business, for Porter, has never been better.

"Hey, Gus," he says to the owner of the diner as he strolls in. Gus, with his shiny bald head and dirty apron, doesn't know much, other than that Porter helped him out with a problem he was having with his liquor license two years ago, so Gus owes him. *I do for you, you do for me*. That pretty much describes Porter's entire way of doing business.

All I need from you, he told Gus, *is once in a while, I might need your office for a meeting. For reasons you can understand, I have to meet privately, off the job, with my operatives from time to time.*

Gus motions toward the back room, signaling that the other attendee at the meeting has already arrived.

Porter passes the kitchen, the glorious smells of fried food and sizzling meat, and opens the office door. Officer Joe Bostwick startles, then stands almost at attention. He is young but looks even younger in civilian gear—a cotton shirt, long shorts, and moccasins.

"At ease," Porter says with a chuckle. "How we doin', Joey?"

"Good, D, good." But he looks anything but good. Nervous as a mouse cornered by a snake.

Porter can't blame him. Bostwick got thrown into the deep end. Oh, he was all up for the occasional skim, diverting some drug proceeds. Victimless stuff. He grew up in a family of cops. He knew the game. But putting down Latham Jackson? That was over and above.

Damn, was his voice trembling when he called Porter that day from Latham's apartment and told him about the video Latham had recorded of the K-Town shooting. *We gotta put that kid down,* Porter had told him. *You up for it, kid? I need a yes or no right now. I'm gonna need this one.*

To his credit, Joey had come through and done the right thing. He put two bullets into Latham and managed to sneak out with an armful of electronics from Latham's bedroom. It looked like a burglary gone bad, just as Porter had told him to set it up.

"How *are* we doing?" Joe asks.

"All good," says Porter. "The Eleventh sees it like a garden-variety B and E. Latham surprised the intruder in his bedroom, and the perp blasted him."

Joe nods, but he's lost all color, reliving it. This kid is still wet behind the ears. He'll learn. "The Eleventh is handling it?" he asks. "Not SOS? Even though it happened across the street from the shooting?"

"It's K-Town, boyo. Not like that shit doesn't happen all the time. And Latham told his mom he was at work that day and didn't see nothin', right?"

Joe nods, finding some relief.

"Right, so there's no connection to the shooting. Just a B and E that went to shit. The Eleventh's looking for a young black kid in the neighborhood. They're not gonna talk to SOS about it."

Porter reaches into the pocket of his jacket, a jacket he didn't want to wear with these temps today, and produces a fat envelope. "This is for your troubles, Joey. It's twenty grand."

"Jesus." He takes the envelope and looks at it.

"Yeah, Jesus." Porter cups a hand behind the kid's head. "Because you did good. Because you did something I normally would never, ever ask you to do. You gotta understand that, boyo. This isn't something that happens every day. Hardly ever, in fact. But you rose to the occasion. So go take that girlfriend of yours, Joann—"

"Jody."

"Take Jody out to a nice place with a white tablecloth. But listen to me now, kid. I want you to understand a couple things. You're listening to me now."

"Yeah, D, I'm listening." God, this kid is young.

"First off, you gotta know, this Latham kid was scum. He was a dealer."

"He didn't look like a dealer."

"Well, he was." He wasn't, of course, but some employee management is in order here. "There are things about this kid Latham you don't need to know. But trust me, you did the world a favor. Really."

Bostwick blows out air. "Yeah?"

"For real, Joey."

"Okay."

"Second thing," says Porter. "You know you can't deposit this cash in a bank account, right?"

"Yeah, I know, D."

"Use a safe-deposit box if you have to, or hide it somewhere, somewhere good. And no extravagant spending. No big purchases. Use it for everyday stuff."

"I got it; I know." Bostwick's heard the speech before. It's not the first envelope he's received, and it won't be the last. Bostwick seems to be warming up now, probably mentally spending that fat wad of cash. "I really appreciate this, D."

Porter smacks him gently on the cheek. "You can be a good cop and be loyal to me. You can do both. You're gonna put a lot of skells away. You're gonna keep the streets safe, and we're gonna help each other out from time to time on stuff that doesn't hurt nobody. The best of both worlds, right, Joey? I'm looking at a future captain right here, sure as I'm breathing."

That stuff always works on Bostwick.

Porter leaves first, already late for his next appointment. That's the one thing that sucks about this gig: the hours. Most of his operatives are inside the various police districts, and he can't meet with them during regular work shifts. So his nights fill up. He tries to fit everything into a few evenings a week to keep Amy happy, to see Jay and Laura once in a while before they grow up and leave.

He takes Lake Shore Drive. Traffic is brutal. He'd use the cherry and drive on the shoulder, but calling attention to himself is one thing Dennis Porter never does.

By the time he's hit the Stevenson, then popped over to I-90, it's running close to eight o'clock. It's half past the hour before he pulls into the alley behind the old bakery.

The other car is there, headlights on, idling. He gets out of his car, squints into the beams, and gets into the other car, passenger side.

"You're late," Carla Griffin says.

CHAPTER 53

CARLA GRIFFIN, one arm slung over the steering wheel, peering straight ahead, looking drawn and haggard. Not one of her better days. She called in sick today, Porter knows—he makes it a point of tracking her and all the others—but he decides not to tell her he knows that. Don't tell 'em anything they don't need to know. That old line: *Treat all of 'em like mushrooms; keep them in the dark and feed them shit.*

That's how he thinks of them, his mushrooms—the cops, dealers, crooks, gangbangers, politicians in his circle. His empire.

"Harney went back to K-Town this morning," she says. "Back to the crime scene."

"Yeah? Why?"

"Not sure."

"You weren't with him? He flew solo?"

"Right. He says he's trying to find the identity of the Jane Doe, the dead junkie. Basic follow-up. But yeah, he didn't seem interested in sharing with me."

Something sinks inside Porter. That's not good. No, that's not good at all. Why would Billy Harney be trying to ID the prostitute? And not tell his partner?

"Victim Services can handle basic follow-up," he says, hearing the edge to his voice, adjusting, not wanting to tell Carla anything more than she needs to know. "That's not the job of an SOS detective. Did you *tell* him that?"

She lets out air, impatient. "It wasn't exactly a linear conversation, Porter, okay? The hell do *you* care about the identity of some Jane Doe?"

Porter doesn't answer right away, drawing Carla's notice. The longer the silence hangs, the greater the import of her question.

"What's going on?" Carla asks, her eyes widening. "You have skin in this game? The K-Town shooting?"

"No, of course not," he says, feeling the seeds of panic rising in him. Shit. He overplayed his hand. "What the hell do I care about gangbangers shooting each other over turf?"

"Exactly my question," Carla says, angling her body toward him, confronting him.

"Listen," he says. "You know Harney pissed off a lotta people on the force. You know a lotta heads rolled on account of him. Including people I worked with in IAB."

"Yeah, I know. So what? You're looking to burn him? I mean, isn't that why you got me assigned to him?"

"To keep tabs on him, yeah."

That's what he told her, at least. The truth? Porter couldn't give any more of a flaming shit about Harney than he does about any other cop. He only cares about cops if they're helping him, like Carla here, or if they're hurting him. And right now, Harney looking into this prostitute, one of Disco's girls, qualifies big-time as hurting him.

Disco goes down, Porter goes down.

"So that's what I'm doing," she says. "I told you what he was up to. I don't see a crime in trying to identify a homicide victim."

"But he's being secretive, sounds like. Like he has a different agenda."

Carla allows for that. "Maybe."

"I want a full report in two days. I want you stuck to him like glue."

"Okay, fine." Carla looks over at him. "You got something for me?"

"Not today," says Porter.

"C'mon, Porter, don't—"

"In two days I will," he says. "After you give me that full report."

Porter leaves Carla, returns to his car, uses his burner phone to call Disco's burner.

Not the way Porter normally does business, using cell phones, even untraceable ones. Whispered conversations are preferred. But Disco needs to hear this fast.

Disco answers quickly, grunting.

"It's me," says Porter. "We have a problem."

CHAPTER 54

"WHERE ARE we going?" Charlotte asks from the back seat. Or at least that's the name they gave her. Disco can't remember her real name anymore. He remembers when she arrived in Chicago, six years ago, from Romania. They had to drag her out of the van, shivering and scared, and shoot her up with tranquilizers just to shut her the fuck up.

She was, what, eighteen then? She's getting old now anyway.

Nicolas, driving, turns off 122nd Street into the old abandoned industrial park.

"This is a personal visit to a special client," Disco tells her. "There are apartments here." He tries to sound calm. He doesn't feel calm, not after that phone call from Dennis Porter.

Nicolas drives past the usual spot, pulls up to the rear of one of the interconnected buildings, the one by the old incinerator.

Nicolas gets out, opens the back door for Charlotte. Together, they walk up to the heavy metal door. Nicolas unlocks it, and they go inside.

Disco stays outside, dials his phone.

Inside the building, behind the heavy door, the first *whump* of contact, followed by a shriek of pain from Charlotte. Disco peeks through the small window. Charlotte is down, her feet trying to gain purchase on the linoleum floor, her hands out in front of her face in defense, Nicolas standing over her, raising his fist, raining down blow after blow.

She's probably wondering what in the hell is going on. She doesn't know the test results. Disco gets them straight from the doctor they use for the girls' monthly STD tests. Charlotte, unfortunately, came back positive. Can't run a high-end business if the girls aren't clean. So he not only has to get rid of Charlotte, he also has to scrub her clients from the list; it's impossible to know which one gave her herpes.

Oh, well. He got six good years out of her. That's more than most.

One last garbled cry from Charlotte. She'll be quiet from here on out.

Porter answers on the third ring. "We can talk now," says Disco.

"SOS is still trying to ID your dead prostitute from K-Town. One of 'em went back to the house where the shooting happened, looking for info."

"And did he find anything?"

"Sounds like no. He got interrupted, I'm hearing. Is there anything *to* find?"

"I cannot know this," says Disco. "Did your people not clean this up? That is *your* job, yes?"

Dead air. For a moment, Disco thinks the signal's lost. He peeks through the window again. Charlotte's body is limp, Nicolas straddling her, hands on her throat, finishing her off.

"First off," says Porter, "I didn't know you were gonna use that house for a fuckin' shooting gallery. I wouldn't have signed up for that."

Which is why I didn't tell you, Disco thinks.

"And number two, the house was never swept. Not for that, at least. The Jane Doe was not the first priority. The solve was."

"Then sweep it now."

"No. My people have already stuck their necks out way too far. My guy put down a witness for you. You got any idea what kinda risk that put him in?"

"I don't care. You are not the only one taking risk."

"Do it yourself," says Porter. "You wanna clean up that house, do it your fuckin' self. And you better do it fast."

CHAPTER 55

THE PLACE is called Briona, which probably means something in some language, but here it means a swanky restaurant I could never afford. The appetizers cost as much as the sport jacket on my back. Even the waiters are better dressed than I am.

Glass walls and glass ceilings. A view of the city skyline. Expensive cologne, plastic surgery, cufflinks, diamonds. Viagra, too, I'd wager, had I brought a search warrant with me.

At one of the tables, a man is wearing linen pants and cream-colored loafers with no socks. Dress shoes but no socks? Is that a thing now? Jesus, seriously? I think that might be the fourth sign of the apocalypse.

In the corner, she's sipping a glass of burgundy and looking pointedly at her companion, a broad-shouldered guy with a lot of hair and a square jawline. I have a seat at the bar where I can watch her. I nurse a glass of bourbon, two fingers of Angel's Envy with one cube of ice, which came with a price tag that would probably get me the whole bottle at the discount liquor store I favor.

I wait twenty minutes. Then her companion gets up from his seat, drops his napkin on the table, and heads for the john. Before he's five steps away, a waiter has folded the napkin properly for his return. I slide into the guy's seat, still warm, a bit of fish and some green sauce smeared on the plate before me.

"Hi," I say to Angela Dupree. "Mind if I sit?"

She looks at me with a combination of surprise and playfulness. She takes her time looking me over. She's fifty-two years old, on her second marriage, and wealthy. She doesn't look fifty-two, but she does look wealthy—the expensive jewelry dangling from her ears and around her neck and wrists, an emerald-green dress with a plunging neckline, some fancy hairdo that allows a few strands of cinnamon hair to caress her impressive cheekbones. She's had some work done, too.

"I don't mind one bit," she says, a twinkle in her eye, suppressing a smile. "But I'm here with someone."

"I know." I flip out my badge long enough for her to see it, for her expression to falter, before I snap it shut discreetly. "You're not in trouble, Mrs. Dupree. Nothing like that. I just have a few questions for you about the murder of your late husband, Nathan."

She recovers, embarrassed that she took me for a flirt, before embarrassment turns to annoyance. "And you came *here*?" she says, cutting that last word with enough force to slice a steel bar.

"You're right," I say. "This is probably the wrong time. You and Mr. Dupree"—I nod behind me—"are entitled to a nice night out. How 'bout—is it okay if I wait till he gets back from the bathroom? And we get out our calendars to find a good time to talk?"

If I touched Angela Dupree's face, it would feel like stone. All except her eyes, shooting daggers at me. "My husband," she says, "doesn't know anything about Nathan's murder. I hadn't even met him yet when Nathan... died."

"I hear you. It's protocol, though. I have to talk to everyone."

She works her jaw, drumming her fingers on the white tablecloth. "Why don't you wait over there?" she says, gesturing toward the corner. "And I'll be with you in a minute? I'd rather not upset my husband about this. I can assure you he doesn't know anything about Nathan's death."

"Sounds like a plan," I say, getting up from the table. She's still pretending that the man with whom she's having dinner is her husband, Matthew Dupree, who is at least twenty years older than her handsome dinner companion tonight. And I'm still pretending that I don't know otherwise.

I head toward the restrooms, which are one flight down, taking the stairs halfway to a landing. Angela Dupree makes me wait a good fifteen minutes. Probably to punish me.

I make a point of enjoying the view as she comes down, because she seems open to that kind of base flattery. I shake my head. "Believe me, I wish this was a social call. Your husband's a lucky guy."

Seems like that got me halfway back in her good graces, but she's still feeling some heat. That's right about where I want her.

I give her a quick rundown. Some follow-up on a closed case, the murder of Nathan Stofer. She comes back quickly—they found his killer, convicted him. He's still in prison, right?

That convicted killer being Antoine Stonewald, Valerie's last client before her death.

"He confessed," she tells me. "He pleaded guilty."

"Right. Let me ask you, Mrs. Dupree—"

"Angela."

"Angela, can you think of any reason why someone would want to hurt Nathan?"

She blinks. "They said it was a robbery. They said it wasn't personal." She's still struggling with why I'm bringing up a subject that she assumed was long closed.

"Humor me."

"I..." She shields her eyes. "I didn't expect to be thinking about *this* tonight," she mumbles. Her eyes closed now, shaking her head, she says, "Nathan put together big deals. Millions of dollars involved. So—I guess money's always a motive. Isn't that what they say?"

"Any deals in particular, before he died?"

She nods, remembering. "Well, the Stratton Tower, obviously."

Stratton. One of the words Valerie had written in her notes. "The Stratton Tower?"

"The . . . you know, the Stratton International Hotel and Tower. By the river."

Oh. Right. That new skyscraper built just north of the Chicago River.

"Every time I walk past that gigantic hunk of steel, I think of him," she says. "He would've loved to have been a part of it. He worked for years on it."

"He was, what, an investor?"

She sighs, like she's talking to an unschooled child. "He was part of an investors' group. They were trying to bring on more investors. He oversaw the due diligence."

My knowledge of high finance begins and ends with *Save what you can, pay your bills on time, and max out your 401(k)*. But even I know what due diligence means.

"Was Nathan running into any problems?" I ask.

I'm taking her back more than five years, and it's not a fun return trip for her. I might have copped an attitude with her, catching her stepping out on her second husband with some young eye candy, but who knows what happens to people? For all I know, her life turned upside down after losing Nathan.

The frown on her face, the teary glaze in her eyes, makes that seem likely. So now I'm feeling guilty for ruining her night, but it's too late to turn back now, and I need this information. And she deserves to know, just as much as I do, what happened.

"There was . . . maybe one thing," she says.

CHAPTER 56

I LEAVE the restaurant with the promise of a name. And a return promise, given as Angela Dupree clutched my arm, her voice full of emotion, to let her know whatever I learn about her husband's death.

Stratton, she said to me.

Stratton, Valerie wrote in her notes.

The Stratton International Hotel and Tower is just a hop down Michigan Avenue from the restaurant where I met Angela Dupree. Pedestrians are everywhere on the Mag Mile tonight, with the early taste of summer in the air. Chicagoans clutch good weather like it's rare oxygen.

There it is, a massive structure of steel and glass towering over the north bank of the Chicago River, with gold-plated awnings, a semicircular drive where valets jockey Jags and Mercedes, where limos unload beautiful people in beautiful clothes.

"Guess it got built without you, Nathan," I mumble.

More to learn about that. I have somewhere else to be right now. A mission I didn't finish, interrupted by Carla. Time to return to K-Town.

There's no more dangerous time on the West Side of Chicago than summer nights. Shootings increase exponentially as people venture outside. It ain't quite summer yet, but it's over eighty degrees, and it's almost ten o'clock.

Clusters of people, mostly young, mostly male, populate the corners, sit on stoops smoking or drinking, laughing and goofing around. Everyone notices my ride, and if they look closely enough, the color of my skin. Am I a cop? If you live on the West Side, you don't have to be committing a crime to fear the police.

I hit Kilbourn and take it down toward the expressway, toward the crime scene, the bullet-riddled house where four people died only days ago, including my Jane Doe, who went by Evie. Just north of that house and across the street, several bouquets of flowers lie against the front door. Someone else died recently, on the same block?

I park my ride, check the house. Dark, of course. Nobody living there since the shooting. I check my surroundings as I walk up the porch, snap on rubber gloves, and slip the key into the lock.

I open the door and hear something inside. Not so much movement as... the abrupt stopping of movement.

Or are my ears playing tricks on me?

Silence.

Then the unmistakable sound of something hitting the floor and breaking.

No tricks. Someone's inside this house. And just heard me enter.

CHAPTER 57

IN THE blink of an eye, every possibility tidal-waves past me. Squatters escaping the elements. Crackheads, preying on vacant property. Low-rent thieves, picking at the carnage of a fallen beast, whatever they can grab and sell for drug money.

Or worse. Much, much worse.

"Police!" I call out as I reach for the weapon at my hip. "Who's there?"

With the window boarded up and the front door closed, the streetlight outside doesn't help. I'm in full darkness. I shuffle along the couch, the one where LaTisha Moreland drew her last breath, but I don't make it to the hallway before I hear violent footfalls, the product of a quick decision to make a run for it.

I turn left toward the kitchen, hoping to cut off whoever it is from the opposite side, running my hand along the wall for a switch, catching it on the thermostat, racing into the small kitchen. A narrow beam of yellow light hits the wall in front of me—

I slam into something, a chair by the kitchen table, and fall forward, face-first, onto cold tile, as the wood above me splinters with multiple impacts. I turn in the direction of the gunfire, the back room, a flashlight now rolling on the floor, a roaming beam only inches off the surface.

But enough to light up the room a little. Enough to see a man, tall and lean, tight haircut, racing out the back door.

He's gone before I can raise my weapon, much less return fire.

I pop to my feet and head toward the back door. There's a window in the back, and I can see two figures running across the lawn, heading south. I stay low, in case they get any ideas about shooting me through the window, but they're in full retreat now. I run through the back door and follow their direction toward the alley, the lighting better, at least, helped by a streetlight and someone turning on a light a few stories above me in the neighboring building.

I stop just short of the alley, stay low, spin, and turn to my right—west—with my weapon up. They're faster than I am, well ahead, nearly out of the alley. The first one turns to his left onto the next street over from Kilbourn. The second one, not far behind him, does a quick half turn and fires a stray shot in my direction, not aiming, just trying to slow me down, but I'm in full chase mode now, as he follows his buddy onto the next street, whichever one of those K streets it is—I can't keep them straight.

It hits me as I'm running. I know which K street. It's Kolmar.

By the time I reach the end of the alley, the two men have hit the next street south, Van Buren, and turned right, increasing their distance. I make it to the intersection of Van Buren and Kolmar; by then, the two men have put far too much real estate between us for me to have any chance of catching them.

I put my hands on my knees and catch my breath, my injured ribs screaming at me. My knee is banged up, too, something I didn't notice during the chase, with the adrenaline flowing, the result of tripping and falling over that kitchen chair. It probably saved my life, probably was the difference between the intruder's bullets hitting the wall and hitting me somewhere from the neck up.

I don't call it in. It'll be too late. And I'll have to answer too many questions.

I have plenty of questions of my own. But I may have an answer or two as well.

I look up at the intersection, at the POD camera, corner of Van Buren and Kolmar.

"I got you, bitches," I whisper.

CHAPTER 58

I HEAD back to Shiv's house, shaky from the adrenaline, limping a bit, but I'll live.

The flashlight the shooter dropped is still on the floor by the back door. I flip on lights as I make my way to the kitchen. I find a brown lunch bag in a cabinet and carefully use it to scoop up the flashlight, just in case he was dumb enough to leave prints. I don't want to touch the flashlight's on-off switch and smudge a possible thumbprint, even with my rubber gloves, so I carry the bag around like it was a luminaria on Christmas.

The bedrooms, not surprisingly, are where the action is. In the first one I enter, the drawers have all been pulled out of the dresser. The bed has been moved, too, no longer aligned with the heavy impressions on the carpet.

But they didn't whip everything out from the drawers willy-nilly or flip the bed over. They didn't ransack the place. They were searching, but they were planning on tidying up afterward. They were hoping for an in-and-out without any sign they'd been there.

They were being careful.

On the floor is a garbage bag containing clothes and papers and effects. I leaf through the items. They are women's clothes.

I work quickly, combing over the bedroom, looking for anything else that might belong to my Jane Doe, anything they hadn't already tossed in the garbage bag.

No, I remind myself, not Jane Doe. Evie, LaTisha's mother said. She went by Evie. Evie-rhymes-with-Chevy.

Then I head to the next bedroom, where there is another garbage bag, this one empty. Apparently they hadn't yet found anything in this bedroom. I check for myself and find nothing. This was obviously Shiv's bedroom, whether he slept here or used it for some other purpose.

So I return to the first bedroom and pick up the garbage bag, look through it again. Some paper with handwriting, clothes, a bottle of women's cologne, a hairbrush.

They weren't squatters or crackheads. They weren't common thieves. They were looking for the same thing I am.

They were trying to remove any evidence of Evie from this house.

CHAPTER 59

IT'S A start. Now let's see how much of a start.

The overnight at SOS is quiet. We don't have much in terms of round-the-clock staff, because we aren't a normal police district. We don't punch a clock. We don't stay in one neighborhood. We go wherever the action is, and we work whatever hours necessary. Only a few detectives and officers are in the squad room when I enter.

I find the room with the POD footage and start working the desktop, searching for the POD camera at Van Buren and Kolmar. I'm not great with this stuff, but the techies are all long gone for the day.

It takes me a while, but I finally find the right camera. I click on the recorded footage for today. Fast-forward through a lot of nothing, a few people walking along sidewalks, one couple making out, all but ripping each other's clothes off. Some car traffic. Mostly an empty intersection at that time of night, in that part of town.

There. The two men, sprinting south down Kolmar, then pivoting, turning onto Van Buren, running right toward the camera.

I lean forward, squint. Black-and-white, grainy, the usual.

But I have their faces. Maybe not enough for facial recognition. But I have them.

The first one is white, a small frame, thick hair that seems dark. Young, I'd say, maybe early to midtwenties. The second one, the one who shot at me—also Caucasian, much taller, solid but trim, his hair buzzed short, looking behind him to gauge my progress, running with a handgun in his left hand.

I pause the recording so I won't be forced to see myself showing up a few moments later, out of shape and winded, catching my breath at the corner.

I rewind and replay. Are they Russian? Could be. Definitely could pass for eastern European. Too hard to tell. Probably too blurry to get facial rec with them.

But if I see them again, I'll recognize them.

I open the garbage bag I took from the house. The clothes don't tell me much, though I see price tags on a couple of items, which tells me that Shiv probably bought Evie some clothes to wear. Makes sense. If I'm right and she escaped from the traffickers, she didn't exactly have time to pack a suitcase.

The only thing I find that could be remotely identifying is a piece of paper with some handwriting on it.

A fost eliberat acum trei luni.
Locatia lui e necunoscuta.

I don't know the language, much less the translation.

On the desktop, I minimize the POD footage and pull up the internet. I type in the words from this note. Several websites cascade down the screen, all of them in a foreign language, most of them beginning with the familiar "www" but ending not with ".gov" or ".com" but with ".ro," which I don't recognize. But it doesn't take long to figure it out. These are Romanian web pages.

A spike of adrenaline. Evie was from Romania.

I pull up an online Romanian-to-English translator and type in the words scribbled on the note. The translation to English:

He was released three months ago. His location is unknown.

I write that down on a notepad. Okay. Now I just have to figure out who "he" is and what he was released from. Prison? Some government facility?

With nothing else to go on from the trash bag, I head to the inventory room, which is closed this time of night. I can't get in without an officer signing evidence in and out. It'll have to wait till tomorrow.

My phone buzzes. I don't recognize the number.

"Officer Harney?"

Close enough. "That's me."

"I'm sorry to call so late. This is Angela Dupree."

"Oh, you're fast." It was only around four hours earlier that we spoke.

"Well, once we talked, I couldn't really think of anything else."

"Sorry about that."

"I looked through some old papers. I think I found the name of the company that my late husband was worried about. It was called KB Investors Group. He called it KBIG. He didn't want them to invest in the Stratton project. He vetoed them."

"Vetoed them?"

"He was in charge of due diligence. He had to say yay or nay. I didn't know a lot about what he did, but that much I understood. He said no to KBIG, and his partners were upset."

And they wouldn't have been the only ones upset.

The folks at KBIG, kicked out of a major deal by Nathan Stofer, might not have been so happy, either.

CHAPTER 60

I LAY it out in the family room, the results from a good night.

- Name: Evie
- Probably from Romania
- Loved one/friend recently released from . . . prison?
- Stratton International Hotel and Tower
- KB Investors Group (KBIG)
- Nathan Stofer, murdered
- Antoine Stonewald, convicted of his murder

Laid out like that, it doesn't sound like much. Still, I reduced the haystack considerably today.

"Well, you had a busy day," Patti says into my earbuds as I pace my family room, giving her the update on my evening. "What should worry you is, how did these guys know you've been searching that house for info on the Jane Doe?"

"Evie," I say. "She has a name."

"Evie, fine, but listen to what I'm saying. Someone tipped them off, Billy. You check out the house this morning, and later that same day, they're in there trying to scrub the place of any trace of her? That's not a coincidence."

"You're thinking Carla," I say.

"Of course. Who else?"

"Plenty of others. I checked out the key from inventory to search the house. Any cop could've found that out. But listen, that's assuming a cop tipped off these guys. I'm not sure of that at all."

"Who else?" she says again.

"If I'm right about this," I say, "and this shooting was all about Evie and not Shiv, then she must have escaped from them. They found her and killed her before she could go to the police, or the FBI, or whoever. But they don't know what Evie took with her, Patti. For all they know, she had information that could bring down their entire organization. They'd want it. They could have been staking out the house, waiting for their opportunity. They could've seen me go in this morning and waited for nightfall to go in and look for themselves."

"Maybe so, brother, but the easy answer's right in front of you. Carla Griffin."

Carla in bed with human traffickers? I don't see it. And especially not after what I learned about her today. She's got plenty else on her mind right now, raising Samuel alone and battling cancer.

"Either way," I say, "it's not like I'm gonna talk about this at work."

"Especially not to Carla."

"Not to anybody."

I walk over to the desk in the corner, boot up my laptop. Time to start searching for "KB Investors Group." It can't be that hard to find the principals behind it.

"This girl Evie was probably trafficked; you're probably right about that," says Patti. "And going after human traffickers—that gets you through the pearly gates any day of the week."

"Hooray for me."

"But do me a favor and just keep one thing in mind," she says. "Just because they're the scum of the earth doesn't mean they killed your wife."

CHAPTER 61

PATTI PUTS her forehead against the window, looks down onto State Street, traffic already gnarled, early morning pedestrians clumped at the corners or kamikaze-ing through cars.

"You haven't answered my question," she says.

"That's because we're supposed to be here about you. Not your brother."

She closes her eyes, feels a bit of vertigo. She hasn't been sleeping. Not hard to figure why.

"We never talked about it," she says. "After Val died. I mean, looking back—we all tried to tell Billy it wasn't his fault. We pulled out all sorts of literature about depression and the lack of warning signs, and suicide during times of grief—you name it."

"Sounds like you *did* talk about it."

"No, but that's the point—it wasn't a conversation. *We* talked. Billy never did. We told him to get counseling; we told him he shouldn't blame himself. But I can't remember a single time when Billy said anything in response. I mean, he'd say, 'I'm fine,' or 'I understand,' that kind of thing."

"He wouldn't discuss his feelings with you."

"Well, that's Billy—he keeps it inside. What I'm saying is, he never talked to us about what *happened*. Never."

"He must have told the police. He must have given a statement."

Patti blows out air harshly, dismissively. Opens her eyes. Watches the pedestrians below, normal people with normal lives, normal concerns—making the mortgage, keeping their kids on the straight and narrow, saving up a little for retirement.

"We're not normal people," says Patti. "We *are* the police. I didn't want him anywhere near a statement."

"You were afraid of what he might say."

"Obviously. So we kept our hands in the investigation and made sure it came out only one way—suicide. We even got the medical examiner to go along."

"So Billy never once told you what happened in that bathroom with Val?"

"Not once. I felt like I was holding my breath for . . . God, for a year, at least. Waiting for the other shoe to drop. It never did. He eventually got better, moved on."

"Seems like you're holding your breath now, Patti."

She turns around. "You still haven't answered my question. Is it possible?"

Dr. Francis Almond, in his standard button-down oxford-cloth shirt, legs crossed in a leather chair, his bony fingers adjusting his eyeglasses, the overhead light in the office shining down on his considerable forehead. "Do you really expect me to say it's impossible?" he asks. "Is anything *impossible* when it comes to the human brain?"

She looks him over, thinks about it. "We can talk about this, right?"

"We can talk about the past, Patti. I've told you that before."

But she needs to hear it again. "Even if it's a crime," she says.

"Even if it's a crime. A crime in the past. I can't reveal it. I'm obligated to report it if a patient tells me she's going to commit a crime in the future. And please don't tell me you're planning on doing *that*."

He smiles as he says it, lets out a nervous chuckle. Watches her.

She doesn't answer. She walks away from the window and sits in the leather chair across from him. Incredibly comfortable, like a soft, warm blanket. Intentionally so. It's hard not to relax in this euphoria of cow skin.

"Well, it sounds like you want a fuller answer," says Dr. Almond. "It's not my area of expertise, but I'll take a shot." He removes his glasses, rubs his eyes. "Patti, the more we learn about memory, the more we learn how unreliable it is. You gave an example yourself about Billy, that Santa Claus story."

She nods. "To this day, he insists it was our father he caught getting into that Santa Claus costume when we were kids, not Uncle Mikey. He swears by it."

"Exactly. He replays it in his head and makes an adjustment for whatever reason, and then that adjustment *becomes* the memory. Then he keeps replaying it as adjusted, and it gets cemented in his brain that way. He'd swear on a Bible that it happened the way he remembers it. But it didn't."

"But this is a little different from being a kid and seeing your uncle dressing up as Santa," she says. "Billy was an adult. And it was the death of his *wife*."

"Sure, but now you're adding trauma to the equation, too. Not just having your illusions about Saint Nick shattered. We're talking about the death of his wife. Immediately preceded, of course, by the death of his *daughter*."

She breaks eye contact, looks over at the ego wall—the diplomas and certifications, the photographs. Feels the knot in her stomach tighten.

"Billy was like a ghost when he walked into his house that day," she says. "You should've seen him. I drove him from the hospital. It was, like, an hour after he'd lost Janey. He sat there in the passenger seat, shaking his head. He just said one thing. 'Valerie was supposed to be there.' He said it so quietly I almost couldn't hear him. Like he didn't want to say it out loud. Like...he felt like he wasn't supposed to be thinking that way about Val, but he was anyway."

She looks down, sees her hands trembling.

"We've only begun to touch on the effects of trauma on memory, Patti. And don't forget Billy's brain injury last year, the gunshot wound. We will probably never fully know the impact on his long-term memory of *that* injury. You put all that together..."

"Right," she says, her voice rough now.

"So you ask me, Patti, as of this moment, today, is it possible that he doesn't remember what happened with Val that day? My answer can only be yes. It's certainly possible that he doesn't remember."

"It doesn't *seem* like he does," she says. "He's all about these Russian sex traffickers. It's ridiculous, but he's got it in his head. Is he... projecting or something?"

Her nerves jangling, she doesn't wait for an answer, pops out of the chair and starts pacing, pulls on her hair. "You have any idea how hard it is to sit there and listen to him speculate that Val might've been murdered and not say something? Not tell him?"

"Very hard, I'd imagine. You feel like you can't?"

She glares at him. "*Course* I can't."

"Have you considered the possibility that he has a right to know?"

"Have you considered the possibility that he'd never speak to me again? That I'd lose him forever?"

Hearing the words, just speaking them aloud, sends a shudder through her.

"So maybe this isn't about Billy after all," says Dr. Almond. "This is about you."

CHAPTER 62

SEVEN TWENTY, bright and early. Sal Argurito's just getting the inventory office open. He seems annoyed that I'm standing there waiting. Like the federal employees at the post office who always loiter in the back, leaving customer-service windows vacant and avoiding the glares of customers piled up in line, he's ignoring me.

"Morning, Sal," I say. He doesn't answer. Or answers differently—by glancing at the clock, which hasn't yet hit half past seven.

I've known Sal since I was a pup in the department. He had his twenty put in even back then. Nobody knows why he's stuck around to do this back-office work when he could be sitting on his porch sipping iced tea with his wife. The only thing we can figure is that he doesn't want to sit on the porch all day sipping iced tea with his wife.

"How 'bout this weather we're havin'?" I say.

Nothing. He puts some forms up on the shelf and busies himself with something, God knows what, out of my sight.

"I need the personal effects for Dwayne Sears," I say. "The Moreland homicide."

He passes by me, stooped and grumpy, with nary a glance in my direction.

"C'mon Sal, I'm on the clock here. I'll buy you some new body wax."

"Hold your damn horses," he mutters.

"I can't remember which scent you prefer. Lavender or Apricot Morning?"

He doesn't think I'm funny. "Moreland?" he calls out.

"Yeah, the multiple homicide. K-Town."

A few minutes later, he returns with a large box. "The one got your name in the papers, you mean."

"Spelled my name right," I say.

"Like that's hard. Try having my name."

"I tried being Italian once, Sal. I felt an overwhelming desire to eat spaghetti and lose a war."

"Sign the receipt, you filthy Mick. If you're sober enough to use a pen."

I sign out the box and take it to an interview room. The box is half full, but all I want is Shiv's cell phone. It's an iPhone like mine, so I assume my charger will work. A tag next to the phone shows the password, which some enterprising officer must have had the foresight to get from somebody, probably LaTisha's mother. The password is 8474, which after a brief game of word scramble tells me spells "Tish."

The phone is dead, but with my charger, it only takes a few minutes before the white Apple icon pops onto the screen. I run through the call history to search for the calls Shiv most recently made. He wouldn't be dumb enough to do drug deals on this phone. He had a burner for that, if he used one at all, but his normal phone is the best bet for what I need.

Most of the recent calls have IDs assigned to them—**Mo**, **Eddie**, **KJ**, **Sheila**—but the ninth and tenth ones stand out, calls made two days before the shooting. They are longer numbers, both beginning with 01140256, followed by different six-digit numbers.

International calls.

I carry the phone and charger to my desk, where I plug the charger back in and jump online on my desktop. Takes me two minutes on a search engine to confirm that 011 is the US exit code for international calls, and 40 is the country code for Romania.

Evie was using Shiv's cell to call home.

CHAPTER 63

AT MY desk, I google the time difference. Romania's eight hours ahead, so it's not quite four in the afternoon there. Then I return to the online English-to-Romanian translator for the phrase "Hello. I'm a police officer in Chicago, the United States. I am sorry, but I only speak English." God bless technology: it spits out a translation, along with a sound icon that speaks the words to me, in robotic Romanian. It seems to be phonetic, so I'll get by.

Then I call the first number, chronologically, that Evie called in Romania.

A woman answers, speaking quickly, presumably in Romanian.

"Bună ziua," I say. *"Sunt ofițer de poliție în Chicago, Statele Unite. Îmi pare rău, dar vorbesc doar engleză."*

"Chicago. American?" the woman says, decent English.

"Yes," I say, relieved.

"You look…for prisoner?"

"Prisoner? I'm calling a prison?"

"Timisoara Penitentiary," she says.

I glance at my notepad, the translation from Evie's piece of paper.

He was released three months ago.

"Yes," I say. "I'm looking for a prisoner who was released three months ago."

"I give you number to call...for English?"

She gives it to me. I read it back to her for confirmation.

Good. Good start. Now I dial the second number that Evie called.

A man answers—more Romanian I couldn't possibly understand. I read him my greeting. I'm a Chicago cop: does anyone speak English?

He says something to me I don't understand, then says, *"Wait."*

Thirty seconds feels like an hour. Then another man's voice comes on the line. *"Hallo? You are from America? You are police?"*

"Yes. I am from the police department in Chicago. What is your name, sir?"

"My name is Peter Dobrescu. I am the director."

"The director of what?"

"I am the director of the...facility." He says the name in Romanian, then realizes I won't understand it. *"Timi's Children,"* he says. *"We are...orphanage."*

"An orphanage?"

Right—that would fit. Evie could have come from an orphanage.

"I am trying to identify a young woman who died," I say slowly. "I am wondering if she came from your orphanage."

"When was she here?"

I don't know. But I can't imagine the traffickers raised Evie from childhood. They brought her over probably, what, a few years ago? I give him my best guess.

"You have her name? Photograph?"

"All I know," I say, "is I believe her first name was Evie. And yes, I have photographs."

He tells me to email him. He gives me the address.

Good; this is good. The universe is getting smaller.

"The Jane Doe? She came from an orphanage?"

I look up, turn. Carla is at her desk, her bag over her shoulder. I didn't notice her come in. And Carla, it seems, didn't so much as place down her bag, not wanting to interrupt me.

She must have seen me on the phone and wanted to know what I was doing. She came around behind me quietly, while I—dumb shit that I am—was focusing on communicating overseas with a guy who was finally leading me somewhere.

I have to be more careful. SOS detectives don't have strict hours. We work our cases when we work our cases. Carla's earlier than usual, here before eight, but I should have had my eyes open, prepared for that. Dumb, dumb, dumb.

"Oh, it sounds like a dead end," I say, a lame attempt to downplay the whole thing.

"What do you got so far?" She drops her bag and looks over at my desk. It's all I can do not to cover it up, which of course would give away how much I don't want her to know what I'm doing.

Especially if Patti's right and Carla's got eyes on me.

What can I do? I have a phone charger strung across my desk that's connected to a cell phone with an evidence tag, plus a pad full of notes.

"I'll help you," she says. "You're right; we should ID her."

"Yeah. I'm just doing it in my spare time. Not a high priority."

She gives me a look. I'm forcing this. I'm obviously making this a priority.

And now she's volunteered to help.

"Hey, we're on for the canvass this morning." Soscia, walking in, changing the subject. "We execute the warrant tonight."

A case Soscia's been working up. We agreed to help.

"Right, right, right," I say.

When all I want to say is *shit, shit, shit.*

CHAPTER 64

"BEEN WORKING this for a month," Sosh says from the front seat. Rodriguez is driving. Mat's no fool. People who've been in a car driven by Lanny Soscia usually volunteer to take the wheel for their own safety. Sosh considers stop signs, traffic lanes, and red lights purely optional, and he has the attention span of a toddler. There are crash-test dummies that have been involved in fewer collisions.

This is Pred turf, the southwest side, Little Village. Los Depredadores Latinos, the Latin Predators, got their name from a press conference Mayor Daley—Richie, not his old man—once held in Pilsen, talking about street gangs preying on our youth. They apparently decided to take it as a compliment.

We drive along 26th Street, where we won't stand out among the heavy traffic, passing colorful murals on brick walls, *panaderías* and Mexican grocery stores, pushcart vendors selling fruity ice cream or corn dipped in butter.

"I could eat," Sosh says. That's a headline right there—Sosh is hungry.

Carla, seated behind Sosh and next to me, elbows me and gestures out the window. "That laundry," she says, pointing to a store with a large green awning bearing the word *lavandería*. "My grandfather used to own that."

"No shit?" I say. Other than having met her son, Samuel, and knowing that she's not married, I don't know a lot about Carla. Does having a grandfather in Little Village mean she's Mexican? My money says she's biracial, but Sosh thinks she's PR, a hundred percent. Neither of us has the stones to ask her. "You grow up here?"

"I moved around. Spent some time by Marshall Square after my parents got divorced."

Rodriguez says something to her in Spanish, so quickly I couldn't make it out, and she returns the volley even more quickly, fluently. They laugh.

So that probably confirms the Latina part. Most cops know some Spanish—I do—but she speaks it like she's been speaking it her whole life.

"Hey, no *habloing* languages I don't understand," says Sosh.

"That rules out English," I say. I turn to Carla. "Bilingual?" Hoping it might give me some further insight, that she might elaborate.

"Tri, actually," she says. "French, too."

French? That muddies things. "I can go as far as *un, deux, trois,*" I say.

"Okay, here we go." Rodriguez hangs a right, and we're in a residential neighborhood now, a large park to our left, brick tenements to our right. Rodriguez takes a left around the other side of the park. "It's on the next corner," he says. "The yellow brick."

He's not gonna pass it. Too noticeable. But Mat pauses the ride for a bit at the stop sign so we can scope it out. Nondescript, just a brick three-flat, an alley behind it. On the front stoop, there's a teenager in long shorts and a T-shirt, wearing an orange bandanna, looking at his phone.

"That's lookout number one," says Sosh. "Unarmed."

"Where's number two?" I ask. We drive away.

"Rooftop," says Carla. I look at her. We haven't worked this case. We're just assisting on the execution of the search warrant.

"Don't look so surprised, Harney. I cut my teeth in Narcotics."

That much I did know about Carla—several years in Narcotics, some undercover.

"She's right," says Rodriguez. "Rooftop. He's not up there now, because the shipment isn't here. It will be tonight. We don't have aerial, but we think he has a twelve-gauge or a Tec-9 up there. We've seen both."

"He probably *has* both," says Sosh.

"What about rear entry?" Carla asks.

"None," Sosh says. "Well, not really. There's one back door you can only open from the inside. Steel-reinforced, looks like. Our intel says it's got an alarm on it. But anyway, the Preds parallel park a truck right up against it. That truck only moves when the shipments come. They take the H in through the back door, park the truck back against it, and set the alarm."

"We can't cut the alarm, either," Rodriguez adds. "Not without it tripping a detector. We might as well call them up and tell them we're coming."

"Roof entry?" I ask.

"Nope. Only way to the roof is the rear fire escape."

"Only way in this place," says Sosh, "is the front door."

"That sounds like fun," I say. "You have diversion?"

"We got two diversions," says Sosh. "We've been running a UC past the place every evening for three weeks. She's from the Fifteenth. She walks some little dog right after eight thirty and stops and flirts. You gotta see this filly in her halter top and tight little shorts."

Carla rolls her eyes. She gets it, but still.

"And the other diversion?" I ask, to change the subject.

"Tonight," says Rodriguez, "they'll be shooting off fireworks in the park at eight thirty. Some spring-fling party or something."

Which explains why we're doing this tonight.

So Carla and I will take out the rooftop lookout while the undercover subdues the kid on the porch. Once the lookouts are out of the picture, the patrols can roll in with the wagon, and Sosh and Rodriguez will lead twenty cops up to the third floor to meet our friendly neighborhood heroin traffickers.

Mat's right about fireworks. We don't get this just right, there's going to be plenty of them.

CHAPTER 65

THE PATROL officers are in full go mode—helmets and vests, handguns and rifles. Sosh gives them a pep talk outside the wagon, then shuts them inside.

"It's humid as shit out here," Carla mumbles, adjusting her vest, checking her piece.

"You good to go on this?" I say to her under my breath, away from the others, only for her ears. My mother had chemo before she died, and it sucked the life out of her. But she was almost twice Carla's age. Carla looks basically okay, if heavy eyes and a drawn expression count as okay. It's how she looks all the time.

She makes a face. "We're not going to do this every day, are we? Just assume I'm fine unless I tell you I'm not. Don't make me sorry I told you."

"Right, got it. I won't bring it up again."

She holsters her weapon, and we jump in our car.

Eight twenty-five. The sun has fallen, and it's near blackness where Carla and I stand in the alley down from the house's rear parking lot. I see the UC pass by, walking the dog she's been walking every night. Even from a distance, I see what Sosh means. Long legs, denim shorts so small they look like underwear, a halter top. That lookout on the front porch is gonna have plenty to occupy his attention.

So is the guy on the roof, if we have any luck here.

"UC's in place," Sosh buzzes in my ear. *"The rooftop is checking her out."*

"We're going," I say.

"Green means we're good. Orange means we're fucked."

Orange being the Predators' color.

Carla and I move down the alley, staying close to the wall, out of view of the rooftop for as long as possible. Carla has jumped in front of me. We didn't really talk about an order. Maybe she feels like she has something to prove.

We stop at the clearing into the parking area behind the building. Peek out. Sure enough, a blue truck is parked sideways across the rear door. Up at the roof level, there's nobody looking down. We just have to get to the fire escape unseen.

I hear the man's voice, up on the roof, calling down, not catching every word but hearing *chiquita*, which tells me he's shouting to our undercover, flirting with her.

Carla and I run on our toes to the fire escape.

We freeze when we hear two quick pops, look at each other until we're sure it was the start of the fireworks, not gunfire. The noise will cover us, but still, we gotta be quiet as mice climbing this fire escape.

And quick, too.

"Ready?" she whispers.

I nod to her. "Don't forget the First Commandment."

Thou shalt not get dead.

I try to move past Carla, but she whispers "Ladies first" and flies up the first set of stairs, again on her toes. She's lighter and nimbler than I am, and it's all I can do to keep up without pounding the stairs and risking announcing our presence.

We're both out of gas after a quick climb up three stories, but the adrenaline is boosting us like a drug. More pops from the fireworks in the park across the street, plus the guy on the rooftop shouting something I can't make out.

The pounding of my pulse drowning out much of the sound.

Carla climbs up the final half set of stairs, crouched low. Looks at me below her, nods. Peeks up over the roof's concrete abutment, pops back down. Nods to me again. It's clear. He's not looking our way.

More pops from more fireworks.

Carla pulls out her sidearm, peeks back up, then hauls her leg over the concrete abutment and disappears from my view onto the roof. A nice fluid movement, better than I could manage.

As I bound up the stairs to follow her, gun drawn, I hear a loud *thump*—

"Motherfuck! *Loco, loco!*" a man's voice cries.

And I know everything's gone to shit.

CHAPTER 66

"ORANGE ON the roof! Orange!" I yell as I raise my head and Glock over the concrete abutment. From the other end of the roof, the lookout is running toward me, a Tec-9 in one hand, a phone in the other, trying to dial, trying to tip off his colleagues inside. When he sees me, he drops the phone and stops, using his second hand to brace the extended magazine of his semiautomatic pistol.

I put two bullets in his chest, center mass, putting him down as a spray of gunfire from his weapon shoots upward at the sky. Then I hike a leg up and jump over the embankment, a fall of a good five feet, more than I'd expected. I land hard, a sharp pain in my shoulder, but bounce up and pivot behind me.

In my ear: *"Unit 4 to the roof! All other units, we are green! We are green! We are green!"*

In front of me: the end of a struggle between Carla and another lookout—a second one on the roof, one we didn't fucking expect. The man, bodybuilder huge, a meaty bicep wrapped around Carla's neck, lifting her off her feet, a gun planted against her temple. Carla half dazed, a bloody gash on her left cheek, blood streaked down her face.

"Drop it!" I shout, getting to a standing position. "You got nowhere to go!"

"Drop the gun or I kill her, *poli*!" He's scared, his eyes searching around, realizing there is no way off this roof other than the fire escape by my position. Scared and cornered, in this situation, isn't good.

And I don't know whether this guy's clean or hyped up on something. Too dark to get a good look at his eyes.

Best move he could make: shoot me, knowing how hard it would be for me to return fire with Carla in the way.

I have a head shot, though. He's taller than Carla by a foot. Am I confident enough in my shot in the half darkness?

My pulse rocking so hard, the *pop-pop-pop* from the fireworks lighting up the sky, adding just enough light for me to see his face for a second, scared and scary, and Carla trying to squirm, the intensity in her eyes.

"Drop your fuckin' gun or I'll do her!" he spits.

"There's no way off this roof!" I yell. "Look around you. Where you gonna go?"

"You want me to do this bitch? Huh! You *want* me to?"

Below us, the squeal of brakes, flashing of police lights. If he thought he was trapped before, now he knows it for sure. He's not getting off this roof. He could surrender or he could go out shooting.

Surrender. Give it up.

He looks over the roof down at the parking lot, panicking, his gun wavering off Carla's temple—

Carla's left hand flies up, pushing his forearm, moving the gun away from her head. His gun goes off, a flash, a bullet whizzing past me.

I fire once, twice, blowing off the top of his head.

CHAPTER 67

THE EMT closes the back door. The ambulance takes off.

Carla's on the bed but sitting up, holding gauze to her face, though it's been taped on. They'll stitch her up at Stroger, which is where we're heading.

"How ya doin'?" I say.

She closes her eyes, angles her head. "Throat hurts more than my face."

We roll along, the siren blaring, slowing at times but never stopping.

"Something for the pain," says the EMT, holding a needle.

"No," says Carla. "No painkillers."

"No?"

"No. I'm fine."

Maybe it's a thing with the cancer medication, some worry about drug interaction. Or maybe she's trying to be tough. If it were me, I'd take all the Demerol they'd give me.

"Sosh says sixteen arrested," I say. "Over eight kilos. About six hundred thousand in cash on hand."

"Sosh said only one lookout on the roof, too."

Apparently, when Carla looked over the embankment, she saw only the one lookout, as promised, standing at the opposite end of the roof, gawking at our eye-candy undercover down on the sidewalk. What she couldn't see, and what we weren't told, is that a second guy was sitting against the back embankment. She all but fell on top of him when she jumped over, and he skulled her with his Ruger, opening a huge, gushing wound on her cheek and nearly knocking her unconscious.

I'm impressed she held him off at all, keeping him from shooting her, wrestling with a guy who could bench-press four of her, all while suffering a concussion.

"That guy was gonna do me," she says, her chest suddenly heaving. "Holy fuck, I thought I was gonna die."

"It's okay; it's okay." I pat her leg. "Relax. We had a happy ending."

Is she right? Hard to say. That guy wasn't getting off that roof. He had to know that. Would he have given up, dropped the weapon? A lot of people would in that situation. But I didn't give him that opportunity. Carla took her chance to knock away the gun from her temple, and I didn't hesitate to fire. It'll be righteous on review, I'm sure, especially because his weapon discharged in my direction, but I'll always wonder if I could've talked him down.

"No maybe about it, Harney." Her momentary panic attack subsiding. "I couldn't breathe. He cut off my oxygen. He had me off the ground. That arm of his was like a noose to me. I had maybe thirty seconds."

"I didn't know. Couldn't see well enough."

Her hand flails out toward me. At first I don't get it, I don't understand, like she's trying to signal me or something.

Then I realize. I reach for her hand. She holds mine tight.

I look at her. Her eyes misty. Her lips trembling.

"Kept thinking of..."

"Samuel," I finish.

"Who'd take care of him, if I died."

I thought she'd mentioned something about a grandmother. "Not his father?"

She makes a noise, not a pleasant one. "Not the child-raising type."

"Right."

"He's an asshole," she says. "Can't have a single thought for anyone but himself. Presents on Samuel's birthday if he remembers. Sometimes Christmas. He wouldn't take him. He wouldn't. I know he wouldn't."

"Well—"

"His mother, my mother-in-law, or ex, I guess—she stays with us. But she's seventy-nine. If I went down..."

With my free hand, I pat our interlocked ones. "But you didn't. Right? You didn't."

She blinks out of it, nods. "Right."

I reach into my pocket for my phone. "Call your boy," I say. "Hear his voice."

"That's okay."

"No, c'mon." I unlock my phone, hand it to her. She dials and holds the phone to her ear.

"*Niño*, it's me. How are you doing? How was your day?" She listens, her eyes filling with tears, her face doing all sorts of contortions to keep from a full-throttle cry.

It's like I've never seen her before, like she's a different person, not guarded and stiff but raw and emotional and vulnerable.

We go over a bump. We're just about to Stroger, where Carla's going to be examined and stitched up, and I'm going to be examined a very different way, by COPA and IAB, over the officer-involved shootings tonight.

"Thank you, partner." Carla hands me the phone. She looks like she's going to say more, or wants to. "Thank you, Billy," she says.

CHAPTER 68

WE END up at Salem's Inn. Nobody feels like hitting the Hole tonight. The patrols are over there, living up the victory, but the four detectives seemed to collectively agree that while booze was in order, a big crowd wasn't.

Even Carla joins us, though she drinks soda water. The left side of her face is bandaged, bruised, and swollen. She got twenty stitches on her cheek at Stroger.

"Only one lookout on the rooftop," I say wistfully, for about the tenth time, as I down my bourbon. The good stuff, best Salem's has, Four Roses Single Barrel, because Soscia's buying, whether he fucking knows it or not.

He knows it. He's feeling good and bad at the same time. Good because the raid was a success. With the fireworks outside, and the noise generated by all the blenders and coffee grinders cutting and mixing the heroin, nobody heard us coming. The rooftop lookout with the Tec-9 and cell phone never completed his phone call before I shot him. The unarmed guy at the front porch didn't know what the hell was going on, apparently, when the undercover flirting with him pulled a small-caliber pistol out of a bag that was supposed to be holding her dog's poop.

The final count: 8.4 kilos of heroin and six hundred and

twenty-five thousand dollars in cash. That's a big take. That's a press conference for Sosh tomorrow.

But Sosh fucked us on the roof, and he knows it. That noise we heard on the fire escape, the backup unit coming to help—the first cop up was Sosh. He'd worked this thing for weeks; this heroin bust was his. But the moment he heard my distress call, he started running for the fire escape. The patrols told me they'd never seen a guy that big move so fast. That's Sosh. He'll try not to let on, but the bad intel he gave us, that's gonna stay with him for a long time.

Rodriguez takes off before the rest of us, but we're too exhausted to give him shit about his wife. Sosh heads to the bar. I look at Carla.

"Don't ask me how I'm doing," she warns. "You can't keep doing that my-poor-sick-partner thing."

"Yeah, but tonight's different."

"Whatever. I'm fine, Detective. Thanks to you."

She tries to smile, but it hurts too much.

Sosh comes back with a couple of shots of Jäger, which is a horrible idea. "All right, Griffin, now that you've shared a near-death experience with us—"

"Not with you I didn't. You *put* me in a near-death experience."

"Ah, semantics," he says. "It's time you tell us whether you're black, Hispanic, Asian, or what-the-fuck."

She almost spits out the club soda in her mouth. She manages to swallow and busts out laughing, touching her bandaged face while doing so. "Ow."

I shoot Soscia a look, and he looks back like he can't understand why I'd be shooting him a look.

"So . . . where's your money?" she asks Sosh.

"I had you as a PR through and through. Harney has you half black, half Hispanic."

By now, my hand is covering my face. Soscia ain't so PC on his best day, and he's thrown a lot of whiskey down the hatch tonight.

"Why Puerto Rican?" she asks.

"Don't answer that, Sosh. Do. Not. Answer." I have no idea what Soscia will say. I just know it won't be good.

"My father was from Jakarta," Carla says. "My mother was Colombian. They met at the University of Chicago, where he was getting a PhD in aeronautical engineering and she was an undergrad. Okay?"

Sosh looks at me. "I don't even know how to make fun of that. Where the hell is Jakarta?"

"Indonesia," she says.

"Where the hell is Indonesia?"

She laughs again. "Southeast Asia, you half-wit."

"Okay, so you're half Asian, half Latina?"

"If that makes it easy for you, Soscia, go for it." She looks over at me. "Everybody good now?"

"And you became a Chicago cop."

"What did you expect me to do? Open a dry cleaner that has salsa dancing?"

Sosh likes that. He points at her. "You're lightening up, Griffin. I knew we'd get there."

"Nah." She stirs her drink. "My mother's father was a cop in Colombia. Bogotá. He was killed by the narcos, in fact. He was one of the first cops who actually tried to stop the Medellín cartel back in the seventies, before it was fashionable to do so. So I always kinda had the cop thing in my blood."

"So your mom must be proud of you," I say.

She thinks about that, and her expression changes, not so easy to read when half her face is swollen and bandaged, but something different, like she was holding something in, and my innocuous comment unlocked the door. Her eyes glisten again with tears, as they did in the ambulance.

She mumbles something about needing the bathroom and rushes away.

CHAPTER 69

PORTER LIKES to catch the Sox from the club-level seats when he can. Sometimes—most of the time—it's good to keep a low profile, but other times, it's good for his mushrooms to see him in a Boss suit or in two-hundred-dollar seats, to let 'em know he has a few bucks in his pocket, which means he must know what he's doing.

This is one of those times.

Giolito's getting shelled by the Astros, and Anderson seems to be the only guy capable of sustaining consistent offense in the entire starting lineup, but so what? It's a mild, breezy night, the Jameson is giving him a warm buzz, and it's a ball game, for chrissake.

"Any trouble getting in?" he asks when Carla Griffin sits down next to him. God, does she look awful. Like she lost a fifteen-round fight.

"No. Not sure why I have to come to the Cell to meet with you."

"Not the Cell anymore, sweetheart. And you have to come here because it's where I am. So talk to me. What's he doing?"

Tilson pops one into short center, ending the fourth, stranding two runners. Chased a bad pitch is what he did.

"You heard about last night," Carla says.

"I did," he says without looking at her. "You're lucky to be alive, sounds like. Harney put down the mutt, yeah? So now you got warm feelings toward him?"

A simple question, but not so simple an answer, apparently. Eventually, Carla says, "Harney seems like a good cop, yeah."

"So tell me about this good cop. He's still tracking the ID of the Jane Doe?"

"Yeah. Thinks he traced her to an orphanage in Romania."

Fuck me, Porter thinks to himself. *I didn't have bad luck, I wouldn't have any at all.* He sips on his whiskey, counts to ten. Disco won't be happy.

"You got my burner, right?" he asks. "I want updates daily now. Probably no good meeting every day. I want to know everything he does with this girl."

"Why, Porter? I mean, shit, what's he doing that's so wrong?"

Maybe he should give her a taste of what's going on. Not everything, but a taste. From her perspective, it doesn't make a lot of sense, Porter being all concerned about some dead prostitute. He doesn't need Carla getting too worked up about this.

Maybe he'll read her in someday. But not today.

"You're my eyes and ears, lady. That's all you are. Unless you don't like our arrangement." He turns and looks at her. "Is that it? You don't like our arrangement?"

She bites back a response. "Just give it to me."

"You holding back on me?"

"I told you—" She catches herself, lowers her voice. "I told you everything. He thinks she came from Romania. He's sending them photos. That's it."

"He didn't say anything about going back to the house and searching it again?"

"What? No," she says.

"You sure?"

"I didn't hear anything like that."

Well, Porter sure heard about it from Disco. Disco was practically busting a nut after his boys went over to that house only to have Harney walk in and nearly catch them. Shots fired and everything—yet Harney never called it in. And apparently didn't mention it to his partner, either.

This is bad.

Porter reaches between his legs and hands her a paper bag. "A week's worth," he says.

"A week?" She reaches into the bag. "What, you're tightening my leash?"

"Maybe I am. The fuck are you doing?"

She's opening the bottle is what she's doing, unscrewing the top, popping one out, looking at it in the palm of her hand. Jesus, why doesn't she just put it up on the jumbotron for the whole fuckin' crowd to see?

"Same as always," Porter says. "Same color, same name. Vit-a-gin. Why the paranoia?"

Carla confirms that for herself, then pops the pill in her mouth, does a dry swallow. "Harney found one," she says.

"He found one of these pills?"

"Apparently I left one on my chair. Or maybe he was snooping. I don't know."

"What'd he say? Does he *know*—"

"No, he doesn't know. He thinks they're ginger pills." She rubs her throat. "His wife took ginger when she was pregnant, for the nausea. He thought *I* was pregnant."

"Which would be a perfectly good thing to tell him," says Porter, "if not for the fact that you'd have to have a big swollen belly soon, and then a baby. So I assume you didn't tell him that."

"Thanks, but I'm not a complete idiot."

"You went with cancer?"

"Yeah." She shrugs, looks away from him, shakes her head.

"I didn't know what else to say. I was on the spot. It worked before, right?"

"So now you have to act like you have cancer."

"Relax," says Carla. "I told him it was in remission but I'm doing follow-up chemo periodically. He won't ask me anything else about it. I mean, the minute I said the c-word, he was like, *None of my business, sorry to pry,* that kinda thing. He won't mention it unless I bring it up. And I won't."

"Jesus, Detective Griffin, the plot thickens."

"I've got it under control."

No, she doesn't.

He gestures to the field, where the manager, Renteria, is out talking to Gio. Two Astros on, another big inning blossoming.

"The pitcher out there, Giolito? He lost his fastball. He's over his pitch count. Coach wants to pull him, but he can't. Know why? Cuz he don't have a bullpen worth shit. So he's gotta stick with a guy can't hardly throw eighty-five."

"Yeah, that's interesting, Porter. You saying I lost my fastball?"

Porter leans forward, elbows on his knees, his head nearly touching Carla's. "I, on the other hand, have a bullpen. A deep one. I got plenty a cops like you. So I sure as hell hope you're not losing your value to me."

"I'm not—"

"I mean, you fuck up with those pills, letting your partner find them. And you're always questioning my motives, asking me questions I shouldn't have to answer. Makes me think you're not on my team anymore. You know what it makes me worry about? It makes me worry about Samuel, growing up in a boys' home, the shit that happens in those places—"

"You don't have to say that to me," she snaps, but he can hear the tension in her voice, the fear. He can smell it coming off her.

He puts his hand on her knee, squeezes it. "I may need your

help with Harney soon. Could be very soon. You're not going to ask why. You're just going to do it. Or your junkie ass goes to prison. You lose your shield, your pension, everything. And by the time you see Samuel again—baby, you won't recognize your sweet little boy."

He pats her knee and leans back in his seat, sips the last of his Jameson.

"We square, Detective?"

Carla shoves the pill bottle into her purse and gets up to leave. "We're square, Captain."

CHAPTER 70

"HOW WE doin' tonight?" I say into the mike. The Hole is packed as usual. Sosh is holding court as always with all the uniforms and disciples who think he's the shit.

It started raining an hour ago, around ten o'clock, really coming down. The Sox barely got their game in before the storm hit out of the blue. If it had come sooner, maybe Gio would've been spared the shellacking the Astros gave him.

The cops who got caught in the rain on the way to the Hole are shaking it off, nursing shots at the bar.

Next to the stage, they put a bucket to catch drops from the ceiling, a decent wet spot. I gesture to it. "Looks like the Hole in the Wall might have a hole in the roof."

They like that, a little warm-up.

"Hey, Morty, I'd lend you a hand, but I haven't had such good luck lately with roofs."

That one works. Most everybody knows about Prince Valentine from K-Town. And Carla's and my adventure with the lookouts on the roof in Little Village last night, not that much more than twenty-four hours ago, is still the talk of the place.

"Most people, they climb onto a roof, the one thing they're thinking is, 'Don't fall.' Me, I'm thinking, 'Duck!' "

Sosh raises a glass to me, makes a comment to his friends.

"Hey, Sosh, am I holding up one or two fingers?"

He flips me just one, the middle one.

"Lanny, he don't count so good," I say. "Just kidding, Sosh. You just had poor intelligence. Same thing the nuns at Brother Rice used to tell you.

"Next time, just remember, Sosh: the number of lookouts on the rooftop equals the number of alimony payments each month."

The crowd likes it. Soscia's an easy foil.

"I know what you're thinking—you can't believe Sosh couldn't make it work with his wives. When he got married the first time, he told me, he never knew what happiness was till he got hitched—but by then, it was too late.

"The second marriage, though—you'd think he would've known better. When the minister asked her to say a few words about him, she said, 'Overweight and cheap.'

"Which isn't fair!" I add, raising a hand. "When the check arrives, Sosh is the first one to put his hand in his pocket. The problem is, it never comes back out.

"No, seriously. Sosh will pick up a bill. He'll pick it up and hand it to someone else."

We laugh at what's true.

"Sosh is so cheap that when his second wife wanted a pearl necklace, he gave her a piece of string and told her to start a collection.

"He's so cheap, he won't even pay attention."

I can do these all night.

"He ordered free-range chicken for dinner because he thought it didn't cost nuthin'.

"Ask Sosh if he has change for a twenty. He'll give you a quarter."

I hit the bar when I'm done. The bartender has a bourbon waiting for me. He says the coppers like it when I do a few minutes, so this one's on the house.

That's me, the funny guy, the comedian. The comedian who's killed three perps in the line of duty in the last week. Ha-freakin'-ha.

"I forgot you had a sense of humor." Marsha Flager takes the seat next to me.

"You did? It's my most endearing quality."

She raises her hands. "Didn't mean to offend. Don't shoot me or anything."

"You're safe; we're not on a roof."

She takes a long, hard look at me, then slides a manila envelope out of her bag and into my hands.

"Are you sure *you're* safe, Billy?" she asks. "Because after reading what I just found, I'm not so sure."

CHAPTER 71

FEELS LIKE a lifetime ago, but Marsha Flager and I went for a spin back in the day, when I was still a patrol officer. That was before I met Valerie and before she met her husband and popped out three kids. Somewhere between the first and second bundles of joy, I think it was, she lost her taste for the street.

"What are you havin'?" I ask her.

"Nah, I hit my limit. Got an early day tomorrow."

"Someone stole a credit card or something?" I wink at her. I understand her move to Financial Crimes. She majored in finance in college, thought she'd do something in that field until she got a yearning for police work and thought, what the hell, put in for the Academy. Turned out she liked the street, had a real talent for it. Misses it, too, even now, but every time she'd roll out on a shift, she told me the other day, when I first called her for help, all she could think about was her children growing up without their mother.

More or less exactly what Carla said to me last night in the ambulance.

"It was good to hear from you," she says. "Even if it was work. Doesn't just have to be work, y'know."

I look at her. She's looking at me. I remember that come-hither expression. It's what got me the first time. Four or five times, actually, before I got transferred and it petered out. She liked to do it in the back of patrol cars, hot and sweaty, legs up in the air.

"Divorced," she says, showing me a finger without a ring.

"Ah, I didn't know. Sorry to hear."

"It's okay. He's good to the kids. We're making it work. Just—y'know, you wanna grab a drink sometime, I might answer the phone." Giving me an out in case I'm not interested. I might be, but not right now.

"Okay, so listen up," Marsha says to me. "This isn't a joke, this guy. I didn't dig all that deep outside of the financial filings, which is what you needed me for. But I saw enough. And what I saw, well..." She nods toward the manila envelope in my hand. "The KB in KB Investors Group is a Ukrainian named Kostyantin Boholyubov."

"That's a mouthful."

"Yeah, nobody can pronounce it. They call him Boho for short."

That's what Valerie called him, in her attorney notes. *Boho.*

"This guy ran the Ukraine secret police for a decade after the Soviet Union fell," she says. "Supported the government, suppressed opposition. Surveillance, interrogations, torture, rape rooms. Had a militia that terrorized the country. Kinda guys who don't knock before they come in. Kinda guys make people disappear, and nobody asks why, or they're next. Amnesty International practically opened up a satellite office in Kiev to complain about him and his thugs."

"And I'll bet nothing stuck."

"Not really, no. And now he's gone legit. On paper, at least. Has his hands in a lotta stuff. Real estate, for one. Also runs a steel export company. Ships it to a lotta places, including America."

I wonder if there's more than steel on those ships. "That must be why Nathan Stofer squeezed him out of the Stratton Tower project," I say.

She turns, gives me a look. “He didn’t squeeze nobody outta nuthin’.”

“No, huh?”

“KB Investors was one of the largest investors in the Stratton Tower,” she says. “Boho made millions.”

“No shit. So the untimely death of Mr. Stofer—”

“Was pretty friggin’ timely for General Boholyubov,” she says.

“Okay, thanks, Marsh.”

She touches my arm. “This guy keeps a personal security detail, Billy. When the secret police was broken up, he hired most of them. This guy doesn’t have a sense of humor. So you’re gonna step into his world? I’d bring body armor and a SWAT team.”

CHAPTER 72

VALERIE, THE GUN under her chin.

Don't come any closer, she says.

What are you doing? Don't—put the gun down, honey. Please, please put it away—

She's gone, isn't she? You wouldn't be here in the middle of the day—you wouldn't have left the hosp—

Yes, she's gone. She just passed.

And I wasn't there.

Give me the gun, Valerie. Give it to me.

I can't do this anymore.

Yes, you can. You know what you can do? You can help me plan the funeral. So we can honor her, together. That's what we're supposed to do.

I... can't.

Yes, you can. Give me the gun.

Don't—don't come any closer.

Give me the gun, Valerie. We'll work through this together. I promise. Just—

What are you—no, don't come any—

Give it to me!

* * *

"No." I pop off the bed, fall to the carpet. Pull the comforter off the bed and wrap it around me, trying to contain an uncontrollable shiver, the fog of the dream fading.

No. That's not what happened. I wasn't there.

No; they killed you, Valerie. They killed you.

They killed you, and I'm gonna prove it.

CHAPTER 73

EVENTUALLY, THE chill inside me wanes, my pulse decelerates. I'm nothing but dried sweat. I grab my phone off the nightstand. Eight o'clock. Shit.

I stumble to the shower, blast the hot water, run a dry razor over my face, let the water scald me, wash it all away.

IAB and fucking COPA—the Civilian Office of Police Accountability—are done interviewing me. Don't see how they can come back negative on me for shooting those two on the rooftop, guys who were about to shoot either me or Carla, all while protecting a major heroin mill, but with civilians and the suits at IAB, who collectively have probably never once had a gun pointed at them, you never know.

I roll in at a quarter past nine.

"Happened to you?" says the intake sergeant, Vitrullo. All these Italians behind their desks while the potato eaters go out and get shot at.

"Shoulda seen the other guy."

"Package for you," he says. "Your partner took it."

She's not at her desk upstairs. I find her in an interview room, watching a—

Watching a video on the flat-screen.

A courier approaches the SUV at the curb. Shots fired from the back window, the screen panning wide to show a massacre.

I'm watching the K-Town shooting.

Carla hears me, turns. "You freakin' believe this?"

"What..." I say. "How..."

She shows me a big brown wrapper, words in black marker: **Detectives Harney and Griffin**.

"Someone dropped it off at the front desk," she says. "Must have seen our names in the papers, knew it was our case." She holds up the remote and rewinds. "You gotta see this from the beginning."

She rewinds it. A 4Runner turning off Van Buren onto Kilbourn, heading north. Pulling up to the curb outside Shiv's house, the courier in the Bears jersey—Frisk, they called him—approaching the vehicle. Camera zooms in on the license plate, tells us what we already knew. Then the camera moves up and tells us something we didn't.

Zooming in on the front-seat occupants. The windows slightly tinted, but the video quality far superior to anything a POD camera could give us, good enough to see two guys wearing baseball caps.

Two white guys.

"Those look like Imperial Gangster Nation to you?" she says. "Like they'd be partners with Prince Valentine and Junior Peppers?"

No, they don't.

But they do look like the guys who shot at me two nights ago inside Shiv's house.

She lets the video keep playing, an explosion of gunfire from the back seat, Frisk shot in the back trying to escape, Shiv and Evie rattled with bullets on the front porch.

"Can't make out the back-seat shooter," she says. "But that wasn't the Nation, Harney."

I drop in a chair.

"Someone was operating that camera," she says. "Working it. Moving in and out."

She picks up a pencil, eraser end down, and uses it to push a piece of paper over to me. Trying not to touch it or infect it.

I look at it without touching it. It's printed off a computer, not handwritten:

Latham took this. I don't want to end up like him. He'd want you to see this.

"Latham," I say. "Any idea?"

Carla shakes her head. Leans back in her chair, looks up at the ceiling. "You know what this means. You know what this means."

Yeah, I know what it means. But I've thought this for a long time. I just never told her. I wanted to handle this myself.

But now she knows.

"It means we didn't solve K-Town," she says.

CHAPTER 74

IT DOESN'T take long.

An hour, tops, to figure out that the Latham in the note is Latham Jackson, who lived just up the street to the north of Shiv's house. According to the notes from the canvass, his mother said he wasn't home during the shooting, and on recanvass, Latham himself claimed not to have seen anything.

It took less than an hour after that to learn that Latham died the same day as the recanvass, found dead only hours after one of our patrol officers interviewed him. The fucking detectives in the Eleventh didn't bother to tell us, seeing it as a run-of-the-mill B and E in K-Town that SOS didn't need to know about. Latham surprised the burglar, apparently, and the offender put two bullets in Latham's chest and skedaddled with his video equipment.

It makes sense. It might be true. But I don't like it. Neither does Carla.

Doesn't take us long, either, to get a look at Latham's email account, courtesy of his mother. Latham sent this video of the K-Town shooting to his cousin Renfro, who works at the DMV. Renfro, obviously, is the one who delivered it to our station house.

We pay him a visit at work downtown, the secretary of state's office. He's not so thrilled to be hearing from us, but we keep it on the down low, not flashing badges or anything, meeting him at his break time midafternoon outside 69 West. He admits he sent us the tape but swears up and down that Latham didn't see anything live, only recorded it, so anything he knows, we know. Carla works him over a little, mentioning the idea of a blackmail scheme and how it would be a shame if Renfro didn't help us right now. Renfro looks like he's going to faint, but he swears there's nothing more to tell. We decide we believe him.

"Now what?" Carla says. "Solving K-Town so fast stopped a riot. We let it out that we got it wrong, that riot's gonna happen. But we can't ignore it, either."

"Talk about riots," I say. "Imagine if it came out that we had a video of white guys shooting up that house and sat on it, let a couple black guys take the fall."

"I wasn't suggesting we sit on it," she says. "I was suggesting we investigate quietly. Like, real quietly. Like, Sosh and Rodriguez don't need to know. Not until we can be sure. We can't let this out until we're ready to arrest those white guys, whoever they are."

Keeping Mat and Sosh in the dark is fine by me. I wanted Carla in the dark, too.

I catch Carla staring at me, her eyes squinting in the sunlight. Or one of her eyes, I should say; the other is all but swollen shut, the left side of her face still puffy and purple, tape and gauze still across her cheek.

"You've been thinking this for a while, haven't you?" she says to me. "That's why you've been so interested in the identity of our Jane Doe. You think this murder is about *her,* not drugs or drug turf."

"Me? No. I don't think that."

"Yeah," she says. "That's why you've been so secretive. Searching the house behind my back. Searching Shiv's phone, finding those calls to Romania—"

"On my own time is all," I say.

But she's warming to her idea. "This girl—Evie, right? She was trafficked. That's what we think, right?"

"Yeah."

"You think the traffickers killed her? Those white guys in the car were sex traffickers?"

"Getting way ahead of ourselves, Detective."

"Yeah, okay." She doesn't look convinced. "Seems like you're way ahead of *me*, though. What happened to no more secrets?"

I open my hands. "What do you want me to say? I'm learning all this at the same time as you."

I've found, over time, that I can bullshit with the best of 'em on the job, certainly when I have a suspect in an interview room or some skell on the street.

Up close and personal, I don't wear the same poker face. Valerie could read me like a book. So can Patti.

"Come clean with me, Harney," Carla says.

"I am. I have."

"If you're worried about Prince Valentine—look, he was selling dope," she says. "He was violating his probation. He ran when we knocked on his door. And he shot at you first. Even if he didn't do K-Town, it was still a righteous shooting—"

"What, you think I'm covering my ass? Covering up a mistake? Gee, thanks a lot, Carla. If I was doing that, the *last* thing I'd be doing is reopening the case and looking at Evie. I'd want this case wrapped up and put behind ten locked doors."

Absolute truth, and not a bad comeback. Until a hint of triumph plays on Carla's face and I realize she played me.

"My point exactly," she says. "You *aren't* locking it behind ten closed doors. You're reopening it and looking at Evie. So maybe it's time you told me why."

"Jesus, you missed your calling," I say, exasperated. "You shoulda been a lawyer."

She allows for that. She goaded me into an admission.

"Well, then I only have one further question of the witness," she says. "Tell me, Harney, once and for all, what the hell is going on?"

CHAPTER 75

I TOLD her, but I didn't tell her.

I told her what she'd already figured out—that I suspect that Evie, not a bunch of drug dealers, was the target in the K-Town shooting.

But I didn't tell her anything else. I didn't tell her that the same human garbage that killed Evie may have killed my wife. She doesn't need to know that.

That part I will handle myself.

"Yeah," Carla says, her face up close to the screen of the footage from two nights ago, the POD camera at Van Buren and Kolmar. "Yeah, looks like the same guys from the front seat of the 4Runner." She sits back in the chair. "So the same guys in the front seat of the shooter's car come back to the house and try to hide all evidence of Evie from us. I mean, shit, Harney." She throws up her hand. "This thing had nothing to do with drugs or turf. It's all about a girl with a black-lily tattoo on her ankle."

"So now you know everything," I say.

Everything except how this involves Valerie. Or General Boholyubov.

But she knows enough. Enough to quietly reopen the K-Town investigation.

"Why didn't you tell me?" she asks.

Because I wanted to find these assholes myself. Because maybe I'm not interested in bringing these slimeballs to justice in the traditional way, with arrests and indictments and prison sentences.

None of that sounds so good.

I say this instead: "Like you said, it's a heater case. The solve prevented a riot. Before I reopened the case officially, I wanted to be sure."

"Yeah, but you could've told *me*. You should've told me."

A smirk plays on her face.

"You didn't trust me," she says.

I didn't trust anybody. But now she knows. I have no choice.

"Let's bring in the Bureau," she says. "Clara Foster, the agent working on human trafficking on that joint task force. She seemed okay."

"The FBI? No," I say.

"Why not? Evie's from Romania, right? Or looks like, at least? This is an international human-trafficking ring, Harney. The Bureau could give us all sorts of resources we don't have."

Yeah, more people who will stop me from handling things my way.

"We don't need Fuck Buddies Incorporated taking this over and cutting us out," I say. "This is our case. If we made a mistake, we'll correct it."

She doesn't like it, but at least she doesn't question my motives. I'm parroting what most cops would say in my position. Nobody in the department trusts the feds, and the feeling is mutual.

"Fine," she says. "Then we do this, just the two of us."

CHAPTER 76

THE AIRPORT is just outside Plainfield. Disco needs GPS to find it.

The jet has already arrived, a sleek, metallic blue, sitting alone out on the runway, gleaming in the late afternoon sun.

"He's here already," Disco says into the phone.

"He didn't say why?" asks Augustina.

No, he didn't say why. He just told Disco to come alone.

Disco parks his car and walks over to the tarmac.

The door opens. A staircase lowers. His heartbeat ratchets up.

He doesn't have a piece with him. Thought about it, but they'd take it off him anyway.

He did wear his best suit, though.

Inside the jet, General Kostyantin Boholyubov sits in a plush leather seat, legs crossed. Dressed in a silver double-breasted suit, crimson tie knotted perfectly, silver cufflinks, Ferragamo loafers shining like mirrors.

Disco stands at attention and salutes. "General."

"At ease, Colonel." The general looks away, as if embarrassed by the show of military display. It's been over for ten years now. The hardheaded general is the same person, with the same tactics, but now he's immaculately coiffed.

If Disco *hadn't* saluted, though, the general would've been furious.

Behind the general are three members of his private security. Two of them, whom Disco doesn't recognize, are armed with Kalashnikov rifles slung over their shoulders. The third, Milton, was Boho's deputy when the general ran the Berkut, the secret police.

Another man stands at attention by the pilot's door, bigger than any of the other men, wide and tall, a neck like a tree stump, a shock of red hair on top with the sides buzzed. To face the general, Disco has to turn his back on this redheaded thug.

Three in front, one behind.

"I have a question for you, Colonel," says Boho. "But first, I'd like you to do something for me."

"Anything, General."

"I want you to strip off your clothes."

A shudder runs through Disco. "My... clothes."

"Yes." The general raises the glass from his armchair, takes a sip of his single-malt Scotch. Always was a big fan of single malt.

"General—"

"Your clothes are still on, Colonel. Perhaps I wasn't clear."

Two of the thugs behind Boho stand. That makes three of them standing, if you count the redhead behind him.

Disco loosens his tie. Unbuttons his shirt. "General, if I have done something wrong..." Trying to avoid a tremble in his voice.

Boho smiles at him, holds eye contact. Doesn't move an inch.

Disco removes his jacket, tie, shirt, undershirt.

"Everything," says Milton, his deputy, his coal-black eyes gleaming.

Disco strips to his underwear. Doesn't make eye contact with Milton, but Milton says it anyway, once more: "Everything."

Disco looks to the general for relief, for mercy, but Boho stares back at him with that stony expression, his blue eyes shiny.

Disco wiggles out of his underwear.

Maybe they just wanted to see if he was wearing a wire. Now that they can see he isn't, they'll let him put his clothes back on.

The general turns toward the men behind him, a curt nod. One of them reaches down to his seat and produces a set of hedge shears—long, sharp blades with black-and-orange leather handles.

"General, *please*." Disco feels himself shrink, his hands over his privates, his heartbeat violent against his chest.

"I haven't asked my question yet, Colonel. Do you want to hear my question?"

"Yes, sir," he whispers, bent over. "Yes, General."

"My question," says Boho, "is why, two days ago, my cousin—the one who operates the orphanage in Timisoara—received a phone call from a Chicago police officer, trying to determine the identity of a dead girl. A girl who had been shot to death in Chicago." The general opens his hands. "Why would this happen?"

"General, I..." His throat closes up involuntarily. Sweat stings his eyes.

"Now," Boho goes on, "I am trying to decide if an answer such as 'I don't know' is better than 'I *do* know, General, but I forgot to mention this problem to you.' I am truly unsure of which answer would upset me more."

"General—"

"Because if you do not know of something going on with one of our girls, from one of our orphanages, then I have to wonder why. Why are things happening without your knowledge? I have to wonder whether you are the right person to be running this operation in Chicago."

"I—"

"But on the other hand, Colonel, if you know of a specific problem but failed to mention it to me, I would have to wonder why you did not bring this problem to my attention." The general holds out his glass. One of the men refreshes it from a decanter of Scotch.

"General, I can explain."

"Ah, he can explain," he says to Milton. "So explain, Colonel."

"I did not... did not want to bother you with a problem I can... take care of myself."

"You wanted to show... what is the American word?... initiative. Yes, that is it. You wanted to show initiative, Colonel, is that correct?"

"Yes, General. I wanted to take care of it without troubling you, sir."

"And yet I am troubled. I am receiving calls from Romanian orphanages. Chicago police officers are sending *photographs of a dead girl* to an orphanage. Do you not think that causes me trouble?"

"I am... sorry, General."

"Do you know why these police are interested in this girl?"

"We... had to kill her, sir. She es—" The throat closure again. This one isn't going to be easy to say.

Boho's eyes bulge in mock curiosity. "She es—she *escaped*? Is that it?"

Disco nods, trying to keep himself from collapsing to the carpet.

"You allowed a girl to escape, and you had to kill her. Yes?"

"Yes."

"But you did not dispose of the body?"

"We couldn't, sir."

"You did not dispose of the body! You left her to be found by the police. And now they are calling one of our best orphanages!" He rises from his chair. "You let all this happen, Colonel."

"Sir, I—"

An arm comes around his neck, lifts him off his feet, arching backward. The two thugs by Boho rush forward, each grabbing a leg. No matter how Disco kicks and rears, it takes them no time whatsoever to hold him still, in midair, spread-eagled.

His body on fire, trembling so hard he couldn't speak if he wanted to, feeling the deepest animal shriek build from his gut.

No no please no God no

Boho, holding the hedge shears, trying them out, opening and closing them, the razor-sharp blades whining.

Disco, subdued and spread-eagled.

"How do I express my disappointment?" Boho asks. "What shall we do now?"

CHAPTER 77

PORTER, SITTING in his office at 35th and Michigan, leans back in his chair, pops a hard candy in his mouth. "Tell him he's gotta wear a wire, he wants to make this thing right."

"He won't go for it, Captain. He says he'll provide information as a CI but won't wire up."

So says Garcia, a new kid, just made sergeant, making his start in the Bureau of Internal Affairs, though everyone still inverts the letters, calls it IAB. He's smart and ambitious, like most of the ones who come here. Porter doesn't know him well enough yet, so he doesn't trust him.

"Tell him he won't wear a wire, we walk him out of the Tenth in bracelets."

"And then we don't build a case, Captain. We don't get the ringleaders."

"Then we don't get the ringleaders," says Porter. "But we send a message. Nobody dictates nuthin' to Internal Affairs. We got this guy by the scrotum, and *he's* telling *us* what he will and won't do? No fuckin' way. Tell him he's got twenty-four hours to decide. Day after tomorrow, he tapes a mike to his chest or we perp-walk him out in front of the whole fuckin' squad room.

A reporter and cameraman from channel 7 might happen to be there, too, just coincidentally, so his wife and kids can see it on the news."

"What if we push him too hard? What if he eats a bullet?"

"C'mon, that's a cliché."

It's a cliché because it's true.

"This guy's got four generations of cop in his family," Garcia says. "You shoulda seen him. He was crying like a little girl, beggin' me for mercy. I wouldn't put it past him to take the exit ramp."

"Then he eats a bullet. That's his choice."

"Jesus, Cap. Remind me not to piss you off."

Porter's phone buzzes in his pocket. His left pocket. His throwaway. Buys a new one every month, which is a pain in the ass, having to give out a new number to his mushrooms, having to input all the numbers again, but it's better than being predictable.

"Beat it, Garcia, would ya?"

The caller ID says it's Carla Griffin. He's supposed to call her today, not the other way around.

He answers the phone. "Call you back in two minutes."

The time it takes him to leave headquarters, at 35th and Michigan, make it onto the street. He sweeps his office every week for bugs, but you never know.

He gets to the street, another scorcher of a day, but nicer now, as the sun falls, close to the end of the workday. Or at least a traditional workday, if Porter ever had one.

He dials Carla.

"We gotta meet," she says, smart enough not to use his name.

"Help me out a little."

"K-Town," she says. "Four dead people. It was about the junkie prostitute, wasn't it? Not a turf war. Not gangs. But a girl. The one Har—the one he's so worried about. The one *you* seem so worried about."

Porter looks around him while his insides swirl. Christ, what happened now?

"Take it easy," he says. "Okay, we'll meet. Say, ten o'clock."

"Where?"

Where, indeed.

He says, "Remember the place we first met?"

CHAPTER 78

PORTER DRIVES through the parking garage. The fourth level is empty, which is good, because that means nobody will be parked on the roof.

This shit is getting out of control, he thinks. First Carla, then Disco, calling him frantically. The lid is coming off, and it's going to take all Porter can muster to shut it back on and screw it tight.

He pulls up the final ramp onto the rooftop. Sees only one vehicle.

He approaches it, prepared to park next to it but facing the opposite direction, so he'd be driver's side to driver's side.

But Disco isn't in the driver's seat. Nobody is. Disco's in the passenger seat.

Porter removes the Beretta from his shoulder holster. Then he pulls up alongside Disco's car the traditional way, so his driver's side is adjacent to Disco's passenger side. They aren't more than three feet from each other as Porter buzzes down the window.

"Where the fuck's the driver?"

Disco's jaw is clenched, eyes narrowed, a blood rush to the face. He's in pain. "Downstairs."

"You sure about that?" Porter looks around him, checks his rear-view mirror. But it's safe. There's no place to hide up here on the roof. Porter checks the seat behind Disco—empty.

"Downstairs," Disco repeats.

"Yeah? He get a look at me?" Their deal is strict, one-on-one only. No friends or associates.

"No," Disco says.

"Then why's he here? What, you can't drive yourself all of a sudden?"

Disco bends forward, reaches down to the floorboard.

"Don't you fucking move!" Porter raises his Beretta, both hands, ready to fire, adrenaline pumping.

Disco just shakes his head, like he doesn't have time for theatrics. He pulls up his leg, showing a right foot that wears no shoe, only a heavy bandage. "This is why I cannot drive," he says.

"The fuck happened to you?"

Disco turns to him. His eyes wander a bit, like there's something wrong. Like he's drugged. Hurting and drugged. "You know the man I work for."

"Yeah, that general guy, Boho-whatever."

"He flew into town to see me."

That's not good.

"He knows about the girl."

Even worse. This thing's turning into a freakin' horror show.

"He put his hands on you," Porter says.

"Not his hands." Disco raises a cigarette to his mouth, his hand trembling, struggles to light it. Blows out smoke. "He gave me a choice. My big toe or my balls."

"Jesus. He cut your fuckin' toe off?"

Disco nods. "He called it 'door number two.' He said in twenty-four hours, he's going with 'door number one.' Unless Harney's dead."

Porter's blood goes cold. "Wait—Harney? Who said anything about Harney? I never told you the SOS cops' names."

He made a point of not doing that. Tell 'em only what they need to know.

Maybe Disco read it in the papers. That coulda happened. There was enough coverage of the K-Town shooting and solve.

"The general gave me his name," he says. "Harney is trying to find out more about the girl. The general says he must be taken out."

"There're other ways of taking someone out. I'm IAB. Let me do it."

The life comes to Disco's eyes now, the druggy haze evaporating. "I have my orders. He must be dead now. You have to help me."

"Whoa, whoa, whoa." Porter raises a hand. "Hold on there, friend. We aren't killing cops."

"We're killing *this* cop," says Disco, his jaw clenched, his eyes watering. "He dies or I die."

"I can't be part of that. I can't be within a hundred miles of that."

Disco shows his teeth, wearing a feral expression, a mix of fear and desperation Porter's never seen. Say what you want about Disco, but he's always been a cool customer. He looks like he's coming unglued.

"I will do it either way, Denny. With or without you. But if I do it without you, it will be messier. If I do it with your help, we can—"

Contain it, Porter thinks. Control it.

Make it look like something other than an assassination.

"Let me think about it," says Porter. "Give me tonight."

He's had an idea percolating along these lines anyway. He's been hoping it wouldn't end in Harney's death, but he probably can't stop that now. This idea, though, now that he thinks about it, is probably the perfect solution.

Let's see what Carla thinks.

CHAPTER 79

PORTER HAS two choices. Hard or soft.

It's all he's thought about since leaving Disco a few hours ago.

He's made his decision. He gets there first, parking as close to the runway at Midway airport as he's allowed, a small lot off the one for general aviation, close to the fire station.

Gangsters like to talk at airports because eavesdropping is nearly impossible and, in many cases, illegal under federal law. But that's not why Porter chose the airport.

He chose it as a reminder. This is where he first met Carla Griffin.

She pulls up five minutes later, gets out of her car, looks around. "Is this your idea of a joke, meeting here?"

"We're past jokes, *chica*."

She stops just short of him. The overhead lights give enough illumination to reveal the gleam in her eye, at least her unswollen eye, but not much more of her expression.

"Why do I feel like I'm the only one who doesn't know what the hell is going on?"

"Probably cuz that's true," says Porter. "That's about to change. But first, tell me what happened today."

She does. The anonymous delivery of a video of the K-Town shooting showing two white guys in the front seat (*Fuck, and after all that work killing Latham Jackson*); the same white guys captured by the POD footage after Harney chased them from Shiv's house (*Motherfuck*); Harney coming clean—or somewhat clean, anyway—about his suspicions and resisting the idea of the FBI being brought in.

As bad as it is to hear this, Porter feels good knowing that his idea, the plan he's formulated, is the right one. He has all this covered.

Okay, here goes. He better keep his lies straight. That's the problem with lies—they're a lot harder to remember than the truth.

"Harney's dirty," he tells her. "He's a wrong cop."

Carla steps back. "Bullshit."

"Doesn't seem like one, does he?"

"No," she says, "he doesn't."

"Right, cuz he's a *smart* wrong cop. But wrong all the same."

"Give it to me, then," she says. "All of it."

He starts to reach for her, thinks better of it. He's decided on soft, not hard, but he doesn't wanna be *too* soft.

"Harney protects a sex-trafficking ring," he says.

He can't see Carla's expression. He wishes he could.

"Jesus," she whispers. "For real? No bullshit?"

"Definitely no bullshit. Could I prove it in court right now? No. But am I sure? Sure as I'm standing here."

"So...he protects the ring that puts black-lily ankle tattoos on their girls?"

"No, no. No, no." He touches her arm, after vowing not to. "No, he protects a rival group. A group that doesn't like competition. This was a turf war, all right. Just not one involving drugs. It involves *girls*."

"So the crew Harney protects, they killed Evie. Because she's a competitor."

"Right."

"So what's Harney doing? What's tracking Evie back to where she came from going to accomplish?"

"Don't you get it?" Porter says. "The crew he protects, they wanna take over the black-lily crew's business. Harney wants to know their supply lines back to other countries. He wants to know anything and everything he can about them. He's using this case as an excuse to get it."

"But without my help," she says. "And without the Bureau's help."

"Exactly. You'll get in his way. The crew he's protecting, they want to take over their rivals' supply line, get their customer lists, grab their girls, then kill the black-lily crew. You wouldn't allow that. Neither would the FBI. You'd want to arrest them, prosecute them. He and his crew want to kill them and swallow their business."

"Wow. That . . . that all fits, I guess."

Of course it all fits. I didn't get where I am by being a mope.

"And Junior Peppers?" she asks. "We found the AR-15 in his car. The murder weapon."

"Yeah. The guy shoots up K-Town, the press goes wild with it, all kinds a heat on him, and he just leaves the assault rifle in the back of his *car*? That never seemed odd to you?"

She allows for that. "So Harney planted it," she says.

Porter did, actually, through one of his mushrooms. But yeah, Carla's taken the hook and bitten down hard.

"And Harney planted the Sig in Prince Valentine's apartment, to tie the whole thing up."

"Now you're getting it." Porter made that happen, too, but Carla's locked in now. "Harney picked Prince well," he says. "An easy scapegoat. A gunner for the Nation, out on MSR—big surprise he might be slinging dope to make ends meet. No surprise at all he'd run when you knocked on his door. And pretty convenient that Harney put him in a coffin so he couldn't defend himself."

"No, Valentine shot at him first," she says. "Saw it with my own eyes."

"Maybe so. That may be how it played out. But either way, Harney wasn't gonna let Valentine leave that roof alive."

"Wow. Wow, really?" She does a little circle. She'll work this over. But it will all fit, as she put it. "Harney knew all along that K-Town wasn't a drug thing. He played me the whole time."

"He played everybody. Mr. Squeaky-Clean Image."

"God." She touches her chest. "I feel like I'm gonna be sick."

"Yeah, on that topic—you don't look so good, lady," he says. "Might be time for some sick leave."

She looks up at him. "Yeah?"

"You got that big-ass wound on your face. Plus, of course, the 'cancer.' Maybe you're having bad nausea."

"Why?" she asks.

"I think this is happening the next day or so," Porter says. "Next twenty-four hours. He's close to finding these guys' identities."

"He is? He didn't tell me that."

"No shit he didn't tell you. But he's got a bead on them. He's about to make his move. And IAB's gonna be there."

"I should be, too."

"And risk getting caught up in this? That's the *last* thing you need, kid. Believe me, a dirty cop gives off skunk spray. You'll stink for years after, even if you didn't do anything wrong."

That seems to make sense to her. "Yeah, it gives me a snitch tag, too."

"Exactly. This way, you can act just as surprised as everybody else. And really, nobody'll think twice, you take a day off after that thing on the rooftop. So disappear tomorrow, okay? That's an order."

She raises her hands. "I got it; I got it."

"Maybe take a long weekend. You and Samuel and the mother-in-law get away, go to a water park or something. Maybe the Dells. Tell you what—my treat."

"C'mon, Porter, you don't have to do that. I feel like an idiot now for doubting you."

"Nonsense." He peels off fifteen bills, fifteen hundred dollars. "You've more than earned it, kiddo. We've had our eye on Harney for a long time. This is great work you've done."

She takes the money, nods.

"Jesus," she says. "Just when I was starting to like the guy."

CHAPTER 80

VALERIE, THE GUN under her chin.

Don't come any closer, she says.

I won't. She's gone. She just died. I just came from the hosp—

And I wasn't there.

I called you, over and over.

But I didn't answer.

Nope—you were busy, looks like. Taking the easy way out.

I'm sorry, Billy, I really am.

I'm not the one needs an apology.

Billy—

Can today be about her? Can at least one day be about our little girl and not you or your sadness or your important cases at work?

I'm… so sorry—

My head pops off the desk in my family room, my arm shooting out, knocking over a glass of water, my other hand gripping paper—research I've compiled on Nathan Stofer and Antoine Stonewald and General Boholyubov.

"No," I say, panting, wiping sweat from my forehead.

No. That's not what happened. None of that happened. I didn't say those things and I didn't *think* those things and you didn't kill yourself.

I didn't believe those things. I never said them to you.

You didn't kill yourself.

They killed you. *They* killed you.

Sunlight streaming into the family room. Well past dawn. I fell asleep at the desk downstairs, doing research. A dream about Valerie, once again, serving as my alarm clock.

I grab my phone. Clock says half past seven.

It buzzes in my hand, as if on cue, startling me. Caller ID says Griffin, Carla.

"Harney," she says, "I hate to do this, but I feel like hell warmed over. I've been tossing my cookies half the night."

I shake out the cobwebs, ignore the icy-cold shiver gripping me, try to get my act together to have a conversation.

"The nausea," I manage to say.

"Yeah. I have to get the bandages on my face changed this morning anyway, and I was thinking maybe I'll take today off, make it a long weekend."

I stand up. "No problem."

"Well, I know we're about to reopen K-Town, so the timing isn't great."

It's more than great. The timing is actually perfect. Now she won't be in my way.

I'll have the next twenty-four hours to myself.

CHAPTER 81

A FEELING of dread swims through my chest as I pull onto the campus of Stateville Correctional Center, near Joliet. I've had more than my share of visits, usually getting background from inmates, sometimes more vital information from snitches, occasionally flipping a guy who'd refused to cooperate but was reconsidering after his initial stretch in this hellhole. It's never a joyride, seeing the dilapidated, overcrowded, overburdened facility, where the inmates are scared, bitter, hopeless, mentally ill, or usually a combination thereof.

But this is the first time I've felt fear.

Antoine Stonewald looks different from his mug shot. He's shaved his head, for one, which a fair number of inmates do. Some for hygienic reasons: better to have no hair than unclean hair. Others for safety reasons: one less thing someone can grab or twist.

He's thicker, too—muscular, not fat, the product of weight lifting, one of the only things to do in here. And he's older. Not because of the passage of four years, but because of the passage of four years inside Stateville.

"What-choo want, po-lice." He doesn't say it as a question. That's learned behavior. Emotion in here is weakness. Weakness gets you a target on your back.

"I want to know if you killed Nathan Stofer."

He looks at me as if we're at a poker table, as if he's trying to read me and doesn't want me reading him. "The fuck you sayin'? Said I did. Pleaded guilty."

"Yeah, I know."

"Yeah, you know. You know a lotta brothers plead guilty to shit they didn't do?"

"Probably," I say. "First-degree with a gun? You were looking at forty-five minimum, and that's assuming the felony murder didn't stick. Probably would've gotten sixty or seventy—black guy kills a rich white guy. So yeah, you took twenty. Doesn't mean you did it."

Antoine works his jaw, controlling his emotions. Twiddles his thumbs. The shackles rake against the desk between us.

"Go the fuck home, cracker po-lice."

"Hey, Antoine, you wanna cut the gangsta smack? You were an honor student at UIC, halfway to an accounting degree, engaged to a nice woman, saving up for a down payment on a condo. You ain't in B unit right now, looking over your shoulder. It's just you and me in here. So lose the hard-ass routine and talk to me."

He chews on his lip, sits back, his expression softening.

"I'm trying to help you, kid."

He lets out a humorless grunt. "A cop wants to help me. That would be a first."

Okay, at least now he's talking to me.

"Help me understand why a kid who worked so hard to make something of himself would do something stupid like shoot a guy in a parking garage."

He shrugs his shoulders, not in a casual, who-knows sort of way, but a violent way. I'm bringing it all back. He's worked through it; he's been dealing it with it for years now, telling himself to keep his time good, get that 15 percent shaved off.

"You pleaded out right after your first lawyer died," I say.

He looks away, remembering. I try not to do the same.

"*Right* after she died," I add. "Four days later."

"So?"

"So? Any judge would give a continuance to someone whose lawyer suddenly died just before trial. There was no rush. Why plead guilty so fast?"

Antoine leans forward, like he's finally willing to engage. The shackles rake along the table as he opens his hands. "Maybe I was already planning on pleading guilty before she died."

"That's not the way I'm hearing it, son. I hear she was going to bat for you. She had some ideas that somebody else killed Nathan Stofer. What was the lawyer's name? Maybe... Valerie?"

"Val," he says. "Val Blinderman. She said only her husband called her Valerie."

I close my eyes, look away. I can't let him know my connection. I reach into my pocket and pull out my phone, check it, anything to busy myself, to keep him from knowing that he just drove a stake into me.

Don't think about her. Think about him.

Another reason, too. You ask an inmate what's the worst part, they don't usually say the violence, the crap food. First thing they usually say is the loneliness. You put a guy in a nice interview room like this, give him a chance to have a conversation, he'll usually take it and run with it.

Takes him a minute, while I stall for time, but then he keeps going.

"Yeah, she was a nice lady," he says. "I mean, she was all business, for sure, but—but y'know, she'd talk to me. Like a human being? Nobody in County would do that. Nobody in here, either. But she did. She made you feel like... like you mattered."

I don't say anything. I can't, the emotion choking my throat.

"Sometimes we'd just talk. Like, she had a sick kid. A little baby girl who had a stroke. She was, like, in a coma, but she wasn't going to come out of it. She'd spend the nights in the hospital and the days working my case. You could tell how tired she was. I told her, go be with her, get someone else to represent me. I mean, she was great, I needed her, but...that's family, man. It's more important."

My eyes bore into the black screen of my phone, my body beginning to tremble.

"What did...she say to that?" I say, hardly more than a whisper.

"She said I sounded like her husband."

I nod, staring into blackness, focusing on anything, anything but the memory. Don't go there. Stay here, in this room, focus on the job.

"She said, 'My daughter's gone. I can't save her. But maybe I can save you.' She said her daughter would want that."

I squeeze my eyes shut. My hand reaches up to my wet face, my shoulders bouncing now, breathing coming in gasps.

She was right. Our little baby girl *would* have wanted that.

"Hey, man, I didn't mean to..."

It takes me a minute, trying to regain composure, because I have a reason to be here, and it's not to blubber and sob like a child, certainly not in front of a man who's had his life stolen from him for a crime he almost certainly did not commit.

And any chance of hiding my connection is long down the toilet now.

"Oh, shit," says Antoine. "Her husband was a cop. You're...Billy."

I do a final wipe of my face, take a deep breath, clear my throat, and nod. "I was the one who called her Valerie, yeah," I say.

"Well, you gotta leave, Billy," he says, his voice different now, stronger, hostile. "I'm sorry, but you gotta leave right now."

CHAPTER 82

"I'M NOT going anywhere," I tell Antoine. "You know what she was doing better than I do. She was looking at alternative suspects for Nathan Stofer's murder."

"No," he says, but he doesn't mean I'm wrong.

"The sex-trafficking ring," I say. "You know she was looking at that, right?"

He turns his head away.

"The Ukrainian general's business, KB Investors Group. The one Nathan Stofer was trying to keep from joining the Stratton Tower project. C'mon, Antoine, you know all this! You know more than I do about—"

"Man, I *can't*." He slams down his fists, the shackles clanging on the table. His words come out as a plea through a choked throat, tears coming now, his turn to cry. "You're already putting my family at risk, just being here."

"They threatened you," I say. What I figured. He pleads guilty four days after Valerie's death. Someone got to him.

He leans forward, pauses, looks over at the prison guard through the glass door, leans farther forward still, his chin only inches from the table. His words spill out in a harsh whisper. "You think I *like* sitting in this shithole for something I didn't do? It's keeping my family alive."

"Your fiancée, Cassietta. Your mother and sister. They threatened them."

He looks at me, defiant, but something else, too. Sympathetic. Apologetic. "How do I know, just being here, you didn't get them killed?"

"Nobody knows I'm here," I say.

He laughs. Shakes his head as if he pities my ignorance. Then turns stone cold. "They can kill a cop's wife and make it look like suicide," he whispers. "They can waltz into County all official and dressed up, like it's nothing, and lay it out for me. Cassie's home address, where she works, how they're gonna take turns on her before they slit her throat. How they're gonna dump gasoline on my sister and light a match while my mama watches. Then the motherfucker walks back out like nothing? They got people everywhere, man."

"It didn't come from you," I say. "I'd never give you up."

"You probably already did, just coming here."

"I'm gonna take them down, Antoine. Every one of them. They won't be able to hurt you or your family."

He pauses. Thinks about it. That thing he's been suppressing, that has secretly plagued him since the first day they locked him up—hope.

"Don't you want out of here, Antoine? Don't you wanna be free? Marry Cassie? See your mother and sister? Have your *life* back?"

He wags a finger at me, cocks his head. "Don't do that, man."

"I can make that happen, Antoine. All I need—"

"Go on now!" he says, slamming back from the table, the shackles sliding off the table as he bounces to his feet. "I got nothin' to say to you, cracker po-lice! I took my twenty cuz I shot that damn fool. I didn't like the look on his smug-ass face, know what I'm sayin'?"

"Just a name, Antoine," I say. "Just a location."

He bangs on the glass window. "Man, I got nothin' to say to this guy!" he calls out. "Let me the fuck outta here!"

I drop my head. It's over.

Two corrections officers enter the room. "Sorry, Detective. If he doesn't want to talk to you..."

...then he doesn't have to. I know.

"What a waste of a morning," I say, loud enough for the guards in the room, and probably the ones outside, to hear. "I come all this way, and this kid doesn't tell me squat."

Antoine, back to his cocky prison-yard attitude, catches my eye. He knows my last comment was for him.

But in fact, Antoine did tell me a couple of things.

One: those dreams of mine are wrong. Valerie didn't kill herself. I wasn't there when she did. They killed her. *They* did this.

And two: the person who delivered the threat to Antoine? The man who waltzed into county lockup in a fancy suit, as he said?

Only a lawyer could have done that.

CHAPTER 83

THE LAST thing Patti feels like doing today is heading to the prison.

She takes a personal day. No way she could justify this trip as official police business.

No way she can justify it, period.

Last night was another restless one, full of nightmares and, worse still, the reality of what happened four years ago.

She can't sleep. Can't do her training runs. Can't eat. Can't focus at work.

All she can think about is Val. And Billy.

And a gun, Billy's service weapon.

The trip to the prison feels like a life sentence itself. She pulls off the highway at one point and retches by the side of the road, but there's no food to vomit. Her body is feverish, though she doubts she's sick.

Her hands tremble on the steering wheel. But she focuses on Billy.

She's doing this for Billy.

She parks in the designated spot and looks up at the imposing structure. "I can't do this," she mumbles. But she doesn't have anywhere else to turn.

She shows her credentials at intake, gives up her weapon and cell phone, endures the pat-down and wanding and warnings, which even cops have to undergo.

They lead her into a private interview room. She finds herself hoping, praying, that the guard will say there's been some glitch, that inmate number 28507-024 isn't available.

She begs for such a glitch.

Then the door opens. She hears the leg irons dragging along the floor, the guard's calm but stern directions. The snap of the lock when the shackles are affixed to the table.

She cries. She swore she wouldn't. Once it comes, there's no use fighting it. She lets it go, covering her face in her hands, shaking so hard she can hardly stay seated in the chair.

She can't bear to look.

But she's doing this for Billy.

"At some point," says the prisoner, "are you going to look at me or say something?"

It sends a chill through her. The voice. The voice she once trusted, the voice that soothed her and guided her.

She looks up at former chief of detectives Daniel Harney.

"Hi, Daddy," she says.

CHAPTER 84

PATTI HAD tried to get it all off her chest before she came. Even spoke it aloud in the car as she drove from Chicago to Terre Haute, Indiana, the federal supermax.

How could you do that to us?

How could you betray us?

We trusted you.

I trusted you.

Variations on that, over and over during the three-hour trip. The man she worshipped, the man who made everything right, in reality a bent cop, corrupt to the core.

She'd hoped to tire herself out on the ride over, have her first—and last—visit be focused on Billy.

But it all floods back, all the hurt, all the insults she wanted to hurl, all the pain she wanted to inflict.

"It's good to see you, honey. I wasn't sure you'd ever come."

Dirty snow atop his head, far whiter than before. He's lost considerable weight, sunken eyes, a skinny stalk for a neck, shoulders drawn tight. Like someone put him in a dryer and shrunk him two sizes.

He was always larger than life to her, the proud, commanding chief of detectives, the baritone voice and erect posture, the man who took over any room he entered. Now he's a soft-spoken, stooped, broken man.

"You look slimmed down," he says. "You've been running again."

"No," she hears herself say, steeling up. "You don't get to do that."

She looks at him. His eyebrows dance. "Okay," he says tentatively. "At least tell me how you're do—"

"No."

"Right, right, I get it. Patti, listen, there's so many things I've wanted to say—"

"No!" She pounds the table. "This isn't a reunion, okay? You can't just..." Her throat chokes up.

Her father gives up, crosses his arms, waits her out. The hurt on his face—so unfair that he can look hurt, that *he* gets to be the victim.

He coughs into his fist, a nasty sputter, deep and wet, the shackles connecting his hands jangling. He doesn't look well. He probably isn't well.

But he doesn't get her pity.

"I'm here about Billy," she says.

He clears his throat, cocks his head. "He okay?"

"He's been talking about Val. He's become convinced she didn't commit suicide."

He brings a hand to his forehead. "Oh, Jay-sus, no. Even with the autopsy report."

"Even with that."

"He never saw the *original* one, did he?"

"No," says Patti. "I actually had a copy, but I burned it."

"Thank Christ for that." Her father opens his hands. "You said he's 'become convinced.' So he doesn't *know*?"

She shakes her head. "He doesn't remember. He says it was all a haze."

Her father nods, takes a deep breath. "He never told us what happened. Never talked about it. Not once, afterward. I figured, maybe the whole thing was like what you said—a haze. Or maybe he remembered it clear as day and just... didn't wanna tell us."

Patti had thought the same thing. She and her father talked about it all the time back then. "And even if he did remember," she says, "he may not now. After, y'know, being shot in the head last year and having those memory issues. That ring a bell?"

He shoots her a look. "We gonna do *that* now? Or talk about Billy?"

He's right. She needs to stay focused. "Well, whether the trauma back then fucked with his memory, or whether he's blocked it out over time, or that gunshot injury from a year ago did it—as of now, he doesn't remember what happened."

"Okay, well, *that's* a blessing," he says. "So why the doubt all of a sudden?"

"He's... he's got it in his head that some sex traffickers killed her, that some case Val was working on—they had to shut her up. It's total nonsense."

"Better than the truth," he says.

"Not if he's going to hunt down the traffickers and kill them."

Her father deflates. "That's what he's gonna do?"

"He says so. You ever know Billy not to keep his word?"

"Jay-sus." His head lolls back. "Tell me about these traffickers."

"He says they come from Ukraine. A former general, a bunch of ex–special operations thugs."

He shakes his head. "He's gonna get his ass killed." He leans forward, looks at her squarely. "There's only one choice," he says. "You have to tell him the truth."

She knows. Deep down, she's known it for a long time. But no matter what else she may feel or think, he's still her father, and maybe she just needed to hear him say it.

"But how in the hell do I do that?" she says. "How do I tell my brother that he killed his own wife?"

BOOK III

CHAPTER 85

FOUR YEARS ago. Patti didn't go far from the house that afternoon.

She wasn't sure why. She'd sat with Billy in the hospital for more than an hour after it was over, after Janey had been pronounced dead, after Billy had said his final good-byes, after Billy had tried, by her count, twelve times to reach Val by phone.

When she dropped him off at his house, he said he wanted to go in alone to break the news to Val.

But Patti didn't go far. Just drove to the coffeehouse a couple of blocks away.

And worried.

Billy had just stared off in the distance on the car ride home. The fog of overwhelming grief, though he'd known this day was coming. But more than grief. Anger, too. No—anger didn't do it justice.

Betrayal—that was it. Billy had held his daughter's hand as she died, told her how much he loved her. Val should have been holding the other hand, should have been whispering in Janey's other ear.

"She should've been there," he said on the ride home from the hospital.

"People deal with this stuff in different ways," Patti said. She felt like a shrink on a TV show, hearing herself, but it didn't make it untrue.

"She should've been there."

At a stoplight, Patti reached into the back seat for a bottle of Jameson she'd been planning to smuggle into the hospital at some point, to help Billy take the edge off during one of his overnight stays. "Have a hit of this," she said.

Billy stared at the bottle as if he'd never seen one before. He hadn't touched the sauce the whole time he'd stood vigil in the hospital, over a month in total.

Then he snatched it from her hand and, like a pro, unscrewed the top, raised the bottle to his mouth, leaned back, and opened his throat.

At least half the bottle was gone before Patti grabbed it from him. "Hey, easy, easy. You're out of practice."

Billy wiped at his mouth and looked out the window. "She couldn't have at least kept her phone by her side in case I called? *That* was too much to ask?"

She looked at him. Didn't know what to say. "This is tough for her, too, Billy. She has that depression thing on her best day. Now, with all this—she's just... dealing with it the best she can." Patti couldn't believe she, of all people, was defending Val. Their roles had been opposite over this last month, Patti and her not-so-veiled criticisms, Billy making excuses for Val. But Billy was too far gone for diplomacy now.

"Let me go in with you," she said when she pulled up to the curb outside Billy's home.

"No."

"You think Val's in there? Or at work?"

"The fuck should I know? Maybe if she'd answer her phone."

"Let me come in with you."

"No." Billy opened the car door, then looked back at Patti. How far he had fallen in this last month, the torture he'd endured, his lifeless, bloodshot eyes rimmed with dark circles, the downturn of his mouth. His whole world had cratered.

"I'll come by later," she promised.

And she didn't go far. She couldn't. She had to hover, stay close, remain on call. She drove to the coffeehouse down the street, nursed an extra-shot cappuccino. Felt the rush of the caffeine buzz. Worried about her brother.

Her cell rang thirty minutes later. Billy. She felt relief.

Then she heard what he had to say. She rushed out of the coffeeshop, jumped into her car.

His front door was unlocked. She bounded up the stairs and into Billy's bedroom.

Felt herself slow. Heard faint breathing.

"Billy," she said for some reason. Some instinctive need to announce her presence. Reached for the weapon at her side. Thought better of it.

She could already sniff it. She'd smelled it a hundred times.

She leaned forward and peered into the bathroom.

Massive blood spatter on the wall, in the freestanding tub, a pool on the floor.

Billy, sitting Indian-style on the floor.

Valerie, eyes wide and vacant, mouth agape, resting in Billy's lap. The entry wound under her chin, a clean contact wound.

Billy, his lap and shirt covered in blood, cradling Valerie.

Holding his Glock, his service weapon, lazily in his hand.

"Oh, no," she heard herself say.

"I... did this." His voice nothing but a whisper of air, pitched high with emotion.

She didn't know what to do, what to say. Her feet wouldn't move.

But her head did. She turned and looked into the bedroom closet. The door open. The gun safe against the back wall. The safe's door open, too.

She looked back at Billy. "She killed herself," she heard herself say. "She couldn't...it was too hard for her. She killed herself."

Billy, staring at the floor, shaking his head. "I did this," he whispered.

Patti looked back at the gun safe, its open door.

And she knew he was right.

CHAPTER 86

LATE MORNING. Carla Griffin locks the front door of her house, wearing sunglasses, a T-shirt, and shorts, looking like summer even with the gauze and tape on her face. She puts the suitcase in the back of her Honda and closes it up. Her mother-in-law, silver-haired and stooped, waddles over to the passenger side and gets in.

The boy, Samuel, belted in behind his grandmother.

Carla jumps in, starts up the car, backs it out of the driveway, and starts heading north. *Wisconsin Dells, here we come!*

This is the last fucking thing Porter should have to be doing, standing on the periphery of a baseball diamond in South Deering, binoculars to his eyes. But this isn't something he can delegate. Delegating it would be bringing in someone else, and he needs another person knowing about this like he needs a third tit.

He lowers the binoculars.

It's time. Carla's out of the way now, taking Porter up on his offer to send her to a water park in Wisconsin. Harney is working alone on this for the time being.

Okay, Harney. You wanted a one-man crusade? You wanted to keep this quiet, do this solo?

Here's your chance, pal.

He pulls out his burner phone and dials it.

"Let's fucking finish this," he tells Disco.

CHAPTER 87

AFTER TALKING to Antoine Stonewald at Stateville, I get on the Stevenson and head to work. I fit in my earbuds and check my phone for J Crew's number, dial it.

"Yo yo yo. To what do I owe this great honorary privilege?"

Jay Herlihy grew up down the street from us, a cop's kid like me. He was built like a linebacker and had the approximate IQ of a football, but he was a good seed overall. Except that one time, second grade, he made the mistake of punching Patti in the mouth. The three Brothers Harney didn't think that was funny. We tackled him after school and rearranged his face. My mother was livid with us but delegated the punishment, as always, to Pop. Pop pulled the three of us into the study, heard our side of it, but you shoulda seen the color his face turned when he heard about Jay giving Patti, his prized possession, a bloody lip.

You boys screwed up, he said. *You shoulda broken his arm.*

Water under the bridge. Jay turned out all right. Ran with my crew, drank with us in the cemeteries, but he got a little wild in college and couldn't make it into the Academy.

So he became a corrections officer.

When the small talk's over, I get to it, lay it out for J.

"This Antoine Stonewald, he was in for murder—so Division 9, right?"

"Right," I say. "Had to be. This would have been four years ago."

"Yeah, well, for maximum—yeah, you're right, some suit shows up unannounced and wants to talk to a detainee, we tell him to pound sand. Ya gotta schedule ahead, ya gotta be on a list, and that list is small—immediate family or the lawyer. But you're saying his lawyer had just died."

"Right."

"Right, so, yeah, if this guy can show us his bar card, we can be sure he's really a lawyer, yeah, we'd sign him in and let him talk to the detainee."

"But he'd sign in," I say.

"Most definitely."

"No other way he gets in, J? Maybe he wants to come in quietly. Maybe a guard would help him sneak in, keep his name off the books?"

"Fuck yourself, Harney."

"Didn't mean you, J. But you know what I mean."

"Yeah, yeah. No, here's the thing. Someone wants to send a message to a detainee, they might try to get to him inside, through another detainee. In the yard or the mess hall. But a visit? No. There's too much security. You couldn't just buy off a guard. You'd have to buy off a dozen."

"Bottom line," I say, "some suit wanted to meet with the detainee, he'd have to go through the front door."

"Most definitely. He'd sign in."

"Good. So can you help me out?"

He sighs. "Division 9? You got an approximate date?"

More than approximate. The date of Valerie's and Janey's death is burned into my brain. And I was decent at math, so I can count out four days later, when Antoine formally pleaded guilty. It had to be within that short interval of time that someone waltzed into Cook County Jail and threatened to kill Antoine's entire family.

"Might take me some time," he says.

"I need this, like, yesterday, J. No fuckin' foolin'. Any chance you can put your foot on the pedal for an old friend?"

I punch out the phone. The traffic finally opens up, and I floor it. Gotta make the most of my time with Carla gone.

I make it to headquarters in less than an hour. Vitrullo, at intake, nods to me. "Someone to see you or Griffin," he says. "Griffin took a sick day, you probably know."

"Right. Where?"

He juts his chin. "Over there. The girl."

I turn. It's a girl, probably late teens. Dirty blond hair back in a ponytail. A tank top, shorts, sandals.

And on her ankle, a tattoo of a black lily.

CHAPTER 88

I WALK the girl to an interview room. I say girl, because I'm guessing late teens, even though she looks more like early twenties. Heroin does that to you. It ages you, weathers you, beats the shit out of you while it loves you.

This girl has user written all over her. Undernourished. Dark, dead eyes. Bad skin.

She has nice features, though, a pretty girl. A party girl, if you tease that hair up, apply some makeup, put her in a nice dress. Sure, she's a hottie, a top-drawer prostitute, when dolled up.

No tracks on her arms, which means she probably smokes, doesn't shoot. Makes sense, if you're projecting glamour. Evie had needle tracks on her arms, but she'd also escaped the clutches of her traffickers for at least the week she spent with Shiv and maybe longer, and it's easier to inject than smoke.

I sit next to her, not across from her, because these interview rooms don't project warmth. This isn't a friendly atmosphere. We want our suspects intimidated, which we can use either way—scare them with our attitude, or be sugary sweet and ingratiate ourselves with them.

I've always known which way to play it. One of my strengths, reading people.

This time, I don't know what to do. So I default to letting it play out.

"My name is Sadie," she says. A thick accent, eastern European.

Not likely, but okay. "Last name?"

"Do I have to tell you that?" She's nervous, fidgeting, scared or upset or both.

"No. That's okay." I put my hand on the table. "Why don't you tell me why you're here?"

Why don't you tell me who put that tattoo of a black lily on you?

"My...friend," she says. "My roommate. She..."

"Something happened to a friend of yours?"

She nods, bites her nails, which are long, manicured, dark purple.

"Okay, what's your friend's name?"

"Evie," she says. Just like I've heard it. Evie-rhymes-with-Chevy.

I hold it back, best I can. "Does *she* have a last name?"

The girl nods. "Her name is Evalina Vacaru," she says.

I don't write it down. I don't have a pad of paper in front of me. Didn't want to spook the girl, make this seem too official.

Evalina Vacaru. Evalina Vacaru.

Our Jane Doe has a name.

"She is from Romania," she says. "Timisoara."

And so is this girl, Sadie—or not far from it. She pronounced the name of the city like a pro.

"I think...she is dead."

"Why do you think that, Sadie?"

She nods, swallows hard. Looks away. "I saw...there is website for missing persons and unidented...unidentif..."

"A website for missing persons and unidentified bodies?"

"Yes, yes."

It's true. When the county doesn't have ID on a dead body, they give out all the information they can—race, gender, height, weight—and post photos from the morgue. You have to go to a

different page, after a warning that what you're about to see will be graphic and shocking, but yeah, usually photos of the dead person will be on that site.

My name would've been posted there, too, as the lead detective. *If you have any information that could lead to the identification of this individual...*

"Evie was on..." Her voice shakes. She wipes away a tear.

Emotion, but this girl is well practiced at the stone expression, suppressing her hurt and fear and sadness.

"You saw Evie on that website? Photos?"

She closes her eyes, nods.

The county would have mentioned the tattoo on Evie's ankle as well, maybe even posted a photo of it. Wouldn't be hard for Sadie to confirm it was her friend.

I grab a tissue and a pen and notepad off the counter at the side of the room. Give her the tissue and slide the paper in front of her. "Could you write her name down?"

She does.

There's no point in my playing totally dumb here. She knows from the website that I'm the lead cop and that Evie was murdered. But I don't have to tell her everything I know, either.

"She was killed when the... little girl was killed?" Sadie asks.

"Yes, she was. Do you know why Evie was in K-Town?"

She shakes her head. "No. She left and did not come back. We did not know."

"*We*," I say. "Who's we?"

"We... live with two other people."

"Who?"

"Friends," she says. "They are friends. Men, but... not boyfriends."

Two men. She and Evie live with two men. The hookers and the pimps.

This prostitution ring is more than two girls. Maybe they house them separately. Not what I figured, but no reason that it couldn't be true.

"Where do you live, Sadie?"

"I just..." She sighs again. "I just wanted you to know her name. So she could be... so the burial..."

"I understand, Sadie. I understand. Can you tell me where you live?"

"I do not... is that... do I have to tell you?"

"No." I try to smile. "No, that's okay."

Sadie. No last name. No known address.

"How can I reach you?" I ask. "If I have questions about your friend?"

She hands me a slip of paper from her pocket. A phone number written in pen. Bogus, no doubt, but she was ready for the question. She doesn't want me calling her.

"Sadie, can I help you in any way?"

"Me? No, is okay."

"You're an addict," I say.

"No." Like she expected that question, too.

"It's okay. You're not in any trouble. But I could help you get treatment."

"No, I am not add—addict."

Sure she is. And that's only the start of her troubles. If her "friends," as she puts it, find out that she came here, they'll be none too happy. She risked a lot coming here.

But I can't tip my hand. I'm not supposed to know any of this. "Okay. Well, can I help you get home?"

"No, is okay. I take bus."

"Okay, then. Let me show you out."

We head downstairs to intake. "Wait here a second," I say.

I walk up to Vitrullo at intake. "Vin," I whisper, "take a few minutes before signing this girl out. I need five minutes. Pretend like you actually work for a living."

He glances over at her, then nods. "I can play a cop on TV."

"Five minutes is all I need."

Seven minutes later, Sadie leaves the station, turns right, heads south on foot, crossing North Avenue.

By now I'm in my car, curbed on Pulaski, slowly crawling forward.

Sadie's about to show me where she lives.

CHAPTER 89

GOOD NEWS. Sadie walks to a bus, the 53 at Pulaski and Division. If she'd hopped on a train, I would've had to ditch my car and follow on foot, leaving me stranded wherever we end up and making me more visible to her.

That's the problem with a solo surveillance. Usually there's a team—you alternate, you communicate, you don't have to expose yourself. Doing it alone ain't easy.

But following a bus is. You never lose sight of it, and Sadie's eyes will presumably be forward. The stops are a bitch, though; I have to keep my eyes peeled for her getting off.

Luckily, I see her jumping off, walking two blocks, and hopping on another bus heading south and west.

At a light, I check my email. I still haven't heard back from the Romanian orphanage, but I have a message in my in-box from the prison I called, giving me a list of inmates released within the last three months.

Names and a lot of other information—probably offenses committed, sentences, amounts of time served—things I can't read in Romanian.

But the names—those I can read.

One of them is Rudolf Vacaru.

Evie—Evalina Vacaru—was calling that prison looking for her brother. Missed him by three months. She had escaped from her traffickers and was trying to find a way home.

The bus ride, in total, is just under an hour, ultimately taking us into a neighborhood that is less residential than industrial.

Sadie gets off the bus and starts walking. Car traffic has lightened, and it's getting harder to follow her without sticking out.

I park my car on 122nd and follow on foot. I keep a one-block distance, but I'm on the opposite side of the street, the north side, giving me a better angle. Sooner or later, she's going to turn, and—

She turns left, disappearing through a large opening with an arched sign connecting the posts on either side. Looks like an old industrial park, long forgotten, shut down and left to wither. Once she's out of my sight, and thus I'm out of hers, I do a hard jog, crossing the street and making up the distance in a few seconds. I hit the wall where she turned and peek around the corner, hand on my service weapon.

Sadie is still walking, the same pace, still no phone, just walking.

It's a risk, following her down this narrow corridor, because this place is deserted. No crowd into which I could disappear, no reason why anyone should be here. If she sees me, it sets off bells and whistles. This whole thing could go to shit.

I follow her anyway. I need to know exactly where she's staying.

This is an old mill of some kind. Most of the structures look like oversize garages, closed and locked now, dusty and rusted, but some structures look like old factories, too.

About four minutes into her walk, Sadie stops at a gate and turns. For a split second, I'm sure she's going to complete that turn, do a one-eighty, and look at me squarely. Instead, she opens a latch, passes through the fence, and closes it.

With Sadie again out of my sight, I hustle up, stopping just short of the gate. I lean over, peek through the grating. It's a loading area, with concrete steps leading up to a door. No cars. No sign of other people.

Sadie walks up the concrete steps, opens a large metal door, and walks in.

I give it a good once-over. I consider using my phone to take some video, but there's nothing complicated here. The fence isn't locked. There's only one way in.

I double back to look for an entrance on the other side. I don't see any. Doesn't mean there isn't one. This was once a company's small industrial village, and there could be all sorts of interconnecting parts, tunnels, and points of entry and egress. No way to know.

But at least I know where she lives now.

"See you all soon," I whisper.

CHAPTER 90

I KILL the afternoon there, sitting in my car, parked a quarter of a mile from the industrial park. Waiting to see who arrives and who leaves. Waiting to see town cars with beautiful young prostitutes coming or going. Waiting to see eastern European thugs coming or going.

Nothing. No action in or out of the industrial park.

Not surprising. I thought I might get lucky, but prostitutes don't see a whole lot of action by day. It's night work.

Which is better anyway. I want to do this in the dark.

I head back to the station, do a little paperwork, chat with the crew, let time pass. I go online to learn about the layout of the industrial park. Don't find much, only that it was once a private boarding school, converted decades ago by an auto-parts company into an industrial park. Then, in the nineties, the company moved out of the city. No architectural drawings. I don't have time to get them through official means, and I don't want to do this officially anyway.

I think of that kid, Rudolf Vacaru, getting out of prison and looking for his sister. I think of Evie, escaping her captors and trying to hook back up with her brother.

I think of Antoine Stonewald, rotting in prison for a crime he did not commit.

I think of Valerie, dealing with the crushing heartbreak of Janey's stroke but staying vigilant, trying to free Antoine, to free girls kidnapped and forced into sexual slavery.

When the shift, such as it is, has ended, when the clock reaches seven and the place is nearly empty, I gear up.

A vest. My Glock at my hip, another at my ankle, a Sig in the small of my back. Spare mags if I run out.

A few other toys, too.

I throw a sport jacket over it all and head out.

When I reach the lot, Patti is standing there, leaning against my car.

CHAPTER 91

PATTI COMES off my car, crosses her arms, looks me up and down, sees my belt, sees the bulge in my ankle. "Looks like you got plans," she says.

"What's it to you?"

"Me? Oh, nothing. You're just my brother."

"Heading home," I say.

"Great. Let's grab a beer first. My treat."

"Not in the mood," I say.

"I'll cook you dinner, then."

"Patti, don't mess with me."

Her chin dips, eyebrows rise. "Then don't mess with *me* and pretend like you're going home when you're armed like you're about to invade bin Laden's compound."

I don't answer. But I don't try to pass, either, to get to my car. Whatever it is, I need to resolve this. I can't have her on my back all night.

"You want to bust a bunch of sex traffickers, fine," she says. "Great. I'll help you. The force will help you. Get Sosh and whatever crew you need, me included, and let's take 'em down. But going in solo to take on who knows what's waiting for you in some kind of pathetic attempt at revenge—"

"Pathetic? They killed Valerie, Patti. I'm supposed to let that go?"

She looks at me, really looks at me, searches my eyes. "You don't know that for a fact, do you? At most, they took credit for her death. I would, too, if I were them. You have questions, fine, let's arrest them and interrogate them. But this suicide mission—"

"I don't have time for this." I angle past her, but she shoves me hard, knocking me off balance, and places herself between me and my car door.

"They didn't kill Val," she says.

"She didn't kill herself. I don't believe it. I don't believe that."

Her eyes narrow. Her head angles to the side. "You really don't remember, do you? You don't remember what happened."

"I..."

A fog. That's all it is now, a fog. A fog that only separates in my dreams, where it comes back with vivid, crashing clarity. But they aren't true. My dreams aren't true. They're just dreams.

Patti answers for me, repeats herself. "You don't remember what happened."

"Okay, so maybe it was a tiny bit traumatic, okay? Is that okay? And maybe that fucking bullet I took to the brain last year didn't help—"

"Of *course* it's okay," she says, tears in her eyes. "Of course it's okay. But Billy, do you remember the aftermath? Do you remember ever asking yourself questions?"

"Do I—did I ask myself *questions*? You mean questions like, why would my wife eat a bullet? Gee, sister, I only asked myself that question about a hundred thousand fucking times. And I got the same answer every time. She killed herself because she was overcome with grief and because I made her feel like shit for not being at the hospital every second of every day. She ran herself ragged trying to be there for our daughter *and* be there for her clients, and I gave her the guilt trip of all guilt trips. Were there other questions I was supposed to ask?"

"Billy—"

"Oh, here's one. Maybe I was supposed to ask if someone had a motive to kill her. Maybe I should've looked through her case files and realized that she was about to expose a major sex-trafficking ring. Maybe if I'd been a little bit more of a *detective* and less of a grieving puddle of guilt and self-pity, I would've figured this out four years ago, and I wouldn't be playing catch-up now." I throw up my hands. "Were there other questions you had in mind?"

Patti closes her eyes, brings her hands together, as if in prayer, against her mouth.

"You came here to say something, Patti. Say it."

She angles her hands toward me, as if sending her prayer my way.

"What question didn't I ask?" I say.

She opens her eyes. Clears her throat.

She says, "How'd your Glock get out of the gun safe?"

CHAPTER 92

I DRAW back. "The—what? The gun? Valerie took it out of the safe."

Even as I say the words, the ground beneath my feet suddenly feels uneven.

"What, the traffickers broke into the house and forced Val to open the safe, so they could kill her but make it look like a suicide, because she used your gun?" she says. "That's your theory, right?"

"Why not?"

"Billy." Her voice trembling. She steps toward me, but I step back. A tear falls down her cheek. "Billy, honey, Val didn't know the combination to the gun safe."

"Well, she..."

"She what? She didn't know, Billy. She didn't *want* to know. Remember? She wanted nothing to do with guns. She hated them. You know that."

"Well, then, I guess I left it open," I say. "I wasn't exactly having the time of my life, either, Patti. All I could think about, day and night, was Janey, lying in the hospital. I was absentminded. Maybe I...I left it...left it open."

Even as I say the words.

An earthquake inside my body.

"Your wife is depressed already, just normally," says Patti. "And now she's dealing with about the most gut-wrenching thing a person can deal with. And you left the safe wide open for her to access that gun? C'mon, Billy."

I stumble backward, reaching out to a patrol car for balance. I shut my eyes and hold on for dear life.

"What are you... what are you saying to me?"

"I'm saying Val didn't know the combo to the safe. She couldn't have opened it for herself or for some intruder who forced her to open it. You didn't even write the combo down, did you? Dad taught us that. Pick a combo you'll never forget, so you don't have to write it down, so it's never written anywhere, so no child or spouse could ever get into that safe. We have the same combo, right? Mom's birthday. Ten twelve forty-nine."

I turn away from her, cover my face with my hands.

This isn't...

No.

It can't be...

No.

"And there's no way in the world you left that safe open, kiddo. C'mon—you told me more than once that the last thing you'd ever want to do is leave your wife, with her history of depression, home alone with a gun. That safe was closed and locked."

I must have. I must have left it open.

My body shaking so hard that the words hardly come out. "You're saying I killed her. I killed my own wife."

My back still turned to her. I hear her footsteps as she walks up behind me.

"I'm *saying* that the person who walked into that bedroom that day may have been you in body. But it wasn't you. It was a man devastated and racked with grief, walking through a fog, probably drunk from the Jameson he downed on the car ride home. And right or wrong, no matter how you beat yourself up about it, it was a man who was hurt and angry that his wife wasn't there for Janey when she died. Put all that together—"

"No." The only word shooting through my brain.

"I don't know how it happened," she continues. "Neither do you. Maybe, maybe, I don't know, you—maybe you said, okay, you're so depressed, you wanna die, go ahead, Val, here's the gun—"

"No. No. She was already dead when I got there."

"That's just not possible, honey."

I spin around, nearly hitting her, she's so close behind me. I grab her by the arms. "How can you say these things to me?"

"You think I *want* to?" All composure lost now, her face all tears, her words garbled.

"You think I'd forget *killing* her? I might forget some details, but you think I'd forget that I removed the Glock from the safe and killed my own wife?"

"That's *exactly* what you'd forget!" she cries. "Because it's too horrible to remember!"

"No. She was already dead." I throw her to the side, open the car door. "She was already dead because they killed her. They killed her! You understand?" I point at her. "Don't follow me! Don't ever talk to me again!"

Patti collapses to the ground, pure torture across her face, tears pouring out, chest heaving.

I put the car in Reverse and drive away.

CHAPTER 93

MY WIFE was already dead when I found her.

Close to eight now. The sun has fallen, at least behind the buildings.

I park in the same spot, around a quarter of a mile from the industrial park.

She was already dead. They killed her.

I wouldn't forget that. No bullet to the brain would make me forget that.

No amount of traumatic exertion on my brain would make me forget *that*.

I punch the steering wheel. They killed her.

The street is all but deserted. No people; almost no traffic.

Then a car approaches from the opposite direction, traveling east, toward me.

Slows by the industrial park.

I raise my binoculars, catch a glimpse of the only person in the car, the driver.

That's one of them. The shorter, stockier of the two guys. The front-seat passenger in the 4Runner in K-Town. The first one of the two caught on the POD camera when I chased them from Shiv's house.

His car turns into the industrial park. I lose my sport jacket, get out of my car, hustle across the street, and make it to the park entrance. Peek down the corridor. The car has stopped by the gate, the same one Sadie opened. The guy gets out to unlatch it, then slides it open wide enough for a car to pass.

That stocky build. Definitely one of the two guys.

He gets in the car and pulls it in. Returns to the gate and slides it closed.

Now I start running, despite the extra weight from the double holster, the three sidearms, and the other accoutrements. But I run like I'm capable, which is pretty fast when I put my mind to it.

I get to the fence and peek in.

The guy is just closing the car door, balancing a pizza box in his hand.

One box. One pizza. Enough for a few people, not a large crew.

Four people. Sadie said four people lived there, if she was telling the truth. Three, minus Evie.

But if she was telling the truth, two men.

This is one of them.

I walk over to the latch, open it slowly, as the man walks up the concrete steps to the front door.

Slide it open just a tiny bit to angle through—the less noise the better—and draw my Glock.

He's pulling on the front-door lever, balancing the pizza box in the other hand, as I race toward the concrete steps.

"Police: don't move," I say it loud and firm enough for him to hear me, not enough for the whole neighborhood to hear.

He doesn't move. I bound up the concrete steps, put the gun against his head.

"What's your name?"

"Sergio."

"Who's inside, Sergio?" I ask.

"Inside here?" Accent, thick. Thick like his neck and shoulders.

"You got two seconds to answer."

"Just me and a girl."

"What girl?"

"Sadie."

"You're lying to me, you're dead. You get that, right?"

"I am not lying."

With my free hand, the one not pressing a Glock into his skull, I grab the pizza box and Frisbee it. Then I clutch his shoulder.

"Go," I say. "But do it slowly."

Sergio opens the door. We walk into a vestibule, a small area with a half door and window, like a ticket window at the movies, boarded up. Otherwise, nothing to do but open another door directly in front of us, a solid wooden door, no window.

"Open it," I say, my pulse banging.

He opens it. I push him forward, gripping his shoulder, pressing the Glock against his skull.

Inside is darkness. An airy feel, like high ceilings; a wide space, but black as pitch.

Can't-see-your-hand-in-front-of-your-face dark.

Sergio keeps walking. After two, three steps, I hold him up.

"Turn on the lights."

"No lights in here."

"What? Bullshit."

"Not bullshit."

"You walk through a dark room?"

"Yes. No choice."

It's possible. Would make for a good hideout, a good place to stow your sex slaves, having a room like this that people wouldn't think to traverse in the pitch dark.

But a slight tremble to his voice, those last words.

This is all wrong.

I throw my arm around his neck, a choke hold, as he tries to slide out of my grasp.

That's when the first bullet buzzes my ear.

CHAPTER 94

I TIGHTEN my choke hold on Sergio as bullets shower down on us, pummeling his body, my human shield. It's only seconds before he goes limp as bullets hit the floor behind us, too, and from different angles.

Muzzle flashes from up high, at ten o'clock and two o'clock.

Two shooters spread maybe thirty yards apart. From a high vantage point. With night vision.

Every advantage.

I can't hold Sergio up forever. So I fall back, pulling him on top of me, and spray bullets from my Glock to my right, having no idea in this darkness where I'm shooting, just my best approximation of the source of the muzzle flash, hoping it's close enough to make the shooter stop and duck for cover, at least temporarily.

The bullets keep coming from the other side, automatic-weapon fire, AR-15 or something, peppering Sergio's dead body, one hitting my forearm around his neck, searing pain, but I let go of Sergio and I'm dead.

A moment of quiet, the after-hum from the gunfire, nothing more.

They're reloading.

I aim my Glock toward the other shooter, the gunman at ten o'clock, and let off a few rounds. Then a few rounds to my right, two o'clock.

Then my clip's empty.

With my free hand, I reach to my belt, every movement of my fingers reminding me of the bullet that just entered my forearm.

I don't reach for a new magazine for the Glock.

I reach for the flashbang and toss it somewhere toward the center of the room.

Close my eyes, cover one ear with my free hand, push my other ear against my shoulder. Duck my head behind Sergio's body.

The grenade drops and goes off, a thundering blast of sound, searing light coloring my eyelids, even with my face pressed into Sergio's back.

Two men wearing night-vision goggles, suddenly blinded.

And immobilized, disoriented, at least for a few seconds, from the blast.

My only chance. I pry myself loose of Sergio and stumble backward, squinting through the harsh light at the door I just entered.

The light from the flashbang suddenly gone, dark again. The flashbang did a number on me, too, no matter how ready I was for it, so I'm not so coordinated, either. I stumble forward into darkness, my chin bouncing on hard tile, my Glock falling to the floor.

Bullets spray the wall near me. They're doing their best, but they're disabled by the blast.

That won't last much longer. They'll recover, and then I'm a sitting duck if I don't make it through that door.

I try to get back up, my head ringing, in total darkness.

More gunfire spray, hitting the door I'm going for.

Then a banging sound somewhere behind me, followed by a loud, efficient hum, and suddenly bright light surrounds me. Not grenade-caliber light but LED lighting. Someone flipped on the overhead lights.

I close my eyes instinctively as fresh gunfire erupts, but different gunfire, in a different direction. Some of the heavy rifle fire, but also some poppy gunfire.

Shots from a handgun.

I force my eyes open, squinting in the overhead lighting, and look to my left. Rafters, just like a gymnasium, at the top of which one of the men drops his rifle, his throat splayed open, and falls backward.

That's the other guy, the taller one, the one who shot at me in Shiv's house, the driver in the 4Runner in K-Town.

I reach for the backup at my ankle and turn, squinting in the direction of the other set of rafters on the other side, my two o'clock, where a man is adiosing the scene, going through some door, some escape hatch, at the top of the rafters. I don't get a look at him, just his back, a heavy limp as he exits.

What, the one guy shot the other? With a handgun?

No, of course not.

I shake my head, get myself together, keeping my backup piece high just in case, and focus. I'm inside an old gymnasium, and a door is open on the other side of it.

With a body leaning against it. A woman's body. A body still moving but wounded, a streak of blood against the door she's propping open.

I jump over Sergio's corpse and run the length of the gym toward her.

She's been hit, but she's still trying to clear the scene.

"Oh, no," I whisper.

The wound is up by her left shoulder, high and wide of the heart, but still a threat to bleed out.

I pull out my cell phone.

"Don't call it in," Carla says through a grimace. "Neither one of us wants to explain this."

CHAPTER 95

"I'M . . . FINE," Carla says through gritted teeth.

"You're not fine."

"You're bleeding, too. Your arm."

I yank off my shirt, buttons flying everywhere, and rip it roughly in half. I tie one half around Carla's shoulder and armpit, the best I can do to put temporary pressure on her wound, Carla crying out in pain as I do it.

She's losing color. Shock is a real possibility as she loses blood.

I tie the other half of my shirt, best as I can with one hand, around my left forearm, which has an entry and exit wound, a clean through-and-through.

I pick Carla up and carry her like a bride across the gym, Carla keeping her weapon out just in case the surviving shooter decides to make a return appearance. We must be quite a sight.

She's toughing it out, but she's in excruciating pain, wincing with every bounce as I run as fast as I can with a hundred pounds in my arms.

The first guy, who called himself Sergio, has been shot so many times he looks more like a broken piñata than a human being. The guy on the rafters hasn't moved an inch after Carla put one through his throat. I don't have time to confirm it, but he's down for the count.

I scoop up my original Glock. Can't leave that here. This place was chosen because it's out of the way. Nobody would hear anything; nobody will be looking around here. This was the perfect ambush site. Also helpful for me, now, buying me some time before anyone knows what happened here.

Just before we're out of the gym, we both hear it behind us. The entrance on the other side, where I found Carla, the gym door banging open again, footsteps bounding on the gym floor toward us.

Carla calls out, in a weak voice, "Don't move," before I spin around and see her.

Sadie, in her tank top and shorts, sandals long gone, in bare feet.

The girl who set us up. She sees Sergio and stops, freaks out, pedals backward. Looks up at the rafters at the other guy.

"Sadie!" I shout. "Look at me! Don't move and look at me!"

She does, though she looks like it wouldn't take much to send her running the other way.

"Come with us. We can help you."

She slowly shakes her head.

"You don't have to be afraid anymore," I say. "We can help you. Will you trust me and come with me?"

She doesn't know, stares at me with doe eyes.

"You can help your friends, too, Sadie. Evie's gone, but you can help the rest of them. They need your help!"

She starts to cry.

"My friend is hurt," I say. "I have to take her to the hospital. You have to decide right now. Will you come with us?"

I can't wait any longer. I turn and get through the door with Carla. It's a long trip to my car, but I do the best I can, running with her, the pain it causes her. Her moans and cries are growing weaker. She's losing blood.

Finally, sweat burning my eyes, my body all but giving out,

we reach my car, parked down the street. I put Carla in the back seat.

"Billy," she says to me, her voice growing fainter, as I'm reaching over to fasten the seat belt. "Billy, I'm sorry."

"Sorry for saving my life? I forgive you." I close the door and get around to the other side. I know there's more, much more to that apology, but now's not the time.

I put the car in gear. Grab my phone and dial it. Patti answers on the first ring.

"Meet me at the ER at Little Company of Mary, Evergreen Park," I say.

I punch out the phone and start driving.

Just as Sadie comes running out of the industrial park toward my car.

CHAPTER 96

DISCO BOUNDS down the back stairs from his escape hatch in the rafters, the pain in his foot screaming out, pure torture with every step.

They will catch him. As slow as he's moving, hobbled as he is, unable to take a step without lightning shots of pain. If they run up the rafters, go through this door, and come down the stairs, they'll catch him within seconds.

Adrenaline pounding through him. Blood oozing through the bandage and dressing with such force that his foot squishes inside the boot.

He reaches the bottom of the stairs, opens the door into a long underground tunnel connected to the next building.

His escape route, part of the plan. The tunnel runs beneath the entire length of the industrial park, nearly half a mile with all the turns and angles, at the end of which he will merely walk up the steps to the exit and find his car.

Half a mile in pure, agonizing pain.

Ahead of him, the tunnel, utter blackness, no lighting, artificial or otherwise.

His night-vision goggles still around his neck. He puts them on. The tunnel lights up in a green glow.

He listens. No footsteps pounding down the staircase behind him. They aren't chasing him. There were injuries: Harney took one in the forearm he wrapped around Trev while using him as a shield. The other one, the woman, was hit by Nicolas.

They're hurt and probably headed to the hospital. He has some time.

He drags his foot, shuffling forward. God, he can hardly move.

This wasn't supposed to be a problem. This was supposed to be a victory lap. Trev and Nicolas, they would carry him through this tunnel like a king after a successful ambush on Harney.

Instead, Trev and Nicolas are dead. And Harney isn't.

He was supposed to come alone.

Porter assured him that Harney would come alone.

Disco's fucked now—he knows it. The general, he doesn't make idle threats. No chance he'll let Disco live after this.

He has to put Chicago in his rearview mirror, right now, and disappear.

He must go on the run, with a severed toe that all but incapacitates him, with a boot full of blood, with pain so excruciating his eyes water, his jaw aches from clenching.

He has to get to his car. He has to get his money.

As he drags himself forward, firearm in one hand, he pulls out his burner phone, the face lighting up. Finds the caller ID for Porter. Dials it...

No cell reception underground.

He puts the phone in his pocket and keeps slogging forward.

CHAPTER 97

PORTER SITS inside the car, the police scanner squawking, staring at the burner phone in his hand.

Twenty-one minutes ago, Disco texted him, told him Harney was on his way into the building, just as they planned.

Twenty-one minutes. And no follow-up.

Nothing from Disco. Nothing from the scanner about an officer-involved shooting or the need for an ambulance.

He sends a text message to Disco. A single question mark.

Did Harney sniff out the ambush? Did he know he was being snookered?

It wouldn't surprise Porter. But it shouldn't matter. Harney was alone, and he was facing heavily armed men with special-ops training.

Edgy, anxious, he busies himself looking over the short dossier he has compiled on Harney, naming him as a dirty cop on the take, protecting human traffickers.

Compiled might be a generous word. Porter made the whole thing up. Pure fiction. But who will contradict it if Harney's dead or "disappears"?

And if Harney somehow survived, well, Porter has *that* covered, too. That's plan B.

Porter always has a plan B.

CHAPTER 98

I PUT the cherry on my dashboard and race to the hospital.

"Keep the pressure on it," I tell Sadie, in the back seat with Carla.

Carla's head is back against the seat cushion, eyes closed, grimacing like she's being tortured, as Sadie puts pressure on Carla's left shoulder wound.

"Who were they, Sadie?" I ask. "Those men who kept you?"

"Trev and Nicolas and Disco," she says, bracing herself in the back seat.

"Which ones are dead?"

"Trev was on floor. Nicolas was... up."

"So Disco got away? What's his name? Full name?"

"I do not know."

"Where does he live?"

"I do not know."

"They sent you to me. It was a setup."

"They sent me, yes. You... knew?"

Not for sure, I didn't. But it felt a little too easy. Either way, it didn't matter. Ambush or otherwise, I wanted to meet them.

We roll up to the drive of the ER. I pop out of the car, wave my star inside, get a gurney and medics to my car within seconds.

I put my hand on Carla's forehead as they place her on the gurney. "I'll be right here," I say.

"Go." She can hardly speak. "Do what you need to do."

They wheel her in, pop her through some doors, leave us behind in the main waiting area.

"You need to be looked at, too, Officer," says a nurse.

My bloody forearm. Hurts like hell. "Give me a minute."

I pull Sadie to the side, whisper in her ear. "When was the last time you scored?"

She shakes her head, denies it.

"Sadie, I'm not looking to jam you up. I'm here to help you. Do you believe me?"

She looks at me. I can imagine what's running through her mind. She's probably never been able to trust a man in her entire life.

She makes a decision. Same one she made by getting into my car.

"What's your real name?" I ask.

"Viviana."

"Viviana, when's the last time you scored?"

"Three hours ago. Is okay. Okay for a while."

For a while. And then she'll start jonesing. Her skin will start to crawl as she itches for another fix.

I dial my phone. "Sosh, are you sober?"

"Unfortunately, yes. I'm at my nephew's baseball game."

"I need a strike team. Tonight. I don't have time to explain. I need you to start mobilizing. I'll give you the details later."

I punch out the phone.

"Officer, we need to look at that arm."

"Fine. She's coming with me."

I take Viviana by the hand as they move me into a room behind a curtain. "You need to tell me everything," I say to her.

CHAPTER 99

THE DOCTOR looks at my forearm. Not a bad place to be shot, if you're gonna be shot. The bullet went clean through, so there's nerve damage—probably physical therapy and maybe surgery down the road. But I'm fine. The doc treats it to avoid an infection and dresses it.

Viviana—"Sadie"—talks to me while I hold her hand. She stutters through her broken English, her tears and sobs. She tells me the different ways the girls come here—they're abducted; they're lured away from orphanages under false pretenses; they're pulled off the street. They're all young girls who won't be missed—runaways or junkies who won't have families looking for them.

The beatings, the rapes, the men they're sold to, night after night, but mostly the drugs.

The drugs tie it all together. Oxycodone, it turns out, not heroin, taken in pill form, so these girls don't rake up their arms with needle marks. Once they're hooked, it's all that matters. They'll do anything for more. You don't need an armada of men to keep them captive in some hideaway. Shit, you probably don't even need to lock the door. You've got the only thing they want, the only thing they need, the only thing in the entire world they care about: the next fix. As long as you let them dress you up fancy, as long as you perform sex acts with some creep every night, those fixes will keep coming.

You think, after you've been a cop for a long time, that nothing can affect you anymore.

I call Sosh again. "How we doin', brother?"

"Getting a team together. Got an unmarked there now."

"Good. Wait for me if you can. Only if you can."

I punch out, hear a woman's voice.

"I'm a cop. And I'm his sister. You better step aside right now."

Patti, fighting her way through the medical staff to get to me. They try to stop her, they're gonna need medical attention, too.

She whips the curtain open and sizes me up, touches my arm, quickly looks me over, puts a hand on my face, studying me. "Just the arm?"

"Yeah, and it's fine."

"Yeah?"

"Yeah."

"Oh, thank Christ." She nods, takes a breath of relief, tears welling up.

I stand up, open my good arm. "C'mere."

She embraces me, dissolves into full-throttle sobbing.

"I'm sorry, Patti. I'm . . . sorry."

The doctor, his work done and not wanting to be a part of this emotional family reunion, holds up a scrip for me and mouths to me about a follow-up with my own doctor. I nod to him and thank him.

"I need your help," I tell Patti when she's finally calmed down. "Carla took one in the shoulder. I think she's fine. But that's two of us, two GSWs."

"Two mandatory reports," she says, wiping her face. "And you want me to be the responding officer."

"Yeah. We'll figure it out tomorrow. We'll get the paperwork cleaned up—"

"Fuck the paperwork and tell me what happened."

I give her the *Reader's Digest* version. The ambush. Two dead, one escaped, only known name is Disco. Sosh putting together a strike team right now.

"And if I told you that you're done for the night, Detective, that you have to go home and take it easy? No—that's what I thought," she says.

"Night's not over," I say. "Stay here with Viviana. We need a patrol officer to keep her here. She's gonna need detox, or in a few hours she's gonna be tearing her skin off."

"I'll make it happen. Where you going?"

I'm going to see Carla, if she can be seen.

Takes me a minute, but I find the trauma doc, an Indian woman named Siddiqui. "It's a clean through-and-through," she says. "We've controlled the bleeding. She won't need surgery."

"I need to see her."

"She'll be groggy. Might be asleep." The doctor leads me down a hall, pulls on the curtain.

Carla is upright on the bed, her head lolled to the right, eyes closed. Peaceful. A large bundle of gauze and tape on her shoulder, still the bandage on the side of her face, too. Beaten and battered. But no longer feeling pain.

She opens her eyes when I walk in. "Hey."

"You're gonna be fine, they say." I take her hand, squeeze it.

"You need to know," she says. "You need to be ready for him."

"Okay. You able to do it right now?"

She nods, faintly.

"Then go," I say. "We don't have time."

"You remember a skell named Trino DeJesus?"

"Trino," I say. "Ran meth in the south suburbs. The meth king. Worked outta Cal City."

She nods.

"Narcotics took him down about, what, three years ago?" I say. "Huge bust. Wiped out his whole operation."

Now I make the connection. She worked undercover in Narcotics.

"So you worked Trino's case," I say. "You were one of the UCs?"

She allows a smile to play on her face, only briefly. "I was *the* UC. I was Trino's girl."

"Whoa. You got next to Trino?"

"Yeah," she says, "and that's where it all went to shit."

CHAPTER 100

IT WAS an unexpected promotion. Carla was undercover as a junkie, cozying up to one of Trino's lieutenants, whatever scraps of information she could vacuum up. But then Trino, he sees her in a nightclub, takes a shine to her, decides that she belongs to him. Even kills the guy she was seeing, one of his own profitable lieutenants, to make sure her loyalty is undivided.

So all of a sudden, she's living with the guy running a twenty-million-dollar meth operation, about as deep as deep undercover gets.

The good news: she learns a lot.

The bad news: she's in role, and if you're playing a meth junkie, you score meth. That's old hat for a UC, buying the dope and dumping it, or transferring it to your handler for evidence. You don't actually take the shit. The department has rules.

There are rules, and there's reality. Especially when your boyfriend is supplying the meth, and he's the protective, jealous type who has eyes on you practically 24-7.

"I started scoring meth," she says. "I couldn't fake it. So next thing I know, the junkie I'm playing? I'm not playing anymore."

You hear about UCs working Narcotics ending up with addiction problems themselves. The department feigns sympathy, puts you in rehab, but that sticker goes on your file. You're damaged goods.

You get a brick on your career.

Doesn't matter you had to take the dope to keep your cover. Doesn't matter you got inside the operation, a tremendous coup for the department. Doesn't matter you risked your life every second of every minute of every day, smuggling information out to your people. Doesn't matter you're almost single-handedly responsible for taking down one of the most notorious drug empires in the last decade.

No—if people find out you're a junkie, you're radioactive on the job.

"So what did you do when it was over?" I ask. "After the bust?"

"I kept using, that's what I did. I was a cop with a drug habit. Didn't take long before I was caught. Got me on video, buying it and scoring it."

"The feds?"

"IAB," she says. "Denny Porter."

Porter. Don't know him. Heard the name, heard some bad things.

"He gave me two choices. Door number one, I go down. Maybe some time in prison, but either way, I lose my star, my pension, my benefits. But most of all..." She can't even finish the sentence.

"Most of all, Samuel," I say. "And door number two?" As if I don't know.

"He puts me to work. Be his eyes and ears. I gotta get well first, though. Three months of rehab, such as it was. Porter arranged it himself."

"Sweet of him."

"Right, but I'm no good to him with a rehab sticker on my file. So we call it cancer. I take a leave for chemotherapy, come back, and say I'm cured. Porter had a doctor who played ball, signed all the paperwork." She smirks. "All he really did was transfer my addiction from one thing to another."

Ah. Okay. "So those pills you take, they aren't ginger pills. There's no cancer or chemotherapy."

"No better liar in the world than an addict," she says. "But I'm clean of meth. I haven't scored since that rehab. Three years clean."

"Good. That's great."

"The pills are dextroamphetamine."

"Dex," I say. Speed. Uppers. Makes sense. You can get addicted, but you're far more functional than a meth head would ever be.

"Porter's my supplier. Even makes them *look* like ginger pills. Probably uses the same doctor who did the bullshit paperwork. He must have something on that guy."

"They help, those pills?"

"They help with the cravings, yeah," she says.

"You still have cravings for meth?"

She almost laughs. "Harney," she says, "I crave meth every waking hour of every day. Only now I crave dex, too."

"Jesus, kid. Jesus, I'm sorry."

"No, *I'm* the one who's sorry." She breaks eye contact, blinks away the tears. "Porter's had his eye on you. He's been real concerned about your interest in Evie. I was feeding him updates. I didn't think much of it. I mean, the K-Town shooting was a turf war, right? Evie, she was just collateral damage. That's what I thought, at least. Until that video from Latham Jackson."

The video that made it pretty damn clear that the shooters had nothing to do with warring street gangs.

"So I went to Porter and called bullshit. I said now it looked like K-Town was all about the dead girl, not a drug war."

"And I bet he had an answer," I say. "Let me guess. I was a corrupt cop."

"Fronting for a rival sex-trafficking ring," she says. "He says he's this close to busting you and I should steer far away from it. Told me to call in sick. Gave me some money and sent me to a water park in Wisconsin for a long weekend. He said it would all be over by then."

"But you didn't go."

"I pretended to. I drove my mother-in-law and Samuel to Rockford, put them up in a hotel for a few days until I could figure this out." She lifts her good shoulder. "I didn't trust Porter. And I trusted you."

And she saved my ass. I'm dead on that gymnasium floor if not for her.

But she fucked herself. She just betrayed Porter. There's no walking that back.

"Then we have to take down Porter," I say.

She makes a face. "Seems so, yeah."

"You don't sound too happy about that."

"You don't get it, Harney," she says. "Porter goes down, I lose everything."

CHAPTER 101

"PORTER HAS me by the short hairs," Carla says. "We pinch him, he'll give me up without thinking twice. Probably a lot of people, to get leniency. But me included. He drops that video, I'm toast."

"He's got you on video taking meth one time three years ago? C'mon, Carla, that's not a great thing, but it's not the end of the—"

"No, Harney, you're not thinking it through. Number one, the moment Porter fingers me, they make me do a urine drop. And now I don't have Porter protecting me with a fake piss result. I'm positive for dex. So there'll be a video of me smoking meth *and* a positive, *current* drug test for amphetamines. And there were at least a couple times over the years when Porter had someone else deliver me the dex, not him. Some skell who must have been in his pocket. I'll give you ten to one he recorded those handoffs, too. He's got those videos tucked away along with the one of me smoking meth."

Her head falls back on the pillow. Her secrets, her shame, laid bare. But more important than that, her fear of the consequences.

"The story will be I've been a junkie all along. For years. Oh, he'll have some story cooked up that paints him as the hero, how he's been running a larger investigation into drug use by cops or something. He'll fuck me and cover himself. He plays a long game, believe me. He's gamed this whole thing out."

"We'll think of something. You might come out of this okay."

"Harney." She says it like, once again, I'm missing something. "It's not me I'm worried about."

Samuel, she means, the reason for the fresh tears forming in her eyes.

"Even if you do a stretch," I say, "your mother-in-law can take care of Sam—"

"My mother-in-law's illegal," she says. "They pinch me, DCFS takes a look, they see an undocumented immigrant as his caregiver. She gets deported. His father sure as hell won't take him. Samuel goes into the system. He goes into a home."

Shit. She's probably right about that.

"And don't think I haven't thought of putting that asshole Porter in the ground," she says. "I would. For Samuel, I would. But Porter's too smart for that. He's told me, more than once, he has an IAB file on me with a copy of that video. Anything happens to him, the next guy up in IAB will just have to pop a disk into a computer and see Detective Carla Griffin, in all her glory, smoking meth in an alley and scoring dex from some gangbanger. Then it's a mandatory urine drop, and I'm done." Her eyes close. "I'm fucked. I am."

I touch her leg. "Are you telling me to lay off Porter? Try to get this done without touching him?"

She tries to smile. "I think we've passed that point, Detective. I think I passed it when I didn't go to Wisconsin."

"Then why tell me about Porter at all?"

"Because you need to know," she says. "You're going after those traffickers, you're going after Porter, too. You can't go in there with one eye closed."

I drop down in a chair, the magnitude of what she's done settling in on me. Carla could've taken the easy road. She could've done what Porter asked, headed up to Wisconsin, buried her head in the sand, and kept the status quo.

She risked everything to come back here and save me.

"I won't let anything happen to Samuel," I say. "That's a promise."

"Oh, c'mon, Harney—"

I take her hand. "That's a promise."

She gives me a look that only a mother could give, full of love, full of fear and concern for her son, fierce and protective and vulnerable all at once. "Don't say something like that if you—"

"Look at me." I bring my face close to hers. "Anything happens to you, I'll take care of him."

She searches my eyes. "You'd...I can't ask you to do that," she whispers.

"You didn't ask."

"You...hardly even know me."

"I know enough. I know what you put on the line for me." I squeeze her hand. "We're in this together, partner. Okay? Besides, who else is gonna teach that kid to throw a curveball?"

I've seen plenty of women cry over the years, but never like Carla does now, relief and emotion releasing like an avalanche.

When I reach the waiting room, Patti's there. "Viviana's with a patrol officer. They're treating her."

"Thanks."

"I'm going with you," she says.

I start to shake my head, think better of it.

"We do it my way, Patti. Or go home right now."

She nods. "We do it your way," she says.

CHAPTER 102

PATTI DRIVES; I'm the passenger. We race across town.

I grab my phone to dial Sosh and see a voice mail from half an hour ago; I must have missed it while getting stitched up. The message is from Jay Herlihy, Cook County Corrections.

"J Crew," I tell Patti.

"The asshole who punched me in second grade?"

"Yeah, and he's really sorry. Shut up and listen." I play the message on speakerphone.

"Hey, bro, those tickets better be center ice. I couldn't access it externally, so I drove over to Division 9 after my shift. Anyway, you're right, my friend—your guy Antoine Stonewald had one visitor during that week. It was a lawyer—you're gonna love this—V-a-s-y-l first name, last name D-i-s-c-o-v-e-t-s-k-y. Got an address and phone, too.

"Vasyl Discovetsky is his name, player."

I write down the phone and address.

"Want me to head there?" Patti asks.

"No. Go where we're going. It's more important."

"More important than finding Disco?"

I look at her. "Yeah," I say. "More important than finding Disco."

I search my phone for the number for Clara Foster.

"Special Agent Foster," I say when she answers. "Billy Harney, Chicago PD. Remember the girl in K-Town? Well, I hope you didn't have plans tonight, because I'm about to ruin your evening."

CHAPTER 103

DISCO REACHES the end of the labyrinthine tunnel system and shoves through the flimsy push door into the final building, at the other end of the industrial park. The trip felt like an endless journey. Three times, he dropped to the floor out of sheer agony, propping up his foot to relieve the pressure and the excruciating pain.

Took over an hour and hurt like hell, but it gave him some time to think.

A lot of time to think.

He hops up the short staircase on one foot and reaches ground level. Looks at his phone, which has some cell reception again.

A single text message pops up, from Porter. A single question mark.

He removes his night-vision goggles and props the exit door open, welcoming fresh air into his lungs. Looks out over the small parking area.

All clear. Weapon still out, he hobbles to his car, starts it up, filled with relief that he's done moving on foot and that he can get distance between him and this industrial park.

He has to find some way to get a new dressing on his foot, stop the bleeding.

And get his money. Most of all, the money.

He sends a text message to Porter:

We have to meet now

The reply comes back before he can take a breath. Porter's been eagerly awaiting Disco's update, apparently. Success? Fail?

Disco responds.

Shit, he writes, then hits Send.

Abort, he writes, and hits Send.

Meet now, he writes. Same place. He hits Send.

The reply comes quickly.

We can still fix this, Porter tells him. I have a plan.

You better, Disco writes back. He puts the car in gear and starts driving.

CHAPTER 104

THE BUILDING is on Rockwell, south of 26th Street. Large, two stories, wooden frame, red paint on the front.

The alley to the side of the building is wide enough for a car, with maybe ten feet to spare. I've seen this alley before.

I saw it in the photos Valerie took and clipped inside Antoine Stonewald's file a few days before she died.

A black Lincoln Town Car pulls past the building and stops, backs into the alley, and aligns itself alongside a door on the side of the building. A tall guy, dressed in black, opens the back door of the vehicle.

On cue, the building's alley door opens, and a young woman, in a long dress and heels, hair done up high, steps out of the door and into the Town Car.

Just like in Valerie's photos.

"Crime in progress," I say into my collar. "Let's do it. Go! That's a go!"

A screech of tires, and an unmarked vehicle bounds into the alley, cherry lit up on the dashboard, nose to nose with the town car, before the chauffeur's even back in the driver's seat. Patti pulls our car up from the rear, pinning in the town car.

Officers will be kicking in the front door of the building right now, others taking the rear entrance by force. I'm the first one to the alley door.

I rush in—"Chicago police!"—and see an older woman, matronly, bright red hair, trying to get away in her flip-flops. I grab her by her shirt and force her down.

"Any men in here?" I shout. "Any men?"

"No, no men."

"You sure? Anybody gets shot, you take the blame, lady."

"No men."

"What about Disco? Disco here?"

"No. No!"

Officers, plainclothes detectives from the Tenth, rushing in. "Take her," I tell one of the patrols. "Cuff her and put her in a chair."

I race downstairs. There's an upstairs, but I'm thinking downstairs.

"Chicago police!" I run down padded stairs into a basement. Turn with my weapon up.

A dim, filthy space reeking of body odor and urine and vomit. A mop and pail of dirty water in the corner. Sleeping cots lining the other half of the basement.

Dozens of pairs of eyes staring up at me. Twenty, maybe thirty young girls, some in their early teens at best. Dressed in rags. Sitting on a stained, broken concrete floor or lying on battered couches, the foam stuffing sticking through the cheap fabric. A few girls in a circle on the floor with a deck of cards. Some huddled around an old television watching a show about animals. Several clutching beaten old teddy bears or scuzzy blankets.

One girl, who couldn't yet be a teenager, sitting in the corner, staring at me through stringy, unwashed hair and sucking her thumb.

They sleep down here. They live down here. When they're not cleaned and prettied up to perform sex acts for strangers, they live down here in a dirty, disgusting cave like animals.

"Chicago police!" I say. "Everyone get down." I pantomime the motion, assuming many of them can't understand me. "Down. Down on floor."

I don't want any cops getting the wrong idea, amped up as they are, coming down the stairs.

The girls get down, lie flat. They don't understand yet, but they understand doing what a man tells them to do. They've been doing that their whole lives.

I catch a few glimpses. Tattoos of black lilies on each girl's ankle.

"Hold your fire; hold your fire," I say to the officers pouring down the stairs. "They're not a threat. They're just . . ."

My throat chokes on that sentence.

They're just children.

I open my phone, which is already linked to an online English-to-Romanian translator. I do my best to repeat the words. Some of them are trying to understand me, but I'm probably botching it.

The translator has an audio component, so I turn up the volume and play it, let the robot voice pronounce the Romanian words better than I ever could.

Nu ai probleme. Sunteți victime. Oamenii ăștia nu te vor mai răni. Suntem aici să te ajutăm să ajungi acasă.

You are not in trouble. You are victims. These men will not hurt you anymore. We are here to help you get home.

I play it once, twice, a third time.

Several of them understand and start talking to the others, rapid bursts of words I couldn't possibly understand. Before long, the news seems to spread across the room in a few languages. The girls are hugging each other, crying, some of them even smiling.

"We . . . go home?" one of the girls says to me.

"Yes," I say, squatting down. "We will help you."

A detective starts collecting the girls, any semblance of a threat now gone. They line up, not for the first time in their lives, but probably for the first time willingly and happily.

"Take them to SOS and call Protective Services," I say. "These girls are gonna need detox, too."

I watch the girls file up the stairs, most of them underage by several years, dressed in ripped, ill-fitting clothes, dirty and sick and abused beyond comprehension.

Sometimes there are no words.

But I have a few more. Not for the cops or for the girls. They're only for one person, one person who isn't here.

This is what you were trying to stop.

We finally did. Thanks to you.

CHAPTER 105

THE MATRONLY woman with the fiery red hair and chubby face is apparently named Augustina, last name currently unknown.

She's the only one in the house. The upstairs was clear. Vanities covered with makeup, closets full of fancy dresses and kinky costumes, even a tanning bed in one of the rooms.

"You're under arrest," I tell her, "for running a house of prostitution. Probably kidnapping, rape, and a lot of other things, too. We could be here all night just listing the charges."

Her chin up, defiant. "I want lawyer." The thick accent.

"I know a good one," I say. "His name is Vasyl Discovetsky. Ring a bell?"

That stops her a moment, but she won't say so.

"You know Disco, do you?"

"I do not know that person."

"What about Trev? What about Nicolas? You know those boys?"

"No," she whips out. Cuffed to a chair, caught dead to rights, but still fighting.

"Trev and Nicolas are dead," I say.

Her expression breaks, but I'm not getting anywhere using those names. Disco runs the show, Viviana told me.

"Disco's on the run," I say. "Though last time I saw him, he was limping more than running."

She looks at me. That bought me something with her; that detail gives me some cred. Still, she won't budge.

"You don't seem nervous, Augustina. But you know who is?" I lean up close. "General Boholyubov."

I pull back. She doesn't look quite as hard, quite as collected.

"Boho must be getting really nervous right now. Nervous enough to make sure nobody talks. That's what you're thinking right now, isn't it? You keep your mouth shut, maybe you do some time, maybe you get deported back to wherever you're from. But ask yourself, Augustina: Is he really gonna let you live? I'm thinking no way."

"We can help with that," says Clara Foster. She shows her badge. "FBI, Augustina. I'm working on a joint federal and county task force to combat sex trafficking. Tonight was a big break for us"—she nods to me in thanks—"but we want to stop this thing at its source. We want General Boholyubov.

"You tell us what you know, we put you in WITSEC. Witness protection. You get a new identity and a new life. If"—she wags a finger—"*if* you can help us take down the general. You help us break up this sex-trafficking ring, you get your life back. You sit there like your mouth doesn't work, we throw you into the system, and the general takes care of you sooner or later."

"Still want that lawyer, Augustina?" I ask. "Or do you wanna tell us where Disco is and have a chance to stay out of prison and live a normal life?"

"You have one minute to make a decision," says Agent Foster. "Make a smart one."

Augustina looks back and forth between us, doing the math in her head, the pros and cons. "I do not know where he is," she says. "He is afraid. Afraid of the general. He will... he will run."

"Run where?"

"I do not know where he will run."

I give that a moment. It's her instinct to clam up, but how far her loyalty to Disco goes is something I can't know.

"Disco's in a world of shit right now," I remind her. "Everything's crashing around him. Your operation here is down the toilet. And yet he didn't reach out to you, did he? Didn't warn you. Didn't call or text you. Didn't say 'Run, Augustina, get the hell out, the cops are coming.' Nothing like that."

I hold up her cell phone, which I've already reviewed—no recent communications from Disco or any unidentified caller.

"Why not?" I ask. "I'll tell you why not. Because he doesn't care about you. He doesn't give one shit about you."

She breaks eye contact. Hard words to hear, but she can't argue with the logic.

I bend over, hands on my knees, so we are eye to eye.

"So, Augustina," I say, "why are you protecting *him*?"

CHAPTER 106

DISCO DRIVES toward the house on Mayfield Avenue, on the southwest side of town, slowing as he gets within a block, listening for sirens, looking up at the dark sky for any illuminations or flashing colors. Nothing. Nothing but dark sky.

He passes Mayfield Avenue, where he'd normally turn, and instead turns into the alley on the next block over. He kills the lights, rolls the car forward, and stops.

Limps between two houses on the opposite side of Mayfield, peeks out to his left, to the house where he keeps his money. A small A-frame bungalow with a detached garage.

The front porch light is off.

The light over the garage is off.

The house is completely dark.

Disco limps back to his car, lights still off, backs out of the alley. He once again passes Mayfield, this time to the east, and turns down that alley.

Again, no sign of police.

He kills the lights, gets out of the car. Puts on his night-vision goggles again. Checks again that the suppressor is securely attached to his handgun.

Limps toward the middle of the alley, toward the back of his stash house. Stops when he reaches it. Turns and looks.

The small backyard of the house. The detached garage. Empty.

He listens. No sounds, at least nothing out of the ordinary. A plane passes low overhead on its way to Midway airport. He uses the cover of that sound to inch forward along the side of the garage, everything lit up in fluorescent green.

Sweat dripping inside his goggles. His foot screaming at him again, intense pain, but he can't let it affect him now.

He reaches the edge of the garage, seeing the concrete driveway where he'd normally park his car before getting out to open the locked garage door.

But there's no car there, obviously, because he came around the back way on foot.

Nothing but a dark driveway.

And a man crouched down among the bushes on the other side, gun in his right hand, flashlight in the left. A cop.

A cop who didn't consider that Disco might have night vision.

Disco takes a breath, readies himself, and steps into the clearing. He fires twice, *thwip-thwip* with the suppressor, aiming for the upper right torso.

Dennis Porter yelps in pain and falls backward. Little chance he could still hold the gun with two gunshot wounds to the right shoulder, but Disco takes no chances, moving as quickly as his bum foot will allow, shooting Porter in the left foot, then the right foot, *thwip-thwip,* to occupy him while Disco closes the distance.

Porter cries out in pain again as Disco reaches him.

The gun is clear of Porter's hand.

"Wait, wait... wait... we can figure this out."

Disco falls to his knees, grateful to relieve the stress on his foot, and puts the muzzle of the gun against Porter's cheek.

"Tying up loose ends?" he asks. "Was this the idea, Denny? I pull up in my car and you ambush me? This was your plan?"

"No, no, that wasn't—"

Disco leans forward. "That garage light is never off, Denny. If you hadn't unscrewed it, *then* you might have surprised me."

"Listen to me, lis—"

Disco sticks the gun in Porter's mouth to shut him up. "I don't have time, Denny. I have to leave. I don't want to kill you. It would make no sense. It does not help me. But I need to know. Does Harney know my name yet?"

Porter shakes his head.

"Did you tell him about the ambush, Denny? Did he know we were waiting for him?"

He shakes his head again.

"No? He brought someone along. A woman. Did you not assure me that Harney would be coming alone?"

Porter tries to talk, which isn't easy to do with the gun's suppressor in his mouth. So Disco pulls back the weapon.

"I don't know. His sister, maybe. His partner left town."

Hard to know if he can believe him. Doesn't really matter at this point.

"I'm the only one... can help you outta this," Porter says, two clean holes in his shoulder, just outside the bulletproof vest, his sweaty face balled up in pain and desperation. "I can misdirect everything. Keep them off your scent. Keep them off *mine,* too. Please, just—*please* let me do that."

Disco puts the gun back in Porter's mouth.

"Denny, I'm going to leave now. For good. But someday, my friend, when it's safe, I'm going to come back here. I'm going to find your family. Your wife, your daughter, your son."

Porter shakes his head, tries to scream, gags as Disco shoves the gun further still into his mouth.

"Your wife, she'll beg me to spare the children. She will do anything I ask. And I will ask, Denny. I am going to violate her every way a man can violate a woman. And when I am done, when my cock is so sore I cannot possibly penetrate her again, she is going to watch while I set your children on fire."

Porter tries to lunge forward, but there's nothing he can do but make begging sounds.

"And I will tell your children, while I am raping their mother, that all this is because of their father, Captain Dennis Porter."

He leans forward, so close he's almost nose to nose.

"Their *late* father," he says.

He pulls the trigger.

CHAPTER 107

DISCO LEAVES Porter dead in the bushes. This house isn't registered in Disco's name. Disco has no connection to it.

He limps over to the garage door, grateful now that Porter went to the trouble to unscrew the light above the garage. Better to do this in darkness, so nobody can see him but, with his night vision, he can see everyone.

He punches the code on the garage's keypad, unlocking the door and disabling the alarm. He lifts the door and enters the garage, grabs the ladder off a hook on the wall, and places it in the center of the floor.

He climbs up to the ceiling, hard as it is with his bad foot, unlocks the bolt, and pulls down the door. Reaches up and feels for the gym bag, pulls it closer.

Inside the bag, a fake passport, baseball cap and glasses, a travel set of toiletries. And thirty thousand in cash.

He climbs down, doesn't bother moving the ladder. The bag in one hand, his handgun in the other.

His phone buzzes in his pocket. Not his normal one—his burner. A text message.

He hikes the gym bag over his shoulder. Porter's dead. Nicolas and Trev, too. There's only one other person who has the number for this burner.

He pulls out his phone, the screen lighting up in the darkness, normally a yellow color but through his night-vision goggles, the color is grassy green.

You haven't checked in, Augustina writes. Is everything ok?

Disco takes a moment, staring at the message. What are the odds, he wonders, that the police have already made it as far as the house on Rockwell where they keep the girls, and thus to Augustina? What are the chances that the police, not Augustina, are sending this message?

No reason not to be cautious, he decides. Be vague and, more important still, give a fake location. His law office, sure, on the other side of the city.

Leave right now and meet me at law office, he writes. I will be there in about twenty min

That's all he types before he hears the squeal of tires, the roar of an engine.

The phone falls from his hands as an SUV turns and bounces into the driveway, headlights on. Headlights changing to high-beam brights.

Blinding him with his night-vision goggles. He fires anyway, shooting in the direction of the vehicle, *thwip-thwip-thwip* and *thunk-thunk* of hitting metal, the splintering of glass, as the vehicle screeches to a halt on the driveway.

CHAPTER 108

I CREEP between two houses and look across the street. The house is dark. No car in the driveway. But the garage door is open. I can't see in. Is there someone in there? Maybe a ladder? Too hard to tell. Too dark.

So I shield Augustina's phone with my hand to cover the light while I type out the text message. You haven't checked in. Is everything ok?

I hit Send. Drop her phone in my pocket. Ready my Glock. Get into a sprinter's position, ready to pounce.

A small square of light appears in the garage, illuminating a man. Disco, limping forward in the garage, reading my text message from Augustina's phone. Goggles covering his eyes.

"It's him," I say into my phone to Patti, who has crawled her SUV toward the house but still kept a half-block distance. "He's got night vision, so use the brights."

It's not quite the flashbang I used at the industrial park, but it should help once again to turn his advantage into a disadvantage.

"Go!" I tell her.

I run between the houses and across the street, Patti's vehicle beating me by only a second.

Her Jeep bounces onto the driveway, lighting up the garage, the high beams blinding Disco, but he fires indiscriminately, bullets hitting the Jeep, metal and glass, forcing me to drop low as the Jeep screeches to a halt.

"You okay?" I shout as Patti's door opens.

"Yeah, yeah."

Disco's already disappeared around the corner of the garage, into what I assume is the backyard. We had no time to stake this place out—we just got here five minutes ago, after Augustina told us this is where he'd come—so I have no idea what's awaiting us back there.

His goggles will adjust any second now, and he'll have the advantage again in the darkness.

I run double-fisted, my Maglite at chin level to shine a path forward, my Glock in the other hand.

I turn the corner, and I can see instantly that he's hobbled, that he can't run well. He's still well within my sight, moving down the concrete pathway toward the alley.

"Chicago police, Disco!"

Still with his back turned, he swings his arm back, an expert move, shooting behind him. I feel a bullet whiz past me as I shoot, by instinct, even though I want him alive, aiming low to the extent I'm aiming much at all.

Patti grunts and falls behind me, a thump in the grass.

I stop, shine the light on her. "Are you hit?"

"I'm okay, the vest," she says. I shine the light on the bullet, square in the chest, stopped by the vest. A nasty bruise will be the worst she gets.

I shine the light forward again. Disco's disappeared once more, but a smear of blood paints the side of the garage where he turned into the alley. I must have hit him.

I race to that blood smear, to that corner, cautiously in case he pops back around and fires. I reach the corner, stop, crouch down, and peek around the corner.

A bullet blasts the wood above me, right where my head was supposed to be. This guy can shoot. But he can't run. He's limping toward a car, but he won't get there.

I shoot again and hit him again, this time in the right shoulder blade. The alley lights are enough for me to see that he has two wounds now, one close to the left kidney, the other in the right shoulder blade.

Already hobbled, now with two gunshot wounds, he can't make it much longer. I'm surprised he's still upright.

But he's got nowhere to go.

"You're done, Disco!" I shout. "You know it. Drop the gun or I drop you!"

Which in his world might be preferable to being caught.

He keeps moving forward, nothing more than an awkward shuffle, but still firing his weapon behind him, a bullet ricocheting off the pavement, another splintering the wood of the garage.

I stay low, size him up, and put one in his left calf.

He crumples to the ground. His gun bounces out of his grip. His hand scrabbles for the weapon, but he's not going to reach it. Not before I reach him.

I raise a hand as I hear Patti coming around the corner, loaded and ready.

"He's down," I tell her.

"He's not dead."

"I know. I got him. There was a body back there by the driveway," I say. "In the bushes. Check it out. And call in a 10-52."

"You sure you wanna do that?" she asks.

I look at her. She's got one eye on Disco, as do I, but he isn't going anywhere.

"My way, right?" I say.

She nods. "Your way."

"Then do it," I say. "And hurry back. I need you as a witness."

She rushes through the backyard toward the driveway.

I walk over to Disco, who can't move laterally but has managed to roll himself over. I keep a close eye on him, making sure he doesn't have another weapon.

He doesn't. He's done.

"I need... ambulance," he says.

"You do," I agree. "No question about it."

The shoulder wound is survivable. The other bullet probably hit a kidney. So he probably doesn't have a great deal of time.

And he probably knows that.

His breathing growing shallower now. I reach down and remove the night-vision goggles off his face, toss them. "Who's the guy in the bushes?" I ask. "Porter?"

He closes his eyes, nods faintly. He grimaces, tries to adjust himself, but can't prop himself up anymore. His head falls back against the pavement of the alley.

Patti comes jogging around the corner. "He's dead. It's Dennis Porter."

I look at Disco, nudge him with my foot.

"Okay, Disco, it's just us now," I say. "Let's see if you get that ambulance."

CHAPTER 109

"YOU HAVE a chance to live," I tell Disco. "You have a chance to get a deal that will give you witness protection if you help us catch the general. But none of that happens—I don't even call that ambulance—until you give me some answers."

He stares at me, fading. He's out of options. And his fear of self-incrimination can't be that high. He knows Augustina flipped on him. He must realize we already have him on any number of state and federal human-trafficking charges, not to mention attempted murder charges, that will put him away for decades. He'll never see daylight again. Admitting to one more crime isn't gonna make a difference.

The only question is his will to live. Some people in his position would rather bleed out, end it right there, than suffer the penal consequences.

"Ask him, Billy," Patti whispers. "C'mon, there's no time."

I turn on my handheld recorder. "Vasyl Discovetsky, do you know a man named Nathan Stofer?"

"Nathan Stofer?" Patti says. "*That's* your question?"

I glare at her. "My way," I remind her. "My call."

Disco coughs, sputtering.

"Disco, how do you know Nathan Stofer?"

His head lolls to the side. "I... killed that man."

"How?" I ask. "Where? Why?"

"I shot him . . . in parking garage downtown."

"Why?"

"The general . . ."

"Give me his name."

"I need . . . ambul—"

"Tell me the general's name!"

"General . . . Kostyantin . . . Boholyubov."

"What about him?"

"This man Sto—Stofer . . . was stopping the general from being in . . . business deal. The . . . Stratton hotel."

"And what did the general do about that?"

"He . . . told me . . . to kill him."

"And you did?"

He nods.

I nudge his shoulder. "Give a verbal answer for the recording device."

"Yes," says Disco, "I did."

"Billy, what are you doing?" Patti says. "We don't have *time*."

"Do you know why Antoine Stonewald pleaded guilty to Nathan Stofer's murder?" I ask.

Disco nods. "I threatened . . . his family . . . if he did not."

"Did Antoine Stonewald have anything to do with Nathan Stofer's murder?"

"No."

I turn off the recorder.

Just as the faint sounds of an ambulance's siren grow louder, having responded to Patti's call for a 10-52—an ambulance.

Disco hears it, trains his fading eyes on me. "You . . . already called . . . ambulance." His words a bare whisper. A small smile crosses his face, as if he admires the deception, one bullshitter conning another.

"Did you kill Val?" Patti shouts at Disco. "Did you kill Billy's wife?"

She kicks his foot, some boot he's wearing. Disco faintly grimaces and shuts his eyes. He may not make it to the ambulance.

As he lies on his back, the blood follows the path of gravity back through the entrance wound by his kidney, forming a pool beneath him.

"Did you kill Billy's wife?" Patti shouts again.

The paramedics rush through the backyard and get to work on Disco. Patti and I back up and let them do their work.

"You didn't ask him," she says, half question, half accusation.

"Ran out of time," I say. "I went in order of importance."

"Order of *importance*? Suddenly something's more important than knowing how Val died?"

"As a matter of fact, yes," I say.

Because I can't bring Valerie back. But I can save Antoine, precisely the thing Valerie was trying to do before she died.

It's what she would have wanted.

This audio recording, with both Patti and me as witnesses, will exonerate Antoine Stonewald. And help take down General Boholyubov, if he hasn't escaped to some country without an extradition treaty. Valerie wanted to free Antoine, save these girls, and punish the traffickers. It took me four years, but I finally completed her mission.

"You said you were gonna kill him." She flips a hand. "Instead, you get him medical care."

"Right."

Patti gives me a sidelong glance. "I suppose you're gonna say Val would've wanted that, too."

That's exactly right. But suddenly I can't speak, too choked up with emotion. Patti, using her twin superpower detector, finally gets it, pulls me into a hug.

"She was a better person than I am," I whisper. "She was stronger than me. God, I miss her so much."

I say those words without tears, feeling some strength in a newfound connection with Valerie. Regret, no doubt, that I didn't do more to understand what she was going through at the time. But cognizant enough, objective enough with the benefit of hindsight, to cut myself a little slack, too—I was focused on our beautiful little Janey.

Both of us, in our different ways, were doing the best we could.

That's gonna have to be enough.

The paramedics working behind us lift Disco onto a gurney and rush off with him. Maybe they can save him. I don't love his chances.

"Maybe he pulls through," says Patti. "And maybe he'll tell you the truth."

"That's a lot of maybes," I say. "In the meantime, we have work to do. We have to see about all those girls, make sure they're getting treatment and help them find their way home. Plus," I add, "tomorrow we go see Antoine in prison and deliver him the good news."

Patti raises her eyebrows, makes a face. "After all this, you didn't even ask him the question."

I watch the ambulance pull away. Police squadrols pulling up, too. This sleepy little corner of the city is about to turn into a circus.

"I didn't need to ask him," I say. "I already know what happened to Valerie."

CHAPTER 110

THE PRISON just came off lockdown today, apparently, so most inmate visits had been canceled. But when I told them it was official police business, not just some social call, they allowed me a visit.

Patti's with me, sitting in the private interview room, her legs bobbing up and down nervously.

Neither of us has slept. It was a long night. Every one of the girls we rescued from that basement—official count of thirty-two—is addicted to Oxy, so Social Services has been working overtime, literally, to try to locate any next of kin while making sure they're going through detox.

The truth is that the path forward for these girls will be rough. Some may never overcome their addictions, not to mention their years of sexual abuse. And many of them may not have any family to which they can return.

All we could do is give them a chance.

The questions last night came from every which way as the department tried to sort out this mess. Principal among them is why a decorated police captain such as Dennis Porter was found dead next to a house linked to a human trafficker, and why the two of them seemed to have so much to say to each other over burner cell phones.

They can't ask Porter that question, obviously. And it remains in doubt whether Disco will ever answer that question. He's still in a coma following surgery.

There's gonna be a lot to talk about today at SOS—not to mention headquarters, at 35th and Michigan. But for now, we're here in the prison for me to deliver some news.

The door opens. His leg irons drag along the floor. He stops when he first sees me, then Patti. He takes his seat as the guard locks his wrist shackles to the table.

"So you didn't get yourself killed after all," my father says to me.

It's the first time I've seen Pop since he was hauled off to prison. He looks like a shrunken version of himself, weak and tired, pale and weathered.

His eyes travel to my lap, to the book resting there.

"I came here to thank you," I say.

CHAPTER 111

MY FATHER being who he is, the circumstances being what they are, Daniel Collins Harney is unsure how to respond. "Thank me," he says.

"I want to thank you for covering up what happened to Valerie. You were concerned that the authorities might think it was a homicide, so you steered it toward a suicide finding. Called in a favor with the medical examiner, right? He was suspicious, but you leaned on him to call it suicide."

Pop looks at Patti, realizes she gave up that info to me.

"You were the chief of detectives, after all," I say. "You could control as much as you wanted. So you basically hijacked the whole investigation and drove it to only one conclusion."

Pop gives me a sidelong glance. "We wanted to protect you," he says.

"*Patti* wanted to protect me. *Patti* did. You had someone else's protection in mind, didn't you, Pop?"

He folds his arms. "I don't know what you've cooked up about me, son, but whatever it is—"

"Personally," I continue, "I feel kinda stupid for not giving it more thought myself. I mean, really, how *did* that gun safe get opened? But, in my shoes, it never remotely occurred to me that someone murdered Valerie. Never once. I walked in and found her dead, holding my gun in her hand. After everything we'd been going through, and her depression, it wasn't exactly a huge stretch to believe the wound was self-inflicted, was it? So I never doubted suicide as the cause of death. Which meant I must have left that gun safe open, right?"

"Right," he says.

"Sure," I say. "At the time, it was the only reasonable conclusion. At the time."

A little tic plays at the corner of Pop's mouth, a trait he always had. Maybe a tell, if I was reading him, and I've read a lot of people in my time, but never my father. My father wasn't someone I read. He was just my father.

"No matter how strung out I was back then, keeping vigil at the hospital," I say, "I never would've left my depressed wife alone in our house with a fucking handgun. Someone got into that safe. Someone who knew that combination. And only three people in the world knew it, because we all had the same one—Mom's birthday. Ten twelve forty-nine."

Pop shakes his head.

"I didn't give it up, and Patti didn't give it up. That leaves you, Pop."

"No," he says.

"Don't worry—I'm not looking to bust you. You're spending the rest of your life in prison as it is. You're never getting out. I'm not wasting my time on you. You're not worth it to me. I just wanted you to know that I know. And I wanted to see if you're man enough to admit it."

Balled into a shell now, eyes downcast, face reddening, my father looks up at me. "You don't know anything."

"Tell you what, Pop. Let's make it easy. Invoke your right to counsel."

"What?"

"Go ahead, invoke. Say you want a lawyer. Then anything you say to me afterward is a violation of your rights, inadmissible in a court of law."

"Billy—"

"Invoke, Pop. Protect yourself. I'm not gonna bust you. I just want to hear you admit it."

"This is ridiculous," he says. "If this is all you—"

"Look what I found when we were cleaning up the house, getting ready to put it on the market." I pick up the book from my lap, the red ledger the feds never found, where Pop kept a list of the criminals he was protecting and how current they were on their payoffs.

"I've never seen that before in my life," he says.

"Course not," I say. "Someone *else* must have stuck it behind the water heater in the basement, tucked into that little slot where I used to keep my *Playboy*."

He works his jaw, fuming.

"Parsing through these cryptic references to clients," I say, "I couldn't help but notice one in particular." I flip to the page I've dog-eared, including this entry:

- S2607R—V Disc—300

"I couldn't help but notice," I say, "that Vasyl Discovetsky ran a prostitution house located at 2607 Rockwell. And I'm guessing this says he paid you three hundred dollars a month for protection. Or was it three hundred dollars a week?"

"This conversation is over."

"Speaking of conversations," I continue, "I had a nice one with Mr. Discovetsky last night, after I caught him."

Pop closes his eyes.

"Disco says he killed Valerie. And you gave him the combination to the safe, so he could use my gun and make the whole thing look like a suicide."

A lie, of course, that last part. Disco's still in a coma. So sue me.

"How could you do that, Daddy?" Patti's voice trembles. She gets to her feet. "You had Val... *killed*."

Pop's expression breaks at Patti's plea. He always had a soft spot for her, his princess.

We're doing a version of good cop, bad cop, even if Patti doesn't realize it.

"Honey, no, it wasn't like that," says Pop.

"Then what *was* it like?" I ask.

Pop, cornered, breaks eye contact. Runs a hand over his thinning, snowy hair, the shackles clanging on the table. He takes a deep breath, blows out.

"I want a lawyer," he says.

As always: more worried about himself than anyone else.

I get to my feet. "That's enough," I say. "That's all I wanted to hear. I don't want to hear your excuses."

"Son—"

"I'm not your son anymore. You're nothing to me. Live with that."

I push through the door. I don't look back.

CHAPTER 112

"DETECTIVE BILLY Harney for the superintendent."

The receptionist waves me in. Superintendent Tristan Driscoll doesn't look happy to see me.

"Long time no see," I say to him, because we saw each other a week ago, the day after the bust, when the superintendent, in all his resplendent glory, announced the breaking up of an international human-trafficking ring on the city's southwest side. He sold the media some bullshit about a long-running investigation, and I didn't bother to stop him. I was there at the presser—didn't have a choice—but I just stood in the background, sucking in my gut.

I drop today's *Tribune* on his desk. The story above the fold: US INDICTS UKRAINIANS IN SEX-TRAFFICKING SCHEME. A nice photo of General Kostyantin Boholyubov, in full military garb, back when he ran the secret police.

"Department's gotten some nice coverage over this," I say.

"You as well, I noticed," he says.

"Dennis Porter, too."

Tristan loses his smirk.

"Captain Dennis Porter, killed in the line of duty, trying to take down a sex-trafficking ring. It's a nice story to tell. Spares you the embarrassment of having yet another crooked cop in our wonderful

Bureau of Internal Affairs. Another scandal on your watch. That'd be kinda hard to explain to the mayor, I suppose."

The superintendent sits back in his chair, crosses a leg.

"I mean, imagine if that came out, Tristan: one of the chief officers in IAB, *protecting* a sex-trafficking ring. A lot of us, we were surprised the new mayor didn't toss you on your ass over the last scandal. But however you managed to survive, you wouldn't survive another one. So Denny Porter goes out a hero."

"Why don't you tell me what the fuck you want?" he says, his face hardening.

"My partner, Carla Griffin," I say. "Great cop. Done some great work for the department. But she's got a problem she has to lick."

"So I hear. I believe we politely refer to it as 'substance abuse.'" He enjoys that, shows me his teeth. "Saw some very entertaining videos of her in one of Porter's files, by the way, looking like the junkie she is."

"Anyway," I say, "she's going into rehab."

"Yes."

"And when she gets out—"

"When she gets out," he says, "like any other cop, she'll be placed on an interim assignment and evaluated." He shrugs. "Maybe someday, I'll let her be a real cop again. Or maybe not."

I snap my fingers. "That's where you're wrong, Mr. Superintendent. She's going to be reassigned to SOS as my partner. Immediately. No delay."

He shakes his head slowly. Even smiles.

"You won't shit-can her career over this," I say. "She comes straight back to SOS after rehab. Or the media hears all about Captain Dennis Porter. And about how you covered it up."

"Your word against mine."

"You sure about that?" I say. "You sure I don't have evidence of Porter's crimes?"

He tries to maintain his composure, but he's not doing a very good job.

"Carla comes back to SOS, or I fucking bury you, Tristan. That clear enough?"

"And here I figured you for playing a long game." The superintendent stands, straightens the uniform he never earned. "You really want to make an enemy of me?"

I wink at him. "I thought you already were."

CHAPTER 113

"WELL, WE don't have many days like this." Judge Horatio Nunez puts down the papers in front of him, looks over at the defense table. "I suppose we could call this a terrible moment in the system of justice, or we could call it a great moment. Kind of depends on your perspective. Mr. Stonewald," he says, removing his eyeglasses, "I hope you're able to see it as a great moment. I hope you're able, somehow, to put this ordeal behind you and move on with your life."

Antoine, seated at the defense table, nods emphatically but doesn't speak.

"And I would commend the Conviction Integrity Unit of the state's attorney's office for acting on this as swiftly as it did. There seems to be no doubt whatsoever that you were wrongly convicted, Mr. Stonewald. We don't usually use the word *innocent*. We normally just say 'guilty,' or we say 'not guilty' if the burden of proof is not met. This is one of those rare instances, sir, where I think we can all safely say that you are completely innocent."

The buzz in the courtroom is palpable. Antoine's family, his fiancée, his mother and sister, his cousins and aunts and uncles, all sit behind him struggling to restrain themselves.

"The defendant's conviction for first-degree murder is vacated. He shall be released from custody immediately."

The gavel bangs, the judge rises with a smile, and bedlam ensues. His family rushes around Antoine as if he were a rock star, hugging and kissing him, rubbing his bald head, laughing and crying and shouting and clapping and dancing.

I'm in the back row with Carla and her boy, Samuel. Only ten years old, and even as the son of a cop, Samuel is awed by the courtroom itself, not to mention the magnitude of what he's witnessing here. Carla wanted him to see this. Samuel himself is part African American—as is his father—and apparently strongly favors his father in appearance. He is viewed, at least generally by his peers, as black. Carla wanted him to see a black man get justice.

Through the crowd that all but lifts him on their shoulders, Antoine manages to catch my eye. We've talked plenty over the last two weeks, when I broke the news of Disco's confession, then kept him updated as I approached the state's attorney's office about reviewing the conviction and righting a wrong.

I give him a salute. He mouths a thank-you to me.

Thank Valerie more than anyone.

We leave the courtroom.

"That was intense," Samuel says.

I chuckle. "Intense" seems a little mature for a kid that age, but then again, I don't have kids that age.

If Janey had lived, she'd be seven.

"When do you go back?" I ask Carla.

She checks her watch. Her face is no longer bandaged, but she has a scar running along her cheek toward her mouth. "Just call me...Joker!," she's been fond of saying, but it's not as bad as all that.

She's been in rehab since she left the hospital ten days ago. She had to testify this morning at Antoine's hearing, so she got a leave for that purpose only. Now it's back to "camp," as she calls it, for another couple of months.

"I have time for lunch, if you do," she says. "My mother-in-law's meeting us downtown."

"Can't do it," I say. "Headed back to work. Somebody's gotta catch bad guys while you're sipping cucumber water and doing yoga."

She elbows me in the arm.

"But you," I say to Samuel. "Tomorrow night, right? Sox versus Royals? Detwiler's pitching, so it should be entertaining."

He gives me a high five. "For sure."

Outside the courthouse, we say our good-byes.

"See you in, what, nine or ten weeks?" she says, squinting into the sun.

"As long as you need," I say. "Your desk will be waiting."

She smirks. "One day, you'll have to tell me how you persuaded the supe to green-light my return to SOS."

"Turns out I had him all wrong. He's a prince of a guy. Big fan of yours, too."

"Yeah, okay." She lights up.

She looks completely different when she smiles.

CHAPTER 114

"SORRY IF I seem depressed," I say into the mike. "I just came from the Sox game."

The crowd at the Hole in the Wall moans. The game's always on the TVs mounted on the wall. Kansas City 8, good guys 0.

"You know how you can tell when the Sox are gonna lose? When the ump says, 'Play ball!'

"I shoulda known when I went early to watch the Sox take batting practice. The pitching machine threw a no-hitter.

"I mean, the Royals put up four in the first inning and never looked back. I've seen more suspense at a funeral.

"The beer man was handing out cyanide tablets.

"The promotional handout was a blindfold.

"Instead of 'Take Me Out to the Ball Game,' the organist was playing taps."

The lines work with this crowd. Most of these coppers are Sox fans, and we love to insult the things we care about. And a few of these mopes actually like the Cubs, so they don't mind, either.

"Anyway, it didn't help that I was tired. I had a rough night's sleep. I had this nightmare that I was trapped in a room with a lion, a rattlesnake, and a defense attorney, and I had only two bullets in my gun. But it had a happy ending."

"You shot the lawyer twice!" Patti calls out from the crowd.

"Hey, c'mon, now! Sorry, folks, that's my twin sister, Patti. Y'know, it's not easy being a twin. They know your thoughts. They finish your sentences..."

And sometimes, they think you killed your own wife.

"Don't steal my punch lines," I say to her after, by the bar, when I get my free bourbon for the stand-up routine. She's got her low-carb drink, vodka soda or something.

"Find some new material," she says.

She looks better now. We got past our troubles.

As incomprehensible as it is for me to even fathom the idea, if I'm being fair, I can't really blame Patti for thinking, or at least suspecting, that I killed Valerie. I was a mess when I walked into that bedroom. With the gun safe open, me in my broken state making vague statements to Patti about how *I did this, I did this* while holding the gun in my hand, and with Pop prodding her on afterward, Patti had plenty of reasons to think it.

And plenty of reasons not to ask me the question directly, because she was afraid of what I might say. Better, in her view, to protect me, to cover it up just in case there was something *to* cover up. It wasn't going to make a difference, either way, from her perspective. Valerie was still gone. I was still her brother, for whom she'd do anything.

She's lived the last four years putting good money on the fact that I killed my own wife. And stood by me, thick and thin, all the same.

How can I turn my back on her? This girl loves me more than I love myself. This girl is my family.

"Y'know, word about Carla is all over," she tells me. "The pills, the rehab."

I shrug. “Let ’em talk. It was bound to happen. She came clean on it. Didn’t want to hide anything anymore.”

“I guess it’s better not to hide, huh? Kind of a life lesson.”

I tap my glass against hers. “I’ll make you this promise,” I say. “If I ever think you murdered someone, you’ll be the first to know.”

ABOUT THE AUTHORS

JAMES PATTERSON is the world's bestselling author and most trusted storyteller. He has created many enduring fictional characters and series, including Alex Cross, the Women's Murder Club, Michael Bennett, Maximum Ride, Middle School, and I Funny. Among his notable literary collaborations are *The President Is Missing,* with President Bill Clinton, and the Max Einstein series, produced in partnership with the Albert Einstein estate. Patterson's writing career is characterized by a single mission: to prove that there is no such thing as a person who "doesn't like to read," only people who haven't found the right book. He's given over three million books to schoolkids and the military, donated more than seventy million dollars to support education, and endowed over five thousand college scholarships for teachers. For his prodigious imagination and championship of literacy in America, Patterson was awarded the 2019 National Humanities Medal. The National Book Foundation presented him with the Literarian Award for Outstanding Service to the American Literary Community, and he is also the recipient of an Edgar Award and nine Emmy Awards. He lives in Florida with his family.

DAVID ELLIS is a justice of the Illinois Appellate Court and the author of nine novels, including *Line of Vision,* for which he won an Edgar Award, and *The Hidden Man,* which earned him a 2009 Los Angeles Times Book Prize nomination.

TURN THE PAGE FOR A SNEAK PEEK AT THE NEXT THRILLER IN THE BLACK BOOK SERIES...

CHAPTER 1

HE'S HERE somewhere. I know it. And the girl might still be alive.

The girl: fifteen-year-old Bridget Leone, abducted off the streets of Hyde Park forty-four hours ago.

Bing. Bing. Bing. Bing.

The ALPR sounds on the dashboard of our unmarked car, registering every license plate we pass, searching for any plate beginning with the letters *F* and *D*. But our witness told us the letters might have appeared the other way around, *D* and *F*, and maybe not even next to each other.

If we have this right, the same man who kidnapped Bridget Leone has abducted four other girls between the ages of thirteen and sixteen, all African American, around the Chicagoland area over the last eighteen months. None of those four girls has been found. All four of them were runaways, homeless—meaning they were easily overlooked and forgotten by overworked and understaffed suburban police departments dealing with cold trails of girls gone missing.

Bridget Leone was different. African American and age fifteen, yes, but far from homeless or runaway. Still, her parents said she dressed "far too provocatively" for her age and often ran with some "wild kids," typical teenage rebellion stuff that her abductor could have misconstrued. And just before she was abducted, we eventually learned from her reluctant friends, she and some classmates had been smoking weed in an alley only a few blocks from the elite magnet high school she'd attended.

When Bridget disappeared, her father—a real estate developer worth millions—called his good pal Tristan Driscoll, the Chicago police superintendent, who in turn immediately deployed the Special Operations Section to find her. That meant Carla and me, at least as the lead detectives.

The computer mounted on the dash buzzes. A hit. My partner, Carla Griffin, leans forward in the passenger seat and checks it. "False alarm," she says.

These automated license plate readers aren't perfect, natch. Sometimes a *D* is mistaken for a zero or an *O*, or an *E* is mistaken for an *F*.

Bing. Bing. Bing. Bing.

"I feel like I'm in a freakin' arcade," I say as I pull our unmarked car into a heavily wooded subdivision called Equestrian Lakes. Giant houses; wide, grassy lots.

Carla smirks. "Well, this is definitely a game of luck, not skill."

She's right. We have so little to go on. Nobody saw the direction in which the offender drove his car after he scooped Bridget off the street. The route he took didn't hit any PODs—our police observation cameras mounted in various places along the streets. The only witness was a homeless guy who had no phone, so he couldn't snap a photo or call it in. And he could only recall two possible digits of the license plate on a "dark" SUV and give us a vague profile of a white male who is "slightly hunched," probably five nine or five ten, with a long scar on the left side of his face.

We have AMBER alerts, community alerts, investigative alerts, and flash messages on every cop's screen in northern Illinois. The Illinois State Police are patrolling the highways. The night Bridget was abducted, we ran a check of ALPRs for those letters—*D* and *F,* next to each other—and picked up a Ford Explorer on South Archer Avenue. The registration traced to someone in Missouri who died six months ago.

We've cleared every registered sex offender in the area. So far, nothing. Nothing but hope for a little luck. Unless by some chance my gut call was right and he's here, on the southwest end of unincorporated Cook County.

My thinking: this largely vacant area would be close to the place where the ALPR picked up the Ford Explorer. There are some nice subdivisions, sure, but it has a rural feel, lots of woods and houses set back deep into the lots, no sidewalks or curbs or streetlights. Lots of privacy. Perfect for a predator.

So instead of running everything from the Special Operations headquarters, at North and Pulaski, Carla and I are here, taking phone calls and issuing orders while patrolling in an unmarked vehicle—unmarked unless you notice the tiny camera, the ALPR, on the roof.

Nothing unusual in Equestrian Lakes, a fancy subdivision, so I get back onto the main road, Rawlings, and follow the bend, the ALPR *bing-bing-binging* as cars pass.

The terrain gets more remote, more wooded. It feels like lake country out here, reminding me of the trips we'd take to Michigan when I was a kid. It's not yet dusk when I take a left turn down an unmarked narrow dirt road, hooded by tall trees, PRIVATE PROPERTY signs nailed to the trunks, glimpses of houses down paths. Beams of sun so infrequently break through the trees that my headlights switch on automatically. I'll do a quick tour before I—

A quarter mile ahead, a white van turns toward us onto the road. Carla's on her phone, talking with the state police, but she drops it from her ear and goes quiet.

I slow the car. The van continues to approach, going the speed limit, its headlights on us.

Bing. The ALPR picks up the plate.

"Commercial van," Carla reads off the mounted computer. "Registered to LTV, LLC. Registration's up to date."

The van moves slowly, giving us a wide berth, nearly driving onto the uneven shoulder.

I stop my car entirely, putting it in Park, and put on my hazards. Just to see what the driver will do.

The van seems to slow but doesn't stop. Carla and I lean down to look out the window at the driver, who's up higher than we are in his van.

White guy, roughly shaved, dark-framed glasses, baseball cap, bandage on his left cheek. Both hands gripping the wheel. His eyes stay straight forward, not even sneaking a peek in our direction, despite the fact that we have stopped in the middle of the road and put on our hazards.

Carla's voice is low. "That look like a white guy, five nine, hunched, scar on his face?"

Yeah, it sure as hell does. Not a Ford Explorer, no *F* or *D* on the plates, but a guy fitting the description in a creepy van. "Let's check it out."

I put the car in Drive and do a U-turn, following the van.

CHAPTER 2

THE VAN rolls along the dirt road, slowing even further as we pull up behind it. So far, it's guilty of nothing. Not speeding. No busted taillights. No apparent malfunctions that would warrant a stop.

"No PC," Carla says. A summary and a warning. We stop the car. Without probable cause, we have a problem in court.

But we don't need probable cause to follow it for a while. It's a free country.

I figure he's headed for the main road from which we just came, Rawlings. But he isn't. The van turns left down an unmarked path. Another dirt road.

No crime in that. And he used his blinker.

Still. I glance at Carla, the expression on her face probably the same as mine, gearing up.

"Baird Salt," she says, noting the logo visible on the side panel of the van when it turned.

I follow the van onto the turnoff. It hardly qualifies as a road—it's more like a clearing through the foliage and heavy tree cover, enough for a single lane of traffic, barely. The bumps are enough to challenge our Taurus's suspension and the fillings in my teeth. The canopy of trees keeps it dark, but the piercing beams of the lowering sun manage to penetrate here and there.

The van keeps moving at a normal clip down a path that wasn't meant to be noticed, much less traveled. I feel like I'm driving through a jungle, overhanging branches tapping our windshield and scraping the sides of the Taurus.

We still haven't taken any official police action, but there's no longer any doubt that we're following. If this guy's innocent, he has to be wondering about our intentions.

But he's not, I think to myself, my pulse banging. *This is our guy.*

And he knows we know.

"Sosh, where are you?" Carla says into her radio. Another SOS team, Detectives Lanny Soscia and Mat Rodriguez, are in this area doing the same thing we are.

"West of Archer near... Hogan?"

"We're just south of Rawlings, traveling westbound on an unmarked dirt road. We're following a white van, driver fits the description. We need assistance."

"Where on Rawlings?" Sosh calls back.

Carla cusses at the GPS, which is spinning right now, unable to connect. "We're the first turnoff west of the Equestrian Lakes subdivision, south side. West of... Addendale, I think."

"On our way."

I keep a distance of two or three car lengths as the van bounces along.

The van begins to slow. I nudge Carla, who nods.

Up ahead, a clearing, sunlight blanketing the ground. No tree coverage.

A road of some kind? An intersection?

"What's that up ahead?" I ask Carla, not wanting to take my eyes off the road.

"Can't get GPS to pull up yet," she answers. Then, into her radio, she calls to the state police chopper: "Air 6, this is CPD 5210. Do you copy?"

"Air 6 to 5210, what's your twenty?"

These state troopers and their formality. Carla repeats our location, best she can.

"We'll try to find you," the pilot calls back. *"GPS is a nightmare out here."*

No shit. The van slows still further, so I do, too.

Then the van reaches the clearing, suddenly cast in the glow of sunlight, while we remain in the darkness of the trees.

The van rolls carefully up onto a small incline, a tiny hill, then comes to a complete stop.

"He stopped," I tell Carla, who's busy banging the GPS on the laptop. "What the hell's he doing? What's he on? Are those..." I lean forward, squinting.

"Wait—GPS is up," says Carla.

We say it at the same time: "They're railroad tracks."

Not a public right-of-way. No crossbucks or gates or flashing lights. "One of those old crossings, out of use for decades," says Carla.

"So what the hell is he doing?" I mumble.

"Parking on the tracks."

Then we both hear it, from our right, the north. The rumbling sound of a train coming.

"Shit."

"He's done and he knows it," Carla says. "Suicide by train."

With a fifteen-year-old girl inside.

We burst out of the car.

CHAPTER 3

WE RUSH toward the van, feeling the vibration of the oncoming train underfoot, fanning out on each side as the train horn bellows its warning. The screeching sound of metal on metal as the train tries in vain to halt ahead of the van stopped in its path.

"Chicago police! Chicago police!" I shout as I approach the driver's door, the side panel emblazoned with the salt-company logo.

In the rectangular side mirror, I catch sight of the man's face, his eyes intense. The van's tires screech as they spin into motion, blasting the vehicle off the platform and over the tracks. Just as the train barrels past us, the deep blare of its horn, sparks flying, a high-pitched screech from the brakes.

I'm blown backwards and almost lose my balance. Carla is calling into her radio to the state police chopper, to all units, as we lose sight of the van on the other side of the tracks, blocked now by the freight train

The train shudders to a halt. "No!" I yell. "Keep moving! Clear this crossing!"

That will take forever. The conductor has protocols. And he's well down the track. He probably can't hear me. He's probably cursing the idiot van driver who just played chicken with him.

Carla drops to the ground, looks under the train. "Can't see anything underneath!"

I look around me, a tree branch raking across my face.

A tree.

I grab onto the thickest low branch I can find and do something I haven't done in twenty-five years. I pull myself up onto the branch and look out. No view. Still blocked by the idled train. I find another branch, pull myself up, and straddle it. There.

I spot the van just as it's turning left through what looks like a cornfield. "He turned south a few hundred yards up!"

I lose sight of him. But at least I know the direction he's heading. I climb back down, jumping from the branch and scraping my hands, falling face-first into some foliage that may or may not be poison ivy. "C'mon," I shout, heading back to the car.

We get into the car. I drop it into gear. I turn the same direction the van is headed, south, and drive along the sloped gravel right-of-way next to the train tracks on my right.

"Air 6, you got this asshole?" Carla shouts. "We're near Rawlings and the train tracks! A white van. It's heading southbound now, probably a half mile southwest of the tracks and Rawlings."

"CPD 5210, we are responding."

We race along the sloped gravel, our tires slipping and sliding.

"Twelve o'clock," Carla says to me.

I see it: a large structure on the right-of-way, a big black junction box mounted in the gravel. I can't plow over it. To the left is unknown terrain, and we could be screwed. Only choice is to go right, nearly hitting the train tracks. Carla braces herself.

"Hope all those years of video games paid off," I say.

I speed up and swerve to the right, the angle dangerously sharp, Carla nearly falling into me from the passenger seat. We scrape the embankment of the railroad tracks, bouncing downward against the junction box, but the momentum carries us past, the Taurus nearly nosediving into the very terrain I wanted to avoid to the left. We kick up rocks and dust, but the Taurus rights itself, and we barrel forward again.

"Air 6 to 5210, we have a twenty on the white van."

So do we. Up ahead, maybe a hundred yards. Flying across the train tracks again, back to the side that we're on, the Baird Salt logo unmistakable.

He's driving in a square. He's heading back where he came from.

"CPD 5210 is in pursuit," Carla says.

"CPD 5210, we can't track him in those woods."

Which is why he came back. He knows these woods. He knows where to hide.

We're on him, at least. But he has a head start. I can only go so fast without losing control of the Taurus on this uneven gravel.

After ninety seconds that feel like an hour, we reach the road where the van crossed back over the tracks. Carla is cool and calm as she relays the developments. "All units, we need to seal off this perimeter. Sheriff 1, you call it; you know this area."

I floor the Taurus, which responds with its souped-up police-model engine. At least this road is paved, so we can make progress. But so can the van. With the cherry lit up on the dashboard and the siren blaring, I hit nearly ninety miles an hour, hoping nobody or no *thing* jumps out into our path. I can't afford to lose the van. We've probably got it pinned down now, but that's not the problem.

The problem is the girl and what he'll do to her if he feels cornered.

"There, Harney, there—"

We catch a glimpse of the van, turning left yet again. Completing the square.

He's going back home?

"Suspect is heading north," Carla calls in. "Air 6, you got it?"

I push the Taurus as hard it can go, then skid into a left turn onto a dirt road, nearly wiping out. “This is the same road,” I say. “The same one where we first saw him.”

Carla calls it in, now on familiar ground. But the driver has the advantage.

We see the van make its final turn up ahead.

“He did all this just to circle back and get home,” says Carla. “What’s so special about back home?”

I pound the brake as we slide into a turn, reaching the turnoff the van just took.

“We’re about to find out,” I say.

CHAPTER 4

WHEN WE reach the turnoff, we see a DO NOT ENTER sign chained across the path. That makes no sense. How did the suspect get through it and reattach it?

Whatever. I blast the Taurus through, the sign splitting apart before I could hit it.

"Some kind of automatic gate," says Carla, checking her weapon, adjusting her vest. "Who the hell *is* this guy?"

We follow a winding road, slowing to navigate the turns. Too slow to overtake the van.

"C'mon..."

Up ahead, the van pulls up to a house of brick and stone, the garage door opening. The van roars inside. Behind us, the sirens of law enforcement—state, county, city—come blaring from Rawlings Road.

The van screeches into the garage. The man pops out. The van's back doors open. He reaches in and pulls out...

...a girl, African American, tied at the hands and feet. Bridget Leone.

Carrying the girl in his arms, the man rushes into the house as we reach the property and squeal to a halt.

I run into the garage, seeing the door to the house ajar. My Glock out and high, I push the door open and shout, "Chicago police!"

I'm in a kitchen, red light flashing in a high corner. An intruder alert?

We race into a sparsely furnished family room—a couch and chair but not much else. A door to the left. To the right, a sliding glass door onto a patio.

And another red light flashing in the corner.

"Bridget! Bridget Leone?" Carla calls out. She tries the door. It opens into a staircase leading down.

Out of the corner of my eye, I see a figure running through the back yard. It's our offender, the ball cap and build matching the description.

"Bridget!"

A faint but clear "Yes!" comes from the basement.

"I got the perp; you get the girl," I say to Carla.

I push open the sliding glass door and leap off the patio onto the grass a good ten feet below. I ignore the pain in my ankle and start running.

It's a thick net of trees, a natural fencing, but I saw where he went in, and I see his hat on the path. I run with my Glock at my side. The path is narrow, the footing uneven. I try to watch for an ambush while running at top speed in an area this asshole knows and I don't.

Advantage: asshole. But I have some wheels when I'm motivated, and I get the sense this guy does not.

Then I hear him up ahead, his labored breathing, the sound of his footfalls. He comes into my view, running with all he's got, but it isn't enough.

"Police!" I shout as best I can while sprinting, my chest burning, my ankle throbbing. I make a decision, stop, aim, and fire at a tree in front of him.

The wood splinters. The man cowers, slowing down.

Then he stops.

"Hands up and turn around!" I shout, shuffling toward him, both hands on the Glock.

He raises his hands. Turns around.

Beady eyes, greasy dark hair, thick nose. A large head rising from a long, skinny neck and sloping shoulders. Big ears protruding off his head like those of some cartoon character. The bandage dangling from his face, the sweat overpowering the adhesive, revealing a decent scar.

"Drop to your knees!" I command.

He doesn't. Instead, with a poker face, he makes a word with his lips.

"Boo."

Then he looks over my shoulder, past me.

"Drop to your—"

Then I realize he wasn't saying *boo*.

He was saying *boom*.

My phone buzzes in my pocket.

Behind me, a deep, thundering explosion. I turn to see the roof blowing off the house, a massive ball of orange and black, the sides of the house caving in.

The entire house, reduced to ash and rubble within five seconds.

I turn back. The suspect has started running again, turning into the thicket of trees and disappearing.

I look back and forth, then holster my weapon and start running back to the house.

CHAPTER 5

I BAT away tree branches and stumble over a hole along the path as black smoke fills the sky. I feel the searing heat before I reach the clearing.

When I push through the final branches into the back yard, I'm hit with an oven blast of heat and dark soot and dust. I nearly stumble over a young African American girl lying in the grass, facedown, wearing a T-shirt and shorts.

"Bridget?" I bend down, touch her neck for a pulse. "Bridget Leone?"

She opens her eyes, nods, looks up at me.

I cover my hand with my mouth so I can breathe. "Are you okay? Can you move?"

She manages to nod, squint at me, cough.

Around the other side of the house, a state police trooper and a county sheriff's unit come running. I flag them down. Eventually, they see me through the smoke. "This is Bridget," I say, while my eyes whip back and forth for Carla. "Get her out of here!" But before I do, I lean into her ear. "Bridget, where's my partner?"

Still dazed, she shakes her head. She doesn't know.

The troopers gather her in their arms and rush her away from the blaze, the poisonous soot, the scalding heat.

"Suspect went through that clearing!" I shout to the sheriff's deputies, pointing. "I don't think he was armed, but I can't be sure! Go! And get the chopper on him! Go!"

I push them as I soldier forward, my mouth covered by the crook of my arm, taking quick, greedy breaths as I move forward. "Carla!" I shout. "Carla!" Each time breaking into a coughing spasm.

By now, more than a dozen officers are on the scene in their various uniforms. I grab two and yell, "There's a Chicago police detective here somewhere!"

Mini fires are scattered around the rubble, but the house was all brick and concrete, mostly stamping them out. The real problem is the air quality—beyond treacherous and making it almost impossible to see through the thick blanket of dust and soot.

What I can see: a house, leveled. Parts of a roof and walls scattered about. Utter wreckage. Carla could be anywhere.

"Carla!" I call out, and others join me, calling out her name. Knowing without acknowledging it that if she was still inside the house, she has no chance. But the girl got away, so she probably did, too.

It gets darker by the second. I pull out my Maglite and shine it around. A rescue squad is spraying the remaining fires.

"Billy, you okay?"

I turn. Lanny Soscia, part of the SOS squad. "Can't find Carla!" I shout.

We look through the debris, pieces of roof, wall, furniture. I break into another coughing spasm. Someone hands me a gas mask.

Then I remember my phone, buzzing just before the explosion. I check it; the call came from Carla. I press the button to call her back and look around.

Through the darkness, only a few feet to my right, a phone lights up.

"Over here!" I rush over, slide down. Carla is lying underneath a slab of concrete that covers her body up to her shoulders.

Her eyes are shut. She looks...she doesn't look...

"I'm here, kiddo, I'm here." Her face is painted soot black. I touch her neck and feel a faint pulse.

"Over here!" I yell. "Officer down! We need a medevac!"

Carla coughs, spraying blood, and opens her eyes. I put my hand over her face, trying to shield her as I lie down on the ground next to her. "You're gonna be fine," I lie.

Her eyes narrow, a smile without a smile.

Sosh runs up with several officers.

"We gotta get this thing off her," I say. I try to push on it. Heavy is an understatement, but all we need to do is raise it enough for someone else to pull her out.

"Should we be moving her?" Sosh asks, bent down.

He might be right. You don't move someone with suspected spinal injuries if you don't have to. "We can at least get this thing off her," I say. "Everyone at once; we can do it."

I bend down to Carla. "Put on this mask, Carla, so you don't have to breathe this shit."

I lower the mask to her face. In her weakened state, she manages to bat it away. "Tell Darryl...I love him and I'm...counting...counting on him now."

"*You* tell him," I say. "When you see him later."

Even in her dazed, battered condition, she manages to shoot me a knowing look. "Tell my baby...his mama loves him."

"He knows that," I say, choking up. "Samuel knows, but you're gonna tell him yourself, goddamn it!"

Officers scramble around us, trying to figure out how to remove this massive concrete wall off Carla's body.

She winces. "Did the girl...did..."

"The girl's fine," I tell her. "You saved her, Carla."

She rests her head back on the ground, closes her eyes.

"Put on the mask," I say, "and we'll get this thing off you."

Officers have placed tire jacks on each side of the concrete slab, while the others prepare to move the concrete.

Carla wets her lips and tries to speak. "Come... closer."

I get as close as I can, practically nose to nose on the grass. My hand wiping the soot from her face, caressing her cheek. "I'm here," I manage, hardly able to speak.

"You saved... my life," she whispers. "You... know that." She grimaces from the pain. Tears well up and fall sideways to the grass.

The concrete slab starts to lift, the tire jacks raising it off the ground and a dozen officers struggling to get purchase under it.

"You saved mine, too," I tell her, making my voice work. "That's what partners do. We stick together." I take her hand in mine. "We're always gonna stick together. You think I'm gonna let you off this easy? You and me, we're gonna retire together. You and me and Darryl, we're gonna sit in rocking chairs and tell war stories."

With the help of the tire jacks, the officers get enough momentum, pushing the concrete up to a ninety-degree angle and then toppling it over in the other direction.

Revealing an area of grass untouched by the soot. But covered with Carla's blood.

"That's better," Carla whispers, her eyes closed.

"Good," I say. "Medevac's on its way. Hang with me, kid. C'mon, hang with me."

She doesn't answer.

She doesn't open her eyes.

"Carla!" I shout.

"Carla," I whisper.

For a complete list of books by

JAMES PATTERSON

VISIT
JamesPatterson.com

Follow James Patterson on Facebook
@JamesPatterson

Follow James Patterson on Twitter
@JP_Books

Follow James Patterson on Instagram
@jamespattersonbooks